MARIE
FERRARELLA

Dear Reader,

The editors at Harlequin and Silhouette are thrilled to be able to bring you a brand-new featured author program beginning in 2005! Signature Select aims to single out outstanding stories, contemporary themes and oft-requested classics by some of your favorite series authors and present them to you in a variety of formats bound by truly striking covers.

We plan to provide several different types of reading experiences in the new Signature Select program. The Spotlight books will offer a single "big read" by a talented series author, the Collections will present three novellas on a selected theme in one volume, the Sagas will contain sprawling, sometimes multigenerational family tales (often related to a favorite family first introduced in series), and the Miniseries will feature requested, previously published books, with two or, occasionally, three complete stories in one volume. The Signature Select program will offer one book in each of these categories per month, and fans of limited continuity series will also find these continuing stories under the Signature Select umbrella.

In addition, these volumes will bring you bonus features...different in every single book! You may learn more about the author in an extended interview, more about the setting or inspiration for the book, more about subjects related to the theme and, often, a bonus short read will be included.

Watch for new stories from Janelle Denison, Donna Kauffman, Leslie Kelly, Marie Ferrarella, Suzanne Forster, Stephanie Bond, Christine Rimmer and scores more of the brightest talents in romance fiction!

We have an exciting year ahead!

Warm wishes for happy reading,

Marsha Zinberg

Marsha Zinberg
Executive Editor
The Signature Select Program

MINISERIES

THE BEST MEDICINE

MARIE FERRARELLA

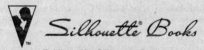

Published by Silhouette Books

America's Publisher of Contemporary Romance

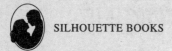 SILHOUETTE BOOKS

ISBN 0-373-21762-5

THE BEST MEDICINE

Copyright © 2005 by Harlequin Books S.A.

The publisher acknowledges the copyright holder of the individual works as follows:

IN GRAYWOLF'S HANDS
Copyright © 2002 by Marie Rydzynski-Ferrarella

M.D. MOST WANTED
Copyright © 2002 by Marie Rydzynski-Ferrarella

This edition published by arrangement with Harlequin Books S.A.

® and TM are trademarks of the publisher. Trademarks indicated with ® are registered in the United States Patent and Trademark Office, the Canadian Trade Marks Office and in other countries.

Visit Silhouette Books at www.eHarlequin.com

Printed in U.S.A.

CONTENTS

Dearest Reader,

For those of you who are visiting for the first time, welcome. For those of you who have read these stories before, welcome back. I've missed you.

You have before you two stories. *In Graywolf's Hands* gives you the backstory to Christian Graywolf's brother, Lukas, and how he met his wife, Lydia, an FBI agent. Lydia was guarding a man accused of setting off a bomb in a mall, not exactly your typical "meet." I have a special spot in my heart for doctors, law enforcement agents and native Americans, so I was really in my element working on this story. I loved every minute I spent writing it. If Lydia and Lukas's romance seems a little like a whirlwind to you, part of it was carried out against a backdrop of life-or-death conditions where emotions are bound to run high. It makes you come to grips with your true feelings quickly.

The other story, *M.D. Most Wanted,* is about Dr. Reese Bendenetti, an internist who becomes involved with London Merriweather, the daughter of an ambassador, who wants nothing more than to escape the trappings of wealth and live a normal life. But the man stalking her has other ideas—until the good doctor who initially treated her for injuries sustained in a car accident comes to her aid once more. Saving her, he brings her love in the bargain, always a good thing.

I hope you enjoy reading these two stories as much as I enjoyed writing them. And as always, above all else, I wish you love.

Marie Ferrarella

IN GRAYWOLF'S HANDS

To Patricia Smith
and
fairy tales that come true

Chapter 1

He was going to live.

Jacob Lindstrom was going to live to see his first grandchild born. Maybe even his first great-grandchild, if the man played his cards right. All because he, Lukas Graywolf, the first in his family to graduate from college, let alone medical school, had decided to make cardiac surgery his field of expertise.

That, and because Jacob's wife had nagged him into taking a treadmill test, whose alarming results had sent the middle-aged corporate CEO to the operating table almost faster than he could blink an eye.

With excellent results.

Walking out of the alcove where friends and family were told to wait for news about the outcome of surgeries, Lukas let the door close behind him and took a deep breath. Never mind that it was basically recycled hospital air, it felt good, sweet, life-giving. And soon, Lukas thought, a hint of a smile finding its way to his lips and softening his chiseled features, Jacob Lindstrom would be able to say the same thing.

It was a good feeling to know that he had been instrumental in freeing another human from the grasp of death. His smile deepened ever so slightly as he turned down the long corridor.

This was probably the way his forefathers had felt. Those ancestors who, more than a handful of generations ago, had relied on the knowledge of plants and spiritual power to heal the sick and injured. There had been more than one shaman found in his family tree and, if he were to believe his mother's stories, a few gifted "seers" and "healers" across the ocean in Ireland, as well.

It was a heady legacy, indeed, he mused. Lukas was one-quarter Irish, three-quarters Navaho but right now he was four-quarters exhausted. It had been a taxing surgery, not without its complications.

Turning a corner, he entered the doctors' lounge. Shedding his scrubs, he put on his own clothes by rote, leaving behind his white lab coat. He was off duty, had technically been off duty for the past two hours. Except that Mr. Lindstrom's surgery hadn't exactly gone as planned. They'd almost lost the man twice.

Lindstrom's vital signs were good now and there was every chance for a strong, rapid recovery.

Lukas had said as much to the man's wife and grown children, who had spent the last few hours contemplating the possible demise of a man they had heretofore regarded as indestructible. He had barely finished talking when Mrs. Lindstrom had hugged him and blessed him.

He wasn't much for physical contact, but he knew the

woman needed it so he had stood still and allowed himself to be embraced, had even patted her on the shoulder. He'd left the woman with tears of joy in her eyes, counting the minutes until she could see her husband again.

Lukas's mouth curved a little more as he shut his locker door. This was why he'd become a surgeon in the first place, why he had set his sights on heart surgery. The heart was the center of everything within a human being.

His goal was simple: to heal and preserve as many lives as he could. He figured the reason he'd been put on earth was to make a difference and he intended to do just that.

The rush that came over him was incredible and he paused beside the locker for a moment to savor it. He was one of the lucky ones, he knew. He could still feel the overwhelming elation after each surgery that went well. There were many in the medical community who had burned out, who performed surgery by the numbers and felt none of the gratification that he was feeling now.

They didn't know what they were missing, Lukas thought, pity wafting through him. He picked up his windbreaker, feeling as if he could pretty near walk on water. Or at the very least, on some very deep puddles.

As he started to open the door to leave, it swung open. Allan Pierce, a first-year intern, stumbled in on the long end of a thirty-six-hour shift. His eyes brightened slightly, the way a private's did in the presence of a four-star general.

"You on duty tonight, Dr. Graywolf?"

"Off," Lukas told him crisply.

He could already visualize his bed, visualize his body sprawled out on top of it, the comforter lying in a crumpled heap on one or the other side of his body. Though it was only a year in his past, he'd gotten completely out of the habit of the long hours that interning and residency demanded. It wasn't something he cared to revisit on a regular basis.

"Wish I were," Allan mumbled. His shaggy blond hair drooped into his eyes, making him seem years younger than he was.

"You will be," Lukas promised, feeling uncustomarily lighthearted. As a rule, he was distant with the interns. "In about five years. 'Night."

So saying, Lukas walked out of the lounge and directly into the path of turmoil.

The rear doors of the emergency room sprang open as two ambulance attendants rushed in. A gust of leaves, chasing one another in the late autumn wind, swirled around the wheels of the gurney. The wounded man strapped to its board was screaming obscenities at anyone within earshot, but most were directed at the slender, no-nonsense blonde keeping pace with the attendants.

For just a second, as the wind lifted the edge of her jacket, Lukas thought he saw the hilt of a revolver. But then her jacket fell closed again and he found himself wondering if he'd just imagined the weapon.

Another man, older than the woman by at least a decade and wearing a three-piece suit, followed slightly behind her.

The man looked winded as he vainly attempted to catch up to the woman. Carrying a little too much weight for his age and height, Lukas judged. He wondered when the man had last had a treadmill test.

But there was little time for extraneous thoughts. The noise level and tension rose with each passing second. Nurses and attendants began to converge around the incoming gurney. From where he stood, Lukas had a clear view. He could see all the blood the man had lost. And the handcuffs that tethered him to the gurney.

One of the attendants was rattling off vital signs to the nearest nurse while the blonde interrupted with orders of her own. The screaming man on the gurney was a gunshot victim.

And then suddenly the patient fell eerily silent, pale in his stillness. He sank back against the gurney.

Lukas lost no time cutting the distance between himself and the injured man, pushing his way into the center of what looked as if it could easily become a mob scene.

Out of the corner of his eye, he saw the blonde frown at him. Placing his fingers on the artery in the man's neck, he found no pulse.

The blonde grabbed his arm. "Who are you?" she demanded.

Lukas saw no reason to waste time answering her. There was a life at stake.

"Crash cart," he ordered the closest nurse to him. "Now!" The dark-haired woman quickly disappeared into the crowd.

"Is he dead?" The blonde wanted to know. When Lukas didn't say anything, she moved so that he was forced to look at her. Her hand gripped his wrist, her intent clear. She was going to hold it still until she got her answer. The strength he felt there didn't surprise him. "Is he dead?" she repeated.

"Not yet," Lukas snapped, jerking his wrist away.

The nurse he'd sent for the crash cart returned, hurrying to position it next to the gurney. There was no time to get the man to a room. What had to be done was going to be done in the corridor, with everyone looking on.

"Someone get his shirt open!" Lukas ordered.

He was surprised when the blonde was the first to comply, ripping the man's shirt down the center. He saw the blood on her hands and arm then. Lukas pushed the questions back as he held the paddles up to have the lubricant applied. Directing the amount of voltage to be used, he held the paddles ready as he announced the customary, "Clear." At the last second he jerked back the paddles when he saw that the blonde had one hand on the victim.

What was she doing, playing games? "Clear!" Lukas shouted at her angrily. "That means get your hands away from the patient unless you want to feel the roots of your hair stand on end."

Glaring at him, the blonde elaborately raised both her hands up and away from the man on the gurney.

The monitor continued to display a flat line as Lukas tried once and then again to bring the man around. Raising the voltage, Lukas tried a third time and was rewarded with a faint blip on the screen.

He held his breath as he watched the monitor. The blip grew stronger. Lukas began to breathe again. He replaced the paddles on the cart.

"Get him to Room Twelve," he instructed Pierce, who had been hovering at his elbow the entire time.

"Right away."

Lukas took another deep breath as his adrenaline began to level off. From the looks of it, his night had just gotten a whole lot longer. By the time they could get another heart specialist down to the hospital, it might be too late for the man they'd just brought in. Casting no aspersions on the doctor on duty, Lukas knew he was better at this sort of thing than Carlucci was.

As with every patient he came in contact with, he felt responsible. He blamed it in part on his grandmother's stories about the endless circle of life, how each person touched another. Was responsible for another. Between his grandmother and the Hippocratic oath, there wasn't much margin for indifference.

He paused only long enough to wash his hands and slip on the disposable yellow gown the nurse—who seemed to materialize from out of nowhere—was holding up for him. The surgical gloves slid on like a second skin. They very nearly were.

Entering Room Twelve, Lukas nodded at Harrison MacKenzie, surprised to see the man there. He must have been in the area when he heard about the gunshot victim. Following the light in Harrison's eyes, Lukas became aware of the woman again. She was shadowing his every move. Or rather, the man on the gurney's every move.

Lukas spared her a glare as the paramedics and attendants transferred the patient onto the examination table. "You're not supposed to be here."

The blonde didn't budge a fraction of an inch. Even as the gurney was being removed. They went around her. "He's here, I'm here."

Lukas assessed the damage quickly. There was a bullet lodged dangerously close to the man's heart. "I take it that it's not filial loyalty that's keeping you in my way."

The term almost made her choke. Her eyes glinted with loathing, the kind displayed for a creature that was many levels beneath human and dangerous.

"He and his friends just tried to blow up most of the Crossways Mall," the blonde informed him grimly. "His friends got away. I'm not letting this one out of my sight."

"The windows aren't made of lead." His hands full, Lukas nodded toward the swinging doors. "You can keep him in your sight from the hallway." The fact that she remained standing where she was threatened to unravel the temper he usually kept securely under wraps. "The man's losing blood at a rate that could shortly kill him, he's shackled to a bed and he's unconscious. Take it from me, he's not going anywhere in the next hour. Maybe two. Now I'm not going to tell you again. Get outside."

Frustrated, Special Agent Lydia Wakefield spun on her heel. The flat of her hand slapped against the swinging door as she pushed it open and stormed out of the room. The older man who had come in with her followed silently in her shadow.

"I'd say someone needs to work on their people skills," Harrison observed.

Lukas looked up at the man who had befriended him in medical school, the man he felt closer to than anyone, other than his uncle Henry. There was a mask covering his face, but Lukas could feel the other man's grin. "You talking about me, or her?"

The smile reached Harrison's blue eyes, crinkling them. "A little of both." He looked down at the patient. "I heard the commotion all the way to the elevator. I thought I'd offer you an extra set of hands, but it doesn't look like you'll be needing me."

Harrison's field of expertise was plastic surgery. He specialized in trauma victims.

If he knew Harry, the man probably had a hot date stashed somewhere. There was no need to keep him from her. Lukas shook his head. "Not unless he intends to wear his heart on his sleeve."

Harrison remained a few minutes longer, just in case. "Did I hear her right?" He nodded at the man on the table. "You operating on a bomber?"

"I'm operating on a man," Lukas corrected. "Whatever else he is is between him and his god. I'm not here to play judge and jury. I just patch up bodies."

Harrison stepped back, undoing his mask. Drooping, it hung around his neck. "Well, I see that, as usual, you're keeping things light." He looked at his watch. If he bent a few speeding rules, he could still make his date on time. "I've got cold champagne and a hot woman waiting for me, so I'll just leave you to your jigsaw puzzle." Shedding the yellow paper gown, he tossed it into the bin in the corner.

Walking out, Harrison stopped to talk to the blonde, who was standing inches away from the swinging door. He had a weakness for determined women.

"Don't worry, he's as good as they make 'em," he assured her.

She frowned. Right now, she wasn't all that concerned about tapping into miracles to prolong the life of a man she considered pure scum.

"Just means the taxpayers are going to have to spend more money," she said without looking at the doctor at her side.

"Come again?"

Standing at the window, she watched as people ran back and forth, getting what looked to be units of blood, doing things she wasn't even vaguely familiar with. "If your friend saves his life, there's going to be a lengthy trial."

Harrison glanced at the man who had come in with the blonde before looking back at her. "Everybody deserves his day in court."

She had thought that once, too. Before the job had gotten to her. Before she'd seen what she had today. She turned from the window to glare at the doctor spouting ideologies.

Her eyes were cold. "A man who would blow up innocent people to vent his anger or to carry out some kind of private war doesn't deserve anything."

Harrison took quiet measure of her. The woman appeared to be a handful by anyone's standards. Probably gave her superiors grief. Not unlike Lukas on a good day, he mused.

"Odd philosophy for a law enforcement agent."

"Oh, really?" Tired and in no mood for pretty-boy doctors who probably saw themselves as several cuts above the average man and only slightly below God, she fisted her hand at her waist. "And what makes you such an expert on law enforcement agents?"

"I'm not," Harrison said. A seductive smile spread along his lips as he regarded her. "But give me time and I could be."

Lydia saw her partner move closer and held up her hand to stop him in his place. "I think you'd better go now."

Harrison raised his hands in complete surrender, taking one step back, and then another. He had places to be, anyway. With a woman who was perhaps not as exciting as this one, but who, he was willing to bet, was a whole lot more accommodating.

"Okay, but go easy on my friend." He nodded toward the room he'd just vacated. "His head doesn't grow back if you rip it off."

She glared at the doctor's back as he walked quickly away. It was easy to be flippant, to espouse mercy and understanding if you were ignorant of the circumstances. If you hadn't just seen a teenage boy destroyed, a life that was far too short snuffed out right before your eyes.

Restless, Lydia couldn't settle down, couldn't keep from moving. If only she and Elliot had gotten there earlier.

But the tip they'd received had been too late. It had sent them to Conroy's house, where they had uncovered enough powder and detonating devices to blow up half the state. It was by chance that they'd stumbled across the intended target: the Crossroads Mall exhibit honoring Native American history.

They'd rushed to the Crossroads, calling in local police, calling ahead to the mall's security guards. To no avail. She couldn't stop the bombing, couldn't get the mall evacuated in time. She tried to console herself with the fact that things could have been worse. If this had happened at an earlier hour, the damage would have been far greater in terms of lives lost. And fortunately, it had happened in the middle of the week, which didn't see as much foot traffic at the mall as a Friday or Saturday night.

The bombing, according to a note sent to the local news station and received within the past hour, had been meant as a warning.

For Lydia, even one life lost because of some crazed supremacy group's idea of justice was one too many. And there had been a life lost. Not to mention the number of people injured and maimed. The ambulances had arrived en masse, and the victims were being taken to three trauma hospitals in the area.

Knowing that only Blair Memorial had an area set aside for prisoners, the paramedics had brought them here.

And now the doctor with the solemn face and gaunt, high cheekbones was trying to save the life of a man who had no regard for other lives.

It was a hell of a strange world she lived in.

Lydia leaned her forehead against the glass, absorbing the coolness, wishing her headache would go away.

"I can take it from here, Lyd," Elliot was saying behind her. "You're beat. Why don't you go home, get some rest?"

She turned to the man who had been her partner from the first day she'd walked into the Santa Ana FBI building. At the time she'd felt she was being adopted rather than partnered. Elliot Peterson looked more like someone who should be behind a counter, selling toys, not a man who regularly went to target practice and had two guns strapped to his body for most of each day. He was ten years older than her, and acted as if he were double that. Elliot took on the role of the father she'd lost more than a dozen years ago. At times, that got in the way.

He was always trying to make her job easier.

Lydia smiled as she shook her head. She wasn't about to go anywhere. "You're the one with a wife and kids waiting for you. All I've got waiting for me is a television set."

"And whose fault is that?" It was no secret that he and his wife had tried to play matchmaker for her, to no avail. Loose, wide shoulders lifted in a half shrug. There was no denying that he wanted to get home himself.

"Yeah, but…"

There was no need for both of them to remain here.

"How long since you and Janice had some quality time together?"

Elliot pretended to consider the question. "Does the birthing room at the hospital count?"

Lydia laughed. "No."

"Then I don't remember."

She looked at him knowingly. "That's what I thought. Go home, Elliot. Kiss your wife and hug your kids and tell them all to stay out of malls for a while."

The warning hit too close to home. His oldest daughter, Jamie, liked to hang out with her friends at the Crossroads on weekends. If this had been Saturday morning instead of Wednesday night…

He didn't want to go there. Suddenly ten paces beyond weary, Elliot decided to take Lydia up on her offer. "You sure?"

This job could easily be turned over to someone in a lower position for now, but she wouldn't feel right about leaving until she knew what condition the bomber was in.

She started to gesture toward the closed doors behind her. Pain shot through her arm and she carefully lowered it, hoping Elliot hadn't noticed. He could fuss more than a mother hen once he got going.

She nodded toward the room. "As the good doctor pointed out, that guy's not going anywhere tonight. I can handle it from here. If anything breaks, I can always page you."

Grateful for the reprieve, Elliot patted her shoulder. "Night or day." He glanced through the window. The medical team was still going full steam. "From the looks of it, it might be a while. Want me to get you some coffee before I go, maybe find you something clean to put on?"

She glanced down at her bloodied jacket. "My dry

cleaner is not going to be happy about this. And, thanks, but I'll find the coffee myself." She didn't like to be waited on. Besides, Elliot had put in just as full a day as she had. "You just go home to Janice before she starts thinking I have designs on you."

Looking back at his life, he sometimes thought he'd been born married. Janice had been his first sweetheart in junior high. "Not a chance. Janice knows there isn't an unfaithful bone in my body."

That makes you one of the rare ones, Elliot, Lydia thought as she watched her partner walk down the long corridor. She vaguely wondered if there would ever be someone like that in her life, then dismissed the thought. She was married to her job, which was just the way she wanted it. No one to worry about her and no one to worry about when she put herself on the line. Clean and neat. She was too busy to be lonely.

"You'd think a state-of-the-art hospital would keep coffee machines in plain sight," she muttered to herself, looking up and down the corridor. About to approach the receptionist at the emergency admissions desk, she heard the doors behind her swoosh open.

Turning, she saw the doctor who had earlier hustled her out of Room Twelve hurrying alongside an uncon-scious, gurneyed Conroy. They had transferred the sus-pect back onto a gurney and he was being wheeled out.

She lost no time falling in beside the doctor. "Is he stable?" she asked. "Can I question him?"

Stopping at the service elevator, Lukas pressed the up button. He'd never cared for authority, had found it daunting and confining as a teenager. The run-ins he had had with the law before his uncle had taken him under his wing and straightened him out had left a bad taste in his mouth.

"You can if you don't want any answers." The elevator doors opened. The orderly with him pushed the gurney inside and Lukas took his place beside it. "He needs immediate surgery, not a game of Twenty Questions."

"What floor?" she demanded as the doors began to close.

Lukas pretended to cock his head as if he hadn't heard her. "What?"

Irritated, she raised her voice. "What floor are you taking him to?"

The doors closed before he gave her an answer. Not that he looked as if he was going to, she thought angrily. What was his problem? Did he have an affinity for men who tried to blow up young girls and cut down young boys for sport because of some half-baked ideas about supremacy?

Her temper on the verge of a major explosion, Lydia hurried back to the emergency room admissions desk and cornered the clerk before he could get away.

"That tall, dark-haired doctor who was just here, the one who was working on my prisoner—"

"You mean Dr. Graywolf?" the older man asked.

Well, ain't that a kick in the head? Conroy and his people had blown up the exhibit because of contempt for the people it honored and here he was, his life in the hands of one of the very people to whom he felt superior.

Graywolf. She rolled the name over in her mind. It sounded as if it suited him, she thought. He looked like a wolf, a cunning animal that could never quite be tamed. But even a cunning animal met its match.

Lydia nodded. "That's the one. He just took my pris-

oner upstairs to be operated on—where was he going
with him?"

"Fifth floor," the man told her. "Dr. Graywolf's a
heart surgeon."

A heart surgeon. Before this is over, Dr. Graywolf
might need one himself if he doesn't learn to get out of
my way, Lydia vowed silently as she hurried back to the
bank of elevators.

Chapter 2

Lydia looked around the long corridor. After more than three hours, she could probably draw it from memory, as she could the waiting room she had long since vacated.

Blowing out an impatient breath, she dragged her hand through her long, straight hair. It was at times like this that she wished she smoked. Or practiced some kind of transcendental exercises that could somehow help her find a soothing, inner calm. Pacing and drinking cold coffee to which the most charitable adjective that could be applied was godawful, didn't begin to do the trick.

She knew what was at the root of her restlessness. She was worried that somehow John Conroy would manage to get away, that his condition wasn't nearly as grave as that tall, surly doctor had made it out to be. And when no one was looking, he'd escape, the way Lock-

wood had. Jonas Lockwood had been the very first prisoner she'd been put in charge of. His escape had almost
cost her her career before it had begun.

She and Elliot had managed to recapture the fugitive
within eighteen hours, but not before Lockwood had
seriously wounded another special agent. It was a les-
son in laxness she never forgot. It had made her extra
cautious.

Something, she had been told time and again by her
mother, that her beloved father hadn't been. Had Bryan
Wakefield been more cautious with his own life, he
might not have lost it in the line of duty. The ensuing
funeral, with full honors, had done little to fill the huge
gap her father's death had left in both her life and her
mother's.

Lydia crumpled the empty, soggy coffee container in
her hand and tossed it into the wastebasket.

The corridor was almost silent, and memories tiptoed
in, sneaking up on her. Pushing their way into her mind.

She could still remember the look on her mother's
face when she'd told her that she wasn't going to become a lawyer because her heart just wasn't in it.

Lydia smiled without realizing it. Her heart had been
bent on following three generations of Wakefields into
law enforcement. Her great-grandfather and grandfather
had both patrolled the streets of Los Angeles and her father had risen to the rank of detective on the same force,
doing *his* father proud.

Her mother had argued that she could become part
of the D.A.'s office. That way, she would still be in law
enforcement, only in the safer end of it. But Lydia had
remained firm. Sitting behind a desk with dusty books
or standing up in court in front of a judge whose bout

of indigestion or argument with a spouse might color the rulings of the day was not for her.

With tears in her eyes, her mother had called her her father's daughter and reluctantly given her blessing while praying to every saint who would listen to keep her daughter safe. Lydia had no doubt that her mother bombarded heaven on a daily basis.

Mercifully, Louise Wakefield remarried six months after Lydia had successfully completed her courses at Quantico. Her stepfather, Arthur Evans, was a kind, genteel man who ran a quaint antique shop. Her mother made him lunch every day and always knew where to find him and what time he'd be home. It was a good marriage. For the first time in nearly thirty years, Lydia knew her mother was at peace.

Lydia looked at the wall clock as she passed it. She sincerely wished she could lay claim to some of that peace herself right now. Glancing at the clock again, she frowned. It announced a time that was five minutes ahead of her own watch. Not that it mattered in the larger scheme of things. It just meant that her prisoner had now been in surgery for three hours and forty minutes, give or take five.

She rotated her neck and felt a hot twinge in her shoulder. It had been bothering her the entire time she'd been here. She couldn't wait for this night to be over. All she wanted to do was to go and soak in a hot tub.

It was her bullet they were digging out of Conroy. If he hadn't moved the way he had, it would have been lodged in his shoulder, not his chest. Though she was filled with loathing for what he'd done, she'd only meant to disarm him. Cornered, the man had trained his weapon on Elliot. There'd been no time to debate a course of action. It was either shoot or see Elliot go down.

Lydia felt no remorse for what had happened. This kind of thing went with the territory and she had long ago hardened her heart to it. If there was pity to be felt, it went to the parents of the boy whose life had been lost and to the people who, simply going about their business, had been injured in the blast.

Lydia sighed. The world seemed to be making less sense every day.

She found herself in front of the coffee machine again. If she had another cup, she seriously ran the danger of sloshing as she moved. But what else was there to do? There was no reading material around and even if there had been, she wouldn't be able to keep her mind on it. She was too agitated to concentrate.

Digging into her pocket, she winced. Damn the shoulder anyway. It felt as if it was on fire. Probably a hell of a bruise there. When she'd shot him, Conroy's weapon had discharged as he'd fallen to the ground. She'd immediately ducked to keep from getting struck by the stray bullet. As near as she could figure, she must have injured her shoulder when she hit the floor.

Lydia glanced down at herself. The jacket and pants she had on were both discolored with the prisoner's blood. Shot, he'd still tried to put up a fight. It had taken Elliot and her to subdue him. For a relatively small man, Conroy was amazingly strong. She supposed hate did that to you.

She looked accusingly at the operating room doors. Damn it, what was taking so long? Were they rebuilding Conroy from the ground up?

Lydia stifled a curse. She knew she could have someone from the Bureau stationed here in her place, but she didn't want to leave until she had a status report on the bomber's condition. She wanted to know exactly what she was up against. There was no way she was going to lose this one, even for a blink of an eye.

Her stomach rumbled, reminding her that not even she could live on coffee alone. She tried to recall when her last meal had been. The day had taken on an endless quality.

Lydia jerked her head around as she heard the operating room doors being pushed open. The sound of her heels echoed down the corridor as she quickly returned to her point of origin.

The physician who had given her such a hard time emerged, untying his mask. He looked tired. That made two of them.

"Well?" she demanded with no preamble.

It didn't surprise Lukas to find the blonde standing here like some kind of sentry. Gorgeous, the woman still bore a strong resemblance to a bull terrier, at least in her attitude. Their earlier exchange had convinced him that she wasn't someone who would let go easily. Or probably at all, for that matter.

Lukas took his time in answering her, walking over to the row of seats in the waiting area and sinking down onto the closest one. The woman, he noted, remained standing.

"Well, is he alive?" she pressed.

Lukas pulled off his surgical cap and looked at her. "Yes. He's lucky. The bullet was very close to his heart. Less than a sixteenth of an inch closer and he'd be on a slab in the morgue."

Her mouth twisted. Whether the word lucky was appropriate or not was a matter of opinion. "Too bad the boy his bomb blew up wasn't as lucky."

Lukas didn't feel like being drawn into a debate. Weary, he rose to tower over the woman. It gave him an advantage. He found he preferred it that way. "Look, I don't want to know what he did. My job is to patch him up as best I can."

Her eyes grew into small points of green fire. "How can you not care?" she asked heatedly. "How can you just divorce yourself from the fact that the man you just saved killed a teenage boy? That he might have killed more people had his timing been a little more fine-tuned."

The woman was a firebrand. The kind his uncle always gravitated toward. Too bad Uncle Henry wasn't here to appreciate this, Lukas thought.

"Because I'm a doctor, not a judge and jury." The look in his eyes challenged her. He knew all about hasty judgments. "Are you sure you have the right man?"

She laughed shortly. The tip they had gotten had specifically named John Conroy as the mastermind of the new supremacy group whose goal was to "purify" the country. The explosives they'd found in his house erased any doubts that might have existed. What they hadn't found, until it was too late, was the man himself.

"Oh, I'm sure."

There was something in her voice that caught his attention. "That was your bullet I took out."

"Yes." And he was going to condemn her for it, she thought. She could see it coming. There was a time for compassion and a time for justice. This was the latter. Lydia raised her chin. "We chased him down into the rear loading dock behind the mall. I shot him because he was about to shoot my partner."

The hour was late and he should be on his way. But something kept Lukas where he was a moment longer.

"I didn't ask you why you shot him. Figured that was part of your job."

She didn't like the way he said that. "You weren't there."

"No, I wasn't. Now if you'll excuse me, I have a life to get back to. Or at least a bed."

Finished, he brushed past her and accidentally came into contact with her shoulder. The woman bit back a moan, but he heard it. Lukas stopped and took a closer look at the bloodied area around her shoulder. When she'd first come in, he'd assumed that the blood belonged to the prisoner. Now he had his doubts.

"Take your jacket off."

Startled by the blunt order, she stared at him. "What?"

"I thought that was pretty clear." There was a no-nonsense tone to his voice. "Take your jacket off," he repeated.

Even as a child, she had never liked being ordered to do anything. It raised the hairs on the back of her neck. "Why?"

The last thing he wanted right now was to go head-to-head with a stubborn woman. "Because I think that's your blood, not his."

Lydia turned her head toward her shoulder. Very gingerly, she felt the area around the stain. Flickers of fire raced up and down her arm. Now that he said it, she had a sinking feeling he was right.

Dropping her hand, she gave a dismissive shrug with her uninjured shoulder. "Maybe you're right. I can take care of it."

Lukas glanced over her head. The operating room was free now. The orderly had wheeled his patient into the recovery room. Administration had sent in a security guard to watch him. That should please Ms. Law and Order, he thought.

"So can I. Come with me." It wasn't a suggestion. He caught her hand and dragged her behind him.

She had no choice but to accompany him. "You have a real attitude problem, you know that?"

Lukas spared her a glance. "I was going to say the same thing about you." He released her hand and gestured toward a gurney. "Sit there."

Lydia looked around the empty room, panic materializing. "Where's the prisoner?"

Opening a drawer in a side cabinet, he took out what he needed. "They took him to recovery."

Lydia turned on her heel, about to leave by the rear door, the way she assumed Conroy had. "Then I have to—"

He caught her hand again. This woman took work, he thought.

"Stay right here and let me have a look at that shoulder before it becomes infected," he instructed. "Relax, your prisoner's not about to regain consciousness for at least an hour."

She frowned, torn. Her shoulder was beginning to feel a great deal worse now than it had earlier. "You know that for a fact?"

The surgical pack in place, Lukas slipped on a pair of latex gloves. "Pretty much."

Maybe she was overreacting, at that. "Is he still handcuffed to the railing?"

In reply, Lukas nodded toward the metal bracelets lying on the countertop. "They're right there." He saw her look and watched her face cloud over. Like a storm capturing the prairie. "I figured you might be needing these for someone else."

She bit back a curse. Unconscious or not, she would have felt a great deal better if Conroy were still tethered to the railing on his bed. "This isn't a game."

"No one said it was." He nodded at her apparel. "Now take your jacket off. I'm not going to tell you again."

Tell, not ask. The man had a hell of a nerve. Setting her jaw, Lydia began to shrug out of the jacket, then abruptly stopped. The pain that flared through her left shoulder prevented any smooth motion. Acutely aware that the physician was watching her every move, she pulled her right arm out first, then slid the sleeve off the other arm. She tossed the jacket aside, then looked at her blouse. It was beyond saving.

She sighed. The Wedgwood blue blouse had been her favorite. "What a mess."

"Bullets will do that." Very carefully, he swabbed the area and then began to probe it. He saw her eyes water, but heard no sound. The woman was a great deal tougher than he'd assumed. He knew more than a couple who would have caused a greater fuss over a hangnail. "How is it you didn't realize you were shot?"

She measured out every word, afraid she was going to scream. "The excitement of the moment," she guessed. "I hit the floor when he fired. I just thought I banged my shoulder." Lydia sucked in a breath, telling herself it would be over soon. "It wouldn't have been the first time."

"And not the first time you were shot, either," he noted as he began to clean off the area. There was a scar just below her wound that looked to be about a year or so old.

Lydia pressed her lips together as she watched him prepare a needle. "No, not the first. What's that for?"

"That's to numb the area. I have to stitch you up."
He injected the serum. "How many times have you
been shot?"

She hated needles. It was a childhood aversion she'd
never managed to get over. Lydia counted to ten before
answering, afraid her voice would quiver if she said
something immediately.

"Not enough to make me resign, if that's what you
mean."

He couldn't decide if she was doing a Clint Eastwood
impression or a John Wayne. Tossing out the syringe,
Lukas reached for a needle. "You have family?"

Watching him sew made her stomach lurch. She concentrated on his cheekbones instead. They gave him a
regal appearance, she grudgingly conceded. "There's
my mother and a stepfather." She paused to take a
breath. "And my grandfather."

That made her an only child, he thought, making another stitch. "What do they have to say about people
playing target practice with your body?"

Did he think she was a pin cushion? Just how many
stitches was this going to take? "My mother doesn't
know." She'd never told her mother about the times
she'd gotten shot. "She thinks I live a charmed life. My
father was killed in the line of duty. I don't see any reason to make her worry any more than she already does."

Lukas glanced at her. She looked a little pale. Maybe
she was human, after all. "What about your grandfather?"

"He worries about me." Lydia kept her eyes forward,
wishing him done with it. "But he's also proud. He
walked a beat for thirty years."

"So that makes you what, third generation cop?"

"Fourth," she corrected. "My great-grandfather

walked the same beat before him." Lydia looked at him sharply. He was asking an awful lot of questions. "Why? Does this have to go on some form, or are you just being curious?"

Lukas took another stitch before answering. "Just trying to distract you while I work on your shoulder, that's all."

She didn't want any pity from him. "You don't have to bother. It doesn't hurt."

He raised his eyes to her face. "I thought FBI agents weren't supposed to lie."

His eyes held hers for a minute. She relented. "It doesn't hurt much," she amended.

He knew it had to hurt a lot, but he allowed her the lie without contradiction. "That's because the wound was clean." He paused to dab on a little more antiseptic. It went deep. "The bullet cut a groove in your shoulder but didn't go into it. That's why you probably didn't realize it. That and, as you said, the excitement of what was happening. They say that when Reagan was shot, he didn't know it until someone told him."

It felt as if he was turning her arm into a quilting project. Just how long was this supposed to take? The last time she'd been stitched up, the doctor had hardly paused to knot the thread. "Maybe I should run for president then."

The crack made him smile. "Maybe. You'd probably get the under-twenty-five vote. They don't examine things too closely."

Another slam. Did he get his kicks that way? Or was it because she didn't crumble in front of his authority? "Anyone ever tell you your bedside manner leaves something to be desired?"

He found that her feistiness amused him despite the fact that he was bone-weary. "Most of my patients are unconscious when I work on them." He cut the thread. "There, done."

Gingerly, she tested her shoulder, moving it slowly in a concentric circle. She felt the pain shoot up to her ear. "It feels worse."

"It will for a couple of days." Rising, he set the remaining sutures aside, then preceded her to the door. He held it open for her. "If you ride down to the first floor with me, I'll write you a prescription."

She paused long enough to pick up her now ruined jacket before following him to the door. "I told you, I don't need anything for the pain."

He began to lead the way to the elevators, only to find that she wasn't behind him. "But you might need something to fight an infection."

She looked down at her shoulder, then at him accusingly. "It's infected?"

"The medicine is to keep that from happening," he told her, coming dangerously close to using up his supply of patience.

"I have to go guard the prisoner." And to do that, she needed to know where the recovery room was located. She had a feeling he wasn't going to volunteer the information.

She was right. "There's a security guard posted outside the recovery room. You need to get home and get some rest."

The security guards she'd come across were usually little more than doormen. They didn't get paid enough to risk their lives. Conroy was part of a militant group, not some misguided man who had accidentally blown up a chem lab. "You ever watch *Star Trek*?"

The question had come out of the blue. "Once or twice, why?"

"Security guards are always the first to die."

"Your point being?"

"Someone professional needs to be posted outside his room," she told him impatiently.

That was easily solved. "So call somebody professional." He saw her open her mouth. "As long as it's not you." The issue was non-negotiable. "Doctor's orders."

Certainly took a lot for granted, didn't he? "So now you're my doctor?"

Taking her good arm, he physically led her over to the elevator bank.

"I patched you up, that makes me your doctor for the time being. And I'm telling you that you need some rest." He jabbed the down button, still holding on to her. "You can bend steel in your bare hands tomorrow after you get a good night's sleep."

She pulled her arm out of his grasp, then took a step to the side in case he had any ideas of taking hold of her again. "Look, thanks for the needlepoint, but that doesn't give you the right to tell me what to do."

"Yeah, it does." The elevator bell rang a moment before the doors opened. He stepped inside, looking at her expectantly. She entered a beat later, though grudgingly, judging by the look on her face. "Your mother has gray hair, doesn't she?"

"Does yours?"

He inclined his head. "As a matter of fact, it's still midnight-black." After writing out a prescription for both an antibiotic and a painkiller, he tore the sheet off the pad.

"Then you must have left home early." She folded the

prescription slip he had handed her. "I'll fill this in the morning."

"The pharmacy here stays open all night. I'll ride down with you if you like."

He certainly was going out of his way. But then, she knew what it was like to be dedicated to getting your job done. She couldn't fault him for that. "I thought you had a bed you wanted to get to."

"Like your prisoner, it's not going anywhere." He pressed the letter *B* on the elevator keypad. "A few more minutes won't matter."

Lydia had always been one to pick her battles, and she decided that maybe it would be easier just to go along with this dictator-in-a-lab-coat than to argue with him.

With a sigh, she nodded her head in agreement as the elevator took them down to the basement.

Chapter 3

The scent of vanilla slowly enveloped her, began to soothe her.

Ever so slowly, Lydia eased herself into the suds-filled water. Leaning back, she frowned at her left shoulder. The cellophane crinkled, straining at the tape she'd used to keep the wrap in place.

Graywolf had warned her about getting her stitches wet just before she left him and, though she'd pretended to dismiss his words, she wasn't about to do anything that might impede her immediate and complete recovery. There was no question in her mind that she'd go stir crazy inside of a week if the Bureau forced her to go on some sort of disability leave. She had no actual hobbies to fill up her time, no books piling up on her desk, waiting to be read, just a few articles on state-of-the-art surveillance. Nothing she couldn't get through in a few hours.

Her work was her life and it took up all of her time.
Yes, there was the occasional program she watched on
television outside of the news and, once in a while, she
took in a movie, usually with her mother or grandfather.
There was even the theater every year or so. But for the
most part, she ate and slept her job and she truly liked
it that way. Liked the challenge of fitting the pieces of
a puzzle together to create a whole, no matter how long
it took.

It hadn't taken all that long this time, she thought,
watching bubbles already begin to dissipate. The tip they'd
gotten from Elliot's source had been right on the money.

Looking back, she thought, things seemed to have happened in lightning succession. An informer in the New
World supremacy group they had been keeping tabs on
had tipped off the Bureau that a bombing at a populated
area was in the works. Initially, that had been it: a populated area. No specifics. That could have meant a museum,
an amusement park, anyplace. For a week, with the clock
ticking, they'd all sweated it out, having nothing to go on.

And then they'd gotten lucky. Very lucky, she
thought, swishing the water lazily with her hand, letting
the heat relax her. If that informant hadn't had a run-in
with Conroy and been nursing a grudge against him,
they would have never been able to piece things together. Even so, they'd gotten to the mall only seconds
before the explosion had rocked the western end, the site
that had just been newly renovated and expanded and
had been filled with Native American art and artifacts.

As Elliot had driven through the city streets, trying
to get there in time, she'd been on her phone, frantically
calling the local police and alerting mall security to
evacuate as many people as possible.

It been an exercise in futility. They'd reached the mall ahead of the police. She'd scanned the parking lot, taking in the amount of cars there, appalled at the number, even though by weekend standards, it was low.

The explosion had hit just as they'd parked. The force had sent one teenager flying into the air. He was dead by the time she'd reached him. It was then that she and Elliot had spotted Conroy running around the rear of what was left of that part of the structure.

She barely remembered yelling out a warning. All she could focus on was Conroy turning and aiming his gun in Elliot's direction. The rest had happened in blurry slow motion.

And try as she might, she still didn't remember being hit.

There were others involved; she knew that they were going to be caught. It was a silent promise she made to the teenager who wouldn't be going home tonight. Or ever.

Lydia sank down farther into her tub, the one luxury she had allowed herself when she moved in, replacing the fourteen-inch high bathtub with one that could easily submerge a hippo if necessary. Some people took quick, hot showers to wash away the tension of the day; she took baths when she had the time. Long, steamy, soul-restoring baths.

The phone rang, intruding.

Glancing at the portable receiver she'd brought in with her, Lydia debated just letting her machine pick up the call. But the shrill ringing had destroyed the tranquillity that had begun seeping into her soul.

Besides, it might be about Conroy.

Stretching, she reached over the side of the tub for the receiver and pressed the talk button. "Wakefield."

"Don't you ever say hello anymore?" The voice on the other end had a soft twang to it.

She smiled, sinking back against the tub again, envisioning the soft, rosy face, the gentle, kind eyes that were too often set beneath worried brows. "Hi, Mom. What's up?"

"Nothing, darling. I was just lonely for the sound of your voice."

Lydia knew evasion when she heard it. For now she played along. "Well, here it is, in its full glory."

"You sound tired."

Her mother was slowly working up to whatever had prompted her to call, Lydia thought. That was the difference between them. She pounced, her mother waltzed. Slowly. "It's been a long day."

There was just the slightest bit of hesitation. "Anything you can tell me about?"

Her mother knew better than that. "Just lots of paperwork, that's all," Lydia told her. Idly, she moved her toe around, stirring the water. Bubbles began fading faster. The scent of vanilla clung.

She heard her mother laugh shortly. "You lie as badly as your father did."

Lydia glanced at her shoulder to make sure it was still above the waterline. Keeping it up wasn't easy even if she was leaning against the soap holder.

"You don't want to know details, Mom." It was supposed to be an unspoken agreement between them. Her mother didn't ask and she didn't have to lie. Her mother was slipping. "All you need to know is that I'm okay. I'm soaking in a tub right now."

"Alone?"

Half asleep she still would have been able to hear the

hopeful note in her mother's voice. "Yes, unless you count Dean Martin on the radio."

Her mother made no effort to silence the sigh that escaped. "Sorry, I was just hoping…"

She knew what her mother was hoping. It was an old refrain. "Mom, don't take this the wrong way, but not tonight, all right?"

"Something happened, didn't it? I heard about the bombing."

Here it comes, Lydia thought. The real reason for the call.

"Was that you—"

"Doing the bombing?" Lydia cut in cheerfully. "No." She decided to toss her mother a bone. Even the Bureau wasn't entirely heartless. "Doing the picking up of pieces? Yes. We've got a suspect in custody—that's all I can tell you."

There was disappointment and frustration in her mother's voice. "I can get more from the evening news, Lydia."

When she was small, her mother had been her first confidante. They would talk all the time. But she wasn't small anymore. On an intellectual level, she knew her mother understood why she couldn't say anything. It was the heart that gave them both trouble.

For a second her thoughts sidelined to the surgeon who had pushed her out of the operating room. Who had insisted on stitching her up. She forced her mind back to the conversation.

"They're at liberty to talk, Mom, I'm not. They don't have a possible case to jeopardize."

She heard her mother sigh. Louise Wakefield Evans had been both the daughter and the wife of a policeman.

She, better than anyone, knew about procedures that had to be followed.

Still, she said, "I hate being shut out this way, Lydia."

Lydia shifted in the tub, then quickly sat up. She'd nearly gotten the bandage wet.

"I'm not shutting you out, Mom. I'm shutting evidence in." The water was turning cool. "Mom, I'm turning pruney, I'd better go."

Her mother knew when to take her cue. "All right. Good night, Lydia. I love you."

"Love you, too, Mom."

Before her mother could change her mind, Lydia pressed the talk button, breaking the connection and ushering in silence. She dropped the receiver onto the mat.

Lydia felt bad that she couldn't share what had happened to her today with her mother, but she knew it would only have served to agitate and worry Louise. In the long run, she'd rather her mother had semipeace of mind by remaining in the dark than live with daily terrors—even if she could give her details, which she couldn't.

Her mouth curved slightly as a question her mother had asked echoed in her brain.

Was she alone?

That would place her mother among the eternal optimists. Louise still nursed the hope that Lydia would be swept off her feet, marry and chuck this whole FBI special agent business.

Lucky for her, Louise hadn't seen that surgeon tonight. There was no doubt in Lydia's mind that her mother would have been all over Graywolf, plying him with questions, inviting him over for Sunday dinner. Louise Wakefield Evans was desperate for grandchildren and Lydia was the only one who could provide her with them. She'd had a brother, born first, but he had died before his first birthday, a victim of infant crib death syndrome. With no other siblings available, Lydia was the only one left to fulfill her mother's hopes.

"Sorry, Mom," Lydia murmured as she leaned forward to open up the faucet again.

The next moment, hot water flowed into the tub again, merging with the cooling liquid that was already there.

First chance she had, she was going to talk to Arthur about getting her mother a puppy. She knew her stepfather was sympathetic to her. A new puppy should occupy her mother, at least temporarily.

Closing her eyes, Lydia let her head fall back against the inflated pillow lodged against the back of the tub. An image of the surgeon materialized behind her lids.

Startled, she pried her eyes open.

What was she doing, thinking about him? She was supposed to be trying to make her mind a blank.

Maybe it was the medicine, making her woozy.

Lydia blew out a breath, ruffling her bangs. She decided that soaking in the tub might not be the smartest thing to do if she were truly sleepy. Death by suds was not the way she wanted to go.

Lydia reached for a towel.

The rhythmic staccato of high heels meeting the freshly washed hospital floor had Lukas looking up from the chart he was writing on. Half a beat before he did, he knew it was her. He'd picked up on the cadence last night. Fast, no nonsense, no hesitancy. A woman with a mission.

Closing the chart, he replaced it on the nurse's desk, still watching the woman approach. He wondered vaguely if Ms. Special Agent was focused like that all the time or if it was the job that brought it out. Did she know how to kick back after hours? Did she even *have* "after hours"?

Lukas had a sneaking suspicion she didn't.

That made two of them.

Even after he'd gone home last night to catch a few hours of well-deserved sleep, he'd wound up calling the hospital to check on Jacob Lindstrom, the patient he'd operated on before Ms. Special Agent had thundered into his life.

Lukas's eyes swept over her as she walked toward him. The woman was wearing another suit, a powder blue one; but this time she had on a skirt instead of pants. The skirt brushed against her thighs as she walked and gave him the opportunity to note that her legs were as near perfect as any he'd ever seen. Long, sleek, and just curved enough to trigger a man's fantasies.

It made him wonder why Harrison hadn't hit on her last night. Special agent or not, she looked to be right up his best friend's alley.

But then, maybe Harrison *had* hit on her and she'd set him straight. That would have been a first. Lukas made a mental note to catch up with Harrison to ask for details when he got the chance. If there had been a conquest last night, something told him he would have known it. One way or another.

"You're here bright and early," he commented as she came up to him.

He didn't look as tired, she observed. His sharp, blue eyes seemed to be taking in everything about her. She'd always thought that Native Americans had brown eyes. "So are you."

Her mouth looked pouty when she said the word "you." Something stirred within him, but he dismissed it. He'd been around Harrison too long. Maybe the other man's ways had rubbed off on him. "I have patients to see."

Lydia inclined her head, as if going him one better. "I have a prisoner to interrogate."

And here, Lukas thought, was where they came to loggerheads. It hadn't taken long. Less than a minute, by his estimate.

"Not until he's up to it."

"If he's conscious, he's up to it, Dr.…." Lydia paused and, though she knew his name, made a show of looking at the badge that hung from a dark blue cord around his neck. Since the back of the badge faced her, she turned it around. "Graywolf." Releasing the badge, she raised her eyes to his face. "This wasn't some spur-of-the-moment, impulsive act by a deranged man acting out some sick fantasy. This was a carefully planned act of terrorism. This man is part of a group that call themselves the New World Supremacists. I assure you, he wasn't alone at the mall last night. I want to make sure his friends don't go scurrying off to their garages to concoct some more pipe bombs to kill more innocent people. The only way I'm going to do that is to get names."

He understood all that, but he was coming at this from another angle. He had to put the welfare of his patient first. "Ms. Wakefield—"

"That's Special Agent Wakefield," she corrected him. Taking out her wallet, she opened it for him. "It says so right here on my ID."

Holding her wallet for a moment, Lukas looked at the photograph. She looked better in person. The photograph made her look too hard, too unforgiving. There was something in her eyes that told him that might not be the entire picture.

He dropped his hand to his side. "I always wondered about that. Is 'special' a title, like lieutenant colonel?" he deadpanned. "Are there any regular, nonspecial agents at the agency?"

"We're all special," she informed him, finding that she was gritting her teeth.

"In our own way," he allowed magnanimously. "Even people accused of crimes."

Not in her book. "Just why are you yanking my chain, Doctor?"

Because it was there, he realized. But he gave her a more reasonable answer.

"Maybe it's because you insist on getting in my way. The man you shot almost died on the table last night. Twice. I'd like to make sure he doesn't. Having you go at him like a representative of the Spanish Inquisition isn't going to help his recovery. I think it might be better if you hold off asking any questions."

Not hardly. And she didn't particularly like being told what to do. "I don't give a damn about his recovery, Doctor. I just want him to live long enough to give me the names of his buddies." She watched him shiver and then turn up the collar of his lab coat. It wasn't particularly cold. "What are you doing?"

"Trying to protect myself from frostbite." He slid his collar back into place. "You always come off this cold-blooded?"

She could almost literally feel her patience breaking in two.

"I happen to be a very warm person," Lydia snapped, then realized how ridiculous that sounded coming in the form of a growl. A smile slowly emerged to replace her frown. "Ask anyone."

It was amazing. He wouldn't have thought that a simple smile could transform someone's face so much. But it did. The woman in front of him seemed light-years removed from the one he'd just been talking to. This one looked younger, softer. Way softer.

"Maybe I will."

He was being nice. So why did she feel so uneasy all of a sudden? And why was he still looking at her as if he was dissecting her a layer at a time? "What are you staring at?"

"Your smile."

Instinctively she began to press her lips together to blot out her smile, then stopped. The smile was replaced by a glare. "What's wrong with my smile?"

He spread his hands. "Nothing. Absolutely nothing. Makes you look like a completely different person, in my opinion."

As if she gave a damn about his opinion. "I'll remember that the next time I need a disguise." It was getting late and she had to get down to business. "Have you moved my prisoner since last night?"

She had remained long enough for Conroy to be transferred from recovery to a single-unit room, where she'd made certain that a policeman from the Bedford police force was stationed.

Lukas was about to remind her that the man was his patient before he was her prisoner, but he let the matter drop. He'd learned early on that butting his head against a stone wall never brought victory.

"I wouldn't dare. I left him just where I found him this morning."

She could do without the sarcasm. "How is he?"

It was Conroy's chart he'd been writing on when he heard her approach. "Still weak."

That was a relative term in her opinion. "I don't want him to dance, I just want him to talk."

"That might be difficult. He's on a great deal of pain medication—speaking of which," he segued smoothly, "how's your shoulder?"

Graywolf's question only reminded her of how much the shoulder ached. "If I was a bird, I'd have to postpone flying south for the winter, but under the circumstances, I guess it's all right."

Lukas nodded. "I need to see you back in a week to take the stitches out." She was favoring her left side. Would it have killed her to follow his instructions? "I see you're not wearing a sling."

She'd actually toyed with the idea this morning, arranging and adjusting several colorful scars around her arm and shoulder. They'd only made her feel like an invalid. "I don't want to attract attention."

Too late, Lukas thought. Three orderlies had passed by since she'd stopped to talk to him and all three had been in danger of severely spraining their necks as they turned to look at her. "Then maybe you should wear a paper bag over your head."

"What?"

Was she fishing for a compliment, or was she wound up so tightly about her job that she didn't see her own reflection in the morning? "I'm just saying that a woman who looks like you do always attracts attention."

Her eyes narrowed in surprise. "Are you coming on to me, Doctor?" She'd dabbled in profiling. Graywolf didn't seem the type.

"Me?" He raised both hands, fingers pointed to the ceiling. "I wouldn't have the nerve to come on to someone like you. I'm just making an observation, that's all." He looked at his watch. "Now, if you'll excuse me, I've got the rest of my rounds to make."

He was turning away from her when she called after him. "You mean you're not going to hover over me while I try to question the prisoner?"

Lukas stopped to look at her one last time. "Would it do any good?"

A smile crept back to her lips as Lydia shook her head. "No."

"Then I won't." He crossed back to her, fishing into his coat pocket. He took out a card and pressed it into her hand. "There's my number if you need me."

She glanced down at the card. Three numbers were neatly printed above one another. "Pager, cell phone and office number." Lydia raised her eyes from the card. "What about your home number?"

"Unlisted. On a need-to-know basis," he added just before he left.

Looking after him, Lydia thoughtfully folded the card between her thumb and forefinger and tucked it into her jacket pocket.

"Damn but I never thought I'd live to see the day."

Roused from her thoughts, Lydia spun around to face Elliot. "See what day?"

He was grinning. *Wait until Janice hears about this!* "The day you were flirting."

"Flirting?" Lydia echoed incredulously. "Are you out of your mind? I was not flirting."

"No?" Elliot crossed his arms at his chest, waiting to be convinced. "Then what do you call it?"

In Graywolf's Hands

"Talking."

"I see."

There were times when her partner got on her nerves—royally. "Don't give me that smug smile."

He made no attempt to eliminate it. "I wasn't aware that it was smug."

"Well it is," she told him. Because one of the nurses had stopped what she was doing and was obviously eavesdropping, Lydia pulled her partner aside, out of earshot. "What is this, a conspiracy? My mother calls to find out if I'm alone in the bathtub and then you come along and tell me you think I'm flirting."

Elliot made a mental note to later ask her what had prompted her mother's question. For now, he shrugged innocently. "Can't help it. In spring a person's mind often turns to thoughts of love, remember?"

What did that have to do with anything? "It's autumn. Remember?"

Unruffled, Elliot laughed. "I'm late, it's been a busy year."

Okay, she'd been a good sport long enough. This had to stop. "Elliot, I'm packing a gun."

The look he gave her was completely unimpressed. "I'm shaking."

This was getting them nowhere. And the day stretched out in front of her, long and unaccommodating. "Let's go, we have a prisoner to interrogate."

"Lead the way." Her partner's expression had turned appropriately serious, but there was a twinkle in his eye she had trouble ignoring.

Chapter 4

John Conroy was not a particularly large man. The height of five foot eight listed on his driver's license was charitably stretching the truth. Bandaged, bruised and buffered by white sheets in a bed, he looked small and non-threatening.

Looking at him, it was almost hard for Lydia to believe that this was the man who had helped to carry out an attack whose ultimate goal was to kill as many people as possible. Which made her wonder why he had picked a weeknight. Was it that he couldn't wait, or that he had thought there was less of a chance of being caught?

There was something to be said for impatience, she thought as Elliot closed the door behind them.

"Evil comes in all sorts of packages, doesn't it?" Elliot commented, noticing the way she was looking at the man in the hospital bed.

"The Bible says that Satan was the most beautiful of all the archangels," she murmured, moving closer to the prisoner.

She noted with satisfaction that along with the various devices hooking Conroy up to vigilant monitors, a tarnished steel bracelet encircled his wrist, chaining him to the railing, keeping him from escaping if he could somehow summon the strength. She'd made a point of putting it back on him last night. Nice to see that the doctor hadn't removed it again.

Conroy looked as though he was unconscious. Lydia studied his face intently, watching for a telltale flutter of his lashes that would give his game away. There was none.

"Not that," she added, "this puny, unimpressive piece of work could have ever been remotely placed in that category."

Not getting a reaction to her insult, Lydia bent until her face was level with Conroy's.

Elliot came closer. "What are you doing?"

"Getting in his face." She spared her partner a momentary glance before looking back to Conroy. "Seeing if he's really unconscious. Are you, Conroy?" she asked loudly. "Are you really out, or just playing possum? Not going to do you any good, you know. You have to come up for air sometime."

Elliot laughed to himself. "Well, those golden tones would certainly rouse me right up." Finding a place for himself in the single-care unit, Elliot took a pistachio nut from his jacket pocket and began to work at it with his nails.

Straightening, she saw Elliot shell the nut. For as long as she'd known him, he'd always carried a supply of pistachio nuts in his pocket. With the understanding of a loving wife, Janice replenished his supply every morning. "Isn't it kind of early for that?"

He shrugged. "Gives me something to do." Seeing the wastebasket, he tossed the shell into it and took out another nut. "I think he's out, Lyd."

She nodded, annoyed. Frustrated. "Looks like the good doctor was right." So much for questioning Conroy now. Though Elliot had seniority, the assistant director had made her lead on this case. "Why don't you go back to the office and see about running down some of those phone calls that have been coming in? Take Burkowitz with you," she said, naming one of the agents appointed to the special task force. "And while you're at it, find out if the bomb squad has found something useful." She knew there'd been evidence galore, but whether or not it led anywhere was another story. Most of the time they were left with a plethora of puzzle pieces and no unifying tray to place them in. "No sense in both of us hanging around until Mr. Wizard here wakes up."

She'd get no argument from him on that. Elliot was already crossing to the door. "That might be a while, Lyd. Sure you want to hang around, waiting?" He'd never met anyone who hated waiting more than Lydia. "We could have Rodriguez page us."

He nodded toward the door and the man they had posted at the desk out front. It was one of their own now, instead of a local policeman, something the Bedford chief hadn't been overly happy about. As always, there was professional jealousy and the matter of jurisdiction clouding things up. But at bottom, they all wanted the same thing. Not to have this kind of thing happen in Bedford ever again.

She looked back at Conroy. Unlike Elliot's endless supply of pistachios, the supremacist was going to be a difficult nut to crack. She wanted to be sure that she got first chance at him. "I'd feel better being here."

After four years he could pretty much read her like a book. "Lyd, the bombing wasn't your fault."

Logically, no. But emotionally it was another story. "Thanks, but it might have been prevented if I'd been a little faster, dug a little deeper. We ignored that first rumor."

"Because it *was* a rumor, one of over a dozen—the rest of which were bogus," he reminded her. "Hell, Lyd, we had our hands full." He also knew her well enough to know that he was wasting his breath. "The term's 'special agent' not 'super agent.'"

The comment succeeded in evoking a smile from her. "Who says?"

Elliot had his hand on the door, and he was shaking his head. "You're getting more stubborn every day."

She looked at him significantly. "I had a damn good teacher."

"Haven't got the faintest idea what you're talking about," he deadpanned as he left the room.

Lydia heard the door close as she turned back to look at the man in the bed. He hadn't moved a muscle since they'd walked in. The only sounds in the room were the ones made by the machines arranged in a metallic semi-circle around his bedside.

He looked almost peaceful. It made her physically ill to be in the same room with him.

"What kind of a sick pervert blows up women and children?" she demanded of the unconscious man in a low, steely voice that seethed with anger.

Only the sound of the monitor answered her question.

Impatient, she blew out a sigh. "You've got to wake up sometime," she told him. "And when you do, I'm going to be right here to squeeze the names of those other men out of you. You're going down for this, my friend, and you're not going down alone."

She knew that would be little comfort to the parents of the teenager who'd senselessly died, but maybe it would keep others from following Conroy's example. Lydia already knew for a fact that this kind of thing had never happened in Bedford before and she wanted to make sure that it never would again. She wanted to do more than send a message to the New World supremacy group who'd been behind this, she wanted to smash it into unrecognizable bits.

With Elliot gone, there was no one to distract her. Unable to remain any longer in the room with a man she loathed with every fiber of her being, she turned on her heel and walked out. She paused long enough to talk to the agent who was sitting at the desk less than five feet from the door.

"I want to know the second he opens his eyes, Special Agent," she told him. "Not the minute, the second. Clear?"

The dark head bobbed up and down. This was his first assignment. "Absolutely, Special Agent Wakefield."

Had she ever been that eager? she wondered. When she'd first come to the Bureau, had she seemed this wet behind the ears?

Somehow, she doubted it. There were times when she thought she'd been born old. At other times she knew it was her father's death and the job that had done this to her.

Her voice softened. "Do you have my pager number, Ethan?"

He looked surprised to be addressed by his given name rather than by the neutral title the Bureau had bestowed on all of its operatives. He patted his pocket where he'd put the card she'd handed him before she'd entered the hospital room. "Right here."

"I'm going to the cafeteria to get some coffee," she told the man. "Remember, the *second*."

He nodded solemnly.

Satisfied, Lydia walked down the corridor to the elevators. The cafeteria was located in the basement. Breakfast was probably still being served. Not that she really wanted any. She normally didn't eat until around noon, a holdover from her college days when she'd stayed in bed until the last possible moment. Then there would only be enough time to get to class. Food took second place to sleep.

This had all the earmarks of a long day, she thought. But Conroy had to come to sooner or later. With any luck, it would be sooner. She had every confidence that he could be broken and made to give up the names of the others. The man was small-time, small-minded; he wasn't going to want to go down alone.

One militant group down, only a million or so more to root out. When she thought of it in those terms, it was a daunting task. But a journey always begins with the first step and Conroy was their first step.

"So, did he say anything?"

Startled by the question coming from behind her, Lydia was caught off guard. She turned around, her hand to her gun before she recognized the deep, resonant voice.

Graywolf.

She relaxed, dropping her hand from the hilt of her weapon. "Are you following me?"

"You're walking around in my hospital," he pointed out. "These are my stomping grounds, not yours. And given that you're hovering around my patient, I'd say the odds are pretty good that our paths are going to cross with a fair amount of regularity." He crossed his arms in front of him. "You didn't answer my question. Did he say anything?"

For a split second the image of Lukas wearing full headdress, stripped down to fringed leggings and war paint, flashed through her mind.

Where had that come from? If there was anyone who didn't deal in stereotypes, it would be her.

Annoyed, unsettled, she shoved her hands into her pockets and lifted her shoulders in a moderate shrug that instantly reminded her she should be favoring the left one.

"You were right," she admitted grudgingly. "He was still unconscious."

A hint of a smile played along his lips. That had to cost her, he mused. She didn't strike him as someone who liked to admit she was wrong. He supposed if he were being honest, he could more than identify with that.

Lukas nodded. "Big of you to admit it. And I'll be equally big and not say I told you so. So, heading back to the office?"

"No, the cafeteria," she corrected. Since no elevator had appeared to rescue her from this conversation, Lydia pressed the down button again, harder this time. "I figure you have to have better coffee down there than in the vending machines."

A logical conclusion, but in this case, not a valid one. "Liquid tar would taste better than the coffee in the vending machines. Although if you really want better coffee…" He debated for a minute, then inclined his head. "Follow me."

She looked at him, not taking a step. "To where?"

Pausing, amused despite himself, he studied her. "You always this suspicious?"

Lydia raised her chin. "It's kept me alive so far."

The woman was definitely defensive. He wasn't aware that he had said anything to trigger that response. "The doctors' lounge on the first floor," he replied in answer to her initial question. "We keep a pot of the real stuff down there." Lukas began leading the way. This time, she followed. "How do you think we keep going all those hours?"

She shrugged indifferently. "Never gave it any thought."

He slanted a look at her. She had almost a perfect profile, he decided. "What do you give thought to?"

He was challenging her, she thought. "Ways to keep terrorists from blowing up innocent people."

He took her words apart. "What if they blow up guilty people?"

She sidestepped a couple coming out of a small gift shop, nearly walking into the large arrangement of sunflowers the man was carrying. "What?"

"In their minds," he explained, then backtracked when he saw she wasn't following his conversation. Or maybe it was disapproval he saw on her face. "Maybe they think they're getting back at people who they feel are guilty of something."

Was he a bleeding heart? It didn't go with the image

he projected. "Doesn't matter what they think. They're not supposed to act as judge and jury." She stopped abruptly. Maybe he *was* some sort of bleeding heart. What a waste that would be. "You're not defending the actions of these people, are you?"

He looked at her mildly. She couldn't read the expression in his eyes. He brought her to a bank of service elevators and pressed for one. It arrived before he took his finger from the button.

"No."

She stepped in ahead of him. He reached around her and pressed the ground floor button. "Then what are you doing?" she asked impatiently. She had no time for word games if that was what Graywolf was playing.

"Just trying to see how your mind works," he answered mildly. "Getting a dialogue going on your home territory."

"Why?"

"Because we're riding in an elevator together and I'd rather listen to you talk than put up with the music the hospital insists on piping in."

She had no idea why that made her feel like smiling. "So I'm better than a Muzak tape?"

"At the very least." The elevator doors opened and he took the lead again. "This way." He reached for her instinctively as two orderlies guided a gurney past them, heading in the opposite direction. Lukas noticed that she pulled away. "So how's your shoulder?"

"Sore."

He was surprised at the admission. He'd half expected her to say that she'd forgotten all about it. Maybe she was human, after all. This time, the thought made him smile.

"It's going to be that way for several days. I'll need to see you again in about a week to take out the stitches."

Lydia wasn't pleased with the idea of having to take off her blouse around him again. She knew he was a doctor, but there was something far too intimate about the whole thing.

"Won't they just dissolve on their own?"

He turned down another corridor. "They're not those kinds of stitches."

Where were they going, to Oz? Maybe this was a mistake. "Why not?"

"These hold better. The other kind we use for internal sewing." Reaching the lounge, he opened the door for her, then stopped. "Does this insult you?"

Lydia gave him a dismissive look as she walked by him. "If you're trying to be politically correct, it's too late for that," she informed him. "And no, having a man hold open a door for me doesn't send me off into an emotional tailspin." She tended to think of it in terms of equality. "If I'd gotten to the door first, I would have held it open for you."

"Fair enough." He crossed to the small island that housed a coffee machine and all the ingredients necessary to make a decent cup of smoldering caffeine. "How do you take your coffee? No, don't tell me," he interrupted himself. "Black, right?"

She wasn't a purist. She didn't drink coffee for the taste, but for what it could accomplish. "Depends on how bad it is."

"It's good."

The man, she realized, was standing too close to her. She liked having space around her, keeping everyone at a decent distance. Whether it was her training coming to the fore, or her own preferences, she never bothered analyzing. The end desire was still the same.

She took a step back. "Then black."

"Black it is," he replied.

Skittish, he decided, noting the way Lydia stepped back from him. As a boy, he'd seen a horse like that, a mare that had been mistreated. Winning her trust had been a challenge. He wondered how Ms. Special Agent would take to being compared to a skittish mare. Not well, if he was any judge.

She watched him pour rich, black liquid into one mug, then another. She assumed that the one he took was his. Accepting the other, she looked down at it. "Whose is this?"

"Someone who's not on duty right now." He took a long sip from his mug. "He won't mind. Don't worry, it's clean," he assured her, amused. "He rinses it out once every fourth Wednesday of the month. That was last night, so you lucked out."

With a shrug, she took a long sip herself. The hot liquid cut a path through her insides. But he was right, it was good.

"You always this flippant?"

"No, actually I'm not. Must be the company." He looked at her significantly before sitting at the table to the left of the coffee station.

After a beat, she joined him. The table seated two and there wasn't all that much room under the table once he put his long legs beneath it. "How long before Conroy regains consciousness?"

He didn't even need to give the answer any thought. "Hard to tell."

She put her own interpretation on the answer. "Are you deliberately keeping him drugged?"

He set his mug down on the table. "Now why would I do that?"

She took the bleeding-heart scenario one step further. "So I won't interrogate him and possibly upset your precious patient."

He was actually more attuned to her feelings that he was letting on. There was something about her that had him rallying to the other side just to watch her reaction. He supposed there was possibly a small boy within him yet.

"He's my patient but he's far from precious." He took another long sip and waited until the liquid hit bottom. "Don't get me wrong, 'Special Agent,' there's no love lost here. I don't pretend to cast a blind eye to what Conroy's done, but I've got to stay above my emotions when I'm doing what I was trained to do. Impartiality is what keeps me sharp." He studied her face. "I imagine it's the same for you."

"Sometimes." The way he looked at her made strange things happen in her stomach. She'd faced down a shooter who'd gunned down another special agent with far less activity transpiring below her waist. "And sometimes, I can't help feeling the way I feel. Passion is what spurs me on."

"'Passion,'" he repeated. He raised a brow. "Are you a passionate person, Special Agent?"

It took her a second to drag her eyes away from his lips. "Why do I feel you're mocking me every time you say that?"

His eyes held hers. "Could be because you're not comfortable with the title."

She ignored the small shiver that zigzagged down her spine, telling herself it was cool within the lounge. "Oh, but I am. See, you're not always right."

He shrugged, the soul of innocence. "Never claimed to be."

She redirected the conversation toward a topic she felt more comfortable with. "How long before Conroy can be transferred?"

To his ear, there was more than a little disdain in her voice. "To where, a dungeon?"

She resented what she took to be his condescending tone. "To a maximum security holding area in the county jail."

He finished his coffee and set down the mug. "Depends on how fast he responds and stabilizes."

She wrapped her hands around her own mug, her eyes intent on his face. If he lied, she thought she could detect it. "In your humble, expert opinion—"

His mouth curved slightly as he looked at her. "Now who's mocking who? And after I let you drink our coffee, too."

She didn't know if he was being sarcastic, or merely teasing. Lydia reserved judgment. "Turnabout is fair play. Answer the question."

"In my humble opinion," he repeated, "I'd say probably a week. Could be sooner." He looked at his empty mug, debating another serving. He'd already had four cups since he'd first opened his eyes this morning. "Could be longer."

He was giving her the runaround. She decided to goad him a little to see where it went. "Are you always this unsure of yourself?"

"I am never unsure of myself," he corrected. "I just don't try to second-guess my patients." Lukas raised a brow as he looked directly at her. "Even patients with fire in their eyes."

Lydia squared her shoulders. The action was not without its price. "What are you trying to second-guess about me?"

"Why someone who looks like you would choose to put her life on the line every day."

Her back went up. She'd had to fight to overcome the handicap of her looks all her life. No one took her seriously at first, thinking that she'd gotten where she had solely because of her appearance. The Hollywood-perpetrated image of an empty-headed blonde was something she found herself fighting time and again.

"Instead of what, becoming a model?"

The barely veiled anger took him by surprise. And then he smiled slightly, understanding. She'd encountered prejudice. It gave them something else in common.

"That might be one way to go," he allowed. "I was thinking more along the lines of being a teacher, maybe making impressionable young boys study harder to make points with their beautiful instructor."

She relented, but only a little. "Now you're beginning to sound like my mother. I already told you last night, my father was a policeman. So was my grandfather and my great-grandfather."

Lukas studied her for a moment before saying anything. "So you went into the family business."

She looked up at the door as a man in a lab coat walked in. "So to speak." Lydia set down her mug. She was wasting time with small talk. "Look, is there any way to bring him to consciousness?"

Yes, there were ways, but Lukas thought it best to take a conservative approach. "We prefer to let nature take its course."

As far as she was concerned, that was nothing more than a convenient excuse. "Nature didn't operate on him last night, or pump him full of drugs."

"Nature needed a little kick start," he told her mildly. "But if it makes you feel any better, in all likelihood Conroy should be waking up in another couple of hours, although I don't think he'll be up to answering any questions. His mind will most likely be too fuzzy."

He *had* been giving her the runaround. "Why didn't you say so to begin with?"

"And miss the scintillating conversation we've just had? Not likely."

Lydia pressed her lips together to keep from telling him what she thought of him. "You know, I'm not sure I like you, Doctor."

He looked at her knowingly. "But I'm making you think, aren't I?"

Her eyes narrowed. "Among other things."

The sound of his resonant laughter curled into her empty stomach. Reminding her that she hadn't had breakfast yet.

Lydia rose to her feet. It was time to go. "Thanks for the coffee." She tossed the words off as she walked out through the swinging door.

Trevor Patrick, an eye surgeon and the other doctor Lukas had initially recruited to take part in his annual medical trips to the reservation, took the opportunity to sit in the seat Lydia had just vacated.

"Harrison was right." Lukas raised a brow, waiting for Trevor to explain. "That is one fine specimen of womanhood, Lukas."

"That she is, Trevor, that she is. But don't let her catch you saying that."

"Why?"

"Long story." Lukas rose. "And I've got patients waiting at the office. See you around."

Trevor watched him leave, a thoughtful expression on his face.

Chapter 5

Elliot looked up, surprised to see Lydia pushing the door open and briskly striding into the field office.

"What are you doing here?" He half rose in his chair in anticipation, ready to roll. "Did the suspect finally wake up?"

With more than a touch of disgusted disappointment, Lydia shook her head. Elliot sat again, silently repeating the first question he'd put to her by the way he looked at her.

With a fresh wave of adrenaline coursing through her veins thanks to both the coffee from the doctors' lounge and in a minor way, she supposed, from the doctor himself, Lydia had given John Conroy exactly fifteen minutes to wake up. When he hadn't, she'd renewed her previous instructions to the special agent on duty to call her the second the unconscious man moved so much as an eyelash and then left the hospital.

"Suspect," she echoed Elliot's term with contempt. "I hate calling him that when we've got the guy dead to rights."

Elliot wasn't all that crazy about the label himself, though he did acknowledge the need for it. "Makes everything equal," Elliot told her as he made himself comfortable behind the computer. The back injury that had sent him under the surgeon's knife and then to rehab for six weeks was beginning to act up. He reached for a painkiller.

Lydia noticed but pretended not to. "Not hardly," she muttered. "No, Conroy's still out. But I need to do something more useful than grow roots in the vinyl floor covering." She nodded toward the open door and the offices that were laid out down the corridor. "How's the crime scene investigation coming?"

Wondering the same thing, Elliot had just gotten off the phone with the head of that department of the Bureau less than ten minutes ago.

"They're still bringing the pieces in. I hear they've got enough fragments tagged to keep a team of five busy from now until Christmas."

Lydia frowned. Seeing as how it was September, that didn't sound overly promising.

"Great," she muttered under her breath. "How about something new on the man himself? Anything?"

"Nothing new, just the usual." He indicated the file he'd just compiled from various pieces of information he'd lifted from the local police database. "John Conroy's a wizard with explosives. The service loved him, then things went a little sour when he decided to be a maverick. Peacetime is hell for militant types. Didn't obey the rules, barely avoided a dishonorable discharge."

It was an old, familiar tune, one she'd heard more than once during her time with the Bureau.

"From the looks of it, he couldn't really find a niche for himself in civilian life." Elliot held up what looked to be a résumé. "He held down a string of jobs as a guard, which he got on the strength of his service record.

"His domestic life is a shambles, probably because of his beliefs. Divorced twice, most recently a year ago. Here's a tidbit you might find interesting." He swung the folder around one hundred and eighty degrees so that she could see for herself. "Says that his only daughter ran off with some guy she hooked up with from New Mexico. She died of a drug overdose this spring. The guy was Native American and 'daddy' highly disapproved."

"Seeing as how the New World group believes that only White Anglo-Saxon Protestants deserve to live in this country, I can see why. I guess the Native American exhibit sent him off the deep end."

Elliot knew she was just thinking out loud, not looking for his input. "More than likely. But if it hadn't been that, he and his group might have set off a bomb in Little Tokyo, Figueroa Street, or for that matter, Knotts Berry Farm. I hear they have Native American dancers performing ritual dances every day." He took the folder back. "You never know with types like that."

But it was their job to know, to crawl into the minds of terrorists, be they foreign or domestic, to discover what it was that started the whole dreadful process by which lives were lost and property destroyed. In the back of the mind of every special agent attached to the terrorist division was the specter of another World Trade Center or Oklahoma City bombing.

"Find out everything you can about Conroy. Who his

friends in the service were, who he hangs around with. Somewhere in there has to be the names of the people responsible for this." She knew she was asking him to find needles in a haystack, but they needed those needles. "Put everything down, no matter how small." She smiled as she recalled something he had said to her on their very first investigation together. "No information is extraneous in the long run, remember?"

Elliot sighed. "I've got to learn to keep my mouth shut around you."

She laughed. He'd been her partner for four years, she'd been to his house for dinner countless time, played with his children, kept vigil and comforted his wife when he'd gone under the knife to correct a back problem. There was a bond between them that transcended their professional relationship. She knew him inside and out. As he did her.

"Never happen. You'd explode."

Elliot looked over the rim of the glasses he'd only recently been forced to wear for close-up work. "A little respect for your elders."

"Ten years does not make you my elder, Elliot," she scoffed, rising. "It just gives you more candles to blow out on your birthday cake, that's all."

He turned his chair to get a better view as she paused in the doorway. "And just what are you going to be doing while I'm doing all this mind-numbing research and legwork, oh, fearless leader?"

She jerked her thumb down the corridor just beyond the door. "Well, for one thing, I'm going to see what the diligent people at the bomb investigation unit have come up with for me. Maybe we'll get lucky and can trace where he bought the detonating devices. Better yet, maybe he didn't buy it and one of his group did. Oh, and one more thing." She paused in the doorway. "See if you can get a line on your snitch."

"So far, I haven't been able to contact him."

"Keep trying."

He nodded. There was no question that Lydia worked harder than any three people he knew, but that didn't stop him from pretending to complain about his own workload. "Next time Zane asks for lead, remind me to raise my hand first."

"Next time," she echoed with a nod of her head as she walked out.

As someone who had suddenly become aware that they had fallen asleep without meaning to, Lydia realized that her mind wasn't on her work. Somehow, while she had been trying to understand the lengthy technical data reports spread out in front of her, her thoughts had strayed to the tall, imposing surgeon who had been able to pull Conroy through.

It wasn't like her to not focus on her work, but then, maybe she'd been too focused and this was her mind's way of telling her she desperately needed a break. The data had begun to swim before her eyes.

Exhausted, Lydia rose from behind the cramped computer desk where she was sitting and stretched. She needed air and food, and she wanted to feel a little like a human being again rather than some kind of a machine that processed information, searching for the piece that would pull everything together.

What she needed most of all, she thought grudgingly, was a break in this case. She was always dogged about her assignments, but this one was going to haunt her for a long time. The boy was already dead when she'd reached him, but his eyes seemed to have looked straight at her. It may be cliché, but she felt as if his spirit wouldn't rest until she brought all the people involved in the bombing to trial.

To make things worse, Elliot still hadn't been able to reach the man who had provided them with their lead in the first place. She had a very bad feeling about that.

Just as she rose to her feet, feeling an annoying stiffness in the shoulder that had been wounded, her pager came to life. Glancing at it, she recognized the number on the screen. Rodriguez.

"You going somewhere?" Elliot asked as he walked in with two huge, covered containers of coffee he'd just bought at the new café on the next corner. The chain of coffee shops, he'd commented to her earlier, seemed to be multiplying like rabbits, with stores springing up all over.

"Rodriguez just paged us." Grabbing the jacket she'd long since discarded, she pulled it on while simultaneously digging out her cell phone. She didn't want to waste any time calling Rodriguez from the office when she could do it on her way to the hospital. "The 'suspect' is either awake, or dead. In either case, it's a change."

Elliot set the containers down on his desk. "Want me to come with you?"

Elliot was beat, she could see that. He still hadn't fully recovered from the surgery that had landed him on a six-week medical disability leave, and the hour was late. "I can handle it. You close up for the night here." She was already at the door. "I'll call you later if there's anything to report."

Elliot had been with the Bureau for more than fifteen years. He didn't like being maneuvered into the background, even when he knew the motive behind it. "You don't have to baby me, Lyd."

In a hurry, she paused in the doorway to look at her partner. She hadn't meant to wound his pride. "I know, that's Janice's job." There was affection in her voice. "Go home and let her do it."

"And who's going to baby you when the time comes?"

Lydia was grateful that he didn't know about the wound Graywolf had sewn up for her. There was no question in her mind that if he did, Elliot would pull seniority and go in her place.

"The person hasn't been born who's man enough for the job," she called over her shoulder before she finally hurried out.

Elliot could always make her smile, she thought. And he was right, she was babying him. She would have balked if anyone had tried it with her. But there were extenuating reasons for that. She was determined to stand up for herself. This was still, by and large, a man's world and she had to work twice as hard to get one half the respect a man would get. That meant being on top of things and finding the answers first.

And never letting her guard down, the way her father had for that split second that had cost him his life, she thought darkly as she hurried into the parking structure for her vehicle.

He'd died on a day like this, dark and rainy. Died on a day like this and was buried on a day like this. Rain always made her feel sad and lonely.

She tried to shrug off the feeling as she got behind the wheel of her '99 silver Honda.

The mild drizzle was a full-fledged storm by the time she'd driven her car out onto Santa Ana's city streets. Logically, she knew that after several dry years, they could certainly stand the rain, but that didn't mean she had to like it. Besides, for the most part, native Californians always acted as if rain was some kind of plague sent down to chastise them for transgressions, and they drove as if they were trying to escape the drops as quickly as possible. Accidents always doubled on rainy days.

Tension infused her body as she drove to the hospital. She decided to postpone calling Rodriguez until she was almost there. No sense in taking unnecessary chances.

Despite the unexpected storm, Lukas found the day to be uneventful and tranquil. There'd been no life-saving surgeries to perform, no patients to rescue from the jaws of death. The most exciting thing he'd encountered in his day, he had to admit, had been the special agent with the attitude. Thinking of her made him smile.

As he filled out his reports, he thought of another determined, dedicated woman—his mother. He decided to take time during his lunch period to call her.

A far more dutiful son now that he had entered his third decade of life than he had been during the other two, especially his early teen years, Lukas had begun to understand his mother more and more and to appreciate the sacrifices she'd made to give him the kind of life he'd aspired to and ultimately achieved.

"What's wrong?" she asked the moment she'd recognized his voice on the phone. "Are you sick?"

If he closed his eyes, he could see her sitting in the

tiny office that served as a teachers' lounge and principal's office all in one. Her thick black hair, still without any flecks of gray and plaited in two long strands, reached almost to her waist. Very much the modern woman, she was most comfortable in her native dress and always taught school that way.

"Don't worry so much, Mother. If I was, I could heal myself. I'm a doctor, remember?"

"Remember?" Juanita Graywolf laughed softly. "How could I forget? It took my holding down two jobs for twelve years to get you there."

He fully appreciated that and wished she would let him take care of her now. Or at least have her agree to slow down. Her concession to his entreaties had been to relinquish her second job and retain only one. The one she adored. Teaching at the reservation school.

Before he could say anything else to her, she repeated, "Why are you calling?"

"Do I need a reason?"

"Need one, no. Usually have one, yes." He heard a bell ringing in the background. Lunch was over. The children would be filing into her small classroom soon. "So, what's up?"

It was good to hear her voice. It occurred to him that he hadn't seen her in some time. How did life keep getting so busy? "Nothing, I just ran into someone who kind of reminded me of you, that's all. Stubborn, plows right through everything, knows best."

There was a smile in her voice. "Sounds like a lovely woman."

"I didn't say she was a woman." But he might have known she'd figure it out.

"You didn't have to. You said the person reminded you of me. If it had been a man, you wouldn't have thought to call."

"Maybe I would have," he countered, absently looking at his calendar. September. What happened to his summer? "I'm overdue."

"Yes, I know. And right now, so am I." He could hear voices behind her. Young voices. "Call me tonight. Or better yet, tomorrow night. Your uncle's going off on a fishing trip and I'll be alone. It'll be nice to hear another voice."

"You've got it, Mother," he promised. "Talk to you then."

"I'll hold you to that." There was a slight hesitation. "Lukas, nothing's wrong, is it?"

"No, nothing." He could probably never cure her of worrying. But then, he'd given her a great deal to be worried about when he was younger: running with the gang on the reservation, collecting him at the local jail for joyriding in a vehicle that, unknown to him, one of the other boys had stolen. "Really."

"Good. I'll be waiting tomorrow night." With that, she hung up.

Lukas smiled to himself as he returned the receiver to its cradle and reached for his umpteenth cup of coffee. Pulling it closer, he settled back to dictate the notes he'd made while examining Mrs. Halloway. Eighty-seven years old and the heart of a young cheerleader. She made a semi-annual pilgrimage to his office at the insistence of her children and grandchildren—and to flirt with him. He only hoped that he was half as energetic when he reached her age.

He paused when he realized that he'd dictated

"Wakefield" instead of "Halloway" into the machine. Lukas rewound the tape to the point where he'd made his mistake. He was accustomed to strong, powerful women who took charge as if it were their God-given right. Coming from a matriarchal society, Lukas had encountered women of Special Agent Wakefield's persuasion since he'd begun walking and talking. He'd learned how to integrate his own life with theirs without losing any of his own self-respect or his convictions, or surrendering any of his masculinity. Rather than waste time butting heads, he chose other ways to get things done his own way.

He had to admit, though, that he hadn't encountered someone like Lydia since he'd left the reservation for good. There hadn't been anyone quite like her in the large world he'd been moving through since he graduated from medical school and earned his position on Blair Memorial's staff.

Maybe that was why he found himself thinking about her, why she seemed to linger on his mind, popping up during the course of the day. It made him think that perhaps she was someone who might bear further exploring, if for no other reason than nostalgia.

"In the meantime," he murmured, aware of the time, "Mrs. Halloway's notes aren't going to dictate themselves." He pressed the record button and began to dictate again.

Finished with his visits at the office and his rounds at the hospital for the day, Lukas was on his way out, walking through the hospital lobby when he saw her.

Lydia had just entered the building. The phrase "woman with a mission" popped into his head again.

Even with distance between them, he could see that determination was written all over her face. She'd burst into the lobby through the electronic doors a scant half a second after they began to open.

Amused, he quickened his pace and caught up to her. "What's up?"

Lydia jerked around. She was so focused on the reason for her return to the hospital that she hadn't seen him approach. Annoyed with the oversight, she silently upbraided herself. She was supposed to be aware of her surroundings at all times, not oblivious to them. She was going to have to work on that.

"Conroy's conscious," she told him, heading for the bank of elevators.

When she'd finally placed the call to Rodriguez from her car, he'd told her that Conroy had opened his eyes, but that he wasn't really awake or responsive. She figured by the time she arrived, the supremacist would be. If not, there were ways to help him along. She'd always regarded herself as a kind, fair person. But kindness abruptly terminated when it came face-to-face with a coldblooded killer.

This was a new development, Lukas thought. When he'd looked in on Conroy earlier in the afternoon, the man had still been unconscious.

"Maybe I'd better come along then." There was nothing pressing waiting for him tonight beyond a program on television he wanted to catch at ten.

Lydia broke stride for a second before resuming her pace. "Why? To check up on me?"

For a woman who wasn't overly tall, she covered a lot of ground quickly. He lengthen his stride. "No, on him. Why, should I be checking up on you?" His gaze swept over her. "You don't look as if you're carrying any rubber hoses or brass knuckles on you."

She stopped at the elevator and jabbed the up button. She looked at him, annoyed. "How can you joke?"

"Because humor is what keeps us sane, Special Agent." The elevator car arrived and he followed her in, letting her press the button for their floor. "Tell me, if I get to know you any better, do I get to call you just 'Special'?"

She blew out a breath. Among other things, she'd done a little background research on Graywolf this afternoon, saying it was just to help fill in the gaps. What she'd learned had roused grudging respect. He'd come up the hard way, living on a Navaho reservation, raised by his mother and a maternal uncle after his father had died in less than noble circumstances. She also knew that Lukas had run with a bad crowd as a young teen before he'd abruptly turned around.

Maybe he felt some sort of kinship with the man they had in custody, something along the lines of "There but for the grace of God go I." Whatever it was, she didn't have time to let it get in her way.

"No," she replied tersely, wishing someone else had gotten on the elevator with them, "you can't." Lydia shifted slightly. It was entirely too confining in here with him.

His eyes seemed to look deep into her being and she found herself struggling not to fidget. That he could actually create this feeling within her annoyed her no end.

"Is that because you're not special or because I'm not privileged?"

She weighed her words carefully, pausing before answering. "A little bit of both, maybe."

The elevator stopped on the second floor, but no one got on. Another car must have arrived just before them, she surmised. Pity.

"What's your name?" Lukas asked her suddenly. "You flashed your ID by me so fast, I didn't get a chance to read it."

Why was this damn car stopping on every floor? she wondered as it opened for the third floor. Again, no one got on. "Wakefield."

"No, I mean your first name."

Lydia turned to look at him, debating the merits of telling him. She had no idea why allowing him this harmless piece of information felt suddenly as if she were opening a door to something. Still, she couldn't exactly refuse to tell him. That would have been childish. Besides, it was written on her ID. "Lydia."

"Lydia," he repeated. "Pretty."

Was he going to make some inane comment about her matching her name next? She stared straight ahead, willing the elevator to bypass the fourth floor and go straight to the fifth. It didn't.

"Never gave it any thought."

"It is," he assured her quietly. She felt something rippling along her skin and wondered how a draft could have gotten into the elevator. Mercifully, the doors opened on five and she all but barreled out.

He kept abreast. "So, what's the plan, Lydia?"

She spared him a cold look, this man who had been playing hide-and-seek with her thoughts today. "Plan? There is no 'plan.' I ask questions, you stand in the background. End of story."

"I'm not much for standing in the background."

His voice was low, quiet, and she had the unshakable

feeling he was putting her on some kind of notice. Probably accustomed to having everything his way. Well, not in an FBI investigation.

She halted in front of the Coronary Care Unit door. "All right, stand anywhere you want, just not in my way. He's your patient, but he's my prisoner and as far as I see it, that takes precedence."

He stopped her just before she pushed open the door to the CCU, placing his hand over hers. "It doesn't take anything if he dies."

She dropped her hand and turned to face him. "What do you think I'm going to do, torture him until he talks?"

She was standing so close, he could smell the soap she'd used that morning, catch the light shampoo fragrance that clung to her hair. And feel the heat of her anger. A woman like this would be magnificent, he caught himself thinking. Under the right circumstances.

"I'm not sure what you're capable of, Special Agent Wakefield. But I think I'd like to find out."

Definitely on notice, she thought. She wanted to dress him down, but found that her tongue had suddenly turned leaden and uncooperative, as had her lips. And as for the thoughts suddenly coursing through her head, they had no place here, certainly not in an ongoing investigation. A small thrill fluttered through her, stubbornly refusing to go.

Just as stubbornly, she refused to acknowledge it. Like the flu, it would leave eventually. "Then watch, if you like. But unless he goes into cardiac arrest, stay clear."

Lukas inclined his head. "Yes, ma'am."

He was mocking her, but she would have to put him in his place later. Right now, nothing was more important than getting Conroy to talk.

Rodriguez rose from the chair he'd been occupying near Conroy's bed the moment she walked in, the magazine he'd been reading falling to the floor. "No change."

Lydia frowned, looking at the sleeping figure. "I thought you said he woke up."

"Like I said, he opened his eyes," Rodriguez verified. "Then closed them again."

Moving around Lydia, Lukas crossed to the bed and took readings from the monitors on either side of Conroy. "Vital signs are getting stronger," he told her.

"Good," she bit off. She looked at the man in the bed, his face a pale, milky white, the color making him all but blend with his pillow. "Are you awake, Conroy?" There was no indication that he heard her despite her clear enunciation. "I know about her, Conroy. I know about Sally."

Lukas was about to tell her that just because the man's signs were good didn't mean he was conscious when he saw John Conroy open his eyes and look directly at Lydia.

There was hatred in them.

Chapter 6

Color suddenly materialized in the form of wide streaks that continued to grow along Conroy's cold, pale skin. His eyes were fathomless in their darkness as they scowled at her. Lydia felt as if was looking into the face of pure evil.

"Leave Sally out of this!"

Yes! Triumph telegraphed its way through her. She'd found a way to get to him. This had to be the key, but to what door? Watching his expression, Lydia moved cautiously—for Lydia.

"How would she have felt, knowing you did this terrible thing? That you picked a place where young kids hang out, maybe even some of her friends." According to the information they had, Sally had attended a local school before running off. "How would she have felt, knowing that her father could kill scores of people, scores of kids without any compunction—"

"How would she have felt?" Conroy interrupted, raising his head from the pillow. His voice, sharp, angry, sounded as if it had torturously crawled up the length of his throat. "Damn you to hell! She wouldn't have *felt* anything. She can't *feel* because she's dead! My daughter's dead, do you understand?" Incensed, he tried to prop himself up on his elbows. Tubes tangled along his arms, pulling at their source. "And those kids…those kids—"

Abruptly, the tirade stopped. The streaks along his skin had turned a bright red. His eyes suddenly glazed over and he clutched at his chest. The sound coming from his lips was a gurgling, strangling noise.

"Move!" Lukas ordered. Not waiting for her to comply, he elbowed a stunned Lydia out of his way.

Lydia stumbled backward, half in response to his command, half from the force of his push. Her eyes never left the suddenly rigid features of the man who had just cursed her. The bright blue lines running across one of the monitors had all leveled out after spiking. Conroy's chest wasn't moving.

Lukas pressed a button beside the bed. A loud, jarring noise began echoing through the room and down the hall, declaring a Code Blue. In less than thirty seconds, two nurses, an orderly and an intern came running into the room. One of the nurses was pushing a crash cart.

The glass-enclosed room, one of twelve within the CCU, was small, with most of its space already eaten up by the monitors. It was filling to capacity.

Lydia jockeyed for position, trying to stay out of the way, but still within view of what was going on. With the others converging around Conroy, orders and hands flying, it was hard for her to see.

She could feel Rodriguez shifting behind her. "It's getting too crowded in here. Step out into the hall," she told the agent.

Despite all the commotion surrounding the patient, Lukas could still make out her voice. He injected a small dose of medication into Conroy's IV to stimulate the man's heart.

"Maybe you should do the same," he told her, raising his voice without looking up.

Lydia didn't waste time responding to the barely veiled order, or arguing her position. She quietly and stubbornly simply remained where she was. Watching. And praying that her zeal hadn't pushed Conroy over the edge. She needed him. Once he gave her what she wanted, the system could have him. Despite what Lukas had said to her the other day, she had no desire to act as judge and jury. That would put her in the same category as Conroy, a space she didn't want to occupy.

"I've got a pulse," one of the nurses declared. Her words were shadowed by the blue line on the monitor that transformed into a continuous steady wave as it snaked its way across the screen.

The pulse grew stronger.

The patient was going to live. At least for now. Lukas stepped back to let the others around him take care of the details. Stripping off the gloves he'd hastily pulled on, he looked at Lydia still standing by the entrance. Though she hadn't said a word, he'd known she was there. She wasn't a woman who could be ordered around, even in the heat of a life-and-death moment.

Tossing the gloves into the wastebasket, Lukas made

his way around the milling bodies to her side. He wasn't feeling very magnanimous at the moment.

"That's twice you almost killed him. Maybe you should ask to be replaced before there's a third."

Choice words came rushing to her lips, but Lydia forced herself to swallow them, struggling to see things from his point of view. It was better to have allies than enemies; you never knew when you might need someone's help.

It wasn't easy, but she curbed her tongue. It was even harder to sound contrite, especially when what she truly regretted was not getting any answers.

"You're right." She forced the words out of her mouth. "It was too soon, I shouldn't have pushed so hard."

Though he was surprised at her admission, Lukas wasn't through being angry. If he hadn't been here, Conroy could have died. "Damn straight you shouldn't have. I can't have him getting excited."

So much for getting more flies with honey. "And I can't have him, or any of his friends, blowing up shopping malls, or churches, or *hospitals* just because they don't like the people in them," she said heatedly. "Or whatever else they get it into their heads to blow up 'for the good of the country.'" The last phrase was a quote from the note she and Elliot had found in Conroy's garage that had tipped them off to the suspect's target. Beneath it had been a tirade about the drain people of color put on the country, except that the term Conroy had used hadn't been nearly as polite.

Lukas crossed his arms in front of him and looked at her solemnly as he worked at controlling his own anger.

She had an inkling of how his forefathers must have appeared, decked out in chief's regalia, glaring down at the white settlers in their fragile wagons as they crossed into the merciless Arizona territory.

At any other time, the irony of it all would have struck her as amusing.

"Right now, I don't think Conroy's in any condition to blow up a milk carton, much less anything else."

"But his friends are," she pointed out. "And they're the ones who got away."

Part of what had gotten him on the right path and ultimately off the reservation was cultivating a positive attitude. He reverted to it now, though not with a great deal of conviction. "Maybe they'll stop here. Maybe blowing up the mall was the point."

He was being incredibly naive, she thought. "And maybe not." In fact, she was willing to bet on it. "I can't take that chance. The people who live around here can't take that chance," she emphasized. "Besides, those so-called supremacists have got to be punished for what they did." She thought that he, of all people, would understand that. Didn't his tribe have some rule along the lines of the old biblical eye for an eye? "They can't just be allowed to get away with it. The Bureau can't say, 'Boys'll be boys, but just don't do it again.' That'll just open the floodgates for every whacko in the country to 'even the score,' or to push their own violent agenda."

"How do you know it's a boy?" he asked her quietly.

What was he doing, nit-picking now? "Boys, men, what's the difference?" She realized she'd raised her voice again when one of the nurses, the one who had brought in the cart, glanced at her. Lydia pressed her lips together, annoyed that this man kept making her lose her temper.

"A lot," he answered. And something within him

suddenly wanted to show her exactly how different. "But that's not what I meant." He saw her raise a questioning eyebrow. "What makes you think there are no women involved in this bombing?"

A ready retort faded as she first opened her mouth to answer, and then shut it again. Damn him, he had a point. That should have occurred to her, not him. Granted there was all that profiling data to fall back on, but that didn't mean anything was written in stone. Things were only one way until they changed and were another.

Conceding the round to him, Lydia raised her eyes to his. "Want to join our team?"

His somber expression melted a little around the edges and then he laughed at the suggestion.

"Maybe in an advisory capacity." He grew serious again. "And my first piece of advice is, don't kill the golden goose. You're not going to get any eggs if you do."

"Aesop's Fables?" she asked in surprise. She would have expected something different from him. "Isn't there any comparable Navaho legend to bring the same point home?"

As soon as the words were out, she bit her lower lip. That was stereotyping, something she ordinarily wasn't guilty of. But then, he was her first Native American anything and she had grown up watching old-fashioned Westerns with her father on television. It wasn't an excuse, but it was a reason.

His eyes narrowed. Was she checking up on him? "How did you know I was Navaho?"

She gave him the truth, knowing he wouldn't stand for anything less. "Conroy's not the only person I researched last night."

Her honesty surprised him. The annoyance abated. "Afraid I'll blow something up?"

He didn't like having his privacy invaded, she thought. The funny thing was, she could wholeheartedly sympathize with that. But niceties had to take a back seat when terrorists and dangerous, bomb-wielding supremacists were concerned.

"No. I just like knowing who I'm dealing with. Fewer surprises that way."

He inclined his head, accepting the explanation. "You could try asking."

She didn't know him, yet she knew better. "Would you have told me?"

The smile that look his lips was slow. And unnervingly sensual as she watched it spread. "Maybe over dinner. Now we'll never know."

"It wasn't an in-depth search I conducted last night," she heard herself telling him. God help her, she was flirting again, Lydia realized. But that didn't change any of the words that followed. "There's at least enough left to discuss over dessert."

Amusement lifted the corners of his mouth again. "Are you asking me out?"

Lydia became acutely aware that they were being overheard. Even so, she kept on, trying not to incriminate herself.

Her answer was neither yes nor no. "I'm expanding on your scenario—and asking for cooperation."

He moved aside as the young nurse pushed the crash cart out of the room. "With the scenario?"

"With the situation." Damn it, what was the matter with her? She was supposed to be concentrating on her job, on the man in the bed, not on the tall man in front of her. "Never mind," she said abruptly. "Forget I said anything." She nodded toward the bed. "Is he going to be all right?"

Experience had taught Lukas to be cautious in his optimism.

"He's stable. For the moment," he qualified. "But I'm going to have to ask you to give me your word that you won't talk to him tonight. And that you won't agitate him when you finally do talk to him."

She didn't like being talked to as if she were slow-witted. "I'll bring incense and candles," Lydia retorted.

"And don't growl."

She looked at him sharply, aware of the grin on the orderly's face. "I don't growl."

"You growl," Lukas contradicted. "You're just so intent, you don't hear it."

He glanced over his shoulder at the monitors. Everything looked to be all right. For now, they were out of the woods. But he knew how quickly that could change. So much for catching that program tonight. Maybe the television in the doctors' lounge had been repaired—but he doubted it.

"I'll hang around for a little while," he told the intern. "Call me if he takes a turn for the worse."

The intern dragged his eyes away from the special agent and nodded with enthusiasm.

Taking hold of Lydia's good arm, Lukas ushered her from the room.

Caught off guard, she found herself moving out the door before she could stop him. Lydia saw Rodriguez looking at them oddly, then averting his eyes the instant he realized she saw him.

"What are you doing?" she rasped at Lukas.

He pulled the door closed behind them. "Making sure he doesn't take a turn for the worse."

Lydia pulled her arm away. "Look, his well-being is important to me."

Lukas loomed over her. "No," he contradicted, "it's not. You just want him conscious long enough to get the information you're after."

She wasn't about to get into an argument with Graywolf. It had been a long time since she'd felt the need to justify herself to anyone. "Is that so bad?"

Yes, it was bad. It meant she had no conscience, but that was her problem, not his. "For one thing, that puts you on a collision course with my oath."

She decided that the best way to handle this—and him—was with humor. Otherwise, they were both going to butt heads throughout Conroy's stay at Blair Memorial. "Which oath? The one you took in medical school, or the one I saw you swallowing when you pushed me out of the way."

"The former, and I didn't push you," he corrected her. "I moved you."

"You certainly 'move' hard." Overhearing, Rodriguez raised a brow as he looked in her direction. Pulling Lukas out of Rodriguez's earshot, she stood, studying the physician for a moment. And then she smiled. "Maybe I've changed my mind, Graywolf. Maybe I do like you."

He covered his heart with his hand. "I can die a happy man now."

She snorted. And maybe she'd been too hasty in her reversal, she thought. "Or at least a sarcastic one."

There it was again, he noted. That spark, that fire in her eyes. He found himself intrigued. "Never knew I was one, until yesterday."

Her eyes swept over him. Whether she liked him or not, there was no denying that he was one hell of a good-looking man. Or that there was something about him that pulled at her. Hard. "Never too late to learn things about yourself."

He looked at her, his thoughts taking a deeper, inward turn. "No, maybe not," he agreed quietly.

The word "magnificent" echoed through his brain as he saw Lydia approach him the following evening. The spark he had witnessed in her eyes had evolved into a full-fledged bonfire and there was anger in each step she took that brought her closer to him. It was obvious she'd come looking for him and it wasn't just to ask after his health.

Anger became her, he decided. Even if that anger was directed against him.

"You, Graywolf," Lydia called to him in case he had any ideas about walking away. "You did this on purpose, didn't you?" It wasn't a question. It was an accusation.

He placed the chart he was signing down on the nurse's desk. Technically, he was through for the night. But not if the look in her eyes had anything to say about it, he thought.

"If you want an answer, you're going to have to be more specific than that."

Did he think he was going to play games with her? That he could just give her what he probably thought was a bone-melting look and she'd forget all about her job? If he did, he had no idea what he was up against, she vowed silently.

"You deliberately placed my prisoner into a drug-induced coma."

She was almost shouting at him and all he could

think about was kissing her, silencing her mouth with his own. "Drug-induced comas are deliberate, yes."

His mild tone nearly drove her up the wall. She felt like a child, being patronized.

"Why?" she demanded. "Why did you do that?"

The action had solid medical reasoning behind it. "Because Conroy'll heal faster that way. He's on a ventilator and has got tubes running all through his body. His body can't deal with everything that's going on and still heal, too. This way, it can focus on the healing process."

All this trouble, all this concern, for a man who was a worthless human being. Sometimes the unfairness of it all turned her stomach. She spoke before she could think to stop herself. But she'd had nightmares. She'd been at the mall and this time, it had been her father she'd been unable to save.

"What about Bobby Richards?"

He stopped to think but the name meant nothing to him. "Who?"

"Bobby Richards," she repeated, banking down a wave of emotion. "The boy Conroy's bomb killed." She'd made it her business to find out his name. And to give his parents her sincerest condolences. "Tell me, Doctor, how's he supposed to focus on getting well?"

They were at an impasse. Lukas blew out a breath. "I can't answer that."

"No, neither can I," she told him honestly. "But I'd like to be able to answer the question 'How are you going to be sure Conroy's New World group isn't going to pull this kind of thing again?'"

Lukas heard the frustration in her voice. He wished she'd realize that, ultimately, they were on the same team and did have the same goal. He didn't want to see teens come in with their limbs torn up, or their lives prematurely cut short, either.

"Don't you have any other sources? Can't the person who gave you Conroy's name get you the names of the others in the group?" It seemed to him that would be the most logical way to proceed.

She closed her eyes for a minute and shook her head. "No, he can't."

Was she just being too stubborn, like some obsessive dog that had caught hold of something, digging in and refusing to let go? "Why not?"

She opened her eyes again. The image wouldn't leave. "It's a little hard to talk with your throat slit. We found his body the morning after the bombing."

They'd found him on the floor of his rented motel room, a drying pool of blood encircling his head. The informant had bled to death. "Somebody must have found out he tipped us off."

The informant, Warren Howard, had been a nondescript man whose life had been a series of wrong turns. There'd been no one to mourn over him. So she had. "So, you see, Conroy's our only hope."

So maybe Ms. Special Agent wasn't obsessive, he relented. Maybe she was just doing her job. "He's not going to do you any good dead," he reminded her.

"No," she admitted, trying to come to terms with her frustration, "he's not."

"And he's not coming out of the coma tonight."

She looked at Lukas hopefully. It had been a long, fruitless day, her shoulder ached and she was tired. She needed something to go on, something to hang on to. "Tomorrow?"

"We'll see. Maybe," he augmented, taking pity on her.

Lydia raised her eyes to his, surprised at the softer tone.

He supposed, looking back, that it was her eyes that had gotten to him. Otherwise, he wasn't really sure what his excuse was, or what it was that prompted him to ask, "When do you get off duty?"

She laughed shortly. The work was never really done. "Never."

He knew how that felt. He took his patients home with him each night, in his head, reviewing their cases in the wee hours of the morning when sleep refused to crawl into bed with him.

"How about technically?"

Lydia glanced at her watch. "An hour ago."

He'd just seen his last patient, written his last note for the evening, barring an emergency. "Would you like to have that dessert now?"

Lydia looked at him, confused. For a moment she didn't know what he was talking about. And then she remembered their conversation from the other morning about sharing things over a meal.

A smile found its way to her lips. "Why, are you going to share some things about yourself?"

He'd bet that she was really good at interrogation once she got going. There were things he found himself wanting to learn about her. "Tell you what, we'll make it a drink instead and it can be an equal trade of information."

The question why hovered on her lips, but never crossed from her mind into the region of sound. Instead, Lydia smiled and inclined her head.

"All right, Doctor, you're on."

They exchanged small talk while they waited for the waiter to return with the drinks they'd ordered. Once the glasses were set in front of them and the waiter retreated, they circled one another mentally, both looking for an opening, a weakness to turn to their advantage.

He raised his glass in a toast. "To discovery."

"Discovery," she echoed, then took a long sip of her screwdriver. She set the glass down. She could almost feel the electricity between them and wondered if he was aware of it, too, and just what it would mean in the long run. "Do I get to go first?"

He nodded. "Ladies usually do."

Chivalry had long been absent from her life. She didn't usually encounter it anymore. "You *are* a throwback."

He didn't consider himself a man who could comfortably live beneath any label. "If you did your research, you'd know that the Navaho tribe is matriarchal."

"A culture of Barbara Stanwycks." The grin that came to her lips was a fond one. "I could identify with that."

The name meant nothing to him. "Who?"

She forgot at times that most people hadn't had the kind of upbringing she had. "A movie star from the forties and fifties," she clarified. "Always played tough, gutsy women making a mark for themselves in a man's world."

He tipped his glass back and let the raw whiskey burn its way slowly down his throat to his stomach. He focused on the sensation and not the fact that he was finding the woman across from him increasingly more attractive, increasingly more desirable. "You watched old movies?"

She nodded. "With my dad. He was a walking encyclopedia of movie trivia. I wanted to please him, so I soaked it up, too." Lydia blinked, suddenly becoming aware of what she'd just said. "You tricked me."

His expression was one of silently protesting innocence. "How?"

"I just gave you two pieces of information." And he hadn't given her any.

Lukas held up his index finger. "Technically, it's one—hyphenated."

She laughed, shaking her head. "You sure you're a doctor and not a lawyer?"

He liked the sound of her laugh. It went straight to his gut and stirred him. Or was that the whiskey? he wondered.

But there hadn't been much of that and there had been a time he could put away a pint and not feel it.

"Where I come from, you have to be a little bit of both, with a few other things thrown in, as well."

She tried to envision him the way he had been as a youth—wild, determined to defy authority. The image pulled her further in.

"Such as?"

"A survivor." His tone was noncommittal. Lukas indicated her glass. "You want a refill?"

She looked down at it. Somehow half of it had disappeared. "I haven't finished this one yet."

He smiled at her over the glass. "I'll wait."

I'll wait. Lydia wrapped both hands around her chunky glass, trying to ignore the very unsettled feeling that had just taken another lunge in her stomach.

Chapter 7

Lydia wasn't accustomed to dealing with nerves, at least, not her own.

It wasn't that she was foolhardy, but for the most part, fear had no place in her life. She wasn't reckless, proceeding through her day with a fair amount of cautious sense, but she never dwelled on what might happen to her, only on what she needed to do. Purpose and duty, that was her focus.

This was different. In every way.

She was sitting across from a man she knew she shouldn't even be near. Because he was dangerous. Not in the typical FBI sense that she was accustomed to dealing with, but dangerous to her.

Personally.

There was something about Lukas Graywolf, something that drew her to him, even though he wasn't the type she was usually attracted to. And never with this intensity. Her instincts told her that interacting with Lukas could and would be different.

If she allowed it to happen.

The problem was, she didn't know whether she should or not.

So then what was she doing here? Exploring?

The truth of it was, she'd gone out for this drink with him on a dare. Her own dare. She'd felt an uneasiness in his presence that was increasingly titillating and had decided to test herself.

Now she wasn't so sure if that was a good idea. Lydia was growing acutely aware of his eyes on her. So blue, even in this light, they made her think of a cloudless sky. And she felt as if they were delving into her very soul.

That would have given him an advantage over her, she thought cryptically.

"So," he was saying after what felt like a long, pregnant pause, "what else should I know about you?"

She regarded her near empty drink rather than look at him. It was called regrouping.

"Seems to me you've had your turn at asking. It's your turn to trade now."

He leaned back, studying her. The warm candlelight made her features that much more sensual. As if the woman needed it, he thought. He wondered if she was even aware of her looks. She certainly didn't act as though she were. He'd known women who were far less attractive than she who'd used their looks like a weapon. Ms. Special Agent seemed oblivious to what the mirror showed her.

"I don't know what it is you know about me already. Maybe if you just ask a question," he suggested, "I'll see if I want to answer."

He was qualifying this. She wasn't surprised. She didn't even blame him. She intended to do the same. "You like your privacy."

"If that's a question, yes." Tilting his glass back, Lukas drained it of the last few amber drops that had mingled with the melting ice.

Lydia couldn't keep her eyes off his hands as he replaced the chunky glass in front of him on the table. They looked to be what they were, a surgeon's hands with long, slender fingers. And yet there was something powerful about them at the same time.

She realized that she was imagining how it would feel to have those same hands stroking her body.

Damn it, she usually had better control over her thoughts than this. What the hell was happening to her discipline?

Lydia cleared her throat, as if that could somehow help clear her mind, as well.

"That was an assumption, actually. I suppose this gives us something in common." She saw him raise a questioning eyebrow. "I like my privacy, too."

Slowly, Lukas stroked the rim of his glass with his thumb, his eyes never leaving her face. "So what are we doing here, playing Twenty Questions when neither one of us likes giving answers?"

She felt her mouth growing dry. "I'm not really sure." As someone determined to be proven fearless, she looked into his eyes. Trying not to allow herself to be drawn into their hypnotic pull. With effort, she reverted to her agent mode, seeking shelter there. "What *are* you doing here?"

"That's easy." He lifted his empty glass in a silent toast. "Having drinks with a woman I find very stimulating."

Amusement brushed along her lips. "Interesting word for a heart surgeon to use."

"Who better?" His curiosity about her growing, Lukas decided to see just how willing she actually was to tell him something about herself. "Do you like what you do, Special Agent? Think carefully now."

She couldn't decide whether or not he was teasing her by using her title, but she had to admit that she liked the sound of it when he said it. And she didn't have to think carefully, she knew.

"Most of the time. I know I like making a difference."

There was a "but" there she wasn't saying, Lukas thought. Waiting, he finally supplied the prompt himself. "But?"

"But sometimes I don't." That's when the job ate at her. It wasn't the pieces of the puzzle that kept her awake at night, it was the failures. "Like this last time. We weren't there in time to stop the bombing."

"But from what I heard, they managed to get most of the people who were there evacuated. Because you called to warn the security guards."

Most, but not all. She shut her eyes. "I guess it could have been worse."

She knew herself very well. She'd never been the type to be satisfied with half a loaf. She wasn't satisfied until she had the keys to the entire bakery in her possession.

Lydia opened her eyes again, looking directly at him, her gaze intense. "But it could have been better. Much better. There could have been no one wounded, no one killed."

He knew she was thinking of that boy. The one whose funeral she'd attended. "Are you including Conroy in that package?"

Her expression sobered and she straightened in her chair. Her voice when she answered was clipped, precise.

"He comes under a different heading." She couldn't gauge what Graywolf was thinking, but she could make a fair guess. "I'm not a cold-blooded woman, Graywolf."

He'd thought that initially, but not anymore. She was far too passionate. "I've already come to that conclusion on my own."

How? a soft voice whispered through her mind. *How did you come to that conclusion?*

She banished the voice, telling herself that it made no difference to her one way or another what he thought or how he had reached his conclusions.

Still, she found herself wanting to make him understand. "But something inside me freezes when I have to deal with people who kill without thought, who think they are so right that there's no room for argument, for differences." She sounded as if she were preaching, she thought. "I don't hate easily, but I do hate bigots."

Half his life had been spent fighting bigots, struggling out of the box that stereotypical thinking insisted on relegating him to. It had been a hard road from there to here. "I guess that gives us something else in common."

She pushed her empty glass away. "I know something else we have in common."

"Oh?"

"Neither one of us should have too much to drink." It was time to leave, she thought. Before things heated up. "You never know when they might need us."

She was right. Besides, he wanted his head clear tonight. "Doesn't leave much room for a personal life, does it?"

She studied him for a second before replying. "Do you really want one?"

"Why, don't you?"

No, she thought, she didn't. Otherwise, she wouldn't spend as much time on the job as she did. For the most part, her job *was* her life.

"I don't really have any hobbies beyond watching old movies." She couldn't remember when she'd taken more than a couple of days off, and that had been to help out with and attend her mother's wedding. "I'd be bored inside of three hours."

As a kid he'd had too much time on his hands and he knew where that had led him then. But he'd come a long way from that troubled youth. Thanks, in no small part, to his uncle Henry and the boxing club Uncle Henry had established on the reservation. Boxing had given him a purpose, a goal and a place to be that didn't involve getting into trouble. Now Lukas wished he could have just part of that time to do all the things he wanted to do.

"Not me. I've got more than enough to keep me occupied."

She knew all about his volunteer work, and the free surgeries he and his friends performed back on his reservation. But to her, that was all part and parcel of the same thing. To her free time meant something completely different from what occupied your time during working hours.

"Then why choose something that makes such a demand on you?"

He found himself telling her things he didn't normally share. And not minding it.

"Because I like the idea that I can save lives, that because of me Mr. Lindstrom will see his grandchild born and Mrs. Halloway will blow out the candles on her ninety-fifth birthday cake and Jon Erickson will live to graduate from high school this year. Besides, I get to give back a little."

"Give back?"

He nodded, thinking of the reservation. Of the people who had grown up with the simplest of amenities, thinking this was the way it was supposed to be because they knew nothing else.

"To the people who put themselves out for me when my life didn't look quite as rosy as—" He stopped, realizing he'd gone a little too far, talked a little too much. "Hey, now who's the underhanded one?"

She laughed at the accusation. "Sorry, part of my training, getting people to talk."

"You're good at it," he allowed.

The simple compliment warmed her.

The waiter approached, his body language making his inquiry for him before he had a chance to form the words. She shook her head at the thought of a second drink. She felt intoxicated enough as it was. Which wasn't like her, she thought. She could hold a great deal more than she'd had tonight.

Lydia had an uneasy feeling that sipping a simple drink comprised of vodka and orange juice wasn't what was sending her head spinning this way, but there was no sense in taking any chances. Alcohol would only make the situation worse.

"You're sure?" Lukas asked.

"I'm sure. It's getting late, anyway. And it wouldn't hurt me to turn in before midnight one night a month." She leaned over to pick up the small purse she kept with her.

Rather than try to talk her into having another, Lukas asked the waiter to bring the check. He paid cash and left a generous tip.

"Was that to impress me?"

Graywolf had left more as a tip than the drinks had cost. He didn't strike her as the kind of man who would go out of his way to impress anyone, but she was the first to agree that she wasn't always infallible in her judgment.

"No, that was to help the waiter with his expenses. He's working his way through school. I treated him in the emergency room," he added when she looked at him curiously. "He collided with another waiter and got some nasty cuts from the broken glasses as a result."

"They have heart surgeons treating lacerations?"

"They do when it's a Sunday night, the E.R. doctor's busy and there's no one else available."

He held the door open for her and they walked out together. There was a full moon and it was painting everything within reach in shades of pale gold. Lukas looked at her and realized that he didn't want the evening to end. Not yet.

"How far away do you live?"

She thought that a strange question, coming out of the blue. "About ten miles, why?"

"My place is closer. It's just three miles from here." Damn it, he was fumbling, he thought. Like some college kid asking a girl up to his place. He wondered if she'd laugh in his face, but it didn't stop him from asking. "Would you like to come over for a nightcap?"

Self-preservation dictated that she turn him down. Politely or flippantly, but either way, firmly. She'd always known when she was in too deep. It was initially a gift that she had honed to perfection over the years. It had managed to save her more than once from a situation that could have turned deadly.

This wouldn't turn deadly, but it was dangerous nonetheless, just as she had already decided that Lukas was.

But that old determination to see how far she could go in any given situation rose to the fore again, daring her to accept his invitation. Daring her to see if she could resist him and ultimately walk away when the time came to leave. Daring her to explore regions that were unfamiliar to her.

"I don't want another drink," she told him. "Do you have coffee?"

For a second he thought she was turning him down. There had been a hint of relief swirling through him. Relief because maybe he wanted to see her just a little more than he should.

But the relief that came with her acceptance was greater.

"If you like." He tried to recall the contents of his refrigerator and vaguely thought he remembered seeing a carton of juice. "I could probably scare up some orange juice if you have a mind to be healthy."

"All right," she allowed, "you're on. Provided neither of our pagers goes off."

"Understood." He led the way into the parking lot. Because it had been fairly crowded when they'd arrived, they had been forced to park in different rows. "Wait here," Lukas told her. "I'll swing around to pick you up."

Lydia nodded and unlocked her car. Sliding in behind the steering wheel, she told herself she had precisely three minutes to do the smart thing and get the hell out of here. Her job tested her enough every day. She didn't need to prove anything more to herself. There was certainly no reason to play Russian roulette with Graywolf this way.

But when his dark blue sedan pulled into her row, Lydia was still sitting where she was, mentally listing pros and cons for doing what she was doing. She'd never been a coward before, she thought, nodding at him. She wasn't about to start being one on a Friday night in late September.

Lydia started up her car and followed the blue sedan out of the lot and into the flow of traffic.

"I thought all heart surgeons were rich." She turned to look at Lukas as he pocketed the key to his third-floor apartment.

Lukas closed the door behind her, locking it. "You mean, why don't I live in a house?" He smiled. His mother asked the same thing, except that she wanted the house to be in Arizona, near her. "There's only me and I'm not around that much. What do I need with a house? This place more than suits my needs. Can I take your jacket?" he offered.

She hesitated, then nodded. "Sure."

When she began to shrug out of it, he moved around behind her to help her. As he slid the sleeves from her arms, she felt something suspiciously like an electrical shock shoot up both limbs. A little voice advised her to run. She ignored it.

"Thanks," she murmured.

He paused, her jacket draped over his arm, humor curving his generous mouth. "I'm not up on my special agent etiquette. Should I ask you for your gun and holster, too?"

"Never ask an FBI special agent for her weapon," she advised him with a smile. "Unless you want the business end of it first."

Removing her holster, she wrapped the belt around it, then placed it on the kitchen counter.

Hanging her jacket on the coatrack, Lukas eyed the weapon. "Well, that'll certainly keep me on my toes. Isn't it uncomfortable, wearing that?"

"I've gotten used to it." These days, it almost felt strange being without it. "Besides—" she thought of the split-second, life-or-death situation she'd been faced with when Conroy had turned his gun on Elliot "—it comes in handy."

"I imagine in your line of work it does." Checking the thermostat, he pressed the keypad. The unit began to rumble as it worked its way up to turning over. "How good are you with that thing?"

Her grandfather had taken her to a target range when she was fifteen. It had become a ritual every Saturday morning for the next three years. She could hit a bull's-eye at a remarkable distance. He called her his Annie Oakley. "I generally hit what I aim for."

"I'll keep that in mind." Lukas crossed to his kitchen. "So, what can I get you?"

She thought back to his offer when they left the restaurant. "Orange juice would be nice."

Moving around the small family room, taking in bits and pieces, she stopped before a collection of framed photographs on the wall—black-and-white and color shots freezing scenes of poverty and groups of dark-haired children with bright, shiny smiles. That had to be home. She tried to pick him out.

Opening the refrigerator, Lukas found the carton on the first shelf. He took it out to read the date stamped along the top, then looked at her. "How do you feel about expiration dates?"

"You're going to have to give me a little more than that to work with."

He raised the carton to underscore his question. "The orange juice stopped being good yesterday."

She shrugged. Drinking orange juice one day past its expiration date was far from the most daring thing she'd ever done. Lydia crossed to him.

"I'll take my chances. If I get sick, luckily there's a doctor in the house." She moved behind him and looked into the interior of his refrigerator for herself. The shelves were almost empty. "I take it that shopping for food isn't high on your priority list."

He let the door close. "I usually get something in the cafeteria."

"But not the coffee," she guessed, opening the cupboard, looking for a glass. She found six cans of coffee instead. Nothing fancy, she noted.

"No, not the coffee. I'm particular about that and I need at least two cups to kick-start my day." He watched her, amused, as she opened the pantry. "There are more closets in the bedroom."

She'd located a glass on her second try, but had decided to continue taking inventory. No wonder the man looked so fit and lean. There was no junk food around to tempt him.

What did tempt him? she wondered.

She realized that he'd said something to her and was waiting for some sort of response. She played back his words in her head and then looked at him over her shoulder. That definitely came under the heading of sarcasm, she thought.

"Excuse me?"

"You look like you're enjoying yourself. I just thought you'd like to look in the closets I've got in the bedroom." He gestured to the small hallway and the two rooms that lay beyond. "I have to warn you, though, there's not much in the way of a wardrobe. I tend to live in jeans and work shirts when I'm not in scrubs or a lab coat."

She let the doors fall. They folded into place. "Sorry, occupational habit. You can learn a lot about a person by what's in their closets. That includes the pantry," she added.

He poured a glass of orange juice for her. "And what did mine tell you?"

She took the glass as he replaced the carton in the refrigerator. Lydia wondered how long he kept things before he threw them out. "That you're a minimalist and that for a man, you're very neat."

She had a strange way of wording things, he thought. His eyes slowly washed over her face.

"Does that mean if I were a woman, you'd consider me messy?"

Her heart was inching its way up her throat. She was having much more trouble catching her breath than she had a few minutes ago, when she'd been alone in her car. "If you were a woman, I would consider it a waste."

He took the glass of orange juice from her hand and placed it on the counter. Even from where he was standing he could feel the heat, the pull that had been haunting him ever since he'd first laid eyes on her. He moved a little closer to the fire.

Slowly he combed his fingers through her hair, clearing it away from her face. "I'd say that puts us in agreement again."

She hardly heard the words, even though she was concentrating on making them out. But it was hard to hear anything with her blood rushing in her ears the way it was.

Chapter 8

Like someone snatching a life preserver tossed to them at the last possible moment as they bobbed up and down in a tempestuous sea that was about to swallow them up whole, Lydia turned her head away from Lukas. One more second and she knew he was going to kiss her. Knew she was going to be lost if he did.

That wasn't what she wanted to happen.

Wasn't it?

Wasn't that why she'd agreed to go out and have a drink with him? To come here with him? Because some part of her was curious? Curious to see if this intense attraction that shimmered between them was really all glitter and no substance—like the elaborate facades that were used to create an illusion on a movie studio back-lot, all front, no sides, no back, no interior.

She was afraid to find out that there wasn't anything more.

She was afraid to find out that there was.

With his hands on either side of her face, Lukas gently turned her head until she looked at him again. His eyes held her more prisoner than his hands. Hypnotized, she watched as he lowered his mouth to hers.

Determined to remain impervious to whatever was coming next, Lydia still felt her eyes closing and her pulse racing in wild anticipation.

She didn't even come close to impervious.

Lights exploded in her head, raining down and bathing her in instant, intense heat, leaving no part untouched. Willing herself to remain still, to somehow maintain distance, did nothing. She wasn't listening.

Lydia rose up on her toes, leaning into him, wrapping her arms around his neck.

And surrendering.

The hunger came full-blown and immediate, surprising him. Lukas was accustomed to exercising extreme control over himself, holding unwanted, complicating feelings at such distances that they never became even a remote threat to his way of life.

That wasn't happening here.

Fissures ripped through his control, cracking it at a mind-numbing speed. Rather than remaining off to the sideline, feelings assaulted him from all sides.

His mouth slanted over hers, taking, giving, reveling in the taste, the feel, of her. Reveling in the excitement that was throbbing all through his body. Her scent, her flavor, was filling every part of him, his head, his senses, his entire being.

And yet he couldn't get enough of her. He wanted more, craved more.

Needed more.

As if they were separate entities, governed only by instincts, his hands skimmed over her, caressing, possessing. Peeling away her garments.

When he relived it later, Lukas wasn't aware of actually undressing her, only of getting closer to what his passions desired.

Lydia moved with each pass of his hand, shrugging out of her cumbersome clothing, divesting him of his. She found herself desperate to get rid of the layers that encompassed his body, keeping it from her.

The closer she came, the more excited she grew, trembling in anticipation of his hands on her naked body and hers on his.

She wanted to touch him. To have him touch her. To waken parts of her that had been dormant for so long, she'd given them up for dead. Making love with someone had always been less than satisfying for her. In the end it was always far more disappointing than exhilarating.

This time she knew the expectations were far greater than ever before. If disappointment came, she knew it would be that much more devastating. The smart thing would be to stop now, while she still could.

But she couldn't.

Because she wanted so much.

Impatience goaded her as she pulled at his jeans. Anticipation tantalized her as she felt him tug away her underwear.

With the last of the clothing gone, she pressed her body to his, glorying in the hardness that she felt against her.

It took her breath away.

And yet, it wasn't his body that caused this all-consuming hunger within her. There was something more, something about the man himself.

Her head was spinning.

She was only vaguely aware that he had lowered her to the floor and that she was twisting beneath him, seeking the heat of his body until it was pressed against hers, hard, demanding.

She moaned as his mouth found hers again. The intimate contact sent her pulse soaring. She pulled him closer to her.

It was like walking into the center of a raging bonfire. Willingly.

What was happening consumed her, burned away the layers of self-preservation that had always cocooned her and exposed the very vulnerable, very tender center that she had always tried to protect.

Where her heart lived.

Lukas could feel his blood rushing through his body, could feel the need slamming through him with the force of a sledgehammer, begging for the final release.

And yet he held off as long as he could, wanting to savor his trip through this uncharted territory, wanting to pleasure her almost more than he wanted to enjoy that pleasure himself.

Damn, what was happening to him? What was she doing to him?

He had no answer, he just didn't want it to stop.

It wasn't enough to explore her body with his hands, Lukas felt the need to taste each part, as well, to sample the flavors there.

Slowly, his breath tantalizing her flesh, he trailed his lips and tongue along the outline of her breasts, the hardened peaks of her nipples, the tempting dip of her quivering belly.

He heard her breathing dissolve into quick, hard

gasps as she moaned his name, reaching for him. Gratified, enthused, he kept on tantalizing her even though he felt as if at any moment, he would self-destruct.

His mouth moved lower, suckling, teasing, until Lukas reached her very core. He heard Lydia catch her breath, felt her stiffen as he drove his tongue into the most sensitive part of her.

Hot ice rained over her, blotting out everything as Lydia tried to grasp hold of something with which to anchor herself. There was nothing. Nothing but this overwhelming sensation.

Building.

An explosion racked her body as the sweet agony of a climax came to her.

Exhausted, she fell back, only now realizing that she had raised herself up on her elbows, the better to absorb the sensation.

A second assault came in the wake of the first, creating waves, making things happen to her she would have sworn weren't possible.

Groaning, panting, she felt herself sinking into the carpet.

"It's a federal offense to kill a special agent," she gasped.

The next moment, she realized that she was looking into his face. He had pulled himself up, snaking along her body until he was over her, his hard torso poised above hers.

"Killing you isn't what I have in mind." His breath undulated along her skin, caressing her.

With her last ounce of strength, she framed his face with her hands and pulled his mouth down to hers, kissing him hard.

She arched her body against his, her flesh calling to his.

He slid into her then, wanting to move slowly, finding he had no say in the matter.

Sheathed within her, Lukas began to move urgently, knowing that the time for hanging back was long since gone. He was no more in control of the situation than she was.

Lydia would have readily testified before the highest court that she had no energy left within her, yet somehow she matched him, moving as urgently, as swiftly, as he. Wanting the same goal.

Wanting more than anything to reduce him to the same quivering mass of flesh to which he had reduced her.

The climax that overtook him was hard, prolonged, and sapped every single ounce of his strength.

With his heart pounding, vibrating throughout every inch of his body, Lukas finally sank down against her. He tried to move off to the side to keep from crushing her, but he wasn't sure if he was able to.

Even so, he wanted her again. He couldn't help wondering if this was somehow tied up to some subconscious death wish.

"So, was it good for you?" she whispered against his ear, trying very hard to sound at least a little flippant. There was no way she wanted him to know just how greatly affected she was.

"Good?" She felt his mouth curve against her cheek in a smile. Something stirred within her belly. And within her loins. "I don't think they've invented the word to describe what just happened here."

Because his pride demanded it, Lukas raised himself up on one elbow. It was about all he could manage for the moment.

Her lips were smudged with the imprint of his mouth, and her eyes seemed slightly unfocused as she looked up at him. He realized that Ms. Special Agent was as devastated by what had taken place here as he had been. Good. He would have hated to think that he'd been the only one flattened here tonight.

Lukas shifted a little to the right. "Am I hurting you?"

Lydia slowly moved her head from side to side. There was no question that she was completely exhausted. And yet, something distant within her was asking for it to happen all over again.

More than that, she wanted to curl her body against Lukas and just take comfort in his presence. As if they were two lovers instead of just two people who had given in to a consuming physical need.

The desire to curl up against him carried implications that were far more intimate than what had just occurred here.

It scared her.

"I'm not sure I'd know it if you were," she told him. "My body's numb."

Lukas shifted again, this time more languidly. He began to trail his fingers over her belly and watched as it quivered in response. If that was numb, then he was a Texas Longhorn.

He grinned at her. "You might want to get a second opinion on that."

She was feeling things again. Deep-seated hunger began to rise. How was that possible? She didn't have enough strength to be poured into a shot glass and yet he was stirring her again. Making her want him again.

This was insane.

She had to get out of here before she made a complete

fool of herself. Lydia began to sit up, her intent to leave clear, but Lukas laid a gentling hand on her shoulder.

His eyes were beginning the process all over again. The one that held her in place.

"You don't have to be anywhere yet, do you?" he asked quietly.

She wanted to lie, to tell him that she had things to do, calls to make. An entire computer database to search through.

But all she could say was, "No."

There was no triumph in his voice, only satisfaction. "Good, neither do I."

Inclining his head, Lukas kissed her softly, touching only his lips to hers.

Knowing what lay ahead, she dissolved just as swiftly.

And then she felt his smile against her mouth. Lydia pulled her head back, looking at him sharply. Was he laughing at her?

But the smile was kind, gentle. Utterly disarming. He cupped her cheek with his hand, his eyes delving into hers. Touching her soul. "What do you say that this time, we go slowly?"

They'd hardly begun and already her breath was growing short, eluding her. Slow would be a very good way to go. Slow, so that she could savor every moment, every nuance.

Even so, she felt an urgency beginning to build and it was going to be a challenge to hold it in check. She didn't want to be the one who seemed eager here.

"We seem to be in agreement again."

He smiled into her eyes. "Good."

And then, Lukas brought his mouth down to hers and made the rest of the room fade into oblivion.

* * *

She never slept more than a few hours at a time any-more. It was because she never knew when she'd have to bounce up, alert and ready to go. She called them cat-naps and made the most of them, training herself to feel refreshed whenever she woke up. It was a case of mind over matter.

When she opened her eyes, night still littered the corners of the room. It took her only a moment to ori-ent herself. She was in Lukas's living room. They'd fallen asleep on the floor, she realized, too exhausted to summon the strength even to make it to his bedroom.

The heavy weight she felt sealing her in place was his arm. It was draped across her chest, not possessively so much as protectively.

She tried not to dwell on that.

God, what had she been thinking, letting this happen? She moved her head, looking around, trying to find a shape that would turn out to be her clothes. Where were they? She hadn't exactly been giving them her full at-tention when he'd undressed her.

This wasn't like her. She should have left hours ago, Lydia upbraided herself.

She didn't want to be here when he woke up. She hadn't the foggiest idea what to say to him. Holding her breath, she eased herself out from beneath his arm. The light hair on his arm tickled her skin, sensitizing it as she wiggled free. She could feel goose bumps forming.

Probably just the cold, she told herself. Rising to her knees, she wondered if her legs were going to be able to support her once she tried to stand. Taking no chances, she braced her hand against the edge of the sofa and slowly rose. Her legs felt like day old Jell-O.

Damn, what had happened to her last night? she wondered, her annoyance growing. And why had she let it happen?

Simple, because she'd had no say in the matter. It was like standing in the path of a storm. Lydia felt as if she'd been broadsided by a force far greater than anything she'd ever encountered.

She didn't like the fact that she'd succumbed so completely. It tarnished her own self-image. She was supposed to be bigger than that, stronger than that. After all, he was just a man.

Granted, he was better-looking than most, more exciting in a sexy, turn-of-the-last-century kind of way, but that wasn't supposed to matter to her. She was an FBI special agent, for God's sake. That was supposed to mean something, wasn't it?

It was supposed to mean that she didn't turn into a plate of mush because some heart-throb heart surgeon kissed her.

She spotted her clothes strewn all over the floor next to the coffee table.

The sooner she got out of here, she told herself, scooping up her bra and blouse, the better.

"Planning to sneak off?"

She spun around, startled, holding the clothes she'd gathered against her. Lukas was propped up on one elbow, looking at her. She blew out a shaky breath, grasping at bravado.

"You're lucky I didn't have a gun on me."

His eyes swept over her very slowly, making her warm. She could literally feel them as they traveled down the length of her body. Could feel his smile as he asked, "Where would you keep it?"

"That's not the point," she retorted. Seeing her skirt, she added it to the pile she held against her. Lydia was more than a little aware of the fact that aside from the clothing she was trying to hold against her, she was completely nude. "You're not supposed to surprise an FBI special agent."

"Why not?" he asked mildly. "The FBI special agent surprised me."

What was that supposed to mean? She was ready for a fight. *Wanted* a fight. Anything that would make her feel in control again.

"Why? Didn't you think I was human?"

"I knew you were human, just not *that* human." Waiting for some kind of crack, she saw him run his tongue along his teeth instead.

"What are you doing?"

"Checking to see if any of my teeth are loose." He pretended to test the soundness with his thumb and forefinger. "I'm surprised we didn't create some kind of vortex last night. It got pretty intense at one point." *At all points,* he thought. If someone had told him the earth moved, he wouldn't have disputed it.

But he still didn't know how he felt about that. Or how he wanted to feel.

Lukas rose, completely unselfconscious in his nakedness. He nodded toward the kitchen. "Want some hot coffee?"

What she wanted was hot, all right, but it didn't have anything to do with coffee. He was testing her, she thought. Well, damn it, she could pass. She could handle any test sent her way. Her eyes never leaving his, she raised her chin defiantly.

"Coffee sounds good." With deliberate nonchalance,

she picked up her underwear and tucked it beneath the skirt she was holding. "Mind if I shower first?"

His jeans in his hand, he turned to look at her. He found himself wanting to join in. But saying so left him open to too much. So instead he shrugged into his jeans, foregoing the briefs that were at his feet. "Go right ahead."

She was staring, she realized. In danger of swallowing her tongue if she formed an answer, Lydia settled for nodding her head and went off to take her shower. A cold one.

Chapter 9

Her hair was damp and curling with riotous carelessness around her face as she came down the hall less than fifteen minutes later. She didn't look like an FBI special agent, but some kind of golden-haired sprite he vaguely recalled his mother telling him about when he was a child and had needed to be lulled to sleep.

The coffeemaker stopped making gurgling sounds. The coffee was ready. Lukas moved two mugs into position and filled each. "You're fast."

"Another occupational habit."

Part of her had debated leaving without even coming into the kitchen. But that would have been cowardly and she didn't tolerate cowardice, least of all her own. Especially since she had no idea what there was to be cowardly about.

She accepted the large mug he placed into her hands

like a sacred vessel containing life-giving liquid. "Thanks."

Holding on to the mug with both hands, Lydia drank deeply, letting the hot, steamy liquid unfurl within her. Hoping it would burn away everything in its path and force her to focus her attention on the heat it generated and nothing else.

Like him.

Like the night they'd spent together.

Her body still felt as if it was vibrating from his touch.

The sigh that escaped her lips as she put the mug on the counter was part contented, part edgy.

Hearing it, Lukas smiled, remembering that the same sound had echoed in the air last night.

So where did they go from here? he wondered. Did they pretend last night hadn't happened, or act as if it was just a casual encounter that had momentarily heated up?

Had it been a casual encounter? He didn't know. He knew he would rather it had been, because that would have meant no complications, but he just wasn't sure.

Right now, his world looked as if it was in jeopardy of being upended and he had no idea how he actually felt about that.

Lukas retreated to safer ground. "Want any breakfast?"

"No, I—"

Sudden rhythmic beeps had her looking down at the pager at her waist. It had taken some doing to locate the device this morning after her shower. Somehow, it had managed to get itself kicked under the sofa.

She recognized the number. It was Elliot's. Why wasn't he calling her on the cell phone?

"I have to make a call," she told Lukas as she reached into her pocket.

Lukas started to nod when he heard his own pager go off. "Looks like we're both in demand this morning."

Lukas couldn't help being relieved that they wouldn't be faced with making small talk over mugs of cooling coffee. He wasn't sure just what he would have said. For the first time in years he felt uncertain about a situation.

The number belonged to the hospital rather than the answering service that took his office calls after hours. Lukas picked up the receiver from the wall phone and pressed the second speed dial button. Cradling the receiver against his neck and ear, he turned to watch Lydia. She had her back to him, her voice low as she spoke on her cell phone. There was a small, zigzag damp spot on her back where her towel hadn't reached.

He wondered what she would have said if he'd followed his first impulse and gotten into the shower with her.

The object wouldn't have been water conservation. He'd wanted to make love to her again. Still wanted to. Last night had been like nothing he could ever remember. So much so that he was beginning to doubt his own memory. Further exploration would be called for if he was ever to have any peace of mind.

He heard someone pick up on the other end. "This is Dr. Graywolf, you paged me?"

"Hi, Dr. Graywolf, this is Wanda," the cheery voice was laced with familiarity. "Sorry to bother you so early but we've got a patient who walked in here and he insists on seeing you."

Her back still to him, Lydia was bending to pick up the pen she'd just dropped. He watched her skirt ride up the back of her legs and felt something tightening in his gut. Definitely hadn't gotten his fill last night, he thought.

"What's this patient's name?"

"That's just it, Doctor," the woman told him, "the man won't give us one. But he refuses to see anyone else except you. Said you would understand once you got here."

"'He,'" Lukas repeated, trying to think of someone he knew who would want to play games like this. But no one came to mind. None of his patients were shy about their identities. This didn't make sense. "What does this 'he' look like?"

"Well, that's the funny thing. He looks a little like you, except a lot older." There was an embarrassed pause. "I mean…"

Wanda was obviously stumbling over her own tongue. She'd been practically the first person he'd met when he'd come to work in the E.R. and he was fond of the older woman. Lukas put her out of her misery.

"I'll be there in twenty minutes. If this mystery patient's suffering any immediate discomfort, have Dr. Reynolds take a look at him," he instructed. A senior cardiac surgeon, Wyatt Reynolds lived across the street from the hospital. Since his wife's untimely passing six years ago, he made himself almost constantly available for any medical emergencies at the hospital if there was no one on duty to take over.

"You got it," Wanda promised. "See you in twenty minutes."

Lukas replaced the receiver just as Lydia turned around, flipping her cell phone closed. Her cheeks were flushed and there was excitement in her eyes. It was different than the kind he'd witnessed last night.

"Good news?" he guessed.

She nodded, tucking the cell phone into her pocket. "I've got to run. My partner thinks we might have a lead on one of the other bombers." She nodded at his pager. "What about you?"

He began to button his shirt. "Somebody came into the E.R. asking for me."

She dragged her eyes away from his chest. The open shirt had been a definite distraction. "A patient?"

Without a name to go by, Lukas couldn't speak for his past association with the man. "In all likelihood, he will be." He could postpone his shower until later, he decided, once he met with the mystery patient. If things got too hectic and he didn't have a chance to get back, he could always use the facilities at the hospital. "Can I give you anything to go?"

Yes, an encore of last night. The response leaped into her mind out of nowhere. Lydia felt her cheeks growing warm a moment before she blocked out the feeling. She didn't know if he'd seen the telltale color.

Lydia tried to distract him. "You have any of those quickie pastries you pop into a toaster? You know the kind I mean, sugar, fat and tinfoil."

"You just named my top three food groups, after coffee." He opened the freezer and pushed a few boxes around. He had three choices to offer her. "Strawberry, blueberry or apple cinnamon?"

She crossed to the refrigerator and stood behind him. "I love apple cinnamon."

"Apple cinnamon it is."

Lukas plucked one out of the box. He didn't bother saying that she'd selected his favorite, or that she was taking the last one. The less talk between them right now, he decided, the better. He needed to sort a few things out and to put them in their proper perspective. He couldn't seem to do that right now. Probably because the memory of last night was too fresh in his mind and because she smelled of his shampoo and his soap and something within him was turning alarmingly and strangely possessive.

All he could think about was kissing her again.

Making love with her again.

She was peeling away the foil, making her way to the door. "Don't you want to toast it?" he asked.

"No time." She took a small bite. "I'll see you at the hospital," she promised.

He hadn't thought about the next time he would see her. "What?"

Her parting comment seemed to surprise him, she realized. Did he think she was just going to cease existing the moment she stepped outside his apartment? "Conroy's got to wake up sometime—unless you plan to keep him permanently doped up."

"No plans," he told her. "See you later."

Almost out the door, Lydia hesitated, then doubled back, took hold of the front of his shirt and pulled him toward her. In a movement that, to varying degrees, took them both by surprise, she planted a quick, intense kiss on his mouth.

"See ya," she repeated, releasing his shirt.

She was gone in a heartbeat. His. His heart slammed against his rib cage at the same time the front door slammed against the doorjamb.

He had absolutely no idea what to make of that. Or her.

But he had someplace to be and no time to waste trying to figure out the actions of one diminutive, mercurial special agent.

Or himself for that matter.

Lukas poured a glass of orange juice and gulped it

down on his way to the front door. One of his shirttails was still sticking out as he got into his car. But then, neatness only counted as far as the stitches he made when working on a patient.

Catching all but one of the lights and managing to squeak through that one, Lukas made it to the hospital in under the promised twenty minutes. The day felt more like spring than fall. The sun was warm early and the sky was an incredible shade of blue. There was no sign of the rain that had hit previously. All in all, it felt like a glorious day to be alive.

For once, the emergency room parking lot was almost empty. He left his car in the last space right beside the wall and hurried in through the electronic doors.

Lukas nodded absently at an orderly he recognized by sight if not by name and went directly to the admitting area. The young woman sitting at the desk was unfamiliar to him. Hospital personnel changed only slightly less frequently than the tides. He flipped his name tag around so that she could see it.

"I'm Dr. Graywolf. There's a patient here asking for me."

From her expression, the woman didn't appear to know what or who he was talking about. Turning in her chair, she called out to the heavy-set woman next to the coffeemaker. "Wanda?"

Wanda Monroe, as dark as the coffee she favored, came forward, a big, bright smile on her lips as she saw Lukas. More than two decades his senior, Wanda treated him the way she treated most of the young doctors at the hospital, as if he were part of her extended family.

"What did you do, Doctor, fly?"

"Caught all the lights," he replied.

"Must have." She set down her spoon and crossed to the desk with a mug of very strong coffee. "Sorry to get you in before your hours, Dr. Graywolf, but he insisted on seeing you. Won't let anyone else near him. Said it had to be you or nobody." Wanda's dark eyes swept over him. "Guess you've got the magic touch, Doctor." Her laugh was deep and completely infectious. "Maybe someday I'll find out for myself if you do or not."

"What would your husband say?"

"Probably, 'pass the remote, honey.'" She winked at him. "As long as we don't televise it, Ed won't know a thing about it," she chuckled, her dark eyes dancing. She indicated the area behind her. "Patient's waiting for you in Room Six."

He nodded his thanks and went back to the rear of the hospital. Room Six was to his left.

He stopped dead just inside the swinging door.

It had to be a joke, he realized, coming forward. One his mother had to be in on, since she was the one who had told him about the bogus fishing trip.

"Uncle Henry, what are you doing here? Why didn't you just come to my apartment?" Genuinely happy to see the man he freely credited with saving him from sure self-destruction, Lukas embraced his uncle, enveloping him in a bear hug.

Henry Spotted Owl returned the hug with a great deal of feeling, hanging on to Lukas for a long moment.

The hug felt almost anemic compared to what Lukas was accustomed to from to his uncle. Something was wrong. He stepped back. His pleasure at the surprise visit died away as he took another, more focused look at his uncle.

Lukas saw that the beloved leathery face, which bore the scars of hard living, looked somewhat pale. The last time he had seen Henry was six months ago. The man had looked robust, as fit as the day he had taken Lukas under his wing at the boxing club he'd started more than fifteen years ago.

The word "robust" was not the first one that came to mind now.

He still wasn't getting the full picture. Lukas sat on the edge of the gurney beside his uncle, placing his arm around the older man's shoulders. When had they gotten to feel so frail? Or had he just been too busy to notice?

"What happened to the fishing trip? I talked to Mother yesterday and she said you were going away on a fishing trip."

Henry shrugged uncomfortably. "I didn't want her to know I was coming here. I didn't want to worry her. I figured if she thought I was going fishing, she wouldn't riddle me with questions about something I don't want to talk about."

The picture was beginning to take shape. And Lukas couldn't say that he particularly liked what he was seeing. "But you'll talk to me about it?"

"You're the doctor."

Lukas remembered other times when they had sat just like this, side by side on a bed in his closet-size bedroom back on the reservation. Then it had been his uncle who was the man with the wisdom. He didn't know if he was comfortable with this reversal.

"Do you need one?"

Henry Spotted Owl frowned. He wanted to say no, that he didn't. That he was as healthy now as the day he'd walked into his sister's house to tame his wild nephew and to make sure they remained a family in every sense of the word. But that would have been a lie. And he wasn't here to lie.

"It's getting to look that way," he told his nephew with a studied casualness that the expression on his face couldn't quite pull off.

There was pride involved here and Lukas knew he had to proceed cautiously to spare his uncle. "Doc Brown send you here?"

Henry laughed harshly. "Doc Brown doesn't know his scalpel from his stethoscope."

Lukas doubted that his uncle would have sought him out in a professional capacity if someone hadn't started him thinking along those lines. His uncle was a fiercely proud, fiercely private man, and asking for help wasn't something he did easily. "Exactly what did Doc Brown say that made you come here?"

There was smoldering anger in the dark eyes as Henry raised them to look at his nephew. "That he doesn't think I'll live to be a hundred."

Since Henry had come to him, there was only one logical conclusion to be drawn. "Your heart?"

Henry nodded. "He thinks I need bypass surgery."

Lukas remembered Doc Brown. The man represented the only medical care available on the reservation until Lukas and his friends had taken to making their semi-annual pilgrimages there. Everyone was certain that Doc Brown had been born old and stoop-shouldered. His idea of practicing medicine was to place a Band-Aid strip over a wound and to browbeat patients into rallying. Lukas knew that the old man wouldn't have bandied about the term "bypass surgery" if he wasn't significantly alarmed.

"What kind of a test did he give you?"

There had been several. The names were all foreign to Henry.

"Made me run with these white round little things glued to my chest until I thought my eyes were going to pop out," Henry informed him moodily.

"A treadmill test." That stood to reason, Lukas thought. "What else?"

Henry shrugged. "Took enough blood out of me to make three vampires happy. Don't remember what else."

"That's okay. Do you have any of the test results with you?"

Henry looked annoyed as he shook his head. "I didn't want to tell him where I was going, either. Man's got a mouth like an old woman, always talking. Nobody's business but mine."

"No problem, I can have him fax the reports over." The last time he'd been on the reservation, he'd brought a fax machine and a renovated computer with him, making the man a gift of them both. Doc Brown had grumbled about progress moving too fast for him.

Lukas thought for a long moment, mentally reviewing the cardiac surgeons on staff. He wanted the best for his uncle.

"Thom Harris is an excellent surgeon." The man had a full calendar. "I'm sure I can get you in to see him."

"Why would I want to see him?" The question was belligerent.

"A consultation is standard before surgery." Henry's finances were tight and Lukas worded this as delicately as he could. "Don't worry about his fee, I'll work something out with him."

"There's not going to be a fee," Henry told him. "Because he's not going to operate on me."

Lukas sighed. This was going to be trickier than he thought. He was beginning to realize that what his uncle had come for was to be assured that he didn't need surgery. "Look, Uncle Henry, I know how you feel. And maybe Doc Brown's wrong, maybe you don't need surgery. But if you do, I want you to have the best."

"So do I, that's why I came here." Henry looked at his nephew, seeing for a moment the scared, defiant, fatherless boy who had given his mother so much grief as he had tried to find a meaning in life amid the poverty that surrounded him. "Doc Brown's not wrong. I haven't felt right for a while now. I already know I need the surgery." He looked at his nephew. "I want you to be the one to do it."

He'd gotten so caught up in wording everything just right and saving his uncle's pride that he hadn't seen this coming. But he should have.

"Uncle Henry, I can't operate on you. I'd be too emotionally involved."

The protest made no sense to the older man. "Of course you'd be emotionally involved. You love me, boy. I want someone who loves me holding that knife, making those cuts." He caught hold of Lukas's arm to emphasize his point. "Because someone who loves me has a high stake in my making it through the surgery."

Rather than shrug out of the hold, Lukas gently placed his hand on top of his uncle's. "Any surgeon who agrees to do the surgery has a high stake in the outcome. And there are rules, Uncle Henry—"

"The hell with rules," Henry interrupted. "They've been bent before. Bend them again. You, I want you to do the surgery." He pulled himself up, a proud, small bull of a man who had lived life hard and enjoyed every moment he had wrenched away from a less than kind fate. "It's you, Lukas, or I go back to the reservation and go on that fishing trip I told your mother I was taking. Whether I make it back or not…" His voice trailed off as he shrugged.

Lukas sighed. He knew he was cornered. There was no way he was letting his uncle go back without conducting a thorough examination. And if the fears of the reservation doctor were correct, he couldn't allow his uncle to leave without having the surgery. Maybe, under the circumstances, he could bend the rules the way his uncle demanded. Or at least be allowed to assist in the surgery. "You always were a stubborn old man."

A slow smile began to work its way to the lips that were drawn back in a harsh, straight line. "Never claimed not to be." He eyed his nephew, knowing he had him. "Do we have a deal?"

Henry held out his hand, waiting for Lukas to take it.

Lukas slid his hand into his uncle's grip, trying not to notice that it felt far weaker than it usually did. It made him acutely aware of Henry's mortality.

"We have a deal." He rose from the gurney, signaling to a nurse. "All right, let's see about getting you healthy enough to live to be ninety-nine."

Henry looked at him indignantly. "One hundred," he corrected.

Lukas laughed. "One hundred," he agreed.

Chapter 10

Elliot stood in the middle of the cavernous loft that held little else than sunlight. This was where the anonymous phone call had sent them hurrying to—an empty loft above an abandoned warehouse in the rundown factory section of Norwalk. Traffic had been a bear, due to all the construction on the 405 freeway. It had taken them twice as long as it should have to get here, apparently all for nothing.

Frustrated, Elliot shook his head, the gun he'd held drawn and ready when they'd entered the deserted loft still in his hand.

"Well, if they were here, they certainly aren't anymore. Maybe it was a bogus tip."

The surge of adrenaline that had shot through Lydia when they'd forced open the door had yet to settle down. It felt as if someone was playing cat and mouse with them. She hated being the mouse.

Lydia scanned the room, squinting against the sunlight. Stooping, she ran her fingers along the floor. "It wasn't bogus. They were here all right."

Curious to see what she'd found, Elliot crossed to her. But unless her vision was a hell of a lot better than his, there was nothing in front of her except scuffed floor. "What makes you so sure?"

She held up her hand. There was no telltale dirt. "When did you ever see a loft this clean?" Rising, she brushed one hand against the other out of habit rather than need. "They cleaned out everything before they took off." She frowned, moving around the empty loft. There was nothing left behind except one sagging sofa, an obvious holdover from the last real tenants. "Tell you one thing, I'd like to hire these characters to do my place."

As Elliot watched, Lydia crossed to the dilapidated sofa and began flipping over the cushions one by one.

Holstering his weapon, he joined her. "What are you doing?"

She tossed the second cushion onto the floor, after the first. "When I was a kid, whenever my parents had people over, this was how I got my spare change after everyone else left the room. Found a wallet this way once. Maybe one of our supremacists left something behind they didn't count on leaving."

It was worth a shot, though it was a long one. But right now, other than a comatose suspect who might or might not come around, they had nothing else to go on. "Anything?"

Tossing the last cushion aside, she took out a handkerchief as she bent to pick up something amid the dirt and stale crumbs of some unidentifiable meal trapped beneath one of the cushions.

"Two dimes and a nickel. And this." Using the handkerchief, Lydia held up a small detonation cap for his inspection. "They were here."

He nodded. They'd gotten lucky after all. "I'll call the crime lab boys, have them dust the whole place." Elliot laughed dryly under his breath. "They ought to love that."

"Probably not, but it's their job. And it's 'techs,'" she corrected.

Phone in hand, ready to call, Elliot stopped to look at her. "What?"

"They're 'crime lab techs,' not 'crime lab boys.' They've got a woman on the team now. Holly Shapiro," she told him, though she doubted it would stick. Elliot had a real problem when it came to remembering names. Faces he never forgot, but names escaped him on a regular basis. "She wouldn't take kindly to being left out."

"Techs," Elliot repeated with an obliging nod of his head as he pressed a series of numbers on the keypad. Contacting the people he was after, he gave them the necessary information and location before ringing off. He flipped the phone shut, then pocketed it. "By the way, where were you this morning?"

Lydia looked out the huge multipaned window. Here the dust had been left undisturbed, acting as a natural curtain to the activities that had to have gone on inside. Was this where it all had begun? The meetings, the hate that was encouraged and urged to feed on itself? It looked not unlike any other loft in any other industrial area. But it wasn't.

Absently she realized that Elliot had asked her a question and was waiting for some kind of an answer. "My cell was off."

"The lab bo—techs'll be here in half an hour, barring any traffic jams," he told her. "You weren't at your place, either," he added casually.

Lydia raised an eyebrow as she looked at Elliot, the questions finally registering. "Checking up on me, Elliot?"

He spread his hands wide, an overly innocent expression on his rounded face. "No, just glad you're getting a life, that's all."

Janice had been talking to him again, Lydia thought with an inward sigh. Why did married people always think you weren't happy unless you were spoken for, too? "I have a life, Elliot. With the FBI, investigating crazies who get carried away with incendiary devices."

He ignored the warning note in her voice. "Can't keep you warm at night."

Very carefully, she placed the detonator cap into a fresh plastic bag she had in her pocket. "That's why God invented electric blankets, Elliot."

He watched her seal the bag. Just as she wanted to seal her life. With a quick, firm, final motion. "Look, I'm not prying…"

The hell he wasn't. "Good," she said dismissively.

Elliot debated withdrawing, but he liked Lydia too much to perpetually respect her privacy at the expense of telling her what she needed to hear for her own good. Moving around so that he was in front of her as she began to head out of the loft, he said, "But just for the record, I think maybe you should admit to yourself that your dad wasn't perfect."

Lydia stopped dead. The look she gave him made him do the same. She did *not* want to listen to anyone, not even Elliot, analyze her behavior for any reason. "Where's this coming from, Elliot?"

"From the heart," he told her with only a hint of hesitation. Lydia exploding was a fearsome thing to witness and she exploded when people pried into her private life. But this had to be said. For her own good. "I've been your partner since the beginning. I know all about your dad, the medals, the decorations for bravery. You thought he was perfect."

She didn't like being placed in a position where she had to defend her father, but if it came down to that, she could. "He damn near was."

"To a fourteen-year-old girl," Elliot stressed. That was how old she'd been when her father was killed. Elliot was losing her and he knew it. He sped up. "My point is that maybe thinking that way is stopping you from finding someone of your own. Your mother found someone." If the widow could, so could the daughter, he was sure of it. "Your stepfather's a great guy."

They'd all gotten together for the last Fourth of July barbecue. Her mother and Arthur, Elliot, his wife and kids. And her. Was that where this was coming from? Because she'd come alone to the barbecue? Well, she'd rather be alone than tied for eternity to someone she didn't want to be tied to, simply to avoid being lonely, which she was not.

She also couldn't picture spending the rest of her life with someone like Arthur, kind though he was. Arthur could put fireflies to sleep.

But because her mother had lived on the edge for all those years, worried that the next time the phone would ring it would be someone to tell her bad news about her husband, Lydia could readily understand why Louise had married Arthur.

"Yes, he is," she readily agreed. "He's just not my father."

She'd be the last to admit it, but Elliot knew there was hero worship involved in the way Lydia felt about her father. The man had died too soon for her to discover the flaws he had, the ones everyone had that made them human.

"No man will live up to your father, Lyd, until you take him off that pedestal."

Elliot was her best friend as well as her partner, but she could feel her patience wearing thin. "Can we talk about something else now? Like about what they're paying us to do?"

He nodded, knowing that it was time to retreat. "I've said my piece."

She pinned him with a look, warning him that he'd better stick to his word. "Good."

Because he was her friend, Elliot couldn't help adding a coda. "For now."

Lydia groaned as she preceded him out of the deserted loft.

Lydia got off the crowded elevator on the fifth floor at Blair Memorial and automatically scanned both sides of the corridor. She wasn't just looking around for anyone suspicious, she was also keeping an eye out for Lukas.

She wasn't at all sure just how she would react the next time she encountered the good doctor after what had happened between them last night, but she knew that an encounter was inevitable. With Elliot going to the office to run down some information regarding the detonator cap she'd discovered, Lydia had elected to return to the hospital to check on Conroy. With the frustration of a near fruitless morning behind her, she wanted something positive to happen. More than anything, she wanted Conroy awake for questioning.

She walked into the glass-partitioned room, nodding at Rodriguez, and found that there was no change in Conroy's status. He was still unconscious, still in the coma he had been medically eased into for his own well-being.

She studied the man's face. He looked dead to the world. Her patience felt as if it was on a short lease. Turning away, she looked at the special agent she'd left watching over the prisoner. "Dr. Graywolf show up this morning?"

Rodriguez tucked away the magazine he'd been perusing. She noted that the cover boldly announced the current football season. "Early."

"And?"

The wide shoulders that had once belonged to a promising college fullback rose and fell. "And then he left."

She blew out an angry breath. "Did he say anything?"

Looking properly intimidated, Rodriguez shook his head. "Not to me."

"Great. Where is he now?" Ethan opened his mouth to reply, but she anticipated his negative answer. "Never mind, I'll have him paged. Just continue doing what you were doing."

Pushing the door open, she left the room.

Nerves were adding to her agitation. Nerves that were dancing like beads of water dropped on a sizzling-hot pan. Why, damn it?

Was it because they'd slept together?

Her mouth curved despite her mood. It was an entire misnomer. Very little sleeping had gone on last night. But even so, it wasn't like her to have any qualms about interacting with someone she'd slept with. It hadn't happened often, but it had happened, and she hadn't been uncomfortable with the situation.

This time, though, it was different. This time she wasn't remotely comfortable with the situation. She would like to blame this state of unrest on Elliot and his pep talk, but she was too good an investigator for that. The nerves had been there before Elliot had ever opened his mouth in the loft. They had sprung up early this morning, the moment she'd opened her eyes, and intensified when she'd discovered she couldn't make good her silent escape.

She didn't like feeling nervous, wasn't used to it. It was like watching the sky, seeing the storm clouds gathering, and waiting for that first loud clap of thunder to shake the earth.

Try as she might, she couldn't seem to smother the feeling and make it go away.

But this was her problem, no one else's, and somehow she was going to have to deal with it.

Coming to the nurses' station, she had a nurse page Lukas, then stood back and waited to confront the source of her unrest about her prisoner. It didn't put her in the best of moods.

Lukas's office was in the medical complex directly across the street from Blair Memorial and, since it was just a little past noon, he decided to forgo making a call and to respond in person to the page.

He came fearing the worst. That the call was about his uncle. He'd had Henry checked into the hospital and, not wanting to rely on whatever Doc Brown's office might eventually fax over, Lukas had left orders for a battery of tests to be done to determine, as accurately as possible, the exact state of his uncle's heart. He had also left strict instructions to page him at the first sign that his uncle was in any immediate danger.

Hurrying out of the elevator, his face an impassive mask to hide the turmoil going on within, Lukas quickly arrived at the nurses' station.

"What's the emergency?" he demanded of the woman behind the counter.

"I am."

Turning, he saw Lydia coming out of the alcove where that floor's coffee machine was housed. There was a paper cup in her hand.

The tension of the morning interfered with what might have been, under any other circumstances, a nice moment. If Lydia had been the one to have him summoned, the problem wasn't about his uncle. Relief hid behind annoyance at being made to rush over.

"What is it?" he asked crisply.

She didn't like his tone. It sounded edgy, bordering on anger. Did he think she'd had him paged for personal reasons? Now that their night of passion was behind them—maybe even a notch on his belt—was he afraid that there might be repercussions? That she'd want something from him, maybe even have some kind of designs on him?

The pompous jerk.

Your own fault. Lydia felt her shoulders stiffen as she cursed the lack of control she'd displayed last night.

"Conroy's still unconscious." Her tone deliberately matched his.

"I know. I checked on him this morning."

Now that he was here, Lukas decided, he would stop

by his uncle's room down the hall to see if any of the
test results had come back. He'd had his uncle admitted to the CCU for obvious reasons: the battery of monitors necessary to watch his condition were all here.

"Well, just how long is this going to go on?" He was
being maddeningly blasé about this.

"As long as it needs to." The fine skeins of his patience unraveled. He walked to the alcove, indicating
that she should follow him. He waited until she joined
him. When she did, he gave it to her with both guns.
"Look, Special Agent Wakefield, I have other patients
to tend to. I've done all I can for Conroy. The rest is up
to him. I can't come running over here like some lackey
every time you want to know 'are we there yet?' like
some kid on a cross-country drive. We'll be there when
we're there. Do I make myself clear?"

For two cents she'd haul off and hit him. Had she
been twenty years younger, she would have. But she
wasn't. And she had a position to maintain, so she kept
silent.

"Perfectly," she stormed, turning on her heel and
walking away.

Angry with her for triggering his outburst, with himself for his uncalled for reaction, and with the anxiety
that was gnawing away at his insides, the fear that his
uncle's problem might be too serious for him to handle,
Lukas silently heaped curses on his own hot head.

He started to go after her, to somehow make amends
and apologize for snapping, but his pager went off
again. This time it was his office.

Torn, he decided that he was in no condition to say
anything to Lydia that she would remotely consider re-
deeming. By the look in her eyes when she turned away,

she was too angry. She'd probably cut off his head if he tried to apologize right now—and with good reason.

He hurried off to answer his page.

She was bored, and her eyes had begun to droop. But the instant she heard the door open, Lydia stiffened, her body alert.

Stiffening was the last thing she needed to do. Her whole body felt as if rigor mortis was setting in. Taking over for Peterson after his shift was over, she'd been sitting beside Conroy for the past two hours in the darkening room, waiting for him to come to. Willing him to open his eyes again.

Trying not to think about what Elliot had said to her earlier about her father.

Trying not to admit that maybe there was a germ of truth in it.

Her hand on the hilt of her service weapon, she stared as she saw what looked to be a white cloth poking through the opening between the door and the frame. What the hell was going on?

Slowly the door opened and then Lukas walked in. He crumpled the cloth in his hand, tossing it aside. "They told me you were here."

"I am," she replied crisply. Angry about the dressing down he'd delivered in the corridor this afternoon, she wasn't about to give him an opening to repeat his performance. Her tone kept him several leagues away.

Well, this is awkward, he thought.

He'd had the rest of the afternoon to chastise himself for his behavior and to try to explain it to himself. The obvious reasons were only partially responsible. There were other, deeper reasons and he didn't know how to go about exploring them without undermining himself. So for now, he left it alone.

But he couldn't leave what he'd done alone. He'd always believed in owning up to his mistakes and in trying to make amends, no matter what it cost him. And this time, it was going to cost him a lot, he thought. Because absolution wasn't going to come easy.

She rose. "If you want to examine him, I'll get out of your way."

He'd never seen a look so stony, which, considering the things he'd done as a youth, was saying a lot, he thought.

Lukas caught her arm as she passed him and realized it was the injured one when she winced. He released his hold immediately. "Sorry."

"It's all right," she muttered, flexing her arm. Wanting nothing more than to leave the room. Calling herself a coward for the very desire.

She was going to leave anyway. Lukas placed himself in her path. "No, I mean I'm sorry. Sorry for this morning."

Lydia lifted her chin, defiant, her eyes almost blazing. "So am I, I should have been gone before you woke up."

She still didn't get it, he realized. "I'm talking about this morning in the hospital." This wasn't easy, but it had to be said. "I had no right to talk to you that way."

"Well, we seem to be in agreement there." She paused. "Look, you had a lot on your mind, it's all right."

He thought of his uncle. The tests had all indicated that Doc Brown knew what he was talking about. His uncle needed bypass surgery. The sooner the better. Not wanting to wait, he'd scheduled it for eleven the next day, giving his uncle enough time to prepare mentally.

Lukas would have rather done the surgery immediately, but it wasn't an all-out emergency and he hadn't wanted to alarm the old man. A calm state of mind could only help Henry.

He squelched a sudden desire to touch her face. It had all but blind-sided him.

"You're right. I did have a lot on my mind, but it's no excuse to take it out on you."

"Fine, you made your apology," she said coolly. "Now examine your patient and then leave so I can go on doing what I'm here to do. My job," she emphasized.

He saw beneath the cool tone. Saw because she employed the same defenses he did. He'd hurt her, he realized. And it was going to take more than a crisp apology to make amends.

"I'm not here to examine the patient. I'm here to apologize and you're not making it easy."

Her eyes scrutinized his, looking for the truth. "I don't make anything easy."

"So I'm learning." He glanced at the overhead clock on the wall. "When do you go off duty?"

She'd brought a copy of the notes on the case with her to read tonight. "I wasn't planning to tonight."

He saw the thick file on the table. Probably her reading material. "Then take a break. I'd like to talk to you in private. Get someone to cover for you." He nodded at the unconscious patient. "This is a baby-sitting detail anyway."

She frowned, looking at him for a long moment. "All right, I'll give you twenty minutes."

"Twenty minutes is fine." He knew he wanted a lot more than twenty minutes. But for the time being, he'd settle for that. At least it was a start.

Chapter 11

She peered into the open area outside Conroy's room and called to Rodriguez. The special agent was busy talking to a young, fresh-faced nurse and making nice progress from the looks of it, Lydia observed.

Rodriguez was at her side instantly, eager to be pressed into service.

She knew she was going to disappoint him. "Stay with the prisoner for a few minutes for me, will you?"

"You got it, Special Agent Wakefield."

She had to keep from smiling. The man made "special agent" sound as though it were a noble title, second only to "queen." "Thanks." Lydia walked outside, through the double doors to the inner corridor that separated the CCU area from the rest of the hospital.

Once there, she had second thoughts about going anywhere with Lukas. He could say what needed to be said here in the corridor. She turned abruptly toward him. "Look, there's no need to apologize, privately or otherwise."

Her voice was distant, detached, but he saw the fire in her eyes. Fire that pulled at him, hypnotically pulling him closer.

"I think there is," he told her quietly. "At least I'd like to explain why I jumped all over you like that earlier."

She felt her back going up. If he was trying to salve his conscience, he wasn't about to get away with it with a few well-chosen words. "You don't have to, I know why."

"You know?"

Just how extensive was her intelligence monitoring? Were the examining rooms bugged now? He knew that was technically against the law because of doctor-patient privilege, but he wasn't naive. There were ways to get around almost anything, openly or covertly.

"Sure I know." Did he think she was born yesterday? "You're afraid that I want to make something of last night."

He suddenly began to realize why she'd reacted the way she had. "And you don't?"

No. Yes. Maybe. The retorts all jumped out at her. She had no real answer to that, but she had only one response she was willing to give him: no.

Seeing someone come through the electronic doors toward the CCU, she moved to the other side of the hall and lowered her voice.

"We're both adults here, both capable of enjoying ourselves, of having a good time without attaching any meaning to whatever happens. You obviously thought when I had you paged this afternoon that I just wanted to see you again or to ask when we could get together."

As she spoke, the ice in her voice dissolved, fueled by the heat of her barely suppressed anger. "Or something equally juvenile and clingy, using Conroy as a convenient excuse. And just as obviously, you don't know me very well. That's not my style."

Though it made no sense, there was something stirring about seeing her angry. When she finished, he crossed his arms in front of his chest, studying her. Amused for the first time that day. "Pretty sure of yourself, aren't you?"

She didn't like the superior attitude he'd assumed. Lydia wasn't about to back away until she put this smug bastard in his place. "I'm generally right."

"And have you ever been juvenile and clingy?"

"I already told you that isn't my style." Her eyes narrowed into glittering green slits. "Not a damn single time."

He hadn't thought so. "Gives us something else in common—along with matching chips on our shoulders." The curve of his mouth faded into a straight, stoic line. "Except the man who taught me how to get rid of mine walked into the hospital this morning looking for me. For my help."

She swallowed the impulse to deny the comparison, to crisply tell him that any chips he thought he saw were fabrications of his imagination, but there was something in his voice that made denial secondary to curiosity. Whoever had come looking for him was someone he felt something for.

"Heart trouble?"

Lukas nodded. His eyes said things to her that his lips hadn't. He was talking about someone who mattered. A great deal. Someone who caused him to leave behind his stoic mask.

This was going to take longer than the twenty minutes she had promised him. Lydia set aside her own wounded pride and took out her cell phone. When he looked at her curiously, she held up her hand to hold back his questions.

"Give me a minute." Within seconds of pressing the familiar number, she was talking to Elliot. She turned her back on Lukas, lowering her voice. "Elliot, I hate asking, but I need you to come down and stay with Conroy."

"You mean in addition to you?"

"No." It took a great deal for her to ask for a favor, even of Elliot, but right now the man she had allowed into her world for the briefest of interludes needed someone and though she wasn't entirely sure why she was doing this, she had elected herself to that position. "I know I said I'd take the first baby-sitting shift but—" She bit her lip. "Trade shifts with me."

There was a pause on the other end. Just when she was about to ask if he had heard her, Elliot responded. "Sure."

She thought she heard Janice in the background, asking him what was wrong. Guilt nibbled away at her. "I wouldn't ask—"

"—if this wasn't important. I already know that, Lyd." He also knew what she was probably thinking. "Janice and I didn't have anything planned for tonight except growing a little older together. I'll be there in fifteen minutes."

"You can take longer than that. Rodriguez is on duty for another half hour." She glanced over her shoulder to where Lukas was waiting for her. "I owe you," she told her partner.

There was a soft chuckle in her ear. "I already know that, too. See you, Lyd."

She snapped down the lid on her cell phone and slid it into her pocket. Elliot would be as good as his word. With Rodriguez still on for another half an hour acting as backup and with Conroy still unconscious, there was nothing to prevent her from leaving with Lukas.

Crossing to him, she felt those same jumpy feelings skittering through her that she'd felt last night. She made a concerted effort to block them out.

"All right," she told him as he looked up at her, "we can go for that coffee now."

They elected to take his car to the small outdoor coffee shop located several blocks away. Nightfall darkened the perimeters of the landscape and the breeze rolling in from the ocean a scant mile and a half away made the evening chilly.

Sitting across from Lukas at a small table that accommodated two, Lydia wrapped her hands around her coffee cup to warm herself. For a man who had wanted to talk, he was rather silent.

She waited until the waiter who had brought them their coffees withdrew.

"So tell me about this patient who walked in this morning. Is he the one they paged you about from the hospital?"

Lukas nodded. "It's my uncle Henry."

The words felt as if they each weighed several pounds as they emerged on his tongue. Why was it so hard for him to share anything personal? People did it all the time. The airwaves abounded with people who called radio talk shows, eager to spill their insides to any stranger with five minutes to spare who was even moderately willing to listen. Here was a woman with whom he had shared the most intimate of acts, and he was hanging back, reticent to say a single word that smacked even remotely of something private.

She waited for him to continue. When he didn't, she coaxed softly, "Tell me about him."

"You mean his condition?" He'd reviewed the tests again just before coming to see her to assure himself that waiting until tomorrow wasn't a mistake. He had a margin, but the surgery had to be performed tomorrow to remain on the safe side of that margin.

"That, too." But she was far more interested in his relationship with his uncle. Far more interested, she realized, in finding out things that she hadn't uncovered in her cursory background check. "You had this look in your eyes when you referred to him in the hospital…" She let her voice trail off.

He remembered referring to Henry only as a patient, not as a relative. "I didn't say his name."

"You didn't have to." Cold, she took a long sip of her coffee and let it slide down her throat. She set the cup down as she studied his face. He had an incredible profile, she thought. Something she would have expected to see in a bronze sculpture by Remington. "The Young Warrior" it would have been called, she decided. "I could tell there was some kind of connection between you two even before you said a word. Did he raise you?"

"How did you know—" And then he stopped as he remembered. "Oh, I forgot. You did a profile on me, or ran an APB or whatever it is you call it when you special agents dig things up on people."

She didn't take offense at the crisp shift in tone. He was throwing up a smoke screen, most likely to protect something vulnerable.

"You make it sound sleazy," she said mildly. "I just wanted to know who I'm dealing with."

Lukas relented. There was no call for him to have said that. That was the private him reacting. But he'd been the one to invite her here, not the other way around, he reminded himself.

"I suppose that's fair. I just don't like people prying."

He had the vague feeling that he was repeating himself. But his mind wasn't on his words. It was on the woman in front of him. The one who had turned to liquid fire in his arms last night. The woman who, despite his best efforts to place this all in perspective and at a distance, made him want to repeat everything he'd done last night—and double it.

Damn it, he should be thinking about the surgery tomorrow, not about making love with her tonight. Especially since the latter wasn't going to happen.

"So tell me about Uncle Henry."

Toying with the remainder of his coffee, he raised his eyes to her. "What don't you know?"

"Pretend I don't know anything." She took another sip, then looked at him. "Start from the beginning."

The beginning. Had there been a beginning? Looking back now, it felt as if Henry had always been part of his life. But, of course, he hadn't.

"He's my mother's older brother. Henry Spotted Owl. She asked him to move in with us about a year after my father died. Told him I was too much for her to handle and that she was…" His voice trailed off as the right words didn't come.

"Afraid you'd come to no good?" Lydia guessed.

He laughed shortly. That was the cleaned-up version, he supposed. "Something like that. I ran with a gang on the reservation. They believed in the old philosophy of might makes right." As he spoke, it almost felt as if he was talking about someone else. Had he really been that wild young kid or had that all just been part of a bad dream?

Her voice, soft, low, brought him back. "Did you get in trouble with the law?"

He shrugged carelessly. "Just minor scrapes." But they had been on their way to major ones. "Until the joy-riding incident."

"Joyriding incident?" she prodded. His juvenile records were sealed, but she'd had her suspicions about what was in them.

He nodded. In his mind's eye, he could see it all again. His friends, the white Mustang they'd all crammed into. The exhilaration of speed as they had careened around corners, heading toward oblivion.

But there was no reason to go into that. Or into the fact that for the first time in his life, driving around at almost one hundred miles an hour, he'd felt free. He gave her the short version.

"I didn't know the car was stolen. Got my behind thrown into the local jail. My mother called for Henry." He laughed. "That was the first time I saw him. Big, old, ugly man, with a scar running down his cheek. Three inches." He held his thumb and index finger apart to underscore the length. It had made Henry seem that much more menacing. "Said it was a knife fight that made him find his way. Called it his Badge of Courage." It saved him from dying in some alley, Henry had added. "Anyway, he came to the jail, bailed me out and took me back to my mother.

"The whole ride back he said nothing." Lukas remembered almost going crazy with the silence. "Just let my imagination run away with me." He drained the remainder of his coffee and set the cup down on the saucer. "I figured once I got home, he'd pound me into the ground the way my father used to. But he didn't." That had been his first surprise.

"What he did do was tell me that from now on, I was going to toe the line. First thing he did was get me to work at the gym he established on the reservation." Lukas had found out later that because of him, his uncle had closed down the gym he'd been running in a neighboring town and brought all his resources to open the one on the reservation. "I was there every morning before school started, sweeping the place out, getting equipment ready for the day ahead. After school he had me training to be a boxer."

She looked at him in surprise. That hadn't been in the background report. "You box?"

There'd been competitions, prizes. He shrugged. "I can hold my own. Won second place in a tournament a couple of times." The prizes weren't important now, but they had been then. He'd wanted to win. And to make Henry proud of him. "He straightened me out, said that boxing saved his life and maybe it could do something for mine." It was a simple approach, but effective. "He was right. I had a punching bag to work out my frustrations on instead of thumbing my nose at the world and seeing how far I could push everybody."

Lukas turned up his collar against the breeze that was becoming colder. She looked unfazed by it, he thought, her face a picture of rapt attention. He wanted to lean over and kiss her.

"I love that old man. And he never asked anything from me." He paused and sighed. "Until this morning."

She could feel his tension, guess what he was feeling. "Can you help him?"

He had done the procedure enough times. But never
on someone he cared so deeply about. "The hospital and
I'd rather someone else do it."

"And he'd rather you do it." It wasn't a guess.

"Yeah." It was more than just a matter of preference.
"He's never cared much for doctors. I can't remember
his ever going to one. The only time he was inside a hospital was to take me to the emergency room when I was
on the wrong end of a right hook. Caught me completely
unaware. I went down hard, cutting open my head." It
had scared the hell out of him. A split second before his
head had hit the canvas, he'd thought he was dead.

Lukas lifted his hair and she saw a small, angry scar
just above his ear. She resisted the urge to trace it with
her fingertips.

"There was blood everywhere. Uncle Henry drove his
old pickup like it was a race car at the Indianapolis 500."
All he'd been aware of was the pain. And jostling from
side to side as his uncle drove. "Did the thirty miles to the
closest hospital in about twelve minutes." Lukas laughed
softly. "Only time I ever saw him look scared." He sighed,
looking at Lydia. "He won't let me recommend anyone."

Lydia put himself in the older man's position. "Why
should he? He wants the best."

Did she have any idea how heavy a burden that was?
"What makes you think I'm the best?"

A smile slid slowly over her lips. "Research,
remember?"

"Yeah, well, this time I might not be the best." The
possibility of what might happen was already haunting
him. "What if I slip—"

His self-doubt surprised her. And made him human in her eyes. It also gave them something in common. She wasn't the only one who had self-doubts in the wee hours of the night.

"You won't," she said with more confidence than he felt. "And the important thing is, he trusts you. I'd say it's a lucky thing that your specialty allows you to help someone you love. Stop resisting and be glad he came to you. The alternative," she added, "is a hell of a lot grimmer."

He let out a deep sigh. "You're right, it is."

She took a last sip of her coffee and made a face. It was cold. She pushed the cup away. "So when's his surgery scheduled?"

"Tomorrow at eleven. Triple bypass." How many times had he written that into a chart without a qualm? But now it was his uncle who was going to go under his knife. Henry, who he loved far more than he had ever loved the man fate had made his father.

Lukas had a lot on his mind. No wonder he'd exploded. She'd done it herself with far less crowding her thoughts. "I'm sorry I got in your face about Conroy this morning."

Her apology struck a raw chord, making him feel guilty again.

"You were just doing your job. I'm the one who should be sorry. I'm supposed to be able to control my emotions better than I did."

His apology made her laugh. He looked at her quizzically for an explanation.

"Sounds like we're both a couple of sorry cases." She felt him slip his hand over hers. This time, rather than stiffen, she held her breath. Waiting. Hoping. Slowly, she raised her eyes to his.

"Come home with me, Lydia."

She felt her heart accelerating. "You don't say my name very often."

"Kind of hard to spill your guts to someone you call 'Special Agent.'" He paused, aware that he was tense, that he was needy even if he didn't want to admit it to himself. "So, will you?"

Lydia was already rising to her feet. "You didn't have to ask."

Silence and small talk filled the interior of Lukas's sedan as he drove her back to the hospital parking lot where she'd left her car.

From there, Lydia followed his vehicle to Lukas's apartment, all the while wondering if she had the slightest idea what she was doing.

What she was doing was getting personally involved, which was against every rule she had ever laid out for herself. Granted, it wasn't as if Lukas was related to her prisoner, but if not for Conroy—more to the point, if not for the shot she'd fired at Conroy, she would have never met Lukas.

And that, she realized, would have been a waste. A waste no matter how this was all destined to end—tonight, tomorrow or a week from tonight. That she was in a finite situation she never questioned. What she questioned was whether or not it would ultimately affect her judgment and her performance on the job.

She told herself it wouldn't. That she was thinking as clearly as ever.

And what she thought—clearly—was that what was happening here was too intense for her not to explore, not to sample. Yes, she was happy with her life, yes she was glad she was an FBI special agent, but being with Lukas made her aware that she needed more than work. It made her aware that there was another Lydia Wakefield, one who occasionally did need the touch of a man's hand along her face. A Lydia who had needs that had not been addressed in a very long time. Hell, she thought, even cacti needed to be watered once in a while to continue growing.

And this was her watering.

Still, she felt unsure as she brought her car to a halt in the guest parking area adjacent to the carport where Lukas parked his own car.

Maybe this was a mistake. Maybe she should just start her car up again and go home to devote herself to going over the case tonight. To get her mind back on her work and not on how a man who moved like a proud god could bring every one of her five senses alive.

She wasn't opening her car door, Lukas realized as he got out of his sedan. She'd slipped into a designated parking space before he'd pulled into his, but she hadn't made a move since then.

Was she having second thoughts? He'd had them himself as he'd led the way to his apartment complex, glancing every so often into the rearview mirror to make sure she was still following him. Each time he saw her, there'd been a sense of relief he couldn't readily ignore.

His second thoughts had melted away the instant he'd begun to replay the moments they'd shared together last night. Moments that made him want her with an intensity that he found unnerving.

Biology was something he was aware of every day, but not on this level. This was something else, something special. This, he only now began to see, made him feel alive.

Not just alive, but real. He couldn't put it in any better terms for himself than that. It was as if he'd been moving through a world filled with shadows for most of his life and had just now wandered into an area that was filled with light.

Light and substance.

And an FBI special agent.

He wondered if it was a coincidence that her last name had the word "wake" in it. Because things were waking up within him.

He was probably making too much of it, he told himself.

And then again, maybe not.

Lukas walked over to where Lydia had parked her car. The driver's door was open, but she was still sitting in her seat, apparently undecided whether she was coming or going. Looking at her, Lukas put out his hand and waited.

After a beat, Lydia placed her hand in his and got out of the car.

Chapter 12

Leaving his keys on the small side table by the front door, Lukas turned on the radio. Soft, bluesy music filled the air.

The music made Lydia feel like swaying. Like kissing him, she thought, turning to look at Lukas. Slowly, she slipped off her jacket and then her holster, draping both over the back of the armchair.

Anticipation rippled through her, finding a resting place within her inner core.

"You seem tense," she noted, moving closer to him. The scent of his cologne, fading now, stirred her nonetheless. Exciting her. "Is it tomorrow's surgery, or me?"

"Both." Lukas held his hands out in front of him. There wasn't so much as a twitch in any of the muscles. But inside? That was where the nerves were doing their thing. Unsettling him. Making him doubt his own abilities.

As if reading his mind, she brushed her hand along his cheek. Suddenly she wanted nothing more than to comfort him.

"Don't spend time doubting yourself and second-guessing tomorrow. You're doing a disservice to both yourself and your uncle."

He didn't take flattery well, she thought. Funny how much they had in common when she thought about it. Glowing words never sat well with her, either. But she sensed that despite this trait, he needed encouragement. Because tomorrow's surgery was different.

"And he needs you to be as good as you were with Conroy." That was the irony of it. He probably hadn't even stopped to think before operating on the prisoner. And no one would have wept if Conroy had died. There was no family, nobody except the other members of his group, all of whom had apparently scattered. "Surely if you can operate on scum like that and bring him back from the dead—twice—" she reminded him "—you can perform the same miracle for someone who deserves it."

That was just it, Lukas thought. When you operated on the heart, it always seemed to involve a miracle or two. But he shrugged, falling back on the oath he'd taken upon graduating. The oath he believed in. "Everyone deserves to be helped."

"Some more than others," she emphasized. Frowning, she tried to block out thoughts of the man she'd left Elliot guarding. She didn't want to waste any time on Conroy tonight. She wanted to carve out a small island, a haven, for herself—and for Lukas—just one more time. "Don't get me started."

He smiled at her, his eyes holding hers. Stirring her up. Again. "I was under the impression that you already were."

Lydia found that her breath was beginning to catch, just as it had last night. It made talking difficult. "That depends on which way you want the evening to go."

"I know my preferences."

Moving her hair back from her neck, Lukas pressed his lips against the sweet slope. He heard her gasp and felt a thrill pass over him.

Her eyes fluttered shut as the sweet sensation proceeded to light a match to everything in its path. This time, because she knew what was coming, because she knew the magnitude of what was about to happen between them and within her, her anticipation was twice as intense, twice as electric.

Swallowing the moan that was struggling for freedom, Lydia laced her fingers together behind Lukas's head and brought his mouth down to hers. Kissing him for all she was worth.

His fingers were already undoing the buttons on her blouse, working them loose swiftly. Beneath them, he could feel the pounding of her heart. As it echoed the beat of his.

Damn, but she excited him. Worried as he was, concerned as he had been all day, just by being with him like this she managed to wipe almost everything from his mind.

Everything except her.

He wanted her so badly he could taste it, feel it in every fiber of his throbbing body. What kind of black magic was this, to ensnare him so? To make his blood rush with a fierceness that he'd never experienced before?

He'd always been able to detach himself from a situation, to view it from a lofty perspective. It was what kept him free, independent. His own person.

But he was too enmeshed here to be able to place any distance between himself and what was happening.

Nor did he want to.

Though it wrested control away from him, Lukas dearly wanted to be immersed in this, wanted to feel and taste and breathe nothing but her.

This, he knew, was nothing short of madness. And he didn't care.

It was as if he'd stepped into another world. One made up entirely of emotions. After a lifetime of holding his own in check, no matter what, to feel this way was liberating.

Hunger beat at him with both fists, urging him on. He came close to ripping her blouse from her body when the last button refused to leave its hole.

Lukas whispered a curse. The outline of the word rippled against her mouth.

Lydia moved her hands beneath his and undid the restrained button. Her lips never left his.

Everything felt as if it were transpiring in a swirling haze that was traveling in a circle through her brain. It was hard for her to think.

It was as before. Except more so.

"Think this time we'll make it to the bedroom?" His question formed waves of warmth against her mouth.

"We can try," she murmured.

It made no difference to her whether they wound up making love in a bed, on the kitchen table or the floor. All that mattered was that they did.

Trembling, she undid the buttons on his shirt and peeled the material away from his chest, yanking it down his arms. The instant her fingertips touched his skin, something shivered through her. She sucked her breath in sharply, as if she'd touched a flame.

Maybe she had.

Each taste of his mouth, each pass of her hand along his skin, only fueled her appetite.

More warm shivers passed over her as Lukas unhooked the clasp at her back. When he eased her bra from her breasts, her body tightened in anticipation. She bit her lower lip, her fingers weaving through his hair, pressing him close as he bought his mouth down to her soft peaks, suckling at each until they became hard.

Moistening her with desires that threatened to explode within her if he didn't hurry.

She'd never wanted anyone like this before. Afraid, she shelved fear to the back of her mind as she raced toward the climax that waited for her only a hairbreadth out of reach.

Divesting Lukas of his jeans and briefs, she surprised him by pushing him to the floor, then straddling him. Smiling at the look of amused surprise on his face, Lydia threaded her fingers through his on either side of his body. Bringing her body tantalizingly down to his.

Moving so as to bring his excitement almost to fruition, she rained small, fleeting butterfly kisses along his upper torso. She could feel his desire ripening beneath her. Unable to check her delight, she laughed with pleasure as she raised her head to look at him.

"Damn, but you are some kind of a witch," he murmured fondly and in awe.

Pushing his hands into her hair, he framed her face and brought her mouth up to his. The kiss deepened and intensified, swallowing them both.

Unable to hold back any longer, Lukas arched and drove himself into her. He felt her stifled yelp of pleasure and approval.

The ride was hard, swift, and rocked them both. He heard her cry his name against his ear before he sought out her mouth again. Pleasure drenched him, mingling with the sweat of his body and hers.

Slowly he felt the tension leave her body as she relaxed against his. The afterglow embraced them both in loving, warm arms, holding tight. Lukas smiled, not trying to figure out any of it.

She could feel his smile forming against her cheek. Still dazed, she raised her head to look at him. His lower lip looked slightly swollen. She realized she must have bitten it. "What?"

"We still haven't made it to the bed." The bedroom seemed a million miles away. And he was growing rather fond of the floor in his living room.

She sighed, her breath tickling his chest. Rousing him. "Maybe next time."

He lifted her hair, then watched as it fell back down like golden rain. "You're giving me an awful lot of credit."

Lacing her fingers together, she rested her hands on his chest and leaned her chin against them, looking into his eyes.

"Just calling it as I see it." She blew softly, watching his skin tighten in response. Glorying in the response. "Feel relaxed yet?"

He laughed, his chest rising and falling, making her move, as well. Lukas stroked her head fondly.

"If I were any more relaxed, they could serve me up as a liquid compound." He wanted her again. Was this normal? Or had she cast some kind of spell over him? "Is this something they taught you in special agent school?"

Lydia moved her head slowly from side to side, the ends of her hair tickling his skin. Arousing him when he'd been certain beyond any doubt that all he had the energy for was to fall asleep.

"This is something that just seemed to happen." She realized that she was smiling and that she felt happy, really happy. She couldn't remember the last time she'd felt like this. "Maybe you bring out the best in me as well as the worst."

Folding his arms around her, he held her close against him, ensuring that she couldn't get up quickly. "What would you say if I told you that I felt like bringing out the best in you again?"

The smile grew as her eyes began to shine. "I'd say you were incredible."

"Right back at you," he murmured. He brushed his lips against hers once, twice, then pulled his head back again. His eyes searched her face, looking for an answer before he asked his question. "Stay the night?"

He was asking her this time rather than taking his chances on it happening because she'd fallen asleep. She pressed her lips together, knowing that the right thing wasn't, at bottom, what she wanted to do.

"I shouldn't."

He heard the hesitation in her voice and felt victory within his grasp.

"We'll put it to a vote." Bringing her hand up to his lips, Lukas turned it over, palm side up and pressed his mouth against the soft flesh. His tongue lightly flicked the center. He saw desire blooming in her eyes and felt her wriggle against him, sending salvos of fresh desire through him. "I vote yes."

She swallowed, knowing the battle was lost. Lost

because she had no desire to fight it. Still, she couldn't go without firing at least a shot in protest. "You're not playing fair."

"Never said I would. I'm rigging the vote," he told her simply.

His tongue swept along her palm, then her wrist. He watched as her eyes closed again.

Delicious sensations hammered their way through her body. Creating riptides of pleasure.

"Oh, what the hell," she laughed, moving up against him, bringing her mouth down to his.

"My sentiments exactly," he told her before there was no more time for talk. Only actions. Only sensations.

And for feelings that were subtly, covertly being unwrapped.

The sound of his even breathing seeped into her consciousness, rousing Lydia from what had been a light sleep at best.

Opening her eyes, she found herself staring at the ceiling. Neither one of them had had the energy to make it to the bed, although Lukas had gallantly offered to carry her. She'd turned him down, knowing he was as exhausted as she was.

He'd fallen asleep within moments of her refusal, proving her right. She'd drifted off herself minutes later.

Now, sleep dissolved like morning mist burned away by a rising sun. She lay beside Lukas, his arm draped protectively over her again, and listened to him breathe. Idly wondering what it would be like to wake up to that sound every morning.

Wondering what it would be like to have someone in her life on a permanent basis.

Whoa, where was this coming from?

Startled, completely awake now, Lydia wrestled with the feeling of well-being that still had its arms wrapped around her. What was the matter with her? There was nothing to wonder about. Nothing permanent to contemplate. She knew that this feeling was only temporary, was already fading away.

To believe otherwise would be to play the part of a fool, and she'd never been that.

There was no place for this to go. Oh, there might be a few more wild, exhilarating couplings ahead for them—maybe—but there was nothing beyond that.

Couldn't be anything beyond that, she insisted silently, forcing herself to turn away from him and to look back up at the ceiling. She already had a significant other. The FBI.

There was no room for any other relationship in her life.

Not that she expected this—whatever *this* was—to even remotely approach the realm of a relationship. It was, as the song went, "Just One of Those Things." Nothing more.

She couldn't let it be anything more. For her own sake. And for his.

Lukas wasn't sure what had wakened him. There was a time when he had been a light sleeper, but in general, when he slept now, he slept soundly, deeply, until his body told him it was time to get up. This time a sound, a feeling, roused him.

For a second, as he opened his eyes, Lukas felt disoriented. A dark foreboding hovered over him, but he couldn't put a name to it.

And then he remembered. He was operating on his uncle today. Consciousness came to him with a vengeance.

Looking around, he saw her. Last night came flooding back to him. Last night and the night before.

But there was no time to dwell on either of the feelings that occupied the battlefield of his mind.

Lydia was fully dressed, he realized. Fully dressed and, by the way she was moving around, apparently trying to leave the apartment without waking him.

Why?

He propped himself up on his elbow. "Is this part of your covert training?" She swung around, a startled expression on her face, to look at him. "Leaving the scene of the crime before the other party has a chance to come to?"

Lydia raised her chin. He was beginning to recognize her defensive movements.

"I wasn't aware that there was a crime."

"Maybe that was the wrong word," Lukas allowed. It bothered him more than he wanted to acknowledge that he'd caught Lydia trying to slip away. He could understand it the first time, but not the second. "I'm not exactly at my best first thing in the morning."

"Neither am I."

Sitting up, he regarded her for a long moment. "So maybe we'd better not say anything that either one of might regret."

Lydia looked at him, weighing her words. Looking for a way out. She had thought she'd come to terms with things yesterday just before she'd entered his apartment, but apparently she hadn't. She didn't know why it was there, but she was aware of a hint of panic pinching her.

"There's nothing to regret." She tried to keep her voice casual. "We made love."

His eyes pinned her, not letting her just shrug off last night and the night before. "Several times."

"Several times," Lydia echoed. She took a breath. "And it was good."

He raised a brow, wondering if he was being cavalierly dismissed, after all. His pride rebelled. "Just good?"

She licked her bottom lip. There was no earthly reason why she should be feeling nervous. These things went on all the time. With no consequences.

"Very good," she allowed. "But not anything that's about to change either one of our lives." She squared her shoulders, daring him to disagree. "I think we're both agreed on that."

He wasn't sure why she was saying what she was saying. But he knew that he wasn't about to argue with her. Not when she was so adamant about downplaying what had been, quite possibly, the best night of his life.

Lukas had felt something last night, really felt something. Somewhere in the middle of their lovemaking, things had changed for him, making him sit up and take stock. Since there was no alcohol involved, he knew that what he'd experienced was rooted in feelings. Making love with her had only made him want to continue.

Not only that, but later, when the roller coaster ride had stopped and he'd lain there, holding her in his arms, the afterglow had been strong, gripping. So much so that he wanted to be able to experience it again.

And again.

It was out of character for him.

And then Lukas realized what she was doing. Why she was protesting so loudly that last night had just been good sex and nothing else. It *had* been something else for her. She *had* felt something and feeling it was out of character for her, too.

She'd felt something just as he had and maybe it scared the hell out of her just the way it did him.

They were both independent, headstrong people and from what he could ascertain, they were both used to being in control and on their own. He wasn't in control here. Whatever had gone on last night had controlled him. Had made him a prisoner just as much as the man in the hospital who was handcuffed to his bed was a prisoner.

Maybe it had made a prisoner of her, too, and that was what she was fighting so hard against.

"Are you sure we're both agreed to that?" he finally asked her.

"Yes," she snapped, then her tone softened just a little. "At least, I'm sure."

As long as she denied that anything of substance had happened between them or existed between them, he couldn't go any further. Pride wouldn't allow it.

"Well, then there's nothing more to talk about, is there?"

A sadness washed over her even as she expected to feel a flare of triumph. The flare didn't come.

"No," she agreed evenly. "I guess there isn't." She hesitated. "Except that I hope your uncle's surgery goes well."

Reaching for his jeans, he tugged them on before getting up. Maybe it was time he got his mind off passion and onto the business of living. And saving his uncle's life.

"Thanks." On his feet, he closed the snap on his jeans. "It will."

His voice was distant. Just as she wanted it to be

had no idea where this sudden wave of frustration and annoyance that surged through her was coming from.

"I'd better go," she told him, beginning to back away from Lukas.

She was reaching for her pager when it went off.

As did his.

Chapter 13

"Say again?"

Suddenly feeling numb, Lydia covered her left ear as she listened intently to the voice on the other end of her cell phone. Hoping that she'd somehow misheard. Rodriguez had been the one to page her. When she'd returned his call, he'd come on the phone almost breathless and extremely agitated, although he was doing his best to control himself.

He took a deep breath now. "Two of Conroy's men disguised themselves as orderlies and managed to slip past the guards."

She tried to read between the lines, anxious to get to the point of the young special agent's call. "They took Conroy?"

"No." In his haste to tell her everything, he was getting ahead of himself. "They're still here. One of the orderlies they stole the uniforms from managed to stagger into the hall and alert security before passing out. The other orderly is dead." His young voice was grim. "When they couldn't escape, Conroy and his people barricaded themselves in the coronary care unit. They're holding the other patients there hostage."

"Do we know who they are?"

"We played back the surveillance tapes on the fifth floor. Crime lab lifted some partial prints. Their names are Marlon Fiske, age twenty-one, and Bobby Johnson, age forty-three."

"Known felons?"

"No, that's the strange part. They're both clean as a whistle."

She didn't understand. "Then how do we have their prints on file?"

"You're not going to believe this. Fiske is a federal employee at the courthouse and Johnson's with an aerospace company that works on the space station."

She'd completely forgotten about federal employees being fingerprinted. Lydia shut her eyes, running her hand over her forehead, massaging a headache in the making. "Terrific. Just what we need. Educated racial supremacists."

Rodriguez broke with protocol and described the scene as he saw it. "All hell's broken loose here, Special Agent."

Out of the corner of her eye, she saw Lukas's shoulders stiffen as he responded to his own page. At any other time, idle curiosity would have made her wonder what was up. But right now, there was only one thing on her mind.

"What about Elliot?" She needed to know.

There was silence on the other end of the line. Lydia

felt a tightness in her chest. She refused to allow herself to think the worst. "What about Elliot?" she repeated, each word underscored.

"They took him hostage." She heard Rodriguez swallowing. "He's wounded."

"How?" she demanded.

"He tried to stop them and Johnson shot him."

She pressed her lips together, grateful for small things. At least Elliot wasn't dead. They still had a chance to get him out of there alive.

"I'll be right there," she promised, not waiting for Rodriguez to say anything further.

Flipping the cell phone closed, Lydia shoved it into the pocket of her jacket. She was already wearing her holster and service revolver.

Damn it, why had she allowed her hormones to seduce her into asking Elliot to trade with her? Why hadn't she been thinking with her head rather than with her other parts? She should have stayed at her post.

Guilt ran riot through her. It was her fault Elliot was in there now in God only knew what condition. If Conroy's men were willing to kill innocent orderlies without compunction, just for their uniforms, what would they do with the patients, with Elliot, once they really became desperate?

She couldn't let herself think about it. It would only paralyze her.

Steeling herself for what was ahead, she turned around. And saw Lukas. His face was a mask of stone. Instantly, Lydia knew he had to have gotten the same message that she had when he'd called the hospital in response to his page.

But she didn't have time to discuss it. Every second

counted. Every second could be Elliot's last. She had to get down to the hospital.

"I have to go," she told him as she hurried by him toward the door.

"They've taken my uncle hostage."

Lydia stopped dead. Guilt ridden about Elliot, she had completely forgotten that his uncle was also in the coronary care unit. Damn, this was just getting worse and worse.

She paused to squeeze his arm. "We'll do everything we can to get him out safely."

He wasn't naive. Promises weren't enough. He knew how these things could go. And even if things could be resolved eventually, Henry didn't have "eventually." Henry needed surgery in a matter of hours, not "eventually."

Grabbing his jacket, Lukas was right behind her. "I'm going with you."

Lydia knew how he had to feel, but he was a civilian and the more civilians around, the more things could go wrong. This was a time when even professionals got in each other's way.

She tried to reason with him. "There's nothing you can do, Lukas. This is a matter for professionals."

His eyes darkened, riveting her in place. "Like the professionals who let them take patients hostage in the first place?"

Lydia blew out a breath. She couldn't argue with him, couldn't waste the time or find the heart. She knew that in his place, nothing in the world would have kept her on the sidelines.

She turned on her heel and threw open his door. "C'mon, I'll drive."

He fell into place beside her.

* * *

For once, Special Agent Rodriguez hadn't exaggerated. If anything, he'd understated the scenario unfolding Blair Memorial Hospital.

The smell of panic, vehicle exhaust and excitement mingled in the air, growing stronger the closer they came to the sprawling compound that encompassed the hospital. Word had already leaked out to the media. News vans and trucks from all the local stations filled the area. Negotiation through early morning traffic had gone from difficult to almost impossible.

For as many reasons as there were vehicles, everyone wanted to be at the heart of what was going on.

Frustrated, Lydia maneuvered her car in as close as possible and left it double parked beside a Channel 12 news van.

"If they want to get out, they're going to have to run over my car," she declared testily as she got out.

There was a sea of people everywhere she looked. In the distance, she saw a dark van opening up and members of a swat team begin to emerge. Reporters making love to the camera as they recited their piece could be seen scattered throughout.

"It's a damn circus," she stormed, angry that tragedy was so marketable. "Don't these people have some meaningless award shows to cover or a celebrity to hound to death?"

Lukas heard the anxiety in her voice. He'd overheard part of her conversation earlier, enough to know that her partner was one of the people who'd been taken hostage. He didn't have to ask to know that she was blaming herself. He would have done the same in her place.

"Looks like for this morning, the supremacists are the celebrities," he told her.

The throng, comprised of reporters, camera personnel, curious onlookers and, more than likely, some family members of the hostages, was thickening to the point that getting through was almost impossible. Lukas saw Lydia elbowing someone out of the way, only to be confronted with another human wall.

"Get behind me," Lukas instructed. Not waiting for her to comply, he stepped around Lydia so that his body was in front of hers. Taking her hand, he forced his way through the crowd, growling a terse, "Get out of the way," to anyone who didn't immediately move as he forged a path for the two of them.

The police stopped them just in front of the front doors. A man who looked as if he were a twenty-year veteran of the force blocked their entrance.

"You can't go in there."

Lydia took out her badge, holding it up to the man's face. "FBI. That's my prisoner upstairs."

"Right now," the policeman said, backing away, "your prisoner has prisoners."

"Dr. Lukas Graywolf," Lukas identified himself, flashing his plastic hospital ID at the man. He left it around his neck. "Those are my patients being held hostage."

"Good luck to both of you." The policeman nodded them on their way, throwing himself in front of the doors the instant the crowd began to swell forward.

Reporters were firing questions at them from all angles, wanting to know everything from the names of the people being held to how something like this could have happened and how did they feel about it.

Lukas's response to that was something that would never make the airwaves.

"Does this mean your job?" a woman asked, shoving her microphone at Lydia.

Lukas shoved it away as he ushered Lydia through the door. "No, but it'll mean yours if you don't get that out of her face. Now," he growled a moment before both he and Lydia disappeared into the building.

Inside, the situation was no better. Nurses, orderlies and several doctors were all milling about, amid the police who had been immediately called in once the assaulted orderlies were discovered.

Lydia sidestepped a woman who had her arms wrapped around herself and was crying. As quickly as possible, they made their way to the elevators.

"I can take care of myself," she told Lukas.

"Nobody's disputing that," he stated in the same tone she'd used.

She opened her mouth, then shut it again. No one had thought to behave like a white knight toward her for a very long time. A small part of her rather liked that. Being looked after. If that was weak of her, she figured she could be forgiven, just this once.

Her tone softened. "Didn't mean to jump all over you."

Lukas shrugged. Maybe he shouldn't have snapped, either.

"Forget it," he told her. "We're both under a lot of pressure."

And it was going to get worse, he thought, before it got better.

Though there were fewer people, the scene on the fifth floor mimicked the one on the ground floor. There seemed to be people everywhere in the hall.

Lukas saw one of the nurses he recognized standing to the side, looking stricken. There were tears streaming down her face. It took him a moment to remember that the woman's husband was an orderly at the hospital. Had he been the one who'd been wounded, or the one who had died? His heart went out to her, but there wasn't time to ask. There was only time to try to save the living.

A policewoman was coming at them, waving them back before they could get very far. "Sorry, this floor's restricted."

Holding her badge up for the woman's benefit, Lydia pushed passed her. She spotted Rodriguez and made her way toward him. Agitated, worried, she was only vaguely aware that Lukas was following in her wake.

"How the hell could this have happened?" she demanded of Rodriguez before she was next to him. "We had people stationed downstairs."

The younger man lifted his shoulders helplessly. "I don't know, Special Agent Wakefield. I was just coming on when someone came up behind me, screaming that people had been killed and that the terrorists were barricaded in the CCU."

"'People'?" she demanded. "Be specific. How many dead?"

Rodriguez tried to compose himself. His inexperience shimmered in his voice. "So far, we only know about the orderly."

Facts, she needed facts. "You said Elliot was hurt. How do you know if you weren't here?"

"One of the nurses on the floor saw him go down when the two orderlies—I mean, terrorists, stormed the corridor in front of the CCU. They dragged him inside with them as the doors closed."

To be used as a bargaining chip. She fought back the angry tears that had sprung to her eyes. Tears weren't going to help Elliot.

"How do you know he's not—how do you know he's just wounded?" Rodriguez said nothing. He didn't know the answers to her questions, she thought, exasperated. The realization stung. For now, to get through, she concentrated on procedure and not on what might be happening behind the barricaded doors. "Did you notify the assistant director?"

"He's on his way down with more manpower. And I called Special Agent Peterson's wife."

Thunderstruck, her eyes widened. "You did what?"

The demand echoed loudly enough to momentarily evoke silence around her as everyone turned toward her and the young special agent.

"I—I called Special Agent Peterson's wife," he repeated, fearfully this time.

"Why in God's name would you do a thing like that? I don't want her here, going through hell—"

"Lydia?"

It was too late. Janice, a small, earthy-looking woman, was hurrying toward her, her face a pale, drawn mask of terror. Behind her, the elevator was just beginning to close.

The policewoman stepped toward her, but Lydia waved the uniformed woman away. "It's all right, she's with me."

"Lydia, is it true?" Janice cried. "Is Elliot in there?"

"Yes." Crossing to the older woman, she embraced her as Janice began to cry. Lydia took a moment to try to comfort her, then motioned a nurse over. "Take care of her," she instructed. "We'll get him out, Janice. I swear to you we will."

Janice could only nod bravely as she pressed her lips together to keep the sobs from emerging.

Lydia turned back to doing what she did best, analyzing the situation. There was no question in her mind that the supremacists had cut the power to the electronic doors that separated the CCU from the rest of the hospital. Otherwise, they would have opened the moment she'd stepped into the sensor's path.

The chair where Rodriguez had sat last night was unoccupied. His desk was devoid of the file box and the visitor registry book that had been on it earlier. The only thing that remained in place was a telephone.

She looked at Rodriguez. "Does the phone still work? We need to be able to communicate with those bastards."

The novice dragged his hand nervously through his dark hair. "I—I don't know."

Raising her voice, she asked, "Anyone know the number?" as she looked around.

Lukas came up behind her, reciting the seven digits that would connect her to the telephone.

"Hold it." Lydia took out her cell phone. "Okay, again." She punched in the numbers he repeated.

A second later, the phone on the desk behind the barricaded glass doors began to ring. It rang a total of twelve times before she saw the doors on the right wall just beyond the desk opening.

At first it looked as if no one was coming out, and then she became aware of movement along the floor. Whoever had come out was snaking his way to the desk like a guerrilla soldier out of a grade-B movie.

Shifting from foot to foot, she waited impatiently for him to pick up the telephone. The second she heard a voice on the other end, she began talking.

It didn't surprise Lukas that the first words out of Lydia's mouth were a demand. "Let me talk to Agent Peterson."

Lukas could almost make out the man's expression. He was scowling and looked as if he'd just started to shave on a semi-regular basis. "Who?"

Was he playing dumb? Lydia wondered irritably. "Peterson. Elliot Peterson. The FBI agent you have in there with you."

It was obvious that the man didn't care for the tone she was using. "Look, lady, you're in no position to make any demands."

She wanted nothing more than to get her hands around the man's neck.

"There's a SWAT team getting off the elevator," she told him. "And a combined force of a hundred guns pointed in your direction from all angles. I'd say you're the one who's not in a position to make demands."

The information didn't rattle the man behind the barricade. On the contrary, it seemed to infuse him with more bravado.

"We can kill everyone here before you can get to us," he bragged.

Terrific, she was dealing with someone whose mind had never made it beyond an elementary school playground. "I'm not about to get into a spitting contest with you. Let me talk to Agent Peterson and then you tell me what you want for Christmas."

He looked up. For a second, despite the distance, their eyes locked. "Sorry, he can't come to the phone right now."

The defiant tone unnerved her. "Why?" she demanded. An answer came to her. *Oh God, please don't let him be dead.*

Lukas saw the look on her face, heard the glimmer of fear in her voice an instant before she valiantly banked it down. There were other patients in there, not just his uncle, and since he was the only doctor who was this close to the scene, that made them his responsibility.

Without asking, he tilted Lydia's cell phone so that he could hear what the other man was saying, as well.

Understanding Lukas's reasons, she didn't even look at him quizzically.

The baby-faced supremacist, whom she assumed had to be Marlon, didn't bother to answer her question. Instead, he made his first demand. "We need a doctor in here. Conroy, he's not doing too well."

She could give a damn about Conroy. "How badly is Agent Peterson hurt?"

The voice on the other end snorted. "We'll let you know once we get that doctor."

It wasn't going to go like that. If she let Fiske get the upper hand in the bargaining, everything would be lost. "You don't get a doctor—you don't get anything—until I see Peterson. Is that clear?" Behind her, she heard Janice sobbing.

"Doctor first," the young man snapped. "It's not negotiable."

Lukas placed his hand over the bottom of the cell phone. "I'll go," he told her.

But Lydia shook her head, vetoing the idea. She had enough to worry about without thinking of him being in there, as well.

"We'll get someone else," she told him. Placing the

cell to her ear again, she returned to negotiations. "Okay, how's this? I'll trade you a special agent for a special agent."

The pause on the other end was ripe with confusion. "No. He stays here."

She had to get Elliot out. Nothing was going to go forward until she saw her partner safely away from the supremacists. She wouldn't allow it.

"Look," she began tersely. "If he dies, he's not going to do you any good and killing a federal agent is punishable by death, I don't have to tell you that. No fancy lawyer is going to be able to get you off. He dies, you die. That's the law and it's written in stone. Now, what'll it be?"

There was a pause on the other end of the line and then Fiske told her, "I've got to talk this over with the others. What's your number?"

She gave it to him. The line went dead.

With a sigh, Lydia snapped the cell phone closed. "He's going to talk it over." She spat the words out. Frustration clawed at her.

"You can't be serious." Lukas's tone rebuked her. She raised her eyes to his, not catching his drift at first. "You can't go in there."

It was her job to go in, to bring about peace at a decent price. Did he think she was just playing at law enforcement?

"You are."

He waved away the comparison as just so much nonsense. "That's different. I'm a doctor. There are people in there who need medical attention."

If there was a difference, she didn't see it. "And one of them's my partner. Who wouldn't be in there if I hadn't suddenly decided to trade with him." She worked her words past the lump in her throat. "Well, I owe him a trade. He said so last night. This is it." She looked at Lukas. "This isn't negotiable, Doctor. He's in there because of me."

Lukas understood that, understood her guilt. But not her recklessness in proposing to change places with the other man.

"I can treat Elliot—"

Lydia looked at him. Was he that naive, or did he simply not understand that the scum beyond the barricade did not subscribe to the same noble principles that he did?

"Conroy's too weak to make it out of here in his present condition. Those men in there with him are not going to let you do anything until you bring about some kind of miracle for Conroy." She saw the impassive look on Lukas's face. She knew it frustrated him that she wasn't listening to reason—his reason, not hers. "I don't answer to you, Lukas. This is something I need to do. We need someone on the inside and that someone is me."

Rodriguez had been standing to the side, listening to the exchange. He moved forward now. "Special Agent Wakefield, I could go in—"

She stopped him before he got any further. "No offense, Rodriguez, but you're still learning."

He did his best to appear as if he was on top of things. "Best place to learn is on the inside."

He was smiling, but she detected the nervousness just beneath the surface. Not that she blamed him. Nerves were healthy. They kept you from doing stupid things and kept you alive.

She placed her hand on his shoulder. "I need you out

here, Ethan. You get to face the assistant director when he comes," she reminded him. "Personally, I'd rather face these maniac supremacists." The phone in her hand rang. She exchanged looks with Lukas. "Looks like it's showtime." She tried one last time before flipping the phone open. "I can't talk you out of this?"

His eyes on hers, Lukas shook his head. "Not a chance."

Lydia sighed. "I didn't think so." She pressed the button on her telephone as she turned to face the man on the other side of the barricade. This time, he was sitting up at the desk, the phone to his ear. "Did you come to a decision?"

"We'll trade the agent for you. As long as we get the doctor, too."

"Smart move," she said, only praying that she was making one that was smarter.

Chapter 14

Back on the telephone, Marlon Fiske made his first demand.

"Send the doctor in first."

"No." Experience had taught Lydia that if Lukas went in before the trade for Elliot was made, no one would be coming out. "We need a show of good faith on your part. Send out Agent Peterson."

Fiske's face contorted. "Do you think we're stupid?"

Worried, angry at the terrorist and at herself for not being here when this had gone down, Lydia looked through the glass directly at the man. Hell, he looked no older than a college freshman. He should be lounging around in a frat house, sneaking in a beer and planning what to do on Friday night, not terrorizing coronary patients.

It was hard holding on to her temper and keeping her voice calm.

"I think you know that you're in a very precarious position. You have other hostages. I already told you that if anything happens to Agent Peterson, you won't be in a position to bargain for anything. Now send him out," she said evenly. "I'll meet you halfway. I'll take a step for every one he takes. An equal trade, like I said. And then you can have the doctor." She couldn't help adding, "That's more of a fair deal than you gave anyone at the mall."

Fiske looked at her angrily from across the barricade, his brow furrowed in indecision.

"Take it or leave it," she told him when his indecision stretched out the silence.

Lukas covered the cell phone in her hand with his own. She might have her agenda, but he had his. He couldn't risk the lives of any of the patients behind the barricade. Jacob Lindstrom, the man he'd operated on just before Conroy arrived in the E.R. had mercifully been transferred to his own room yesterday afternoon, but there were others there, others who had to be terrified by what was happening.

"I've got to go in there, whether or not he agrees to the trade." According to what a nurse had just told him, there were five patients currently in the CCU, not counting Conroy. Four were post-operative and one, his uncle, was pre-operative. All of them required close monitoring. There were hospital staff members trapped inside with them, but he couldn't count on them being able to handle an emergency situation.

Lydia looked into his eyes. She understood where he was coming from, but it didn't change anything. "We have to do it my way. You can only come in from a position of strength, otherwise, we lose them all." She saw the doubt. "I know what I'm talking about, trust me."

It all boiled down to that. Trusting her. Trusting someone else to handle things. It wasn't something he was accustomed to doing.

"What are you two whispering about?" Fiske demanded, his voice rising out of the cell phone.

She turned back to look through the glass. Fiske was peering at them uncertainly. Almost nervously, she thought. She had to use that to their advantage.

"That it's a nice day for a negotiation," she said simply. "So, what'll be?"

"Okay," he barked angrily. "Come ahead."

She placed her hand on the door. It wouldn't budge. There were chairs and a table piled against it. "You're going to have to clear off some of the debris before I can get in."

Fiske took two steps toward them, then stopped. "Back up!" he ordered, loud enough for his voice to carry through the doors. "Stand where I can see you."

"We won't rush you," Lydia promised. There was nothing to be gained if they did. The other man inside the unit could easily kill the hostages in retaliation. "You have my word."

Fiske sneered. "The word of a government pig doesn't go too far."

A smile with no humor behind it curved her mouth. "Pig senior-grade carries some weight on this side of the door, even if not on your side," she assured him, taking several steps back. "Nobody will make a move on you."

Her eyes never left Fiske as the supremacist, balancing his weapon under his arm, managed to pull back one of the barricades.

"Okay, you can come ahead."

But she made no move to go in. "First, get Agent Peterson. Equal steps, remember?"

Frustrated, Fiske backed up, not willing to leave the corridor unmanned now that one of the obstacles had been removed. He kept his gun trained on the doors until his body was level with the second set of double doors. Pushing open the door with one hand, he glanced in, then immediately looked back at the special agent he resented having to deal with.

"You, nurse, bring the wounded guy over here." Sparing only another glance, he motioned to the woman he was addressing with his weapon.

Lukas lowered his head so that only Lydia could hear him. "I don't want you to do anything stupid in there," he whispered in her ear.

She looked at him sharply. She thought of last night. Of how vulnerable she'd made herself, being with him. Who knew how disastrous a mistake that could have been if she hadn't retreated this morning?

"No more stupid than anything I'd do out here."

Lukas thought of the way she'd been with him initially. "That's not very reassuring."

His eyes swept over her. A myriad of emotions pushed their way to the fore. Everything had suddenly taken on a different cast in light of the dire situation. He realized that within moments, she would be at the mercy of men who had next to no regard for human life. And he didn't want her to be at their mercy, he wanted her to be safe.

"I mean it," he told her fiercely. "Don't get them angry."

Too late, she thought. "They were born angry, Graywolf." She paused to smile at him. "You ought to know a little about that. Here, hang on to this." She gave him her cell phone. "He might want to say something to you before you go in."

Movement beyond the glass caught her attention. Lydia sucked in her breath as she saw Elliot emerge from the communal CCU area. Leaning heavily on the young nurse who seemed to be doing more than her share to prop him up, he was taking shaky steps forward. There was blood all along his left pant leg.

Her heart constricted. "Oh, God."

Lukas turned to summon one of the people behind him. "Get a gurney and take Peterson down to E.R. the second he comes out," he ordered.

When he turned back, Lydia was opening the door. Aware that his heart had suddenly lodged in his throat, he caught her by the arm.

Startled, she looked at him quizzically. If she was going to ask what the hell he thought he was doing, she never got the chance. Her mouth was beneath his in a kiss that tasted of concern, of fear, and of other things she didn't have time to decipher. There were too many emotions colliding within her for her to handle any more.

Releasing her, Lukas stepped back, seeing Lydia for the first time. Seeing himself, as well. It crossed his mind that they were living in an insane world where things became clear just when they were the most complicated.

"Be careful."

Nodding, Lydia pushed open the door.

"Okay," she said to Fiske, using her calmest voice. Fiske was watching her every move intently, nervously. She knew she was dealing with a volatile person who could pick any time to go off. It wasn't a comforting thought. "I'm coming toward you. Remember, a step for a step."

"Remind me one more time, bitch," the kid terrorist warned her, "and it'll be the last time you remind anyone of anything."

I'm going to get you, junior, Lukas silently vowed as he watched Lydia slowly make her way toward the other end of the corridor. *And make you eat every damn word out of that smart mouth of yours once this is over.*

When she was halfway there, Fiske's eyes suddenly widened and he snapped to attention as if he'd just been poked in the back by a cattle prod. "Hold it! Take your piece out."

"My piece?" she echoed incredulously. What was he, a veteran couch potato who spent his life watching old crime dramas? Nobody used that word anymore.

He obviously took her repetition as ridicule. "Your gun, bitch," he snarled, shifting from foot to foot. "Take your gun out of your holster and put it on the floor. Now!"

Very slowly, holding her jacket open with one hand, she carefully plucked the service revolver out from its holster with the other. Securing it, she held the gun aloft with two fingers. If she wanted to, the weapon's hilt would have been in her palm in an instant and she could have easily gotten a clear shot at the baby-faced supremacist. But there was the chance that before he went down, he could get off a shot at either Elliot or the nurse who was propping her partner up.

Either way, she couldn't risk it. She needed to get the drop on Fiske when he could do the least amount of damage. And when a shot wouldn't have his partner in the other room reacting and retaliating.

She bent and placed the gun on the floor in front of her.

"Good. Now kick it over here," he ordered. When she did as she was told, he nodded. "Get your hands back up over your head and keep walking." He saw her look toward Elliot. She wasn't taking a step. He cursed roundly, then looked at the nurse. "You, do the same with the lead weight."

Lydia gauged her steps to Elliot's until they were finally parallel to one another. Hands above her head, she spared one glance toward her partner. "I'm really sorry, Elliot."

He offered a weak smile. "Just when I thought it was safe to get off disability." His breathing was labored. The wound hurt like a son of a gun. "It's not your fault, Lyd." He pressed his lips together to lock out the pain. "Watch yourself."

The exchange, too low for Fiske to pick up, only succeeded in agitating him further.

"Hey, hey, hey, no talking. You got something to say, say it out loud so I can hear." To emphasize his point, he waved the gun first at Elliot, then Lydia.

She was almost next to him now. It wasn't easy bridling her contempt as she looked at him. "Okay if I put my hands down now?"

"No, get inside the room." His hand to her back, Fiske pushed her toward the communal area. "And you out there," he shouted into the telephone, "send in the doctor or the FBI agent dies."

Breaking communication, he slammed the receiver down into the cradle.

The moment the outer doors parted and the nurse emerged with Elliot, Lukas waved the gurney forward. Elliot's wife was beside him, grasping her husband's hand even as they laid him on the gurney.

"Get him to the O.R., now," Lukas ordered. "He's lost a lot of blood."

The resident took over. Lukas pushed open the door and stepped inside the inner corridor. Fiske was coming toward him. "I'm Dr. Lukas Graywolf."

Fiske stopped in his tracks. Small, cold, amber eyes looked him over with contempt. For one moment, Lukas was propelled back to his past, looking into the eyes of people who thought themselves superior to him.

Fiske's thin lips curled. "Damn it, you Indians are everywhere, aren't you?" He spat out the words.

Lukas wasn't about to allow himself to be rattled by a low life. He'd endured far more from better men than the one standing in front of him.

"We're all part of some minority or other," Lukas told him mildly. "Even you."

The fair complexion reddened with rage at the insinuation. "My people go way back."

Lukas merely looked at him, not stating the obvious. That his went back further. He wasn't here to antagonize the small-minded man, only to treat the patients.

Fiske used his weapon as an extension of his hand and pointed it toward the black bag Lukas was holding. "What's in there?"

Because he'd learned long ago to suffer fools and endure their stupidity, Lukas remained calm. "Medical supplies." He'd had one of the nurses put it together the second he knew he was going in.

Moving backward, the supremacist motioned him over to the desk.

"Open it."

Lukas complied. With the tip of his weapon, Fiske moved things around within the medical bag, more for a show of strength than anything else. Satisfied that everything appeared to be in order, he indicated the other doors.

"Okay, now get in there and fix Conroy."

The ludicrously simplistic command demanded some sort of response. "He's not a broken toy to be mended," Lukas told him evenly, preceding him into the large room.

A dozen beds separated by Plexiglas walls and sandwiched in between monitoring machinery were arranged in a large semicircle. There was a patient in every other one. His uncle had been put in the bed closest to Conroy's area. The nurses' station was the focal point of the unit. The hospital personnel who had been within them when the two terrorists had rushed the area were huddled by the far wall where they'd been ordered to stay. Three nurses and an orderly.

And Wanda.

Lukas saw the fear in her dark eyes. He nodded at her as reassuringly as he could. "It's going to be all right," he promised.

"Only if you and the government bitch don't mess up," the other supremacist, Bobby Johnson, warned him. A big man, he looked older than his age, with streaks of gray running through his reddish hair. "Otherwise—" Johnson turned his weapon on Lydia. He was holding on to her by her bad arm, Lukas realized. "Bang, she's dead."

Lukas looked at Lydia. She looked completely passive, as if she weren't even listening to what had just been said. Damn it, she shouldn't have to be here. None of them should.

"I thought the whole point of this was for you to get

out of here with Conroy. You kill her and they'll never let you out alive," Lukas said.

"We don't need an Indian lecturing us." Fiske snickered, pleased to be the one who knew something the others didn't. "You believe it, Bobby? They sent us an Indian to treat Conroy. Surprised he doesn't have a rattle and some kind of magic dust with him to sprinkle on Conroy." He shook his head contemptuously. "These hospitals are just falling apart, letting anyone who wants to practice come in here."

She saw anger flare in Lukas's eyes and hurried to prevent a confrontation. The condescension toward Lukas galled her, but she had to pick her fights and right now, that couldn't be one of them. She needed to defuse the situation before it turned ugly.

"You wanted a doctor, you got the best. He saved your friend's life twice."

Her words made no impression on Johnson. "If you stinking FBI people hadn't shot John in the first place and let us get our point across the way we were trying to, none of this would be happening," Johnson yelled at her angrily, shaking her. Lukas saw Lydia try not to wince. "Now get him well enough for us to get out of here."

"And just how do you propose to get out of here?" Lydia asked as Lukas moved past both of them, crossing to Conroy's bed.

"How do you think?" Johnson sneered nastily, his eyes ravaging her. "We've got you for that. You get your people to get us safe passage out of here and onto a jet—"

Maybe they weren't as professional as she'd first thought. They certainly hadn't thought out a decent plan. "There's no place to land one around here," she pointed out. She'd gotten the particulars on Blair Memorial when Conroy had been admitted. "All we have is a helicopter pad on the roof."

Mention of the landing pad evoked a hoot of pleasure from Fiske. "That sounds good. I've never been on a helicopter ride," he said to the older supremacist.

Johnson looked at Fiske with contempt. There was no love lost between them. "Make the call and get one," Johnson ordered.

With all this gun waving going on, Lydia knew it was just a matter of time before one went off. She wished both men would keep their weapons still.

"I left my cell phone outside," she told Johnson, fervently wishing there had been time for her to get fitted for a wire. That way, Rodriguez and the others would have been able to hear what was happening. But Fiske had never taken his eyes off her and she hadn't wanted to risk upsetting the cart by temporarily ducking out of his range of vision.

"I hate careless women," Johnson growled.

His eyes were malevolent as they swept over her. Aerospace engineer or not, there was no doubt in Lydia's mind that the man was unbalanced. She just prayed he wouldn't go off the deep end and start shooting people before she had a change to disarm him.

Crossing to Conroy's room, Lukas passed his uncle's bed. Rather than fear, there was only concern on the older man's face. Despite the impatience of their captors, Lukas paused by Henry's bed. Lukas took his own turn with guilt. If he'd insisted on sending his uncle to another hospital, the man would be having the procedure done now, out of harm's way.

"You all right?"

Too weak to sit up, even with the help of the adjustable bed, Henry still managed to smile at his nephew.

"Don't worry, today is not a good day to die," he joked.

Lukas didn't like the color of his uncle's face. It was far too pale.

The next moment he felt Fiske prodding him with the muzzle of his weapon.

"You two can powwow later," the youngest supremacist sneered condescendingly. "You're here to fix Conroy, remember?"

All he needed was a clear shot at him with his bare hands, Lukas thought. But Fiske was brandishing a weapon while standing too close to Henry. He couldn't afford to do anything yet for fear of Henry getting hurt.

Lukas was forced to do as he was told.

Walking into the small space allotted to Conroy, he paused to check the monitors surrounding his bed. The readings were good. Progress was slow, but that was to be expected, given the circumstances.

"Can't you give me something?" Conroy complained angrily. "It hurts like hell."

Lukas took hold of his wrist, gauging Conroy's pulse. "You were shot and you had heart surgery, you're lucky to be feeling anything."

Unable to remain still for more than a few seconds, Johnson was pacing at the foot of Conroy's bed. "Just fix him so he can travel, medicine man."

He knew that, to buy some time, Lydia wanted to perpetuate the ruse that they were going to be given everything they wanted, but he felt he had to give them the truth about Conroy's condition. The man had still been unconscious as of last night. His being awake was sapping all of his energy for the time being.

Lukas avoided looking at Lydia, knowing her reaction to what he was about to say. "You move him, you do it at your own risk."

Johnson hit the black bag with the muzzle of his weapon. "There's gotta be something in that bag of yours, medicine man, to do the trick. Maybe you just need some incentive. Maybe," his voice grew harder, "if we start eliminating the people in the room, you can see your way clear to doing what I tell you. How about it, medicine man? Who goes first? The old lady—" He swung his weapon toward Wanda, who looked back at him defiantly. Lukas mentally took off his hat to her. "Or maybe your pal, here?"

As he said it, he aimed his gun at Henry. Lukas could feel the muscle in his jaw grow rigid. If they hurt Henry in any way, he was going to kill them with his bare hands.

"Better yet, how about her?" This time Johnson aimed the gun at Lydia. "They can only kill me once and they've already made up their minds to do it because of that kid who died at the mall."

"Worthless punk," Conroy gasped. "Served him right for coming out to see the exhibit. What the hell's wrong with people, coming out to gape at some useless scribbling and calling it a tribute. Tribute, huh. A tribute to dirty, marauding scum." Angry, red-rimmed eyes turned on Lydia. He nodded at Lukas. "You know his kind killed my daughter? Killed Sally? Gave her all sorts of garbage to mess with her head. I found her in the bathroom. My daughter, dead in a pool of vomit on the bathroom floor." He fairly shrieked the words. "They're all worthless, drug-snorting, foul-mouth lowlifes. I wish I'd gotten more of them." His eyes narrowed. "Next time."

"There's not going to be a next time if you go joyriding on a helicopter," Lukas told him.

"I'm touched by your concern," Conroy sneered. "Just give me something to kill the pain and have the government pig get the helicopter," he ordered. "Otherwise, we're going to have ourselves an old-fashioned massacre here." He looked at Lukas with hatred as Lukas took out a syringe and a vial of morphine. "You know all about that word, don't you?"

Lydia had heard just about all she could stand. "I think you could have been forgiven if your scalpel had slipped during his operation," she told Lukas.

"Gimme a gun," he ordered Fiske. The latter handed him Lydia's own weapon. Conroy's lips curled at the sheer irony of it. He'd use her own gun on her. There was justice for you. Weak, his anger strengthened him. "Say your prayers, FBI bitch, we've got ourselves enough hostages, I'm taking you out. An eye for an eye, right? You shot me, I'm shooting you."

With that, he raised the gun and aimed it at Lydia.

Chapter 15

Lukas didn't remember thinking, he merely reacted. He jabbed the needle into Conroy's arm. Jerking, Conroy screamed in surprise and pain. His shot went wild.

Lukas doubled up his fist and swung at Conroy's jaw, knocking him out.

The distraction was all Lydia needed. She swung around and kneed Fiske, who was standing behind her, frozen in place, gaping at what had just transpired. As he doubled up in pain, howling and cursing at her, she grabbed Fiske's gun away from him and spun around to find Johnson, the gun cocked and ready in her hand.

The moment she turned, she saw Johnson backing up, the gun he was holding trained directly at her head.

Triumph shone in his dark eyes.

"Drop the gun," he ordered.

Lydia caught her breath, frustrated beyond words. But the gun remained in her hand, aimed at him.

"Maybe you should follow your own advice," Lukas told him.

Johnson spared a look to the side. He was staring down the muzzle of the weapon Lukas had taken from Conroy. Rather than exhibiting any fear, the supremacist's lips peeled back in an evil smile. He was clearly enjoying himself.

"What we have here is what they used to call a Mexican standoff."

"Wrong," Lukas contradicted evenly, not a single muscle giving away the very real concerns he had. Even if it didn't manage to get Lydia, or him, a stray shot could hit any one of the patients or the staff. He had to get Johnson to drop his weapon. "A Mexican standoff is when there's a balance of power. In case you forgot how to count, it's two to one here. Not in your favor."

"You can't kill both of us, Johnson," Lydia told him, her gun still raised.

The wild look in his eyes intensified as he swung the muzzle of his weapon from Lydia to Lukas and then back again. He cocked the gun. "No, but I sure as hell can kill one of you."

His choice of victim evident, Johnson squeezed the trigger before he finished his words. But the shot went wild, passing through the ceiling as he fell to the floor, dead. His eyes were wide, glazed and unseeing as they stared at Lukas.

Lydia stared, dumbfounded. Lukas had fired his gun before she could even squeeze her weapon's trigger. Training that had been rigorously drummed into her had held her back until the last possible moment.

And that last possible second would have been too late. If it hadn't been for Lukas.

Rounding the bed, Lukas was beside her the next moment, his eyes taking swift inventory of all her parts. "You all right?"

Numbed, she nodded.

"Everybody else okay?" he asked, tossing the question to the room. A murmur of uneven, shaky voices answered in the affirmative.

Crossing to Johnson, Lydia dropped to her knees over his body, feeling for his pulse more out of obligation than expectation. She wasn't surprised not to find any.

But she was surprised by what had just happened. She looked at Lukas, kneeling beside her. "Where did you learn to shoot like that?"

He sat back on his heels. There would be no life-and-death battles waged over Johnson. That fight was over. "The reservation. Billy Standing Bear could get his hands on almost any weapon you could think of."

His life in the wild band he had run with in his youth had included experiences about which he'd told no one, not even Henry, although he figured his uncle had had his suspicions. It was funny how things worked out sometimes. If he hadn't been part of the gang, he wouldn't have known his way around weapons and wouldn't be looking down at a dead man now. And Lydia, in all likelihood, would have been the one on the floor in his place.

Satisfied that Johnson no longer posed a threat, Lydia swung around to check on Fiske. He was still on the floor, writhing in pain. She looked at him with contempt. "We need something to tie up the junior terrorist with before he slithers away on us."

Lukas had a roll of white adhesive tape in his hand. "Way ahead of you." Crouching, he went to work.

Lydia hurried to the door to call in the others and to call off the SWAT team. She glanced over her shoulder and saw that Lukas had Fiske's hands and feet pulled together behind him.

He felt her looking at him. Lukas commented. "Not unlike tying a calf in a rodeo."

She shook her head. The man had hidden talents. "Someday, you're going to have to tell me about that childhood of yours."

Someday. The word shimmered between them as he watched her hurry into the corridor. He took it as a promise, not a slip of the tongue.

"Dr. Graywolf, I think you'd better get over here."

Wanda's voice brought him around. He didn't like the tone he heard. He tested the integrity of the tape he'd just wound around Fiske's hands and feet. Satisfied that Fiske wasn't going anywhere in the near future, Lukas rose. Only then did he realize that Wanda was standing next to a bed.

His uncle's bed.

Adrenaline shot through him like a flare. Rushing over, he felt Henry's neck in an effort to deny what he saw on the monitor. The screen was flat-lining.

"Crash cart. Get me a crash cart!" Lukas shouted, beginning manual CPR. Panic ate away at him the way it hadn't when he'd faced down Johnson an eternity ago. "C'mon, old man, we've been through worse things than this. This was just a little noise, a lot of shouting. It's over. Don't die on me now."

Counting in his mind, Lukas administered one round

of CPR before the nurse came running back with the crash cart.

At the same moment, Lydia returned with Special Agent Rodriguez following behind her like a shadow. Keeping up was the assistant director and several other FBI agents who entered the room in their wake.

"He's all yours." She indicated the hog-tied Fiske on the floor, then nodded toward Johnson. Blood was pooling around his upper torso. "And you'll need a body bag for that one. Conroy was strong enough to hold up a gun, so I think he can be transferred to the medical ward in the county jail."

The assistant director looked down at the unconscious prisoner. "What the hell happened to him?"

"A little doctor-patient interaction," she replied, looking around for Lukas. Any other words faded as she saw Lukas standing over his uncle, charged paddles in his hands. Relief fled as something tightened in her chest. "Lukas?"

Exhaling as he silently rendered a fragment of a prayer of thanks, Lukas replaced the paddles on the cart and waved it back.

"We've got a pulse. Call down for an O.R.," he instructed a nurse beside him. "Tell them I've got a man up here who can't wait."

Closest to the wall phone, Wanda made the call to the first floor. Lukas didn't wait. Taking the safeties off the wheels, he mobilized the bed and began pushing it toward the double doors.

Not waiting to be asked, Lydia quickly took over the other side, helping to guide the bed down the corridor. Between them, the old man lay unconscious, lost to the drama he had instigated.

"Lukas, what happened?"

He hadn't even looked at her. His face was a grim mask. He was afraid that if he allowed himself the slightest bit of emotion, it would crack everything else apart, including his strength.

"He had a heart attack," he answered crisply, punching the button for the elevator. "I guess seeing a gun pointed at me was too much for him."

The service elevator car arrived almost immediately and they pushed the bed in. Lukas pressed for the ground floor. Praying. Praying to remember how to pray.

Unable to help herself, Lydia took the old man's hand in hers even though she knew he wouldn't feel it. Silently she tried to will him her strength. "Is there anything I can do to help?"

Lukas looked at her over his uncle's inert form. "Do you know how to pray?"

She hadn't prayed since her father had been shot. An ocean of prayers had turned out to be useless. Her father had still died. "I'm not sure I remember how."

"You might try remembering," he told her as the doors opened again.

Quickly, they made their way through the throngs in the corridors. Though questions followed them, people got out of their way. The emergency operating rooms were located next to the elevators at the rear of the hospital.

As they arrived at the doors of the first operating room, Lydia reached over the bed to touch Lukas's hand to get his attention. "Is there anyone I should call for him?"

He shook his head. "There's just my mother. She thinks he's off on a fishing trip." He set his mouth grimly, not wanting his thoughts to stray. "It's better that she doesn't know."

Lydia watched helplessly as Lukas disappeared through the double doors. She disagreed with his assessment of the situation, knowing that if she were his mother, she'd want to know that her only brother was on the operating table, fighting for his life. She'd want to move heaven and earth to be there.

But it was Lukas's call to make, not hers. She let out a shaky breath. All she could do was be there for him when it was over.

Suddenly at a loss with what to do with herself, Lydia went to the lounge where family and friends were supposed to wait sedately while those they cared about were half a corridor away being operated on.

The moment she walked in, she was enveloped in an embrace. It took her a second to realize that Elliot's wife was pressing her tear-stained face against hers and hugging her for all she was worth.

"He's going to be all right, Lydia. Elliot's going to be all right." Stepping back, Janice covered her mouth with her hands, physically holding back a sob of joy. "They're admitting him overnight, just to be sure, but the doctor says he's going to be just fine. It looks like he just needs a transfusion. Nothing vital was hit." Fresh tears shimmer in her eyes. "Lydia, I can't thank you enough—"

Lydia shook her head. All she could think of was that if it hadn't been for her, Elliot wouldn't have been shot in the first place. "There's no need to."

"Oh, but there is," Janice insisted. "If you hadn't traded yourself for him, he could be—" She stopped abruptly, unable to say the horrible words.

There was no point in going over everything, assigning blame and denying it. What mattered at this moment was the end result. Elliot was going to be all right. Lydia smiled at the other woman.

"Hey, I'm in no mood to break in a new partner. I had no choice but to get him out of there." She gave the woman a quick, warm hug. "Tell Elliot I'll be up to see him later."

Watching her back away, Janice called after her. "Where are you going?"

"I've got a promise to keep." Lydia commandeered a folding chair and looked at the hospital attendant sitting behind a small desk in the corner. Eyeing her. "Okay if I take this? I'm just going into the hall with it."

Seeing the badge at Lydia's belt, the attendant reluctantly nodded.

"Just the hallway," he emphasized.

Taking the chair back with her to where she and Lukas had parted, Lydia sat beside the operating room doors to keep vigil. And to try to remember how to address a power she had turned her back on.

Rodriguez found her there a few minutes later. The look of concern he was wearing faded from his young face. "The assistant director's looking for you."

A wave of weariness washed over her. She supposed she was derelict in her duty, but she wasn't up to anything further now. Right now, she just wanted to be a woman waiting for her man.

"There's nothing left but paperwork, Special Agent. Tell him I'll get to it when I come in later."

Rodriguez was grinning. "No, what he wanted me to tell you if I found you was 'nice work.'" He laughed softly, shaking his head. "Somebody said that was a first for him."

"Actually, I think you're right." The man was far

from lavish with his praise. She smiled. "Tell him thanks."

Unwilling to leave her side just yet, Rodriguez hovered protectively. "Is there anything I can get you? Something to eat, maybe?"

The thought of food made her queasy. "Coffee would be nice."

Delighted to be of service, Rodriguez was already on his way. "You got it."

There were five empty coffee containers in various stages of crumple lined up beside the metal legs of Lydia's folding chair, one large one that Rodriguez had brought to her from the corner café and four smaller ones obtained from the vending machine down the hall. The coffee there was foul, but it was hot and black and she required little else as the minutes dragged themselves around the circumference of the hall clock, forming hours.

Her whole body felt stiff with tension. She was vaguely aware that bypass surgery took time, but how long she hadn't a clue. And she was afraid to go anywhere beyond the bathroom, which was conveniently located next to the vending machine, to ask someone for fear that she would miss Lukas when he came out.

She wanted to be there for him, to be the first person he saw no matter what the result of the surgery, good or bad.

Despite the massive doses of caffeine that were coursing through her veins, as well as the tension gnawing away at her, Lydia was beginning to feel sleepy. If she felt like this, what did Lukas feel like, she wondered, standing all this time over the body of his uncle, battling for his life?

She tried to put herself in his shoes and couldn't.

Most of all, she wanted to comfort him, to be there for him. But she was at a loss as to exactly what to do, what to say, once he came out.

And then the doors parted.

Seven hours after he'd gone in, Lukas Graywolf slowly walked out of the operating room, a man who had fought the good fight and was exhausted beyond words because of it. He'd taken off his mask. It dangled around his neck.

The moment the doors opened, Lydia was on her feet, almost sending her folding chair crashing to the floor. She caught it just in time, her eyes never leaving Lukas's face.

He looked pale, she thought, and she couldn't read his expression. Was he just tired, or heartsick? Had he won, or lost?

Lydia realized that despite the noise she'd made, he was oblivious to her presence. Afraid of intruding, unwilling to back away, she touched his shoulder.

"Hey," she said quietly.

He looked at her. For a second he felt as if he were still in some kind of a dream. Or was she real?

"Hey," he echoed, then scrubbed his hand over his face. God, but he felt as if he'd been in there a hundred hours. "What time is it, anyway?"

"Almost seven. An eternity since you went in." She bit her lower lip. The question had to be asked, there was no subtle way to find out the results. "How is he?" she asked softly.

"Alive." Even as he said it, Lukas was in awe of the fact. His uncle's heart had stopped and now it was beating again. The wonder of it would remain with him forever. Almost afraid to let it, he could feel joy flooding through him. "Breathing." He allowed himself a hint of a smile. "It looks good."

Relieved, she threw her arms around Lukas and hugged hard. The tears she'd held back for so many years dampened his shoulder. "I'm so glad for you."

He could feel her tears, hear her joy. Both took him by surprise. His uncle was no one to her, yet she was affected by his recovery.

"Yeah, me, too." And then he really looked at her, bits and pieces of reality floating together for him. He hadn't thought it possible, but his heart swelled even more. "What are you still doing here?"

"Waiting to find out if your uncle's all right."

Because it was a great comfort to him, Lukas slipped his arm around her shoulders, holding her close. He'd almost lost her today, too. But he hadn't. She was still alive. And here. The day had turned out to be pretty damn great. "No other reason?"

A hint of a coy smile crept to her lips. "Well, I was waiting for you, too."

He already knew that, and he hadn't been hinting for an admission. "No, I mean it's not because of Conroy, or that other scum—"

"Fiske," she supplied. "No, they're both on their way to jail, Fiske to wait for proper arraignment and Conroy to go to the medical ward at County. A man strong enough to hold a gun doesn't have to be pampered." Suddenly she felt awkward. He looked tired and should be on his way home. She had no idea if there was a place there for her. "Elliot's going to be all right," she told him. "Janice said they were admitting him overnight for observation, but there's every indication that he'll go home tomorrow."

"That's good."

Her awkward feeling intensified. She looked at the chair. "I guess I'd better take this back to the lounge. The attendant didn't look too happy about lending it out when I took it."

But she'd taken it anyway. That sounded like her. He smiled at her. "Lydia, do you have a few minutes?"

She had eternity if he wanted it, she thought. Those few minutes this morning had changed everything for her, had made her reorder her priorities.

If she told him, he'd probably laugh at her, she thought.

"Sure." She waited. "Was there something you wanted to say?"

"Yes." He looked around. Things had gotten back to normal. It was as if there had never been a siege or a hostage situation, as if he'd just had a nightmare and now it was over. Except that she was still here. "But not in the hallway. Want some coffee?"

She laughed, glancing at the battalion of paper cups on the floor. "If you squeeze my hand, you might be able to pour yourself a cup." When he looked at her quizzically, she nodded at the mini-squadron.

"All right then, want to grab some food to go with all that coffee?" He didn't care what the pretext was, he just wanted to get her alone for a few minutes. Just long enough to get something off his chest.

Her stomach rumbled, speaking for her. Lydia laughed. "Sounds good to me."

Shedding his scrubs and leaving them in his locker, Lukas took her to the small café around the corner where Rodriguez had bought the coffee for her hours ago.

He felt edgy as he waited for their orders to be brought to the table. It was like waiting for the stage to be set, for the curtain to finally lift. The way the curtain had finally lifted for him.

He would have thought that, after all he had been through today, there wasn't an ounce of tension left within his body. Apparently, there was an endless supply.

After the second the waiter set down their sandwiches and accompanying beverages and backed away, Lukas took her hand.

"We need to talk," he prefaced, then saw her frown. "What?"

She pulled her hand back. Contact would only make what was coming that much worse.

"That never means anything good." Like an old-fashioned lawman, she headed him off at the pass. "You don't have to worry, Lukas. Just because I kept vigil while you were operating on your uncle doesn't mean I'm trying to lay squatter's rights to some space in your life. What we said this morning goes."

He vaguely remembered the words. And hated what they represented. "No it doesn't," he contradicted. "Not anymore. Things have changed."

She looked at her cola and wished for something stronger, something to temporarily settle her nerves. But that was the coward's way out. She lifted her chin, telling herself she was ready for this no matter how roundabout his path.

"What things?"

How come wrestling a gun away from a madman was easier than speaking his mind? And a hell of a lot easier than speaking his heart?

Taking a deep breath, Lukas plunged in. "You know how when you face death, your life is supposed to pass before your eyes?" She nodded. "Well, when Conroy was about to shoot you, my future passed before my eyes." He reached for her hand again. This time, looking somewhat stunned, she left it in his. "A future without you, and I realized that I didn't want it. Didn't want to go back to what I had because I didn't have anything. It had me." He couldn't say it any plainer than that, he thought. He put his entire fortune into the pot, betting all. "Now I'd like to know if you'll have me."

"Have you?" she echoed. He couldn't possibly be driving at what she thought he was driving at.

The edginess was carving neat little pieces out of him, stacking them by the roadside. "In marriage."

It was only through supreme effort that she didn't gape. "You're asking me to marry you?"

Frustration snapped its jaws around him as he feared the worst. That she'd turn him down. "I guess I wasn't making myself clear."

"No, no," she said quickly, "it's me. My brain just fogged up." Her mouth curved slightly in awe. "And I'm having a fantasy I don't want to wake up from."

She found herself suddenly wanting to share things with him. To give him a part of herself she'd held back, even when they'd made love together.

To bring them closer.

"Elliot said that my problem was that I was looking for a man like my father." She'd always denied it, but at bottom, she knew it was true. "Strong, honorable, decent to the point of being selfless."

Was this her way of gently turning him down? "Hard shoes to fill."

Her eyes reflected the smile she felt within her. "I think they've been filled. And then some."

It was his turn not to grasp what was being said. "Are you saying what I think you're saying?"

Lydia nodded. "I am if you think I'm saying yes." The grin nearly split her face. "The answer is yes. Yes, I'll marry you. I always wanted to find a doctor I could trust." She looked at him significantly, touching her breast. "You see, I've been having some heart trouble lately."

Picking up her tone, he arched his brow. "Is it serious?"

She nodded solemnly. "Very serious."

He kept a straight face, even when he felt like cutting loose with a whoop of joy.

"Bears some looking into."

She could feel her heart accelerating with anticipation. "How soon can you start looking?"

He cupped her cheek with his hand. He was the type, he realized, who had to almost lose something before he became aware of how truly precious it was to him. "The second I get you home."

Her eyes softened, already making love to him. "Sounds good to me."

Because the tables were very small, he had no trouble leaning over the one they were sitting at. Lukas sealed his proposal and both their futures with a long, languid, deep kiss.

M.D. MOST WANTED

To
Dr. John G. Miller,
who answers all my questions,
and is the perfect example of everything
a doctor should be

Chapter 1

There were some days that Reese Bendenetti felt as if he just hit the floor running.

This was one of those days.

He'd been up, dressed and driving before he was fully awake. Normally punctual, Reese was running behind, thanks to an asthmatic alarm clock that had chosen this morning to make a sound more like a cough than a ring when it went off. The sound had barely registered in his consciousness, and he'd fallen back to sleep only to jerk awake more than half an hour later.

When it came to getting up, Reese had been cutting time to the bone as it was, setting the clock to give him just enough leeway to shower, shave and have breakfast—provided he moved at a pace that could easily be mistaken for the fast-forward speed on a VCR.

That had been before his fateful early-morning encounter with the "little alarm clock that couldn't." Consequently, the shower had lasted all of two minutes, his hair had still been wet when he'd gotten behind the wheel of his '94 'Vette—the single indulgence he allowed himself—and his face was fated to remain untouched by a razor until he could find some time at the hospital in between rounds, emergency room patients and whatever else the gods chose to throw at him this morning.

Eating was something he couldn't think about until he came within coin-tossing distance of a vending machine at the aforementioned hospital, Blair Memorial.

Reese knew he only had himself to blame. No one had made him become a doctor, no one had told him to go into general surgery or to specialize in internal medicine. Those had been his own choices. His mother, bless her, would have been satisfied if he'd become a part-time sanitation engineer. As long as he was happy—that was her only criterion. Rachel Bendenetti never placed any demands on him, only on herself.

But healing was the only thing that did make him happy. It was in healing others that Reese felt as if he were healing himself, renewing himself. Building a better Reese Bendenetti.

He never quite understood why, he just knew that making someone else's life a little better, a little easier, always managed to do the same for him.

That was why whenever Lukas Graywolf, a cardiac surgeon, returned to the reservation where he'd been born and raised, Reese always volunteered to go along with him and provide services to people who would otherwise not be able to afford them. The way he saw it, the rewards were priceless. It had never been about money for Reese.

He'd been enamored with medicine ever since he'd applied his first Band-Aid. Almost twenty-five years later he could still remember the circumstances. After calling him a name, Janet Cummings had turned and begun to run away, only to trip on the sidewalk. She'd scraped her knee badly and it had bled. Without hesitating, he'd run into the ground-floor apartment he and his mother were living in at the time, gotten a Band-Aid and peroxide out of the medicine cabinet—the way he'd seen his mother do—and run back outside to come to Janet's aid.

He never stopped to think that she deserved it because she'd been nasty to him, all he could think of was to stop the bleeding. Watching him, Janet had stopped crying. When he was finished, she'd shyly kissed his cheek.

Reese remembered lighting up like a Christmas tree inside. Janet had been six at the time. He'd been almost seven.

It was a feeling that he wanted to have again, and he did. Each time he worked on a patient.

Working on Tomas Morales's perforated ulcer was a little more complex than applying peroxide and a Band-Aid to a scraped knee, but the feeling of satisfaction was still the same.

Taking off his mask, he tossed it into the hamper and sighed, bone weary. The operation had taken longer than he'd expected. As he ran a hand through his hair, holding the green cap he'd just removed in his other hand, his stomach growled. Fiercely.

"I heard that all the way over here," Alix DuCane cracked. She was standing by the sink, putting lotion on her freshly scrubbed hands. The gloves she'd just taken off chafed her flesh. If she wasn't careful, she thought, she was going to wind up with skin like a lizard.

As if in response, his stomach growled again. One of the orderlies chuckled to himself.

Reese shrugged, tossing the paper towel he'd just used to dry his hands into the wastebasket.

"That's what happens when all you've had for breakfast is a small candy bar." It'd been stale at that, he thought. Hazards of war.

Having removed her own surgical cap, Alix shook out her short, curly blond hair as she crossed to him. "It was at least a granola bar, I hope."

Reese grinned and shook his head. "Nope. Chocolate bar. Pure sugar in a sticky wrapper. I think the candy in the vending machine down the hall is melting."

She tended to agree, having hit the machine more than once for an energy surge in the past week. Alix frowned in mock disapproval. "Shame on you, Dr. Bendenetti. What kind of an example are you setting for your patients? You're supposed to know better."

His shrug was careless, loose-limbed. The movement hinted that there was an ache there somewhere, waiting to emerge and make him uncomfortable. He needed a new mattress, he thought. And the time in which to purchase it.

But first things first. "Know where I can get a reliable alarm clock?"

Alix smiled to herself. She knew of several women on staff at the hospital, including two physicians, who would have been more than happy to volunteer to wake Reese up personally, any hour of the day or night. So long as they could occupy the space beside him in the bed right before then.

There was no denying it, Alix thought, looking at her friend with an impartial eye. Reese Bendenetti was one desirable hunk, made more so by the fact that he seemed to be completely unaware of his own attributes. To her knowledge, he rarely socialized. When he did, it was to catch a beer or take a cup of coffee with a group from the hospital. Never one-on-one, except with her, and theirs was a purely platonic friendship. They had a history together, going back to medical school. He'd known her when she was still married to Jeff. Before the boating accident that had taken him away from her.

Alix knew firsthand what a solid friend Reese could be. It seemed to her that it was one of life's wastes that Reese didn't have anyone in his life who could truly appreciate the kind of man he was.

Sometimes, she mused, dedication could be too much of a good thing.

But there was still time. Reese was young. And you never knew what life had in store for you just around the next corner.

"Is that what happened this morning?" she asked as they walked out of the room connecting two of the operating rooms. He raised a brow at her question. "I happened to see you peeling into the parking lot."

Reese smiled ruefully. Driving too fast was a vice of his, and he was trying very hard to curb it.

But this morning there'd been a reason to squeeze through yellow lights that were about to turn red. He absolutely hated being late for anything, most of all his work at the hospital.

"My alarm suddenly decided to turn mute," he confessed. "I woke up fifteen minutes before I was supposed to be here."

She'd been to his apartment on several occasions and knew he lived more than fifteen minutes away from Blair Memorial.

"You can really fly when you want to, can't you?" His stomach growled again. Rotating her shoulders, Alix smiled. "Join me in the cafeteria if you feel like it. I'm having a late breakfast myself. Julie was up all night, cutting a tooth to the sound of the Irish Rovers singing 'Danny Boy.'" She'd played the CD over and over again in hopes of putting Julie to sleep. As it was she'd spent half the night pacing the floor with the eighteen-month-old. "In the meantime I'll see if I can scrounge up a rooster for you."

"You do that." But instead of following her, Reese began heading down the corridor toward the back of the hospital. "I'll see you downstairs in a few minutes," he promised. "There're some people in the E.R. waiting room I have to talk to first."

She nodded. There was protocol to follow. She knew how that was.

Her own stint on the other side of the operating arena had been a negative experience. Reese had been there with her, to hold her hand when the surgeon told her that everything humanly possible had been done, but that Jeff had still expired. Expired. As if he'd been a coupon that hadn't been redeemed in time, or a driver's license that had been allowed to lapse. Each time she'd had to face a grieving family since—which mercifully was not often—she remembered her own feelings and tempered her words accordingly. Neither she nor Reese believed in distancing themselves from their patients. That's what made them such good friends.

"I'll save a bran muffin for you," she called out to Reese.

He made a face. Bran muffins were just about the only things he didn't care for. Knowing that, Alix laughed as she disappeared.

Reese continued down the hall to the emergency waiting room area. This was the part he liked best. Coming out and giving the waiting family good news instead of iffy phrases. Tomas Morales had been to his office late last week. Choosing his words carefully, Reese had cautioned the man that playing the waiting game with his condition was not advisable. Morales hadn't wanted to go under the knife, and while Reese understood the man's fear, he also understood the consequences of waiting and had wanted to make the man painfully aware of them.

Painful being the key word here, he thought, because Morales had been in agony when he was brought into the hospital. His oldest daughter, Jennifer, and his wife had driven him to the emergency room.

This morning, as Reese had run into the hospital, he'd come through the electronic doors just in time to hear himself being paged.

And the rest, he mused, was history.

Mother and daughter stood up in unison the moment he walked into the waiting area. Mrs. Morales looked painfully drawn. There was more than a little fear in her dark eyes. Her daughter was trying to look more positive, but it was clear that both women were frightened of what he had to tell them.

Reese didn't believe in being dramatic or drawing the spotlight to himself, the way he knew some surgeons did. He put them out of their misery even before he reached them.

"He's going to be just fine, Mrs. Morales, Jennifer."

He nodded at the younger woman. Jennifer quickly translated for her mother. But it wasn't necessary. The older woman understood what the look in her husband's doctor's eyes meant.

She grasped his hand between both of hers. Hers were icy cold. The woman kissed the hand that had held the scalpel that had saved her husband's life before Reese had a chance to stop her.

"Gracias," Ava Morales cried, her eyes filling with tears. Then haltingly she said, "Thank you, thank you."

Embarrassed, but greatly pleased to be able to bring the two women good news, Reese gave Jennifer the layman's description of what had happened and paused after each sentence while she relayed the words to her mother. He ended by telling them that they would be able to see Mr. Morales in his room in about two hours, after he was brought up from the recovery room.

"Maybe you and your mother can go down to the cafeteria and get something to eat in the meantime," he suggested. "It's really not bad food, even for a hospital."

Jennifer nodded, her eyes shining with unspoken gratitude. Quickly she translated his words to her mother.

As he began to walk away, he heard the older woman say something to her daughter. He gathered from the intonation that it was a question.

"Please, Dr. Bendenetti, where's the chapel? My mother wants to say a prayer."

"He's out of danger," Reese assured her. Of course, there was always a small chance that things might take a turn for the worse, but the odds were negligible, and he saw no reason to put the women through that kind of added torture.

"The prayer is for you," Mrs. Morales told him halting. "For thank-you."

Surprised, he looked at her. And then he smiled. The woman understood far more than he thought.

Reese nodded his approval. "Can't ever have too many of those," he agreed. Standing beside Mrs. Morales, he pointed down the corridor. "The chapel's to the left of the front admitting desk. Just follow the arrows to the front. You can't miss it."

Thanking him again, the two women left.

And now, Reese thought as he walked out of the waiting room, it was time to tend to his own needs. His stomach was becoming almost aggressively audible. He was just grateful that it hadn't roared while he was talking to the Morales women.

He took a shortcut through the emergency area itself. As he passed the doors that faced the rear parking lot where all the ambulances pulled in, they flew open. Two paramedics he knew by sight came rushing in, pushing a gurney between them.

Instinct and conditioning had Reese taking the situation in before he was even aware that he had turned his head.

There was a woman on the gurney. The first thing he noticed was her long blond hair. It was fanned out about her like a golden blanket and gave almost a surreal quality to the turmoil surrounding her. She was young, well-dressed and conscious. And it was quite obvious that she was in a great deal of pain. There was blood everywhere.

So much for finding time for his stomach.

Reese fell into place beside the gurney. "Exam room four is free," he pointed toward it, then asked, "What happened?" of the attendant closest to him.

The name stitched across his pocket said his name

was Jaime Gordon. The dark-skinned youth had had two years on the job and was born for this kind of work. He rattled off statistics like a pro, giving Reese cause, effect and vitals.

"Car versus pole. Pole won. Prettiest Jag I've ever seen." There was a wistful note in his voice as he flashed a quick, wide grin. "If it'd been mine, I would have treated it like a lady. With respect and a slow, gentle hand."

It was then that the woman on the gurney looked up at him. Reese caught himself thinking that he had never seen eyes quite that shade of green, a moment before the education he'd worked so hard to attain kicked in again. He began seeing her as a physician would, not a man.

The woman was conscious and appeared to be lucid from the way she looked at him, but there was grave danger of internal bleeding. He needed to get her prepped and into X-ray as quickly as possible.

As he trotted alongside the gurney, he leaned in close to the woman so she could hear him above the noise. "Do you know where you are?"

London Merriweather's thoughts kept wanting to float away from her, to dissolve into the cottony region that hovered just a breath away, waiting to absorb her thoughts, her mind.

Ever word took effort. Every breath was excruciating. But she couldn't stop. *Don't stop. You'll die if you stop.* The words throbbed through her head.

"I know where…I'm going to be…once…Wallace…catches up to me," she answered. Her eyes almost fluttered shut then, but she pushed them opened. "Hell."

It had been a stupid, stupid thing to do. But all she'd wanted was a few minutes to herself. To be free. To be normal.

Was that so wrong?

She hadn't seen that pole. She really hadn't.

Officer, the pole just jumped up at me, honest.

Her mind was all jumbled.

It would be so easy to slip away, to release the white-knuckled grasp she had on the thin thread that tethered her to this world of lights and sounds and the smell of disinfectant.

So easy.

But she was afraid.

For the first time in her life, London Merriweather was truly afraid. Afraid if she let go, even for a second, that would be it. She'd be gone. The person she was would be no more.

She was twenty-three years old and she didn't want to lose the chance of becoming twenty-four.

And she would. If she slipped away, she would. She knew that as surely as she knew her name.

More.

Stupid, stupid thing to do. Wallace was only doing his job, guarding your body. That's what bodyguards did. They guarded bodies.

They hovered.

They ate away at your space, bit by bit until there wasn't any left.

Trying to fight her way back to the surface again, London took a breath in. The pain almost ripped her apart. She thought she cried out, but she wasn't sure.

London raised her hand and caught hold of the green-attired man beside her.

Doctor?

Orderly?

Trick-or-treater?

Her mind was winking in and out. Focusing took almost more effort than she had at her disposal.

But she did it. She opened eyes that she hadn't realized had shut again and looked at the man she was holding on to.

"I don't want...to die."

There was no panic in her voice, Reese noted. It was a bare-fact statement she'd just given him. He was amazed at her composure at a time like this.

She found more words and strung them together, then pushed them out, the effort exhausting her. She forced herself to look at the man whose hand was in hers.

"You won't let...that happen...will...you."

It wasn't a question, it was a mandate. A queen politely wording a request she knew in her heart could not be disobeyed.

Who the hell was she?

Reese had the feeling that this wasn't some empty-headed joyrider the paramedics had brought to him but a woman accustomed to being in control of any situation she found herself in.

This must be a hell of a surprise to her, then, he decided.

"No," he told her firmly. "I won't."

He noticed the skeptical look in Jaime's dark eyes, but Jaime didn't command his attention now. The young woman did.

He'd told her what she'd wanted to hear. What he'd wanted to hear, too. Because, to do was first to believe it could be done. That was his mantra, it was what he told himself whenever he was faced with something he felt he couldn't conquer.

Just before he conquered it.

The woman smiled at him then. Just before those incredible green eyes closed, she smiled at him. "Good," she whispered.

And then lost consciousness.

The next moment the rear doors burst open again. A man came running into the E.R. The unbuttoned, black raincoat he wore flapped about him like a black cape. He was at least six foot six, if not more, relatively heavy-set with wide shoulders that reminded Reese of a line-backer he'd once seen on the field. The man had looked like a moving brick wall.

So did this one. And he moved amazingly fast for someone so large.

"Who's in charge here?" he demanded in the voice of a man who was accustomed to being listened to and obeyed. The next moment, not waiting for an answer, the man's eyes shifted to him. "Is it you?"

"I'm Dr. Bendenetti," Reese began.

The man was beside him in an instant. His face was pale, his eyes a little wild. Reese had no doubt that the man could probably reach into his chest and rip out his heart if he took it into his head to do so.

"This is Ambassador Mason Merriweather's daughter. I want the finest surgeons called in for her. When this is over, I want her better than new, Doctor." A good five inches taller, the man had to stoop in order to get into Reese's face. He did so as he growled, "Do I make myself clear?"

Threats had always had a negative effect on Reese. Now was no different. Disengaging his hand from the unconscious woman, his eyes never left the other man's face. They'd brought the gurney to the swinging doors of room four. He waved the team that had clustered around the rolling stretcher into the room.

When the man started to follow, Reese blocked his way, placing his hand on the bigger man's chest. There was no way he was going to allow the other man into the room.

"You'll have to wait outside while we decide what's best for her." Stepping inside, Reese turned away from the man and toward his patient.

The swinging doors closed on the man's stunned, outraged face.

Chapter 2

The next moment, the doors were pushed open again. The bang as they hit the opposite walls resounded through the room.

"There's no way you're going to keep me out," the man informed Reese, his voice commanding even more obedience than his presence.

His hands already in surgical gloves, his attention focused on the unconscious accident victim before him, Reese's back was to the doors. He didn't even bother looking around toward the other man.

Instead, he directed his words to the dark-haired orderly on his left.

"Miguel, call security," he instructed calmly, cutting away London's suit from the site of the largest pool of blood. "Tell them to hurry."

The man stood with a foot inside the room, wavering, immobilized by indecision. A guttural sound of frustration escaped his lips. And then, struggling with his rage, his demeanor became deadly calm.

"I hope for your sake that your affairs are in order, Doctor. You lose her, you don't leave the hospital. Ever." With that, he pushed the doors apart again and stepped outside.

Rose Warren, the senior surgical nurse shivered at the quietly uttered prophesy and glanced toward Reese. "I think he means it."

"I know he does."

Reese finished cutting and examined the wound exposed beneath the blood-soaked material. There was no doubt in Reese's mind that the hulking man behind him could easily snuff out his life if he so chose, but there was no time to consider the situation. He had a patient to try to save, whether or not his own safety had just been put on the line.

He began processing the information coming at him from all sides and issuing orders in conjunction with the findings.

The man scowling just outside the swinging doors, peering through the glass and glaring at their every move, was temporarily forgotten.

The X rays confirmed what Reese already suspected. Miraculously, there were only two fractured ribs. But there was a great deal of internal bleeding going on. If the situation wasn't corrected immediately, it would turn life threatening in less time than it took to contemplate the circumstances or even to explain them to her not-so-silent guardian.

They had to hurry.

The instant the doors parted, the hulking man came to rigid attention. Surprised that they were on the move again, he fell into place beside the gurney, trotting to keep pace.

"How is she?" he demanded. "Where are you taking her?"

"There's internal bleeding," Reese told him.

He took care to keep his own reaction to the man out of his voice. Stress took many forms, and Reese figured that the man's concern might have been expressed in bullying behavior because of the nature of his work. He'd already seen the hilt of the gun the man wore beneath his overcoat and surmised that he was connected to some kind of bodyguard detail associated with the young woman. Either that or the man was her wise guy/hitman/lover.

"We have to stop it," he continued. "We're taking her to the main operating room."

As they turned a corner, Reese glanced toward the man beside the gurney. He saw deep lines of concern etched into his otherwise smooth face. His expression wasn't that of a man who was concerned about his job, but of a man who was worried about the fate of a person he cared about.

Reese wondered what the real connection between the two was and decided in the same moment that it was none of his business. All that mattered to him was doing whatever it took to save the woman's life. Anything beyond that was out of his realm.

Moving swiftly beside the gurney, Wallace Grant took London's small, limp hand into his. This was all his fault.

His fault.

Damn it, why had she driven away like that? It was almost as if she had been playing some elaborate game of chicken, daring him to catch her.

He was supposed to keep her safe, not jeopardize her life.

The ache in his chest grew. He wasn't looking forward to calling her father and reporting this latest turn of events. The man had hired him to make sure that what had happened to the Chilean ambassador's daughter didn't happen to London.

The anger was gone, temporarily leeched out, when Wallace looked up at the man he was forced to place his faith in.

"Is she going to—?"

"Pull through?" Reese supplied, guessing the end of the man's question. "I made her a promise that she would. I like keeping my promises." They'd come to another set of doors. Reese suddenly felt sorry for the man who had threatened him. For a moment the bodyguard looked like a lost hound dog. Compassion filled Reese. "You're going to have to stay outside."

Wallace didn't want to be separated. The irrational fear that she would die if she was out of his sight crowded into his fevered brain. He licked his lips as he looked past the doctor's shoulder into the pristine room that lay just beyond.

"Can't I just…?"

Reese firmly shook his head. There was no room for debate, no time for an argument. "No."

Wallace dragged his hand through slicked-down brown hair. He knew the longer he stood out here arguing, the less time the doctor had to do what needed doing. Saving the ambassador's daughter. Saving the woman he had sworn to protect with his very life.

"Okay," Wallace said breathing heavily, as if dragging his bulk around had suddenly become very difficult for him. "I'll be right out here if you need me."

"There's a waiting room," Reese said, pointing down the hall toward the cheerfully decorated area that was set aside for the families and friends of patients in surgery.

"Right out here," Wallace repeated, stationing himself in the corridor against the opposite wall. From his position he would be able to look directly into the operating room.

Reese shrugged. "Suit yourself."

Maybe the man *was* a relative, Reese thought. Or connected to the woman on some level that went far deeper than first noted. Or maybe the man was one of those people who took their jobs to heart. If so, Reese couldn't fault him. He fell into the same category himself.

The next moment Reese entered the operating room, and all extraneous thoughts about missed breakfasts, silent alarm clocks and strange personal connections were left out in the corridor.

Along with the man with the solemn face and worried eyes.

Three hours later it was over.

The freshly made openings had all been sutured closed, the bleeding had been stopped, the ribs had been taped. She wasn't, as her bodyguard had demanded, better than new, but she would be well.

The woman's vital signs had never faltered once. They'd remained strong throughout the lengthy procedure, as if her will to live was not to be snuffed out by whatever curve life and the road had thrown at her.

He wished all his patients were that resilient.

Weary, hungry, relieved, Reese stripped off his surgical mask and cap for the second time that day. Now that this newest crisis was over, he became aware again of the deep pinched feeling in his gut. It felt as if his stomach was stuck to his spine. He still hadn't had a chance to take in anything more substantial than a stale candy bar.

This time, he promised himself, he didn't care if the paramedics brought in Santa Claus and his eight tiny reindeer laid out on nine stretchers, he was determined to go get something to eat before he literally passed out from hunger.

At this point freshness would no longer play a part in his selection. He didn't care what he ultimately got to eat. His only criterion was that it remain relatively inert long enough for him to consume it.

Even the bran muffin was beginning to sound pretty tempting.

But first, he knew, he had to go out and face the sentry out in the hall. The man who had remained steadfast throughout the entire procedure, standing there like an ancient gargoyle statue, guarding the door and watching the surgeon's every move. Reese hadn't had to look up to know that the deep-set brown eyes were taking in everything that was being done in the small, brightly lit operating room.

"How—" The single word leaped out at him as soon as Reese pushed open the door.

"She's fine," Reese said quickly, cutting the man off. He didn't want to stand around for any more threats or whatever it was that the man had in mind now that the operation was over. "Like I said, she had some internal bleeding, but we found all the openings and sutured them. She had a couple of fractured ribs as well—"

Wallace stopped him right there. "Fractured?" he demanded. "You didn't mention them before."

Reese chose to ignore the accusatory note in the other man's voice. Instead, he cut him some slack. It was pretty clear that they were both a little overwrought, he thought.

"It could have been a great deal worse. The paramedic who brought her in said her car was totaled." Reese saw guilt wash over the wide face. Had that somehow been his fault? he wondered.

"Yeah, it was." And then, just as suddenly, the guilt left his eyes. His expression turned stony. "How soon can she be moved?"

"Why don't we wait and see how she does first?" Reese calmly suggested. The next twenty-four hours would decide that. "In the meantime, maybe you should go to admitting and give them any information you can about her. Administration has forms to keep your mind busy for a while."

"I don't need to have my mind kept busy," the man snapped.

"But I do." With that, Reese turned on his heel and began to walk away.

"Hey, Doc."

For a moment, Reese debated just continuing to walk away. There was no sense in encouraging any further confrontation. But if there was going to be another scene, he might as well get it over with now.

Suppressing a sigh, Reese half turned and looked at the larger man. "Yes?"

There was what passed as a half smile on the man's face. He suddenly didn't look the least bit threatening, but more like an overgrown puppy whose limbs were too big for his body.

"Thanks."

Surprised, it took Reese half a beat to recover. He nodded. "It's what I do."

Mercifully, Reese's stomach had the good grace to wait until he was well down the hall before it let out with a fearsome rumbling.

Each eyelid felt as if it was weighed down with its own full-size anvil.

Either that, or someone had applied glue to her lashes.

Maybe they should apply the same compound to the rest of her, London thought giddily, because she felt as if she had shattered into a million pieces.

A million broken, hurting pieces.

Breathing was almost as much of a challenge as trying to pry her eyes open. It certainly hurt a great deal more.

And right now there was a herd of drunken African elephants playing tag and bumping into one another in her head.

London heard a deep, wrenching moan echoing all around her, engulfing her. It sounded vaguely familiar.

It took her a beat to realize that the noise had come from her.

The pain was making her groan. And why did it feel as if there was a steel cage wrapped around her upper torso?

London opened her eyes or thought she did. The only thing that seemed to be filtering through was white. Lots of white.

Heaven? It didn't feel hot, so it couldn't be hell.

No, it felt cool, very cool.

Was she dead?

Where was the light everyone had always talked about? The light that was supposed to lead her to a better place. Or was that just a lie, a myth like unconditional parental love?

She thought she heard a male voice.

St. Peter?

Lucifer?

Batman?

Her mind jumped around from topic to topic like a frog attempting to reach safe ground using lily pads that kept sinking beneath his weight.

The male voice spoke again. This time she heard real words. A question. "How are you feeling?"

Was he talking to her?

With one last massive effort, London concentrated on pushing her lids open. This time she succeeded and saw—a man.

Not Batman, Superman, she amended. No cape, no blue tights that showed off rows of muscles, but definitely Superman. Right down to the chiseled chin and blue-black hair falling into brilliant blue eyes.

She swallowed. Her throat felt like rawhide. He'd asked her something. What? London searched the vacant caverns that comprised her mind and finally found the words, then laced them together.

Feelings, he'd asked something about feelings. No, wait, he'd asked her how was she feeling, yes, that was it.

It was a damn stupid question. How did she look? If she looked half as bad as she felt, Superman had his answer without her saying a word.

"How are you feeling?" Reese repeated for the third time.

He bent over close to her so she could hear him. He had been in twice before, only to find her still sleeping. This time, as he'd checked her chart, he saw her eyes flutter slightly. She was trying to come to.

London took a breath before answering. It felt like someone had shot an arrow into her ribs. "Like…I've been…run over…by…a…truck."

Was that breathy, scratchy voice coming out of her? It didn't sound like her, London thought. She tried to read Superman's face and see his reaction to the pitiful noise. Was he recoiling in horror?

No, his eyes were kind. They were smiling.

She liked that. Smiling eyes.

"Not quite a truck," Reese told her. "They tell me a pole did this."

The single word brought with it a scene from somewhere within her brain. She and her parents, sitting at a long, white table, watching blond girls in native costumes with wide skirts, black corsets, red boots and wreaths of flowers in their hair, dancing.

Poland, her parents and she had been in Poland.

Poland, the last place her mother had been before she couldn't be anyplace at all.

"Pole?" she echoed. She didn't remember hitting a Polish national.

Reese saw the confusion in her face and wondered if she was suffering a bout of amnesia. Her airbag had failed to deploy and she'd hit her head against the steering wheel. Amnesia wasn't unheard of.

"The one you tried to transplant by running into," he told her gently, taking her pulse. The rhythm was strong.

She had a good constitution. Lucky for her. "The paramedic almost wept over your Jaguar."

The words were filtering into her brain without encountering matching images. Her jaguar. A pet cat? No, car, her car. The man was talking about her car.

Oh God, now she remembered. It all came rushing back at her as fast as she had raced her car to get away from Wallace.

She'd lost control and totaled her beautiful car.

London groaned, the loss hitting her between the eyes—the only spot on her body that didn't hurt.

She raised her eyes to look at him as he released her wrist. "Is it totaled?"

"Like an accordion."

The paramedic, Jaime, was still shaking his head and talking about the colossal waste of metal to anyone within earshot. He drove a small, secondhand foreign car whose odometer had gone full circle twice, and he looked upon the other vehicle as if it was a gift bestowed by the gods. He periodically drooled over Reese's Corvette.

Reese studied London's pale complexion for a moment. There was a bandage on her forehead where flesh had met wheel, but apart from that, she was a gorgeous woman, possibly the most perfect specimen he had ever seen. She could have been forever disfigured. Why had she risked losing all that in the blink of an eye?

"What were you trying to prove?"

"Nothing," she answered quietly. She would have turned her head away if the effort hadn't hurt so much. So she just looked at him steadily, meeting his probing gaze. "Just looking for space."

He laughed shortly under his breath. The woman had

intelligent eyes, and she certainly didn't look stupid, but then, looks could be deceiving.

"You very nearly got it. Six feet by six by six," Reese told her, pausing to write a notation in her chart. "A final space in the family plot."

Beside her mother, she couldn't help thinking. Maybe it would be peaceful there and she could finally find out who she was.

A flicker of rebellion rose from some faraway quarter that hadn't been banged around relentlessly, and London looked at her intrusive surgeon with as much defiance as she could muster.

"A lecture? Save your…breath, doctor…I've heard… it all. "

She'd certainly heard more than her share. From her father, from Wallace, although she preferred the latter because at least Wallace was her friend. Her father, well, she didn't really know what Ambassador Mason Merriweather was or how he figured into her life, other than to impose restrictions on her for as long as she could remember. Even Wallace and the other two bodyguards, Kelly and Andrews, were part of her life because of him.

"Not a lecture, a fact," Reese told her mildly. He slipped her chart back into its slot at the foot of her bed.

She was tired, very tired and there was this wide, soft, inviting region just waiting for her to slip into it. Its pull was becoming irresistible, but London struggled to ask one more question.

"Did you do it?"

The question caught him off guard. Reese looked at her. She appeared to be drifting off again. In another moment she'd be asleep, and the keeper at the gate would have to continue to wait before he would have the opportunity to talk with her.

"Do what?" Reese asked.

Every word was a struggle. Her mind was shutting down again. "Save…my…life."

What he had done was utilize his training, his education and his instincts, not to mention the up-to-date technology that a hospital like Blair Memorial had to offer. There was no doubt in his mind that twenty years ago she would already have been dead. But even now, with all this at his disposal, there remained at bottom the x-factor. That tiny bit of will that somehow triumphs over death.

He allowed himself a small smile, though he doubted she could even detect it. "You saved your own life. I just put the pieces together."

"Modest." The single word came out on a labored breath. "Unusual…for…a…man."

He began to say something in rebuttal, but it seemed that at least for now, his side wasn't to be heard. His patient had fallen asleep again.

Just as well, Reese thought, standing at the foot of the bed and regarding her for one long moment. He didn't feel like getting embroiled in a debate right now.

Not even if the opposing team looked like an angel. An angel, he mused, slipping out of the room, who had gotten banged up falling to Earth.

Very quietly he closed the door behind him.

Chapter 3

The moment Reese stepped out of the ICU, he found himself accosted by the big man who had stood vigil in the hallway all this time. He'd been told that Wallace Grant had been hovering around the nurses' station ever since London had been brought out of recovery. To his credit, he had tried not to get in anyone's way.

The question in the man's eyes telegraphed itself instantly to Reese.

"She's asleep," Reese told him.

Wallace frowned as he sighed, frustration getting the better of him. He'd already put in a call to London's father. The ambassador was scheduled for a meeting with a highly placed official in the Spanish government, but he'd canceled it and was catching the first flight from Madrid to LAX that his secretary could book for him. Wallace wanted to have some good news to give the man who signed his paychecks when he arrived.

Laying a large paw on Reese's shoulder to hold him in place, Wallace blocked his exit.

"Is that normal?" he wanted to know. "I mean, shouldn't she be waking up around now?"

Reese knew for a fact that the man had been looking in on London for his allotted five minutes every hour on the hour. The day nurse had told him so. But it was obvious that each time he did, he'd found the young woman unconscious.

"She did," Reese told him. Surprise and relief washed over the other man's face, followed by a look of suspicion. Wallace was a man who took nothing at face value. "For about five minutes," Reese elaborated. "She's going to be in and out like that for most of the day and part of tomorrow." Very deliberately he removed Reese's hand from his shoulder. "Maybe you should go home."

Wallace looked at him sharply. "And maybe you should do your job and I'll do mine." Wallace didn't appreciate being told what to do by a man who knew nothing about the situation they were in. "Her father pays me to be her bodyguard. I can't exactly accomplish that from my apartment."

Reese didn't care for the man's tone or his attitude. "Seems to me you didn't 'exactly' accomplish it earlier, either, and you were a lot closer then."

To his surprise he saw the anger on the other man's face give way to a flush of embarrassment. His remark had been uncalled for. Reese chastised himself; he was civilized now, at least moderately so, and was supposed to know better.

He chalked it up to his being tired. It wasn't an excuse, but it was a reason.

"Sorry," Reese said. "I didn't mean that the way it sounded." He wasn't up on his celebrities, but it seemed to him that someone so young wouldn't normally need to have her own bodyguard. Her name didn't ring a bell for him, but that, too, was nothing new. For the most part, except for his small circle of friends or his mother, he tended to live and breathe his vocation. "Why does she need a bodyguard?"

The wide shoulders beneath the rumpled brown jacket straightened just a fraction. That was all there was room for. The man had the straightest posture he'd ever seen outside of a military parade, Reese thought. He'd had Grant pegged as a former military man.

"You can ask her father that when he gets here," Wallace told him, his tone formal. "It's not my place to tell you."

Guarded secrets. Definitely a former military man, Reese decided. He shrugged. Whether she had a bodyguard or not didn't really matter to him, as long as the man stayed out of the way.

"Just an idle question. Don't have time for many of those," Reese confessed, more to himself than to the man in front of him. Before he left, he stopped at the nurses' station and looked at the middle-aged woman sitting behind the bank of monitors, each of which represented a patient on the floor. "Page me if the patient in room seven wakes up." He leaned in closer to her and lowered his voice. "And don't forget to tell our semi-friendly green giant here, too."

Slanting a glance at the man who had resumed his

vigil in the hallway, the strawberry blonde raised a silent brow in Reese's direction.

He grinned. "Call it a mercy summoning," he told her just before he left.

Reese was in the doctor's lounge, stretched out in a chair before a television set showing a program that had been popular in the late eighties. He must have seen that particular episode five times, even though he'd rarely watched the show when it was originally on. *Murphy's Law.*

He wasn't really watching now, either. The program was just so much white noise in the background, as were the voices of the two other doctors in the room who were caught up on opposite sides of a political argument that held no interest for Reese.

For his part, Reese was contemplating the benefits of catching a quick catnap, when his pager went off.

Checking it, he recognized the number. He was being summoned to the ICU. He wondered if the nurse was just responding to his instructions, or if London had taken a turn for the worse.

"No rest for the wicked," he murmured under his breath. Rising, he absently nodded at the two physicians, who abruptly terminated their heated discussion as they turned toward him in unison.

"Hey, Reese, you up for a party tonight?" Chick Montgomery, an anesthesiologist who knew his craft far better than he knew his politics in Reese's opinion, asked him enthusiastically. "Joe Albright's application to New York Hospital finally came through, and he's throwing a big bash at his beach house tonight to celebrate."

His hand already on the door, Reese shook his head.

He didn't feel like being lost in a crowd tonight. He had some serious sleeping to catch up on. "I'm not planning to be upright at all tonight."

The other doctor, an up-and-coming pediatrician, leered comically. "Got a hot date? Bring her along, the more the merrier is Joe's motto, remember?"

Reese didn't even feel remotely tempted. "No hot date," he told them. "I'm booking passage for one to dreamland tonight. Maybe I'll actually manage to start catching up on all the sleep I lost while I was in med school," he cracked.

That was the one thing he missed most of all in this career he'd chosen for himself. Sleep. When he was a kid, weekends were always his favorite days. He'd sleep in until ten or eleven, choosing sleep over watching early Saturday-morning cartoon programs the way all his friends did. Sleep had been far more alluring.

It still was.

Trouble was, he didn't get nearly enough anymore. He couldn't remember the last time he'd gotten a full night's sleep. If anything, life after medical school had gotten even more hectic for him. There was always some emergency to keep him at the hospital or to drag him out of bed early.

You asked for it, he thought, walking down the first-floor corridor toward the front of the building.

The ICU was located just beyond the gift shop. As he passed through the electronic doors that isolated the intensive care unit from the rest of the hospital, Reese absently noted that the hulking guardian wasn't hovering around in the vicinity.

He wondered if the man had finally decided to take

a break and go home for a few hours. Diligence could only be stretched so far.

"Jolly green giant on a break?" he asked Mona, the strawberry blonde who'd paged him.

The woman shook her head and pointed toward room seven.

Apparently, Reese thought, diligence could always be stretched just a wee bit further. The man he'd just asked about was now hovering over London Merriweather's bed. To his surprise the booming voice the bodyguard had earlier used on him had been replaced by a voice that was soft and pleading.

A gentle giant, Reese mused. Who would have thought it?

"Promise me you won't do that again, London," he was saying. "I'm only here to look out for you. I'm the good guy."

London only sighed in response, but to Reese it sounded like a repentant sigh. But then, maybe he was reading things into it. He didn't really know the woman. She might just be placating the big guy.

Sensing his presence, Wallace glanced toward the door. The look he gave Reese clearly labeled him as the intruder, rather than the other way around.

Since only five minutes at an ICU patient's bedside was allowed, Wallace had taken to peering periodically into London's room when the nurse's back was turned. Each time he did, he saw that London was still sleeping. His agitation grew with each unfruitful visitation. As did his concern.

So when he'd looked in this time and found that her eyes were open, his heart had leaped up like a newly released dove at a wedding celebration. He'd lost no time in coming in and peppering the young woman for whose safety he was responsible with questions and admonishments.

"You gave me some scare," he'd freely confessed, saying to her what he would never have admitted to another man. "When I saw your car hit that pole, I thought my heart stopped." A small smile had curved his lips. "I found out I still remembered how to pray."

She'd looked at him ruefully then and he could see that she was sorry. When she had that look on her face, he couldn't bring himself to be angry with her, even though they both knew that she'd pulled a stupid stunt by taking off at top speed like that, trying to lose him. London was alive, and that was the bottom line. That was all that counted. The rest could be worked out somehow. He'd make sure of it.

Wallace had said his piece and didn't want London to be upset, with him or with herself so he'd smiled shyly at her and added, "Bet the Big Man Upstairs was surprised to hear from me after all this time." He'd placed his hand over hers, dwarfing it. Letting her know that he would always be there for her. That there was nothing to be afraid of. "But you're going to be okay. The doc who operated on you told me so."

She'd nodded, as if she knew she was going to be all right. Because Wallace had told her so. "Sorry. I just wanted to get away."

And he'd looked at her, his dark eyes pleading once more. The next time could prove fatal. "Not from me, London. Not ever from me. I'm not just your bodyguard, I'm your friend. I'm the guy who's supposed to keep you safe, remember?"

She'd bitten her lip and nodded. He'd almost gotten

her to promise never to take off like that again when the doctor had walked in on them.

Self-conscious about his lapse in protocol, Wallace quickly lifted his hand from London's.

"She woke up," the bodyguard told him. There was a touch of defensiveness in his voice, and the soft tone Reese had heard just a moment earlier was completely gone, vanishing as if it had never existed.

Reese nodded as he approached the bed. "So I see."

His eyes shifted to the woman in the bed. He looked at her with a discerning eye. London still looked very pale, but there was a brightness in her eyes that had been absent earlier. She was definitely coming around, he thought.

"Let me check your vital signs." Reese's tone was light, conversational as he took the stethoscope from around his neck and placed the ends in his ears.

"Vital signs all present and accounted for, Doctor," London cracked. She would have saluted him, but her arms still felt as if they each weighed more than a ton.

"You don't mind if I check for myself." He picked up her wrist and placed his fingers on her pulse. Mentally he began counting off the seconds and beats.

"Feel free." She watched him for a moment. He looked so cool, so calm. Was that just a facade? What did it take to light a fire under him? "Did you know that in some cultures, if you save a person's life, that life belongs to you?"

His eyes met hers briefly. "Makes a casual birthday present seem a little ordinary and rather insignificant, doesn't it?"

Taking a pressure cuff that was attached to the wall, Reese wrapped it around her arm, then increased the pressure until the cuff was tight along her arm. This was something the nurses did periodically, but he liked checking for himself. Nothing like hands-on experience whenever possible.

He kept his eye on the readings as the air was slowly let out. Her blood pressure was excellent. And she was no longer speaking in fragments, which meant that she wasn't having trouble taking in deep breaths. She had amazing recuperative powers.

Satisfied, he removed the cuff, then made a notation in her chart. He was aware that the giant standing on the other side of her bed was watching his every move. "How do you feel?"

She almost felt worse than when she'd first come in on the gurney. But then, she reminded herself, she'd probably been in shock.

"Like Humpty-Dumpty."

He laughed under his breath. "Well, lucky for you we're staffed with something other than all the king's horses and all the king's men." He smiled at her. "So we were able to put Humpty-Dumpty together again." Reese replaced the cuff in its holder on the wall. "Your vital signs are all strong. You keep this up and you can move into the suite that Grant, here—" he nodded at the giant "—insisted on reserving for you."

He was referring to one of the rooms located in what the hospital staff referred to as the tower. Large, sunny rooms that could have easily been mistaken for hotel suites, made to accommodate VIPs who came to the hospital with their own entourages. CEOs, movies stars and, on occasion, politicians made use of the suites whenever circumstances forced them to stay at the hospital.

At present only one of the four rooms was in use.

While checking London in, Wallace had insisted on reserving the largest suite for her once she was well enough to leave the ICU. The tab had begun the moment he'd made the request formally.

London tried to raise herself up on her elbows and discovered that it was yet another stupid move. Pain shot all through her, going off through the top of her head. She winced and immediately chastised herself. She didn't like displaying her vulnerability.

Reese was at her side, adjusting the IV drip that was attached to her left hand. "You feel pain, you can twist this and it'll increase the medication dosage."

She frowned. "I don't do drugs."

"You do for the moment," Reese informed her mildly, stepping back.

London sighed. All she'd wanted was a little control of her life, and now look—she was tethered to a bed, watching some clear substance drip into her body and listening to an Ivy League doctor tell her what to do.

She looked at him. "I don't want a special room. I want to go home."

"Then you shouldn't have tried to break the sound barrier using a Jaguar," Reese informed her mildly, ignoring the glare that was coming from the woman's bodyguard. He replaced her chart, then sank his hands deep into the pockets of his lab coat as he regarded his newest patient. He offered her what he deemed was his encouraging smile. "We'll try not to keep you too long."

She sighed. It was already too long. She knew it was her own fault, but that didn't change the fact that she didn't want to be here. That being in a hospital made her uneasy, restless. She wanted to get up out of bed, walk out the door and just keep walking until she hit the parking lot.

But being tethered to an IV and feeling as if she had the strength of an anesthetized squirrel wasn't conducive to her going anywhere. At least, not for the moment.

She tried to shut out the sadness that threatened to blanket her.

"I called your father." Wallace had been wrestling with the way to tell her since he'd put through the call to the embassy.

They both knew he had to, but he also knew how much she didn't want him to make the call.

London sighed again, more loudly this time. Great. This was just what she needed on top of everything else. To experience her father's disapproval coming down from on high. They hardly had any contact at all, except when her father felt the need to express his disappointment about something she'd done or failed to do.

In the past year she had turned her hand—and successfully at that—to fund-raising for charities. There hadn't been a single word of commendation from her father even though the last affair had raised so much money that it had made all the papers.

She looked at Wallace. She had thought she could trust him. In the past eighteen months, while he'd been heading the security detail for her father that she thought intruded into the life she was still trying to put together, they had become friends.

Obviously, salaries transcended friendships.

"Why?" she asked sharply. "There's no point in worrying him."

Wallace didn't care for the fact that the doctor was privy to this exchange, but he had no say in the matter. Reaching for the newspaper section that was folded and stuffed into his overcoat pocket, he tossed it onto her bed.

"He'd be plenty worried if I hadn't. This was on the bottom of page one in the *L.A. Times.* I figure a story just like it is bound to turn up in the papers or on the news in Madrid." The small brown eyes bored into her. "You know how much your father likes to watch the news."

Almost against her will she looked at the paper. Ambassador's Daughter Nearly Killed In Car Accident.

London frowned. Stupid, stupid. She shouldn't have given in to impulse. But she'd been so tired of having her every move shadowed, of feeling isolated but not alone.

"Yes, I know." Well, there was no undoing what she'd done. She was going to have to pay the piper or face the music or something equally trite. London pressed her lips together. Her eyes shifted toward Reese. "Wallace, I'd like to talk to the doctor alone."

Wallace opened his mouth in protest. The doctor should be the one to leave, not him. But there was clearly nothing he could do. Reluctantly he inclined his head. "I'll be right outside."

Because none of this was his fault, London mustered a smile, resigning herself to the inevitable. And, she supposed, in light of everything, there was a certain comfort in knowing Wallace was around. "Yes, I know."

"Right outside," he repeated, this time for Reese's benefit just before he left the room.

For a moment there was no sound except the gentle noises made by the machines that surrounded the upper portion of her bed, monitoring her progress, assuring the medical staff that all was going as it should.

Reese had places to be, patients to see. He didn't have time to dance attendance on a headstrong young woman who hadn't learned how to curb her desire for speed. "You wanted to say something to me?"

"Yes." She'd never been very good at being humble. Maybe because it made her feel as if she were exposing herself, leaving herself vulnerable.

Finally she said, "Thanks."

She made it sound as if it pained her to utter that, Reese thought. "Like I said earlier, it's my job. And if you really want to thank me, get better." Finished, he began to walk out.

"I don't like hospitals."

The statement came out of nowhere. Stopping just short of the door, Reese turned around to look at her.

For some reason she suddenly looked smaller, almost lost in the bed. He remained where he was. "Not many people are crazy about them," he acknowledged. "But they serve their purpose."

She knew that. Knew that she'd probably be dead if Wallace hadn't summoned the paramedics to get her here in time. But that still didn't change the feelings that were clawing inside of her.

"My mother died in a hospital," she told him quietly.

Reese took a few steps toward her bed. "I'm sorry to hear that."

She barely heard him. Only the sympathy in his voice. She didn't know doctors could be sympathetic. She thought they were supposed to be removed from things like death. "In Brussels. It was a car accident. She wasn't even thirty."

Each halting word brought the incident closer to her. Standing alone on a hospital floor with a large, black-and-white checkerboard pattern, feeling abandoned. Feeling alone. Watching a tall man in a white lab coat talking to her father. Watching her father's proud, rigid shoulders sag. Wanting to reach out to him in her anguish, but being restrained by the woman who had been placed in charge of her.

Something started to make a little sense. "Is that why you—"

She wasn't going to come up with any analogies. She had no death wish. She had a life wish. She wanted to find one. A life she could be content with, if not happy. "No, I was just trying to get away."

He glanced toward the closed door. "From the jolly green giant?"

Wallace was harmless, even though he was an expert marksman and had been the head of security for Donovan Industries before being wooed away by her father when her old bodyguard had retired.

She shook her head and instantly regretted it. "From being London Merriweather, Ambassador Mason Merriweather's wild daughter." That was how her father thought of her, she knew. And how the headlines had once viewed her.

She didn't seem so wild right now, Reese thought. She looked almost frail and vulnerable, although he had a feeling she wouldn't appreciate that observation. "Simpler ways of doing that."

The streak of rebellion that had become her constant companion since the day she lost her mother raised its head at his words. "Such as?"

Seemed obvious to him. "Such as you could do away with the wild part."

Everyone seemed to have an opinion on how she was to live her life. "Will this lecture be itemized on the hospital bill, or does it fall under miscellaneous?"

He had better things to do than spar verbally with a spoiled brat who happened to be very, very lucky as well as extremely gorgeous.

"It falls under common sense." Reese turned and once again began to walk away. "You might think about getting some."

"I don't like people who insult me," she called after him.

He stopped by the door. "And I don't like people who are careless with their lives. Especially when they have everything to live for."

Where did he get off, saying things like that to her? He knew nothing about the pain in her life. Nothing about the emptiness. "How would you know that?"

Reese didn't know why he was bothering. Except that she was his patient and she was in pain. Pain that went deeper than the lacerations and bruising she had sustained in the crash.

"Because most people have everything to live for, Ms. Merriweather. The alternative is rather bleak and, to my knowledge, completely nonreversible."

With that he left the room.

Chapter 4

He'd almost lost her.

For a long moment, his soul troubled, he stared at the mural that dominated one wall of the small studio apartment where he lived. The mural was comprised of all manner of photographs in all sizes, both black-and-white and color. There were newspaper clippings, as well, though those were few.

His eyes lovingly caressed the face he saw before him. The photographs were all of the same woman.

London Merriweather.

London, the daughter of the ambassador to Spain. The daughter of the former ambassador to England. It was there that she was born twenty-three years ago.

Returning to the task that he had begun, he shook his head in mute sympathy as he cut out the latest clipping from the *Times*. It was a relatively small article describing the accident that had almost taken her out of his world. He had larger articles, and better pictures, but he kept everything, every scrap, every word, every photo. They were all precious.

Because they were all of her.

What kind of father names his daughter after a place he's living in? he wondered not for the first time. After something that was associated with his line of work? Where was the love there?

It was simple. There wasn't any.

Her father couldn't love her the way he could. The way he did.

No one could.

He tossed aside the newspaper, smoothing out the clipping he'd just liberated from the rest of the page.

Very carefully he taped the clipping with its accompanying photograph in one of the last free spaces on the wall.

The mural was getting larger. It was taking over the entire wall.

Just like his feelings for London were taking over everything in his life. His feelings were evident in every breath he took, every thought he had. They all revolved around London, around his possessing her.

Loving her.

She was going to be his.

Some way, somehow, she was going to be his. He knew it, sensed it, felt it in his very bones.

He just had to be patient, that was all. Once she realized, once she saw how much he loved her, how he could make her happy, she would be his. And everything would be all right again.

He sat down in his easy chair and felt her image

looking at him from all angles, all sides. He returned her smile, content.

Waiting.

The feeling of oppression hit Reese the moment he stepped off the elevator onto the top floor of the hospital tower.

He was already annoyed. He didn't get that way often, but having his professional authority circumvented was one of the few things that was guaranteed to set him off. His orders had been countermanded by the hospital chief administrator, Seymour Jenkins, because Mason Merriweather had come in and demanded that his daughter be taken out of the ICU and placed in the tower suite that the head of London's bodyguard detail had already reserved for her.

Granted, the woman was getting better and he was about to order the transfer of rooms himself, but he didn't appreciate being second-guessed, or more to the point, ignored, because a VIP was on the scene making demands.

Seymour Jenkins didn't ordinarily interfere in any of his doctors' cases, which was what made this such a complete surprise.

He'd looked infinitely uncomfortable when Reese had burst into his office after having gone to the ICU and found London's bed vacant.

"I would have understood if you'd needed the bed," he'd told Jenkins. "But it was empty. Why the hell did you move my patient without first checking with me?"

A dab of perspiration had formed on Seymour's upper lip. He'd run his hand nervously through the thin strands of his remaining hair. "The ambassador got on the phone himself—"

Reese watched the man's Adam's apple travel up and down his throat like a loose Wiffle ball.

"And what? He threatened to huff and puff and blow the hospital down if you didn't instantly obey him and put her in the tower suite?"

Jenkins rose from his desk and crossed to Reese in an effort to placate him. He was more than a foot shorter than the surgeon. "Please, be reasonable. Look at it from my point of view. Ambassador Merriweather is an influential man, he has connections, and we're a non-profit organization—"

Why did things always have to come down to a matter of money rather than ethics and care?

Thinking better of approaching him, Jenkins decided to keep a desk between them. "I've never seen you like this," the man protested nervously.

Even though not completely seasoned, Reese Bendenetti was still one of the finest surgeons on the staff at Blair Memorial, which was saying a great deal. The ninety-year-old hospital, which had recently undergone a name change from Harris Memorial because of the generous endowment from the late Constance Blair, prided itself on getting the best of the very best. The last thing Jenkins wanted to do, for the sake of the hospital's reputation as well as for practical reasons, was to alienate the young physician. But neither did he want to throw a wrench into possible future contributions from the ambassador and any of his influential friends.

"There's a reason for that. I've never been completely ignored before." Reese leaned over the desk, bringing his face closer to the other man's. "She's my patient, Jenkins."

The man drew himself up, finding a backbone at last, albeit a small one.

"Yes, and this is my hospital—and yours," he pointed out. "Ambassador Merriweather is a former captain of industry." Merriweather's company had made its mark on the stock market before he had resigned from the board to take on the responsibility of a prestigious foreign embassy. "He hobnobs with kings and presidents, not to mention some of the richest people in the world. We can't have him unhappy with us," Jenkins insisted. "Besides, we're not endangering his daughter with the transfer." He'd made a point of checking the Merriweather woman's record—after the fact. "You noted yourself in her chart that her progress is amazing. And we sent up monitors with her, just in case."

Which in itself had probably required a great deal of juggling, Reese surmised. He had said nothing in response to the information meant to placate him. Instead he'd turned on his heel and walked out, heading straight to the tower elevators and straight to London's floor.

Where the wall of noise hit him.

The area appeared to be in the middle of being cordoned off. Men in gray and black suits were everywhere. Reese looked sharply at the nurse who was sitting in the nurses' station.

"What the hell is going on?"

The older woman turned her head and covered her mouth so that only Reese could hear. "Ambassador Merriweather's landed, and from the looks of it, he's brought half his staff with him."

He could see that. That still didn't answer the question. "Why?"

The woman shrugged her wide shoulders. This was causing havoc on her usually smooth-running floor. "Something about keeping his daughter safe."

Reese felt his anger heighten. Maybe he was overre-acting. His quick temper went back to the days when he was growing up and was regarded as someone from the wrong side of the tracks, someone whose opinion—because his mother's bank account was represented by a jar she kept in a box beneath her bed—didn't count. But if his patient's life was in jeopardy from something other than the injuries she'd sustained the other day, someone should have taken the time to inform him.

"What room did you put her in?"

The nurse didn't even have to look. "Room one." She pointed down the hall toward where the activity grew more pronounced. "The largest of the suites."

He was vaguely familiar with it. He remembered thinking that the room was somewhat larger than the first apartment he'd lived in.

Reese nodded his head and made his way down the corridor.

Besides being on the cutting edge of medicine, Blair Memorial prided itself on being uplifting and cheerful in its choice of decor. The tower rooms were designed to go several steps beyond that. Here patient care was conducted in suites that looked as if they were part of an upscale hotel rather than a hospital.

Reese supposed there was no harm in pandering to patients who could afford to waste their money this way, as long as playing along didn't get in the way of more important matters, such as the health of the patient.

As he approached suite one, a tall, unsmiling man stepped forward, his hand automatically reaching out to stop Reese from gaining entry to the room he was guarding.

"I'd put that hand down if I were you," Reese told

him evenly. He'd had just about enough of this cloak-and-dagger VIP nonsense.

Wallace turned from the man he was instructing to see what was going on. Recognizing Reese, he crossed the room to him. "He's okay," he told the bodyguard who was part of his detail. "He's the main doc." His brown eyes shifted to Reese. "This is Kelly. He's on midnight to eight," he stated matter-of-factly.

"Well I'm on round-the-clock when it comes to my patients," Reese replied. He looked at Kelly coolly, waiting. The latter dropped his hand and stepped out of the way.

But as Reese started for the unblocked door, Wallace shook his head and moved to stop him.

"I wouldn't go in there just yet if I were you," he advised.

Was someone in there, brightening up her room, giving her a pedicure? He was in no mood to be dealing with the very rich and their self-indulgence.

"And why not?"

Wallace glanced toward the door, lowering his voice. "The ambassador's in there. He's talking to London, and I think they'd rather keep it private."

Wallace was willing to place bets that London did. If he knew her father, the man was probably giving her a dressing-down for being so reckless. For his part, Wallace would have liked to be there to shield her, but it wasn't his place and he knew it. Still, he couldn't help but feel sorry for her.

It was going to take more than a private chat between the ambassador and his daughter to keep Reese out. He figured he'd wasted enough time as it was.

"I'll keep that in mind," Reese said to the other man as he walked by London's primary bodyguard and into the room.

Mason Merriweather narrowed his piercing blue eyes. He wasn't happy about this. Not happy at all.

He had no idea what to do with her.

Damn it all, being a father shouldn't be this difficult, especially at his age.

He could negotiate contracts and peace treaties that were advantageous to people on both sides of the table, get along in several languages with a host of people and was known for his ability to arrange compromises and defuse the hottest of situations, be they global or, as they were once upon a time, corporate.

But when it came to his own daughter, he hadn't a clue how to behave, what to do, what to say.

It was his considered opinion that he and London had never gone beyond being two strangers whose photographs just happened to turn up in the same family album.

Perhaps part of the problem was that she behaved and looked so much like her late mother. It was like receiving a fresh wound every time he laid eyes on her. Because London made him think of Anne, and Anne wasn't here anymore.

She hadn't been for a very long time.

And now this, a car accident that brought all the old memories back to haunt him. Because Anne had died behind the wheel, taking a turn on a winding road that hadn't allowed her to see the truck coming from the opposite direction—the truck that had snuffed out her vibrant young life and taken the light out of his own.

Anne had never gotten the hang of driving on what

she termed the wrong side of the road. And it was he who had paid the price for that.

But now it was London, not Anne, who was the problem. Just when he thought she was finally settling down. After all, she'd acquiesced to his wishes regarding the bodyguard detail. He'd thought—hoped—that this was a sign that she was finally coming around, finally learning not to make waves in his life.

He should have known better.

The initial words between them when he'd walked into the room had been awkward. They always were. She looked a great deal more frail than he'd thought she would. The IV bottle beside her bed, feeding into her hand had thrown him.

Anne had looked that way. Except her eyes had been closed. And she was gone.

But London wasn't. Thank God.

"How are you feeling?" he managed to ask in a tone he might have used to an underling or even a complete stranger.

"Achy."

London waited to see a sign of some kind of emotion from the man she felt kept himself so tightly under wraps he could have easily passed for an android…or a mummy.

The ambassador had just endured the long plane ride from Madrid to John Wayne Airport with the specter of his daughter's imminent death sitting beside him. Seeing her alive had been a relief, but it was instantly replaced by a feeling of helpless anger.

Throwing decorum to the winds, thinking that he could just as easily have been attending London's funeral right now as standing by her bedside, he demanded hotly, "What the hell were you thinking?"

She wanted comfort, she wanted to hear him say that he was glad she was alive. Not recriminations. But then, after all this time, she should have known better. He hadn't been there when her mother, her whole world, had been taken from her. He hadn't held her, comforted her, cried with her. And she'd been a child then. She was a woman now. Why did she expect him to do things differently?

Her eyes narrowed just the way his did. "I was thinking that I wanted to get away from the bodyguard. That just for once I wanted to be me, driving alone without leading a wagon train through the streets. Is that so much to ask?"

His anger rose at the accusation. He knew she thought it was all his fault. As if he had been the one to kidnap the other ambassador's daughter. Didn't she realize that he was doing this just to keep her safe? That she meant everything to him?

"We've been through this, London," he said sternly. "These men are here for your own protection."

She touched the bandage on her forehead and thought of the one taped to her ribs. She raised her eyes to challenge her father. "Didn't do a very good job, did they?"

It took everything Mason had to keep his temper. He wasn't going to shout at her. He didn't believe in shouting. Shouting was for lowlifes, and he had always striven to raise himself above his own roots.

Spreading his thumb and index finger he smoothed down his pencil-thin mustache. It was still dark, even though his hair had turned silver gray years ago. He liked to joke that he owed the change in color to London. Right now he figured it wasn't that far from the truth.

"They would have, if you didn't travel around think-

ing you were the reincarnation of James Dean, bent on
tearing around the countryside."

"I wasn't tearing, I was driving," she snapped.

It was hard to defend a point when she knew she was
wrong and would have admitted it freely if only he
cared about her.

Why couldn't her father have just come up and
hugged her? Told her that he'd been worried sick about
her when he'd gotten the news? Instead he was carrying on nobly, descending on her with his entourage.

Damn it, just once couldn't he be her father instead
of the ambassador?

Mason sighed. This was getting them nowhere. Nobody could ever tell her what to do, and she'd only gotten worse with age. "Look, I don't want to argue about
this. I've decided to have you transferred to another
hospital—"

Just like that. Without asking, without consulting.
He was treating her like a child. Just the way he'd sent
her away to boarding school right after her mother's
accident. Instead of trying to make things better, he'd
only made them worse. Made her feel more isolated,
more alone.

And more brokenhearted.

Well, she wasn't eight years old anymore. He
couldn't do with her as he willed just because it was
more convenient for him.

"No."

He looked at her sharply. Why couldn't she just accept things for once instead of fighting him at every
turn? "London—"

But she didn't let him get started again. "You've already had me transferred to another room. I'm not play-

ing musical hospitals. The care is good—my doctor is the best, they tell me. I'm staying here."

His voice rose almost against his will. "For once in your life, London, stop fighting me just for the sake of fighting."

Reese picked that moment to walk in.

London's eyes darted toward him, and he saw the momentary flicker of distress there. Maybe he was crazy, but it felt as if she was asking him to come to her aid. He couldn't help wondering if she even knew that plea was in her eyes.

Or maybe it was all in his mind.

"You're upsetting my patient, sir," Reese said, crossing to the bed. "If you can't refrain from doing that, I'm going to have to ask you to leave."

Mason drew himself up to his full height and squared his shoulders. He was somewhat heavier than the man who was challenging him and only half a head shorter. "Do you know who you're talking to, young man?"

Reese never missed a beat as he applied the blood pressure cuff to London's arm. "Yes, someone who's upsetting my patient, and I can't have that."

Mason wasn't accustomed to being addressed this way. He'd been an ambassador for more than thirty years and was always treated with the utmost respect. He'd become used to being listened to and obeyed—except by London.

"I am her father."

"Yes," Reese said mildly, noting the reading he was getting. "I know. That might be a contributing factor to your daughter's reaction, but I don't have time to explore that right now." He replaced the cuff back in its position. "Mr. Merriweather—"

"Ambassador Merriweather," Mason corrected him tersely.

He was never one for titles, but he obliged. "Yes, well, Ambassador, your daughter's not supposed to be agitated this way. It'll impede the progress she's making." He looked at the older man pointedly. "So I suggest that if you have anything else to tell her that will upset her—you keep it to yourself for the time being."

Color crept up the man's aristocratic cheekbones. "I don't appreciate being spoken to in this fashion."

Taking London's hand, Reese placed his fingers over her pulse and mentally counted out the numbers. Her heartrate was higher than it had been. Undoubtedly because of her father's presence.

"No, I don't suppose you do, sir, and I don't particularly enjoy speaking this way myself, but my patient comes first, above and beyond family ties, charitable contributions or political standings." He released London's hand, still looking at the ambassador. "Am I making myself clear?"

He succeeded in unsettling the ambassador. It took the older man a moment to get his bearings. When he did, he slanted a look toward London, then one in Reese's direction.

"I would like to speak to you alone, Doctor—" Mason paused to read Reese's name tag, then raised his eyes to the younger man's face "—Bendenetti."

Reese inclined his head and allowed himself to be led to a corner of the suite. This had better be good, he thought.

"If I find that your care of my daughter is lacking in any manner, *any* manner, you'll have me to answer to, personally, and I guarantee it will not be a pleasant experience."

Reese had no doubt about that at all. But he didn't like being threatened by the ambassador any more than he had liked it when the bodyguard had done it. "I'll have myself to answer to first, Ambassador. My patients receive my full attention and the best care I can offer them, regardless of their standing in the community or," he added pointedly, "any threat that might be issued."

Reese didn't add that in his short career he had already been threatened graphically with vivisection by the brother of one of his patients. It had been in Los Angeles, and the man had been the head of a local gang in the area. He had gone into great detail about what would happen to the surgeon in charge of his sister should she die on the operating table.

Reese deliberately went and opened the door. He held it, looking expectantly at Mason. "Now if you'll excuse me, I have to examine my patient."

Curbing his anger but admiring the spirit that had caused the younger man to stand up to him, Mason inclined his head then looked toward his daughter. "We're not finished yet," he told her, raising his voice. "I'll see you later."

With that he walked out.

London watched the door close. She couldn't remember anyone ever putting her father in his place. "I guess that makes twice you've rescued me. Keep this up and you won't be able to get rid of me."

If she meant that as a threat, even in jest, it didn't have the desired effect, because he could think of things that were a great deal worse than having a beautiful woman in his life, even one who was emotionally wounded, as this one apparently was.

"Do you know that you're the first man who's ever put my father in his place?"

Reese picked up her chart again and read the various notations by the day nurses.

"Wasn't trying to do that, I was only trying to get him out of my face—" Reese looked up from the chart and at her "—and yours for the time being."

"I appreciate that." She smiled at him, and much to his surprise, he realized that his own pulse had stepped up just a tad.

Chapter 5

"You're not getting enough sleep."

Reese smiled at the woman sitting opposite him in the tiny breakfast nook of the house he'd bought for her. He supposed, no matter how old he got, his mother would always fuss over him.

It didn't bother him. In a way he had to admit that there was comfort in knowing that some things remained the same, year in, year out. This was a far cry from the way he'd felt in his teens, when everything his mother said was guaranteed to irritate him, even though he knew he was being unreasonable.

But in the past ten years or so, he and his mother had settled into a pattern mimicking the one that had been in place when he was a boy. The only difference now was that they were individuals rather than a set—independent yet forever bound by mutual affection and caring. He wouldn't have it any other way.

Reese finished off the piece of French toast he was nibbling. Taking breakfast together once a week was a tradition his mother had begun years ago, when both their schedules were hectic beyond belief. He still liked keeping it up.

"Mom, that's the kind of thing I'm supposed to say to people."

Just barely into her fifth decade, Rachel Bendenetti was still an attractive woman by anyone's standards. Her dark hair had a few streaks of gray, but her skin was still smooth and her eyes were as lively as ever. She was a woman who enjoyed life no matter what curves it threw at her.

She turned those lively eyes on her only son now as she slipped another piece of French toast onto his plate.

"Ever hear the one that goes Physician, Heal Thyself? They're not hinting that he should perform surgery on himself, Reese. Just see to his own needs." Her eyes narrowed as she refreshed his empty cup with aromatic coffee, then tended to her own. "Just the way you should."

He took his coffee black, his optimism light. He laughed before taking a sip. "And put you out of business?"

Rachel became serious. She knew he didn't take advice, but she was bound to try. He was working long hours at the hospital and keeping up with his own private practice. That amounted to burning the candle at both ends. Granted, she'd done it herself for far less pay, but that was her and this was Reese. The difference to her was enormous.

"There's no reason for you to work yourself into a frazzle, Reese. You're not the only surgeon around."

He drained his cup and placed it back on the table. "Yes." Rising, Reese pretended not to notice that there was a new piece of French toast on his dish. He was stuffed as it was. Outside of these once-a-week get-togethers, breakfast was a haphazard affair that was comprised of anything coming out of his refrigerator, taken cold. "But I am one of the best."

"*The* best," she corrected firmly and with a great deal of motherly pride, "but that's not going to do anyone any good if you're dead."

Coming around the table, Reese bent over and kissed her cheek. "That's what I love about you, Mom, your flair for drama."

She wasn't sure if he was referring to what she'd just said or to her concern for him, but she honed in on the latter. "No, I'm just looking out for my only son." She pushed aside her own half-empty cup. There was time enough for coffee later, before she went to the shelter. "Take some time off, go on vacation." As long as she was shooting for the moon, she might as well go all the way. "Meet a girl. Make me a grandmother."

So that was where this was headed. Amused, Reese shook his head. "You're too young."

Rachel rose to her feet. "True," she allowed, her eyes sparkling. "But you're not."

He'd never taken a real vacation, nothing beyond a couple of days off here and there. The week he'd been off when he'd had that miserable strain of flu didn't count. Vacations held no allure for him. He liked his work. But to placate his mother he said, "I'll think about taking some time off after I discharge London Merriweather."

About to pick up her plate and take it to the sink, Rachel paused, thinking.

"Where have I heard that name before?" And then, before he could tell her, she suddenly looked at Reese sharply as it came back to her. "The newspaper. I just read about an accident—" Her eyes widened considerably. "You don't mean that the ambassador's daughter is—"

Not his mother, too, he thought, nodding in response. "My patient. They brought her in on my shift."

Without saying another word, Rachel hurried into the next room, which was officially the small, formal dining room. It was also where she kept all the previous days' newspapers until they were picked up for recycling once a week.

Reese heard her searching through the pile. Triumphant, she returned a minute later, a four-day-old A section of the *L.A. Times* in her hand.

"*This* ambassador's daughter?" Rachel pointed to the article at the bottom of the first page.

"That ambassador's daughter," he acknowledged.

Taking the paper from her, Reese glanced at the article. It was the morning edition, and it carried an old photograph of London. She'd worn her hair differently then, he noted, and the photo was grainy. But even the newsprint couldn't detract from the sparkle that seemed to be in her eyes. It was there even when she was angry, the way she'd been when her father had descended on her.

Funny how some things just stuck with you, he thought, handing the paper back to his mother.

Rachel folded it and left the section on the table. "And she's your patient."

A deaf man would have picked up on the wonder in his mother's voice. What was it about these people that caused others to be in awe of them?

"We just established that, Mom." He raised a brow. "Or should I take you in for short-term memory-loss testing?"

With an exasperated squeal, Rachel swatted at him, then looked thoughtfully down at the photograph. "Very pretty girl." She glanced up at Reese. "Article doesn't say anything about a fiancé."

He knew that look. It meant his mother was delving further. It also meant he should get going.

"Far as I know there isn't one. At least, none that I've seen or heard her mention." Because he knew he probably wasn't going to get a chance to stop for lunch, he picked up his glass of orange juice and finished it off. Putting the glass down again, he gave his mother a warning look. "Drop it, Mom."

She couldn't have looked more innocent if she'd been created five minutes ago. "Drop what, dear, the paper?"

The paper was already on the table. And her meaning was out in the air. "The thought."

Her eyes widened further, though it was hard to keep her lips from curving and giving her completely away. "What thought?"

He tapped her forehead with his fingertip. "The one I can see forming in your mind." They'd always been close, he and his mother, and he almost always knew what she was thinking. And right now she was being a very typical mother. "She's my patient."

Rachel grinned. It was an expression that succeeded in transforming her into someone who looked as if she was far too young to have a son as old as Reese. "Exactly."

He took out his car keys. "And there's such a thing as ethics—"

But Rachel was way ahead of him on that score. "She won't always be your patient. That's the beauty of your being a surgeon. You operate, you check, you release." Rachel dusted off her hands. "And then she's not your patient anymore." She looked back at the thumb-nail-size photograph again and smiled. "Really lovely girl. Needs a strong hand, though, according to what I read in the article. Just a little too headstrong." Rachel looked up at her son. "Is that true?"

He thought of London's standoff with her father and the way she tried to maintain her own space within the fishbowl existence that she'd had. You could call that headstrong, he thought. Or you could call it determined to be her own person. Either way, he had no desire to get into that kind of a discussion with his mother right now. Given an inch, he knew she'd be trying to invite the woman over for dinner.

"Don't believe everything you read," was all he said. He began to head for the door. "Gotta go, Mom. Thanks for breakfast."

Placing his dish beside hers on the counter, Rachel turned and accompanied him to the front door. "Maybe what she needs is a good home-cooked meal."

Reese nearly laughed. He'd seen it coming a mile away, he thought. "Maybe."

His mother looked at him brightly. "I cook. At home," she added.

Crossing through the small living room, Reese opened the door. "Hence a home-cooked meal, yes, I know." He made an elaborate show of looking at his watch. "Gotta go, really. It's getting late."

It was not even 7:00 a.m., but she knew he had rounds to make before he went to his office and he was nothing if not conscientious.

Still, she didn't want to give up on this totally. She had a feeling about it. Or maybe she just wanted to have a feeling. "I don't need much notice," she persisted.

"Yes, I know. Ready for anything, that's you."

Opening the door, Reese stopped, realizing that must have sounded flippant. He knew how much this woman had given up so that he could pursue his own dreams. His mother could have remarried, could have been assured of security years before he'd grown up and been able to give it to her. Joe Abernathy had asked her to marry him twelve years ago. Reese knew that she'd loved the man. But Joe had not wanted to be saddled with a child and had wanted her to send him off to a good military school. He could have afforded the best.

She hadn't even taken any time to think it over. She'd refused, and she and Joe had eventually come to a parting of the ways. She'd continued to hold down two jobs so that he would never lack for anything, not even her. Looking back, he didn't think she'd slept much in ten years. His mother was his first experience with a superwoman.

Impulsively, even though he wasn't given to being demonstrative, Reese hugged her to him.

"Thanks, Mom."

Surprised, delighted, it took Rachel a second to collect herself and return the embrace. She felt tears betraying her as they sprang to her eyes. She loved him dearly and, more than anything in the world, she wanted him to be happy.

"Don't be such a stranger," she said as her son released her. "I make other things than breakfast, you know."

Shaking his head, Reese laughed as he walked away. "Yes, I know."

Rachel Bendenetti stood watching her son as he got into his car and drove away. Mentally she crossed her fingers and offered up a few prayers to any saint in the immediate vicinity who had the time to work a miracle or two. She wasn't partial to a particular saint; she appealed to them all. The only thing that interested her at the moment was the end result.

"He's a good boy," she said out loud, although she knew there was no need. There were tallies of these things somewhere. Every good deed was noted and remembered. She figured that her son had a huge volume with his name on it. "It's time he had something more than his medical books to curl up with. See to it," she instructed as she walked back into the house.

She had every hope that she wasn't going to be ignored. After all, it wasn't as if she was always asking for things.

It seemed to Reese that each time he walked into her room, London Merriweather looked a little better, a little more attractive.

The spark in her eyes was the first thing to return, then the color in her cheeks.

Four days into her stay, she'd done something with her hair. At first he'd thought that maybe her father had sent in a hairdresser for her. Under the circumstances, it wouldn't have surprised him. But Betty at the nurses' station on this floor had said that one of the nurses had helped London into the shower and to blow-dry her hair.

The end result was that when he walked in this morning, it took him a moment to remember just what he was supposed to be doing here. He blamed it on his mother, on some kind of posthypnotic suggestion she had probably planted in his brain.

But he still had trouble drawing his eyes away…still had to remind himself that London was his patient and that was all.

London was sitting up in bed, reading, looking like a vision.

She had on an ivory peignoir with lace trim around a scooped-out neckline that flatteringly emphasized her breasts. Her shoulder-length golden-blond hair formed a cloud around her and seemed to sparkle in the morning sunlight that came in through the windows.

The moment he walked in, she raised her head. The preoccupied look on her face faded, to be replaced with a warm, inviting smile.

She closed her book and let it fall on her lap. "Enter, Daniel."

He remember that he was supposed to be able to walk and crossed to her bed. He looked at the title of the book. The words were in red letters, but didn't register. "Daniel?"

Amusement entered her eyes as she slowly nodded her head. The woman knew exactly the kind of power she had and how to wield it, he thought.

"The man who bearded the lion in his den and lived to tell about it."

He forced himself to mentally take a few giant steps back—and to remember that she was his patient and only that. He picked up her chart, though he didn't open it. "You consider yourself a lion?"

London laughed. Tigress, maybe. But not a lion. "Not me, my father." She studied him for a moment. Definitely good lines. She wondered if he was the least bit impressed with her. Or was he one of those equality advocates who was put off by wealthy, powerful people?

She didn't blame him. She felt a little that way herself, even though she'd grown up with them all around her. "He respects you, you know."

Reese remembered the way her father had glared at him, and the warning he'd issued. He figured that London was fabricating things. "How can you tell?"

She indicated the bed and the room. "Because I'm still here."

He took no credit for that. Because he found himself in danger of staring into her liquid green eyes and getting lost there, he looked down at her chart and flipped it open to the last page.

Reese allowed himself a mild smile. "I thought that had more to do with your refusal to leave."

"The ambassador doesn't listen to me and no one tells him what to do unless he is inclined to do it, anyway." She debated keeping the next thing to herself, and then decided to tell him to see his reaction. You could tell a lot of things about a person by his reaction to having his privacy invaded. "He's had you checked out, you know."

Reese didn't care for that, but there was nothing he could do about it. He made an entry in her chart. "I never doubted it."

Because she was curious herself, she'd made Wallace give her that report. The bodyguard hadn't seemed comfortable about releasing the information to her, but she'd overruled him. Wallace was a pussycat. "You graduated at the top of your class."

Reese spared a single glance in her direction. "It was a dirty job, but someone had to do it." With that he placed her chart back in its slot at the foot of her bed. Suite or no suite, some things remained the same.

London cocked her head, looking more closely at the man who she'd dreamed about last night. A very hot, erotic dream that had made her look at him more closely now. It seemed that her subconscious was way ahead of the game. And right on target.

She also noted something else. "You look tired."

The comment surprised him and then he laughed quietly. "My mother said the same thing this morning."

It was still early, that meant he'd had to have come from there. "You live with your mother?" He didn't seem the type.

Was she trying to pigeonhole him, he wondered. "No. Stopped by for breakfast."

"A good son," she approved mockingly, then her tone faded as a question entered her mind, ushered in by a wave of sadness and longing. "What's it like?"

He wasn't following her. Looking at her, he saw that the flippant expression was gone. He couldn't quite fathom the one he saw. "What's what like?"

She supposed he'd probably think she was a loon, but he'd brought it up in the first place. "Having breakfast with your mother?"

Reese remembered she'd said that her mother had died in a hospital. "A lot like this—toast mixed with interrogation. Except that we had French toast."

"Your favorite?"

There was a small shrug. "She likes to make it, I like to eat it."

Noncommittal, she thought. Like most of the people who drifted through her life. She made sure of that. With people who were noncommittal, there was never the danger of wanting to commit to them. You knew where you were at all times. There was no fear of being abandoned, of being left behind. That you would part was a given to begin with.

London laughed, but he could hear a sad echo within the sound.

He came closer to her. "How old were you when your mother died?"

She raised her eyes to his, surprised at the personal question. He didn't strike her as the type to ask. Part of her was happy he did. "Eight."

Reese nodded, taking the information in. He could visualize her, the girl she'd been. Something tugged on his heart. "Rough. I was ten when my father left."

"Left?" She hadn't thought of him having anything but a perfect background, a perfect family. A mother who made breakfast for her busy, successful son and a father who liked to brag about him to his friends, whose chest puffed up at the mention of his son's name. To find out otherwise was surprising.

He'd divorced himself a long time ago from any pain associated with the incident. Even when his father had been there, he hadn't really *felt* like a father. Just a man who lived with them. Who lost himself in a bottle whenever the whim hit.

"Just like that," he told her. "One morning he decided he didn't want to be a family man anymore. Didn't want the responsibility of taking care of a wife and son, not that he really did much of that, anyway," he said more to himself than to her.

His words replayed themselves in his head, surprising him. He generally didn't talk about personal matters, not to the small circle of people he considered his friends, and certainly not to strangers. Maybe it had been the look in London's eyes that had prompted him to share this darker side of his life. She looked as if she needed comforting, even though her mother's death had happened so far back in her past.

London curbed the impulse to place her hand over his. "I'm sorry."

He shrugged. "Nothing to be sorry about. I think in the long run we got along better without him, although my mother had to take on two jobs to make ends meet."

Earning his own way had made him strong. She should have realized that. It had done the same for her father. Except it had worn away any kindness he might have possessed.

"We never had that problem," she told him honestly. "Ours was bigger."

The bewildered expression on his face urged her to explain.

"Your father's leaving brought you and your mother closer together. My mother's 'leaving,'" she said, using a euphemism, "drove my father and me farther apart. He sent me off to boarding school right after the funeral."

Just the way Joe had wanted to do with him, Reese thought. The empathy was immediate, but because it made him feel slightly uncomfortable, he said, "He was probably doing what he thought was best."

"Yes, for him." There was a trace of resentment in her eyes when she looked up at him. "You see, even then I looked like my mother."

"She must have been a beautiful woman." The words came out before he could stop them.

London looked at him in surprise and then smiled. "Why, Doctor, is that a compliment?"

Her smile was seductive, there was no other word for

it. Any more than there was a way to immunize himself against its effects.

Still Reese tried to make his voice sound cool, distant. "I don't give compliments as a rule. I make observations."

She laughed lightly. She'd embarrassed him; she could see that. "What a lovely observation, then." Making up her mind, she scooted to the edge of the bed, then dangled her legs over the side. She winced a little as she did so.

No pain, no gain.

Reese was at her side immediately, taking her hand. "What are you trying to do?"

She wiggled down a little more, trying to get her feet to touch the floor. Getting out of bed now was a far cry from the bouncing exit she was accustomed to.

"I'm supposed to get out of bed and walk a little before breakfast." She looked at him deliberately. "Doctor's orders."

Yes, he knew. They were standard orders. He hesitated a moment. "You could wait until after breakfast."

But London was already wrapping her fingers around his hand tightly as she continued to slowly draw herself out of bed. Her legs felt incredibly wobbly. Just as wobbly as they had the night before when she had attempted a constitutional with the night nurse.

But the sooner she was moving, she thought, the sooner she would return to her life. It was important to her to take back control—what control she'd had—of her life.

She almost fell as she tried to steady herself.

He caught her, wrapping his arms around her just as she was about to sink to the floor.

London looked up at him. "Why wait?"

He felt his heart throbbing in its newfound position: his throat. Maybe this wasn't such a good idea. But then, if he backed away, she would ask why. And see the reason no matter what excuse he tendered.

This morning there was no surgery to claim his attention—barring anything that might be going on in the emergency room. And he had never been a coward. "Once around the corridor?"

She brightened. "That's my goal."

"Admirable." He took her hand and slowly led her out the door.

He caught the reflection of her smile in the windowpane as they passed and felt as if he'd been pierced by an arrow.

Reese shut away the thought, refusing to explore it. He was going to have to make certain that he gave his mother a different topic to occupy her mind the next time he stopped over for breakfast.

Chapter 6

With no undue conceit Reese prided himself on being reasonably intelligent. Added to that he was a physician, a surgeon. He figured that meant he was capable of recognizing electricity when he came up against it. Whether it turned up at the end of a live wire or in the unexpected contact between two people, he knew electricity when he felt it.

He felt it now.

As London took another faltering step forward, she suddenly dipped beside him. He'd only had a light hold of her hand. Instantly his arm went around her waist, drawing her to him and steadying her before she had a chance to sink down completely.

It was the second time in as many minutes that their bodies had touched.

The current that traveled along his at the sudden contact was enough to light up one hotel in Las Vegas for an entire month. Possibly longer.

This jolt was stronger than the one before.

Startled, wondering if he was hallucinating, Reese looked at London in surprise as he gently raised her up. The look in her eyes told him he wasn't the only one who had found himself standing in the middle of an open field during an electrical storm with a lightning rod in his hand. She was as surprised, as affected, as he was.

Careful, Bendenetti, you don't want to do anything dumb, he warned himself sternly. Allowing whatever the hell it was that was now racing through his veins to take even infinitesimal control of him would be dumber than dumb. It would also be asking for trouble with a capital *T.*

Reese took a better hold of London's hand, offering her steadfast support as she struggled to stand up. Maybe his mother was right at that, he thought. Maybe he really needed to get out once in a while. He knew biology, knew that man did not live on work alone.

The problem was he had no time for anything else. Not if he was going to continue to build up an excellent reputation. It was Reese's avowed goal to become one of the top surgeons in the state, not because of any egotism or need for adulation on his part, but because he'd always believed that if you undertook something, you should do it to the very best of your ability.

And along with an excellent reputation came the monetary compensation that would enable him to pay his mother back a small portion of what she'd sacrificed for him over the years. He knew no matter what he did, he could never fully repay her, but at least he could make a dent in his debt.

Damn, London thought, but she hated feeling as if a strong wind could whisk her away with no trouble at all, and silently cursed her own weakness. It had been four days since the accident—wasn't she supposed to be on her way to recovery by now?

And what was this other thing that was going on? This tension, this static charge dancing between them? What was that all about?

Taking a step, her fingers tightened around the doctor's, as if she could somehow channel his strength into her legs. He had very strong hands, she thought, yet they weren't large.

Gentle hands. Like the hands of a lover.

London bit her lower lip, exasperated, refocusing. "How long before I stop doing sudden imitations of a rag doll?"

She sounded annoyed with her progress. He had a feeling she had no patience with weakness, her own especially. London's impatience didn't come as a surprise to him. Given her nature, he'd expected it.

They took another step together toward the door.

"Seems to me that you're doing very well now. Better than expected."

She allowed herself to slant a glance in his direction before looking back at the floor and her feet. "In general…or better than expected of a pampered ambassador's daughter?"

There was a defensive edge to her question that surprised him. It made him wonder about the kind of life she'd led until now. He forced himself to concentrate on her steps and not on any extraneous thoughts he was having, or the fact that her nearness was affecting him in ways that had no place here.

"In general," he replied, keeping his voice mild. "Maybe I'm wrong, but I get the distinct impression that the pampering you're being subjected to is being done against your will."

He was rewarded with a smile that flashed at him like diamonds. It lit up her eyes and made her even more beautiful.

"Handsome, skillful *and* astute," she noted approvingly. "Why hasn't some woman snapped you up, Reese?"

He'd forgotten she had access to the information her father had an investigator gather about him. That gave her an advantage he didn't care for. All he knew about London was what was in her chart. He wasn't obsessively private, but he didn't particularly care to have his life an open book, either.

"Maybe we'd get along better if you called me Dr. Bendenetti," Reese suggested pointedly.

Well, that put her in her place, London thought. "Ah, barriers, I can relate to that. All right, *Dr. Bendenetti,*" she said. "Why haven't you become some lucky lady's trophy?"

They were almost at the door leading to the corridor. "Too busy."

Though it irked her, she paused for a moment to gather her strength. "Too busy to enjoy yourself, or too busy to be tied down?"

His eyes met hers. She was sharp. And into nuances. "Both. And you'd do better to concentrate on your situation, not mine."

His hand against the door, Reese pushed it open. He found himself looking up at the bodyguard who was standing directly in front of the doorway.

"I'll take over from here, Doc." The big man's tone was friendly enough, but there was no room for argument. The bodyguard wasn't making a suggestion, he was stating a fact.

Not that Reese had any intention of opposing him. He had other patients to see, and besides, he had a feeling that it was safer all around if he just surrendered London into the man's waiting arms.

But if the two men were in agreement, London was not. She made no effort to take the arm he offered, but kept hers firmly through Reese's.

"That's all right, Wallace. *Dr.* Bendenetti wants to make sure I'm not doing anything that might impede my progress." She smiled as she added, "But you can watch if it'll make you feel better about doing your job." She turned her face toward Reese. "Ready, *Dr.* Bendenetti?"

Reese noted that she deliberately emphasized his name and title every time she said it.

The right thing to do, he knew, was to hand her off to the hulking bodyguard. Reese had no idea why he acquiesced to her wishes.

Maybe it was because deep down they were his wishes, too. Which made even a stronger argument for his not spending any more time than he had to with this headstrong woman.

But, he reasoned, there was absolutely no opportunity for anything remotely improper to occur. They were under the hawklike gaze of the bodyguard, who gave no indication of turning his attention to anything else, and there was a smattering of hospital personnel milling around. He was safe.

From her and himself.

So Reese inclined his head and gave in. "All right, just once up and down the hall," he agreed.

It was London's natural tendency to balk at restrictions, and she particularly disliked being treated like an invalid. "Oh, but I can do more."

He had no doubt that she could. Much more. Some of it even involved walking. But he didn't think he could afford to allow her to spread her wings beside him. Not while she was his patient. The lady was far too tempting. Reese had always had a very healthy sense of self-preservation. Doctors who became involved with their patients never went far, and deservedly so. He didn't intend to have his name mentioned among the number.

"No point in tiring you out." His tone put an end to the debate. "Ready?"

She nodded, her face turning toward the corridor. Determined. She let him win this round. "Ready."

They took baby steps that he could see irritated her even though she was the one who set the pace.

Her frown deepened with each step she took until he finally asked, "What's the matter?"

She huffed impatiently. "I'm used to sprinting, not crawling."

At least, mercifully, she didn't have to drag around her IV bottle with her anymore, London thought. But she'd expected, once that was a thing of the past, to be making greater strides. Instead she wasn't striding at all.

Reese was accustomed to exercising patience. She obviously was not, he thought. "You have to crawl before you sprint. And when you get discouraged, just think they could be saying words over you right now, sinking your casket into the ground."

Her eyes on the ground, monitoring her own small steps, London shook her head.

"Not me." She gritted her teeth together. Her ribs ached with every step she took, every movement she made. Wasn't that supposed to be a thing of the past by now?

Reese looked at her. "You're never going to die?"

"No." It was getting harder now. She didn't risk looking at him, only the floor. "Never going to be buried," she clarified. "When I go, I want to be cremated. Have my ashes scattered to the wind from the highest point in the country." She allowed herself an enigmatic smile. "That way I can live forever."

"Interesting thought." He watched her put her feet down. She was slow, but she wasn't walking on glass. Which meant that either she was getting better at tolerating pain or the pain was receding. "Which country?"

"What?" Glancing at him, she'd thrown herself off and had to stop for a second. "Sorry," she muttered.

He waved a hand at her apology. She expected perfection from herself, he thought. He expected to find perfection in books, not in life. At least, not in his life.

"From what I've gathered, you've traveled all around the world. I was just wondering which country you'd picked to scatter your ashes in."

London didn't even have to pause to think. There was no hesitation.

"This one." She saw him glance at her, mild surprise on his face. "The other places are all right to visit, but this is home." It always had been, in her mind. She was just an American girl, happiest when she was here. "My mother's buried here. In San Clemente," she added, then flushed. "Guess this a rather a morbid topic to be discussing in a hospital."

He made no comment. The hospital was like life. All about living. And dying.

She was breathing harder and they had yet to reach the end of the corridor. "Want to stop?" he suggested, concerned.

"No." She turned her face toward him proudly before resuming the snail's pace toward the end of the corridor. "I'm a very stubborn woman."

He stuck his tongue in his cheek. "Really? I hadn't noticed."

Wise guy, she thought. Exhausted, she looked to see how much farther she had to go. Too far.

"Another thing you might not have noticed, they've stretched out the hallway since yesterday."

He nodded, playing along. "It's what happens when they steam clean the rugs. The carpet doesn't keep its shape." He looked at her, sympathy getting the best of him. Pushing herself was only good for so long, then it became damaging. "We can stop. I can get a wheelchair for you." There was one down at the end of the hall. He indicated it.

"No." She squared her shoulders, though the movement cost her, telegraphing sharp pain through parts of her body. "You can use the wheelchair if you like. I did this yesterday, I'm doing it today. I'm not about to slide backward."

He couldn't help but admire her.

It gave him something else to think about rather than the electricity that insisted on humming between them like a haunting refrain.

"Made it," she sighed as they reached the end of the corridor.

"Now we go back," he told her, his voice deliberately light.

She responded with something under her breath he didn't quite catch. He thought it better that way.

In the interest of getting through this, Reese kept her arm tucked through his, his hand wrapped around her fingers and his pace achingly slow. Eventually they made it back to Wallace, who had been intently watching their every step, like a chaperon out of an eighteenth-century novella.

"She looks tired." The comment was made to Reese. Wallace's tone was accusatory.

She'd never liked being fussed over. Now more than ever she felt as if it cut into her space.

"There's a reason for that." London sighed and looked longingly toward the bed that was all the way over against the opposite wall in her suite. "I think I've had enough for now." She didn't want Reese to think of her as a weakling. "Maybe I'll do more later."

"No maybe about it," Reese informed London, escorting her back into the room. He could almost feel Wallace's displeasure as the latter fidgeted a step behind them, then halted at the doorway, sensing that he wasn't needed or wanted. "The more you walk, the faster you can get out of here."

She smiled, her relief growing with each step she took toward her bed. She spared a glance toward the doctor. "Anxious to get rid of me?"

The tension shimmering between them didn't abate. "You said you hated hospitals," he reminded her.

A few more steps. Just a few more steps, she cheered herself on. She could do this—even though the idea of turning to the doctor and asking him to carry her the rest of the way was not without appeal. With her luck he'd probably tell Wallace to take over for him. "You pay attention."

He saw her smile blooming and tried not to dwell on it. "It's my job. I believe in the whole picture, not just a section."

Almost there.

Her knees were beginning to feel as if they wanted to buckle again. She willed them not to. "So, I'm more to you than just taped-up ribs and a bruised liver?"

Reese realized that he didn't want her to be, but she was a damn sight more than that. And he had a feeling that she knew it.

"Yes," he answered simply. "If you treat the whole person, the whole person gets well faster." He swept away the cover and gently lowered her onto the bed. She released an unguarded sigh as she made contact with the mattress. Without thinking, he removed her slippers and raised her legs onto the bed, then covered her.

The look of gratitude she gave him went straight to his gut. He chastised himself for his reaction. It changed nothing.

She'd never known that a bed could feel so wonderful. For a moment, London just allowed herself to enjoy the sensation. Then she looked toward Reese. "Admirable philosophy, *Dr.* Bendenetti."

He wondered if she was going to continue to emphasize his title, or if she would tire of the game. In either case he had to get going. Reese crossed to the doorway. "I'll see you later."

London sighed, a touch of restlessness already setting in. "I'm not going anywhere."

But apparently he was.

The moment Reese stepped out of the suite, Wallace took him by the arm, stopping him. Now what? "Something you want, Grant?"

"Not me, the ambassador," the bodyguard clarified. "He'd like to have a few words with you."

This day was not shaping up well. Reese looked around, but the ambassador was nowhere to be seen. "Oh? Where is he?"

Wallace was already leading the way to the tower elevators. He looked over his shoulder expectantly until Reese fell into step. "He's waiting for you in Mr. Jenkins's office."

He didn't have time for this. "I've got patients to see."

But it was evident that he wasn't going to be doing that immediately. Pressing the down button, Wallace turned and looked at him, towering over him. "He wants to see you now."

Reese sighed. "Now it is."

The statement gave every indication of being a royal summons. That might fly in England and in Spain, but it did very little to impress him, Reese thought. The ambassador might have Jenkins in his pocket, but he had no desire to reside in that small place himself.

By the time he arrived on the first floor and was standing before the chief administrator's door, Reese found that he was in a fairly foul mood.

He was beginning to understand why London was the way she was.

But when he walked into Jenkins's office, which he found devoid of the chief administrator, Reese was treated to the sight of a smiling, genial man who had made his mark upon the world with his wit, his charm and his intelligence.

The ambassador rose the moment he saw Reese and extended his hand to him, one professional man approaching another. "Dr. Bendenetti, I'm afraid we might have gotten off on the wrong foot."

That, Reese thought, undoubtedly displayed the ambassador's gift for understatement.

Still, he felt it only polite to demur. "That only counts when you're dancing, or in a three-legged sack race at the county fair."

The ambassador laughed. Reese noted that the man's eyes were smiling.

"I've heard some excellent things about you. I believe in doing my homework," the ambassador added.

Reese inclined his head, taking the statement in stride and waiting for the bomb he felt sure was about to be dropped.

"I won't keep you long," the ambassador promised, "but I thought that perhaps an explanation for my earlier abruptness might be in order."

Reese took the seat that the ambassador indicated, waiting. The man, Reese thought, seemed to make himself far more at home in Jenkins's office than Jenkins ever did.

"You might be wondering about the bodyguard detail," Merriweather began genially.

It was more than a detail, it was a major intrusion. He'd managed to get Jenkins to send away the other members of the ambassador's entourage, but Wallace and the other two men on his team were a fixture.

"It did raise a question in my mind."

Merriweather folded his long, aristocratic hands before him, his tone confidential and intimate. It was a trick he employed successfully in his negotiations.

"Two years ago, the daughter of the ambassador to Chile was kidnapped." His expression was appropriately somber when he said, "They found her body in a shallow grave three months later. Several other daughters of various ambassadors received threatening letters after that—"

"Did your daughter?" Reese interrupted.

Merriweather was honest with him. He'd already sized Reese up as a man who wouldn't react well to being lied to or misled.

"I don't know. She wouldn't tell me if she did. London is very much her own person." He shook his head. There were so many ways in which she reminded him of Anne. "Perhaps too much so. She grew up early." He allowed himself a half smile. "My late wife, Anne, used to say that London was born old." He looked at Reese. "I'd like to see her get to that state in reality. That's why the bodyguards are posted."

Reese could understand the other man's concern. But he could also see how the situation made London feel. She'd told him that she just wanted to have her own space for a little while. In his opinion, being shadowed and protected could get old very quickly.

"But you can't keep that up indefinitely."

Merriweather didn't quite get the response he was hoping for. "I can while I'm part of the diplomatic corps."

Reese was nothing if not practical. "Have there been any more kidnappings or threats recently?"

Merriweather sensed where he was going with this. Where London had gone when she'd made her appeal to terminate the detail.

Until the other thing had begun.

But there was no reason to share that piece of information with the doctor.

"No, but that's not to say that there won't be. I'm telling you this because I think you deserve an explanation and because I don't want you to become a tool for her to use in eluding the bodyguards, Doctor. Mr. Jenkins told me that you were quite annoyed at having the detail on the floor."

He made no apologies for his actions. "They do get in the way."

"I'm willing to pay to compensate for any inconvenience that it might cause you or the hospital." He took out his checkbook to show he was serious and tossed it on the desk beside him. "My daughter is very precious to me."

Reese didn't care for the implication—that his cooperation could be bought. "You might try telling her that."

The ambassador's eyes narrowed. He had the sensation of butting heads with a ram. He was accustomed to being listened to. "I'm quite capable of conducting my own private affairs."

"I'm sure you are," Reese said politely. He rose to his feet. "I have patients to see, Ambassador. So, if there is nothing else—"

Merriweather stood up as well. His look pinned Reese to the wall. "Stay on my side, Dr. Bendenetti, and you won't be sorry."

It was a threat, uttered in a silken voice, placed on a silver tray. But it was a threat nonetheless. "I don't take sides, Ambassador. All I do is try to make my patients well."

With that, he left the office. On his way out, he passed a worried-looking Jenkins, who was out in the hall looking like a displaced person.

"Don't worry, Seymour, your contributions are still all safe," was all Reese said as he kept on walking.

He heard a relieved sigh in his wake.

Chapter 7

Passing the nurses' station, Reese walked toward London's suite.

The chair outside the door was vacant. Absently he wondered where the man who was usually posted outside her door had gone.

According to the head nurse, there were three bodyguards in all, and they worked in shifts. Pleasant enough, they tried to remain as unobtrusive as three six-foot-plus linebackers could be.

But this linebacker was missing. Reese smiled to himself as he entered the suite. Grant was probably going to have the other man's head when he heard the bodyguard was "missing" from his post.

The first thing Reese noticed were the two suitcases packed and ready by the door. The lady didn't travel lightly, even to the hospital. He'd seen Grant carrying in various items that had been deemed indispensable during the past seven days. Somehow he figured there'd be more to pack.

London sat perched on her bed, looking lovelier than should have been legally allowed.

Crossing to her, Reese remembered to pick up the chart. He didn't remember to flip it open. Instead he just stood for a moment, looking at her.

When she turned toward him, Reese finally found his tongue.

"Big day today."

He noticed she was wearing high heels and stockings. And a snug, light-blue skirt.

"Yes, I get 'sprung.'"

"You could have left two days ago," he reminded her. He'd offered then to discharge her early because of the rapid progress she'd made over the course of the past four days. Had she been a patient on one of the lower floors with the usual medical coverage, London would have been sent home within three or four days at the most. Beds were needed and insurance only went so far. Unless there was a major reversal in the patient's recovery, they didn't stay long in the hospital no matter what kind of surgery they had.

But above the drone of the common and the ordinary was the world of the privileged, the world whose populace could afford these inordinately expensive hospital suites without blinking an eye.

The final bill in this case was to be sent to London's father at his insistence. He'd left instructions with the chief hospital administrator that his daughter was to remain in the hospital suite for as long as it was thought necessary and until she was truly ready to go home.

Since there was currently only one other patient on the tower floor, a film star, the hospital administration was not in a hurry to release London if she chose to remain.

She chose to remain.

The fact that she did made Reese wonder, considering what she'd told him previously about her feelings regarding hospitals.

"I wanted to be sure I was well enough to be on my own—" She thought of Wallace and Kelly and Andrews, the two other bodyguards. On her own. Now there was a joke. She was never really alone, not anymore. "In a manner of speaking."

"I thought you said you hated hospitals."

"I do." She looked around the large room. The rug here was more plush than that found in the rest of the hospital, and the walls had been done with Wedgwood-blue-and-white wallpaper. "This was more like being in a resort. Without the cabana boys," she added, a smile curving her lips as she raised her eyes to his.

He took her pulse in self-preservation, then went on to measure her blood pressure. It gave his hands something to do, as well as something to occupy his mind. He didn't like where it was going of its own volition.

Finished, he remembered to make the notations on her chart, then flipped the cover closed. He handed her a pink piece of paper he'd just finished signing.

"A pink slip?" Her smile widened, becoming positively dazzling as she turned the paper around in her hand, studying it. "Are you firing me, *Dr.* Bendenetti?"

She was still emphasizing his title, as if somehow it was a private joke between the two of them. Except that he wasn't exactly sure what they were laughing at.

"From the hospital, yes." He tapped the paper. "Those are your discharge orders."

London placed the slip on top of the purse she'd had Wallace bring her from her apartment. "Kind of like a 'get out of jail' card in Monopoly." She made her way over to Reese until they were standing within a breath of each other. Or closer.

"If you like." He inclined his head. "Now, I want you—" He faltered a moment as he realized just how close he and London were actually standing.

She turned her face up to his, encouragement in her eyes. She liked the way that phrase sounded, all by itself, without any adornments. He wanted her. "Yes?"

If she were standing any closer to him, she would have had to take up residency in his lab pocket. And her breathy question brought home to him what he was wrestling with. He did want her. There was no sense in lying to himself.

Every visit to her room at the hospital, no matter how much he tried to keep a tight rein on his thoughts, made him acutely aware of that desire.

Had they met under different circumstances, London Merriweather might just have been the woman to cause him to find that small island of time that wasn't taken up by patients, responsibilities and duties and then share it with her.

To what end? he demanded silently.

London represented the top of Mt. Everest, and he was just one of the low-lying villages at the base of the peak. They had nothing in common other than existing on the same planet, in the same hemisphere.

He was lucky he couldn't start anything that promised only to end disastrously.

Clearing his throat, he tried to clear his thoughts at the same time. "I want you to come see me in my office in a week."

Her eyes held his. "You want to let a whole week go by?"

They were having two very different conversations here, using the same words. Even in a simple skirt and blouse, she made a tempting seductress, he thought. He was willing to bet that she was a force to be reckoned with at an embassy ball.

He laughed at himself silently. The only kind of ball he was acquainted with was the kind that periodically went by home plate. Their worlds were as different as different could be.

Reese did his best to maintain the boundaries he knew were proper. "That is the customary length of time between discharge and follow-up visit in this kind of case. Of course, if you experience any pain or have any of these symptoms—" he handed her a list of the various things she needed to watch out for and be aware of "—don't hesitate to call me right away."

Taking the paper he gave her, London folded it slowly and then tucked it into her purse. Her eyes remained on him the entire time. A smile curved her mouth. "I'll be sure to do that."

"Otherwise, call my office to arrange for an appointment." As an afterthought, he reached into his shirt pocket beneath the lab coat and took out one of his cards, then handed that to her, as well.

His duty done, he knew he should be leaving. Glancing toward the door, he lingered. "Your father coming by to take you home?"

She shook her head. There had been no long visit, no

clearing of the air between them the way she always se-
cretly hoped there might be. Try as she might not to be
disappointed when it didn't come about, she always
was and called herself a fool because of it.

"Dad's back in Madrid, making the world safe for
flamenco music." And then, hearing her own words,
London flushed. He was an outsider, a stranger, he
shouldn't be subjected to the civilized feud that was
being waged between her and her father. "I'm sorry, did
that sound very bitter?"

There was something soft about her, something vulnerable when she apologized. Even offhandedly, the
way she did now.

"Maybe not bitter," he allowed generously, "but
pretty sarcastic."

He was letting her off easy. Another yes-man? No,
she didn't think so. Unless she was mistaken, Dr. Reese
Bendenetti was his own man and no one else's. It might
be mildly interesting to dawdle with him for a while.

His mouth had been tempting her ever since she
could focus her eyes.

"I don't know what I expected," she admitted honestly. "You'd think at my age it wouldn't matter anymore. Parental bonding," she added, when she realized
that she was rambling.

There was sympathy in his eyes. That threw her. "It
matters at any age. For what it's worth, he told me that
you were very precious to him."

She looked at him in surprise. That didn't sound like
Mason Merriweather. "You didn't strike me as the kind
of man who lied."

"I don't."

Everyone lied, she thought. Everyone said things

they didn't mean to get things they wanted. Men said they loved you just to get you into their beds. But she was immune to all that because she was prepared for lies, expected lies.

But this great big medicine man seemed almost unshakably honest.

It was a great facade, she thought. "Not even little white lies to help patients along?"

He actually considered the question for a moment. "Maybe if you had two minutes to live, I might let you think you had more by not putting a number on it, but as far as I'm concerned, lies do a disservice to the liar and the li-ee."

"Li-ee?" she echoed, laughing.

Her eyes sparkled when she laughed like that. It made her look softer. Not quite the girl next door—he doubted if anything could transform her into that—but definitely softer. "Sometimes there isn't a word to fit the occasion, so I make one up."

"A surgeon and a lexicographer, very impressive." Amusement highlighted her features as she studied his face. "What else can you do, *Dr.* Bendenetti?"

"My rounds."

Reese began to back away—before he couldn't. He had an uneasy feeling that if he didn't put some space between himself and London, there wouldn't be any in a few minutes. Because more than anything else he wanted to kiss this woman who was sorely tempting him and threatening everything he'd always believed in, every rule he'd ever set down for himself.

He paused right before the door. "You'll be all right? There's someone to take you home?"

The amusement didn't abate. It made him wonder if

she was able to read his mind. Probably. Very savvy ladies could do anything they set their minds to.

"Two very different questions, *Dr.* Bendenetti. But to answer your last question first, yes, there's someone to take me home. As for my being all right..." She shrugged philosophically. *"Que sera, sera."*

She'd hit upon one of his mother's favorite songs, and a saying she quoted often enough to become a family logo on their coat of arms, if they had such a thing. "That only worked for Doris Day in *The Man Who Knew Too Much.*"

She was clearly impressed. "Wait, you didn't tell me you were a film buff—"

Hungry for anything American while being shuttled from one country to another when she was a child, and then during her long stay at the boarding school in Switzerland, London had watched any old American movie she could find.

"I'm not," he confessed. "My mother is. She liked to keep the television set on at all times whenever she was home. I kind of absorbed a great deal of the trivia by osmosis." It was time to leave. He couldn't allow himself to be distracted any longer. "No more racing, London," he warned as he began to open the door. And then he added one final instruction. "Be good to yourself."

"Maybe I need someone to show me how."

When he turned around to look at her before leaving, there was that same flippant smile on her face, but her eyes, her eyes didn't have that know-it-all look. They weren't flippant. There was something in them, a sadness that spoke to him for an instant.

And then it was gone.

She hadn't meant to get so serious. It was just that, during off-guard moments, there was something about this doctor who had saved her. Something she couldn't put her finger on. In an odd way, whenever he entered the room, he made her feel safe, as if everything was going to be all right. As if he was going to take care of her.

As if.

She knew it was ridiculous to feel that way. Outside of the follow-up visit, she'd probably never see him again. They clearly existed in two very different worlds. Unless she became involved in some kind of a fundraiser for the hospital, there wasn't a chance in hell that they would stumble across each other again.

Besides, London reminded herself abruptly, she'd made a career of not getting involved with anyone. That included men with soulful eyes, an easy smile and a bedside manner that made it almost worthwhile being in an accident. You never knew when the next abandonment was waiting for you, and she for one wasn't going to be caught by surprise ever again.

Not ever.

There it was again, that electricity. He could feel it crackling all the way from across the room. Trying to console himself that it was only extreme static electricity, nothing more, he nodded toward the door he held ajar. "Should I send in your bodyguard?"

She would rather have him take her home, but she'd laid enough groundwork today. Being overly pushy wasn't her style. She lifted her shoulders and then let them drop carelessly. It was time to get back to business as usual.

"Might as well."

Reese didn't even have to look around when he opened the door. Wallace had reappeared and was taking up all the available space in the doorway. Because of the hour, the man's appearance on the scene surprised him. "I thought Kelly had this shift."

"You've been paying attention, Doc," Wallace approved with a mild smile. "Ms. Merriweather's more comfortable with me, so I volunteered to be the one to take her back home."

Made sense. Maybe. Despite the fact that she'd tried to get away from him, she and this hulk were really friends in a strange sort of way. Wallace seemed to be less on London's level than even he was.

Reese took the opportunity to ask the man to verify something for him. "She said her father was back in Madrid."

Wallace was impatient to get back to his charge, but he nodded. "Left three days ago. Why? Is there something you have to tell him?" He didn't add that he wanted to know if it was about London. If it was, he'd find out soon enough.

This was none of his business, Reese told himself. He wasn't supposed to be getting involved in a patient's private life. This wasn't an underage child in a dangerous home situation, so he had no right to ask anything. He shook his head.

"No."

Wallace's natural tendency toward suspicion raised its head. He regarded the surgeon closely. "Then why the question? You'd do better to remember to keep this on a professional level, Doc."

Wallace's constant vigilance was beginning to really annoy him. "Aren't you overstepping your bounds?"

Wallace didn't see it that way. "The bottom line is

that I protect Ms. Merriweather. From anything," he added significantly.

He couldn't see London putting up with this kind of thing for very long, and he was surprised she hadn't really rebelled before.

"Gotta take the cotton batting off sometime, 'Daddy,'" Reese informed the other man as he walked away.

He was beginning to experience a great deal of sympathy for London. The phrase "poor little rich girl" was starting to take on new meaning.

"So, how's life with the tower set?" Lukas Graywolf asked when Reese ran into him a few minutes later on the fifth floor of the hospital, commonly thought of as the surgical floor. Reese was back making his rounds, looking in on the three patients on whom he had operated earlier in the week. All three, two men and a teenage girl, had come in after London.

Unlike his ancestors, Lukas enjoyed beating around the bush a little. Right now Reese was really not in the mood for it. "If you're asking about the ambassador's daughter, I just discharged her."

Lukas fell into step with him. He had just come from the cardiac floor and had stopped to look in on a friend who'd had surgery forty-eight hours ago. "So you're down here with the rest of us peasants?"

"Just where I belong," Reese pointed out. And then he sobered slightly. "That trip of yours to the reservation still on for next month?"

Lukas, a full-blooded Navaho, was the first of his family to go to college, much less medical school. To placate his mother, he didn't practice on the reservation. To placate his conscience, he returned whenever he could with other doctors in tow, all volunteering their time.

Lukas nodded. "My mother says that by the time we get there, we'll be seeing every living, breathing person on the reservation. Word travels faster there than any other place I've ever been to."

Reese remembered the last time they'd gone. It had been a grueling three days during which he hardly remembered sleeping. But the feeling of satisfaction had been overwhelming. "I guess I'd better stock up on some extra candy bars to keep going."

Lukas slanted him a disparaging look. "There'll be hot food, like always."

As he recalled, Lukas's mother was one fine cook. Thinking of the man's mother turned Reese's thoughts immediately toward the newest development in his friend's life. His engagement to an FBI special agent.

Talk about different worlds, he mused, this one took the prize. And yet it seemed to be working. He'd never seen Lukas happier.

"What's the almost Mrs. Graywolf going to be doing while you're gone?" he wanted to know as he stopped by the nurses' station.

"She's taking some vacation time and coming with us to help." It was her generosity of spirit that made him love her as he did. That and the fact that she moved him the way no other woman ever had. "And to meet my mother. She's already met my uncle," he reminded Reese.

Meeting a mother came under the heading of heavy-duty stuff and could definitely weigh in as an entertainment bonus. For the first time that day Reese grinned. "This promises to be interesting."

"That's one way to put it." Lukas hesitated, then confided his greatest worry, "My mother always wanted me to marry a girl from our tribe."

That wasn't unusual, Reese thought. Several of his friends had parents who wanted their children to marry people of like heritage. That sort of thing had been going on since the beginning of time.

"Mothers are like that." He picked up three charts from the desk and began to head to the first room. Mr. Walker and his gall bladder.

Lukas glanced at him. "Your mother wants you to marry a girl from your tribe, too?"

His mother, bless her, was the exception to every rule, save one. "My mother would be satisfied if I just found someone from my species. She wants grandchildren."

Lukas was already planning on a family. Girls who looked like the woman who had won his heart. "Give her some."

Reese paused in front of Sidney Walker's room. He had no idea why, but he felt a flicker of irritation. "They skip something in your training? I'm missing one important ingredient. A wife. Or at the very least, a significant other." The fact that he would definitely marry the mother of his child if that ever came to pass was something he felt he could keep to himself.

Lukas saw no problem with that. "Shouldn't be hard for a dedicated young surgeon like you to find himself a wife. Word has it that the ambassador's daughter has eyes for you." He'd seen her being transferred from the ICU to the tower suite. "And she certainly is a looker."

Reese shook his head. "I've never seen it fail. Get a guy ready to walk up the aisle and suddenly he starts trying to get his friends to do the same thing."

Lukas's expression sobered and he shook his head. "Not true."

"No?"

"No," the taller man said firmly, then deadpanned, "Since when are you my friend?"

Reese merely laughed and shook his head, his hand on the swinging door. Mr. Walker had waited long enough. The man was itching to be sent home. "Get back to me when you have exact dates."

"The same goes for you."

One foot in the doorway, Reese paused again. "Come again?"

"With that Merriweather woman."

Lukas of all people didn't need to be told this. "She's a patient, Graywolf."

"You just discharged her," his friend reminded him. "One visit and you're home free."

Reese said nothing as he went to look in on his next patient.

But his friend's words accompanied Reese for the remainder of the day, buzzing around his head like annoying summer flies. They followed him home, as well, at the end of the grueling day.

And it bothered him.

Bothered him a great deal that his thoughts kept returning to London at the oddest moments.

He had no business thinking about her except as a patient who had made an amazingly fast recovery. There'd been nothing to learn from her case, no nugget to squirrel away for a time when he had another patient in her condition.

Outside of the fact that her recovery was swift, there was nothing remarkable about her case.

Other than the woman herself.

Chapter 8

She saw them the instant she stepped off the elevator. They were waiting for her.

Flowers.

Roses from an unknown sender. Big, plump ones that the doorman had brought up to her apartment and placed before the door in her absence.

They were always the same. White roses with an unsigned card.

This one read: "Welcome home. Remember to be careful. Someone loves you."

Reading the words created a chill that wrapped itself around her spine, shimmying up and down. London tried to tell herself that the roses could just as easily have come from one of her friends or from one of the myriad people she'd met during her travels both alone and as part of her father's entourage. After all, her hospital room had been filled with flowers. Her work had her interacting with a great number of people.

The flowers and note could have come from any one of them.

They could have, but they didn't. Because anyone else would have signed the note, and this one was unsigned. Just as the other five had been.

Her heart had almost stopped when she'd first seen the roses sitting there before her door, artfully arranged in a lovely blue crystal vase, the florist's logo on the side of the envelope. Blue, because that was her favorite color.

Whoever was sending them had done his homework.

Seeing the vase, Wallace had cursed under his breath. One of the things London liked about him was that he never said anything offensive loudly. He'd started to pick up the flowers—vase, card and all—ready to throw them away.

But she had stopped him, hoping against hope that she was wrong. That the color of the roses was just a coincidence. She held her hand out for the small envelope. "No, I want to see it."

Wallace's expression had registered his doubt over the wisdom of her request. "Ms. London—"

She could tell by his tone that he was trying to change her mind, but he never argued, never tried to browbeat her the way her father did. That, too, was in his favor.

"It might be from a friend," she pointed out.

"Maybe the wrong kind of friend," was all he said politely. He watched her face for a reaction as she opened the card, ready to take his cue.

He saw the brief moment of fear in her eyes and his heart ached.

She slipped the note back into the envelope. "I still

think it might just be someone who's painfully shy. Not everyone who's persistent is a stalker."

But even as she said it, she was beginning to believe in her own explanation less and less. The roses and unsigned notes had begun arriving six weeks ago, strategically placed where she would just happen upon them. At first it was a single rose, then two, three, swiftly blossoming into a bouquet. The vase before her held two dozen.

Ironically, the first rose and note had arrived just as she had almost convinced her father that there was no need for the bodyguard detail that had been following her around like a string of discarded dental floss that had somehow attached itself to the heel of her shoe. But when Wallace called the ambassador and told him about the rose and the card on the doorstep, any hope she had of being rid of her bodyguards was terminated. The ambassador wouldn't hear of it.

Wallace put out his hand. He made her think of a gentle, trained bear.

"Give me the card," he requested. "I'll see if the florist can describe whoever sent the roses." He held the card through his handkerchief. "If he wrote the card, there'll be fingerprints."

She smiled. Good old Wallace. He never gave up, even when it was hopeless. They both knew that there was a pattern being followed. There would be no identification, no prints other than those belonging to the florist or one of his or her assistants.

"That's what you always say, and it always turns out that someone has phoned the order in using someone's else's credit card and that person always turns out to be surprised because they never heard of the florist." She told herself to enjoy the flowers and forget the implications. Wallace wouldn't let anything happen to her, and who knew, maybe whoever was sending them was content with things the way they were. "Face it, my secret admirer's got this thing down pat."

The wide shoulders rose and fell. "Everybody slips up eventually."

"Everybody?" she echoed, a smile curving her mouth. "Even you?"

Wallace returned her smile, suddenly looking like a young boy instead of the seasoned professional he was.

"Almost everyone." He nodded at the flowers. "Want me to toss them out?"

"Oh no, Wallace, why take it out on them? They're beautiful. Whoever this secret admirer is," she refused to label him anything else, even in her mind, "he's got good taste."

Wallace looked at her. "He'd have to, Ms. London. He picked you."

Then, before she could make a response, Wallace unlocked the door for her and turned away to pick up her luggage.

She could have sworn she'd seen him blush.

The man was a positive dear, she thought, crossing her threshold, and she felt guilty about making his job difficult. She just wished that it didn't conflict with her own sense of freedom.

For now she was just going to enjoy being back in her own apartment and not think about anything else.

Except maybe, she thought with a smile as she sank down on her sofa and kicked off her shoes, a very sexy surgeon who did a great deal to get her blood moving.

She sighed with contentment as Wallace placed the vase on top of her baby grand.

* * *

Keeping perpetually busy, Reese had not allowed himself to realize how much he missed seeing London until he walked into examining room number three and saw her sitting on the examining table, waiting for him, her legs dangling over the side.

She looked like an innocent and a temptress all rolled into one.

She looked up when he opened the door. Her eyes met his instantly, taking him prisoner. Reese had to remind himself of the boundaries that still existed, though it wasn't easy.

But then, she wasn't the kind of woman who made things easy on a man.

She just made him glad to be alive.

He'd picked up her chart from the see-through holder on the outside of the door where his nurse had left it. Reese flipped it open now, forcing himself to concentrate on the reason London was here.

Quickly he scanned the few notes that his nurse had made. Everything seemed to be in order.

Closing the folder, he placed it on the counter and looked at London. "So how have you been feeling? Since there haven't been any emergency phone calls, I take it your amazing progress has continued."

She'd been tempted to call him. More than once. But there'd been no reason other than she wanted to hear his deep, masculine voice. She had no symptoms to report, no flare-ups. London indulged in games on occasion, but she didn't believe in outright lies. She supposed that did give them something in common.

"That's me," she affirmed blithely. "Wonder Woman. Or is that Superwoman?"

As far as he was concerned, she was a woman in a class all by herself. "I don't think you need a secret identity. Or me, for that matter." Taking her chin gently in his hand, he turned her head so that he could look at her left temple. Even that minor contact between them sent unsettling ripples undulating through him. "The cut is healing nicely, and the bruise seems to be going away."

She could feel her heart speeding up. The sensation intrigued her. She didn't normally react this way to something so innocent. After all, he was just examining her, not seducing her.

"A little makeup doesn't hurt," she finally managed to say.

Reese gently rubbed his thumb along her temple to see if any telltale powder or cream came off. When he looked, there was nothing on his thumb. But a great deal was going on inside of him.

"No," he replied quietly, his eyes on hers, "no makeup. That's just your body at work, taking care of you." He continued holding her chin for another long moment. Wondering what it would be like to kiss her.

Her nerves felt as if they were tiny beads of water on a hot skillet, bouncing here and there. It took skill to mask her reaction. "Dr. Bendenetti?"

"Yes?"

She smiled then, her temple moving ever so slightly against his fingers. Like a playful kitten rubbing against the hand of someone who was petting it. "Are you through with my face yet?"

He sincerely doubted that he would ever be through with her face. It was the kind of face that haunted a man, the kind that wasn't easily forgotten.

Reese dropped his hand, self-conscious, though he tried not to show it. "You can have it back."

"My ears thank you," she quipped. The smile that rose to her lips was nothing short of wicked. And stimulating. "So, do you want me to disrobe?"

Oh, yes.

The silent response bursting across his brain left him thunderstruck. He'd seen her nude during the operation, when sections of her body had been left uncovered so that he could work. When they'd thrown a fresh sheet over her, there'd been a split second when her undraped body had been exposed. Even with the bandages and the peril of a life-and-death situation, it had registered in the recesses of his mind as damn near perfect.

But that had been a passing, neutral observation. Her suggestion now brought an entirely different response coursing through his veins. Reminding him that he didn't get out very much.

He shook his head, taking a step back from the examination table.

"Won't be necessary. Just lift up your sweater so that I can see how your ribs are healing."

When she raised the left side of her sweater, a potpourri of colors met his eye. Yellow, purple, blue. But none of the colors were as bold as they had been several days after she'd been brought in.

He allowed himself a smile. "Looks like you have a pretty good rainbow going there."

She looked down to the area under scrutiny, acutely aware of his nearness. He was wearing a cologne she was familiar with and liked. It was arousing.

"All the basic colors," she agreed. It still hurt when

she shifted, but not nearly as much as it had before. "And a few not so basic."

Gingerly, Reese touched the area all around the bruises. "Does this hurt?"

The ache she was experiencing intrigued her. It had very little to do with the fact that after two weeks, she was still somewhat sore to the touch and everything to do with the doctor who was touching her. London caught her breath as something hot and demanding zipped through her with an urgency she was unfamiliar with.

"A little," she breathed.

Very gently, Reese dropped the sweater back into place. "That'll pass before you know it. Everything seems to be in order." A smile came into his eyes as he raised his gaze to her face. "Perfect, actually."

Shifting on the table, London adjusted her sweater slightly and looked at him. "So I don't need to come back?"

He was really trying to maintain the lines that were drawn between them—and getting no help from her. "Not unless you start experiencing any of those symptoms on the list I gave you."

She nodded, as if taking everything in slowly. "So, you're discharging me."

"Yes."

"We're no longer doctor-patient." It wasn't so much a question as it was an establishment of the new parameters that existed between them.

He allowed himself a slight smile. "Well, I'm still a doctor, just not yours." He decided to qualify that. "Unless you need me."

She took it one step further. "What if I need you, but not as a doctor?"

Saying nothing, he waited for her to elaborate.

"What if I need someone to talk to? Someone who isn't part of my usual insane existence." She wasn't sure why, but for some reason she didn't completely fathom, she found herself trusting this man, knowing that at least when it came to keeping confidences, she could rely on him. As for the rest, well, she wasn't going to think about that. She wasn't looking for anything permanent anyway. Quite the opposite. "Could I pick up the phone and call you?" she pressed. "Just to talk?"

He was desperately trying to continue thinking like a doctor, but she was making it very hard for him to maintain his boundaries. But then, he *was* discharging her from his care.

He made one last notation on her chart and closed it with finality before looking at her. "If you can reach me."

"I thought doctors could always be reached." She looked significantly at the pager at his waist, then raised her eyes again to his.

There was no doubt about it, the man definitely intrigued her. She'd given him every possible opening, and he hadn't attempted to pursue her, hadn't even remotely attempted to take advantage of the situation, even at the hospital when she had all but poured herself against his side when he'd taken her for a walk down the hallway. Granted she'd been weak, but that didn't change the fact that he hadn't even tried to press her closer to his side. The man was chivalry personified.

Men had always come on to her, ever since she'd reached puberty and suddenly transformed from a mildly pretty little girl into a child-woman in possession of a woman's body. She'd always had more attention than she'd wanted.

Yet this man was restrained by things like ethics and integrity even while he attracted her with such force that she found her teeth being jarred.

Breaking down his reserves seemed like the perfect challenge to her.

"We can," he agreed. "For medical reasons."

Without making a move, she seemed to draw closer to him as she asked, "How about for other reasons?"

He laughed, shaking his head. The woman was definitely one of a kind. "Have you always been a shrinking violet?"

London tossed her hair over her shoulder, her manner just the slightest bit defensive, even though she told herself there was no need to be. She was what she was. "Shrinking violets get stepped on, *Dr.* Bendenetti. I don't intend to be stepped on."

He wondered if anyone actually had, once upon a time, stepped on her, and that was why she came across as she did. "I think, under the circumstances, you can start calling me Reese now."

He watched the smile unfold in her eyes first, slipping down to her lips, curving them appealingly. "Does this mean I made the cut?"

She'd lost him. "Excuse me?"

Very slowly she slipped off the table in one long, languid movement, never taking her eyes off his. "From patient to friend?"

He looked at her for a long moment. He knew only one way of dealing with people, be they patients or just the people he came in contact with, and that was honestly. "I don't toss the term around loosely. Being friends means something to me."

He meant that, she realized. Her smile this time was

not for show. It came from somewhere deep within. "I certainly hope so."

She used her looks to attract, her humor as a defense, he noted, and found himself being intrigued by her as much as he was attracted to her.

That caused him to step out on the limb he'd known all along was waiting for him.

"Would you like to go out to dinner tonight?" He tried to recall his appointments. There were only two patients to see at Blair Memorial. "My rounds at the hospital shouldn't take me too long."

From out of nowhere a little voice exclaimed, *Yes!* as she did her best to remain casual. "Would you like to pick me up at my place, or would you rather that I met you somewhere?"

A thoroughly modern woman, Reese thought. Although he admired that, there was a part of him that still enjoyed the old-fashioned roles that had once been assigned to men and women.

"I'll pick you up." Taking her folder with him, he began to cross to the door. There was another patient waiting for him in the next room. "Eight o'clock all right?"

Her eyes crinkled as anticipation took another pass through her. She marveled at the new sensation. "Eight is perfect."

He hesitated at the door, remembering her hulking shadow. Would Grant be coming along with them, or content to post himself outside the restaurant?

"By the way, should I make the reservation for two or three?"

London laughed, understanding perfectly. "Wallace is about to get the night off."

There was no room for argument in her tone, but Reese still had his doubts. The other man seemed to take his job exceedingly seriously. "Can you dismiss him that easily?"

If either Andrews or Kelly were scheduled to be on duty, London knew she wouldn't have to think twice about her answer. The other two bodyguards took their orders from Wallace, but she had discovered that she could twist them around her finger when she needed to. However, Wallace was the one on evening duty and twisting him was another matter.

He wasn't as easily led around as the other two. But, on the plus side, there hadn't been any flowers on her doorstep or notes in the mail since the ones that arrived the day she'd returned from the hospital. With any luck Wallace was beginning to relax and could be convinced to see things her way at least for a few hours. She wanted to spend the evening with the good doctor without the sensation that someone was looking over her shoulder, observing her every move.

"I can appeal to his sense of fair play." If she really put her heart into it, she felt certain she could get Wallace to listen to her. After all, it was only for one evening and it wasn't as if she and Reese were going to a deserted beach. "You look like you can take care of yourself," she observed. "I can tell him that I'll have you to protect me from being whisked off by third-world terrorists or ninja warriors."

Her flippant choice of culprits aroused his curiosity. Was the truth in there somewhere? "Is that who kidnapped the Chilean ambassador's daughter?"

The question caught her off guard. But only for a moment. "So, you know about that. Who told you? Wallace?"

"Your father."

That shouldn't have surprised her. It was her father's method of getting his way. She'd heard that there'd been a power struggle between the two men as to whether the entourage would remain on the hospital floor.

She nodded. "Terrorist, they think. But there haven't been any incidents or kidnapping threats in eighteen months."

If that was the case, then why was the ambassador spending good money to keep three bodyguards looking after her around the clock? "So why keep the detail in place?"

She shrugged. "He's being overly cautious." More than that, it was a power thing. "And it's a way to keep me in place. So he thinks," she added with a wink. Straightening her shirt, which had hiked up slightly during her descent from the table, she slipped the chain strap of her purse onto her shoulder. "So, I'll see you at eight?"

"Eight." This time, to assure his exit, he opened the door.

"You have the address?"

"It's in your file," he reminded her, indicating the folder in his hand.

"This is smaller." She opened her purse, took out a card and handed it to him.

There were several numbers on the card, covering home, office, cell phone and fax, plus the word "Fundraiser" beneath her embossed name. He looked at her in mild surprise. Up to now, he'd thought of her only as the ambassador's daughter. It never occurred to him that she was anything beyond that. That probably would have irked her, he realized.

"You're a fund-raiser?"

"It's a good excuse for throwing parties." She wiggled past him, making her way out of the room first. "I like to party."

He didn't doubt it for a moment, he thought as he watched his ex-patient walk down the hall to the reception desk. The saunter she added to her step was for his benefit, and he enjoyed it as such.

She knew he was looking and he knew that she knew. He figured that put them on an equal footing.

For the first time in a long time, he found himself looking forward to the evening for reasons that went beyond his just crashing on his bed and getting some well-deserved sleep.

Chapter 9

Reese found himself wrestling with conflicting desires all afternoon.

The temptation to pick up the telephone and cancel their dinner date was great. The temptation to see London again was greater.

Which worried him.

Seeing London again shouldn't have mattered. Not in the way that it did. It should have been one of those things he could take in stride routinely. But going out with beautiful women could not, by any stretch of the imagination, be considered as part of his routine. When he saw women at all, they were not at their best: distraught before surgery, pale and recovering afterward. And he'd never gone out with any of his patients, not even after he'd signed off on their care.

This was different. It *felt* different and if pressed, he couldn't say whether or not he was happy about that.

After leaving the hospital, Reese went home to get dressed. Once he was ready, there was nothing left to do but pick London up at her apartment.

Reese glanced at the pager on his belt and waited for the Fates to intervene. The Fates were sleeping or on vacation. The pager remained silent.

It was either an omen or not. In either case, there was a lovely woman waiting for him on the upscale side of town.

Reese got into his car and drove.

"But I'm giving you the night off, Wallace. Go, have a life."

London had left this clash of wills to the very end, after she'd gotten dressed for the evening. She looked at the man who was giving her such a hard time over her minor request and wondered why she couldn't have been born to someone less ambitious in life. Someone who ran the corner bakery, or worked in insurance. Someone whose life would not have dragged her into the limelight.

Wallace returned her pugnacious look with a patient one. She was dressed simply but elegantly. The lady had style, and it was, he thought, in all likelihood wasted on the man she intended to spend the evening with.

"No disrespect, Ms. London, but I don't answer to you, I answer to the ambassador."

She made a vain attempt to usurp her father's power, knowing she was doomed to fail but bound to try. "There were times at the embassy when I spoke for 'the ambassador.'"

Wallace smiled, seeing right through her. In the eighteen months that he had been head of the detail, he'd gotten to know the way her mind worked pretty well. It was one of his talents. It was what allowed him, at times, to remain ahead of the game.

"We're not talking about choosing a tablecloth or what kind of silverware to use for a reception, we're talking about your life, Ms. London."

She seized the words and tossed them back at him. "Yes, that's exactly it—*my* life. And, Wallace, once in a while, I'd like to live it."

He wouldn't be budged on this. Not with all the dynamite or perturbed looks in the world.

"That's my whole point, Ms. London. I'm here to make sure you *have* a life and that some jerk doesn't steal it away from you." He smiled reassuringly at her. "I won't get in the way. You won't even know I'm there." She should know this by now, he thought. He might be heavyset, but he was very good at disappearing, at blending in.

She threw up her hands. "How can I not know? You'll be watching." The thought left her unsettled. She liked Wallace, but she didn't like the thought of his watching her every move. Bodyguard or not, there was something creepy about that.

"Not you," he reminded her patiently. They'd been through this before. "Everyone else. At a discreet distance," he added though he didn't think, by now, he should have to.

London blew out an exasperated breath, defeat closing in. There was no way around this. Wallace couldn't be cajoled into relenting. The best she could hope for was a compromise. "A discreet distance?"

Wallace raised his hand as if taking a solemn oath. "Yes."

"At all times?" She didn't want to be eating dessert and suddenly look up to see him standing there.

He made no attempt to drop his hand. "Yes."

She cocked her head, watching his eyes. When he tried to hide things, he looked away. "And if he brings me back to my apartment, where will you be?"

His eyes never left hers. He knew what she was doing and was, again, ahead of the game. It was his job. "Outside the building, in my car, same place Kelly is every night."

It was Kelly who was supposed to be on the night shift, but Wallace knew better than to trust the younger man. All London had to do was look at the man and he gave in to her. But for the time being, Kelly suited his purposes, and he wasn't about to terminate him.

London swallowed a sigh. She supposed she couldn't ask for more, not without having Wallace violate some kind of client-employee trust he had going with her father. "Oh, all right, I give up. But if I see any sign of that crewcut of yours—"

He grinned his small-boy grin at her. "You can have me replaced."

She knew the man actually meant what he said. And that he only had her well-being in mind. London put out her hand. "Deal."

His large hand swallowed hers up. His handshake was firm, binding. "Deal."

At exactly eight o'clock London heard the doorbell ring. Habit had her looking at her watch. The man was incredibly punctual, she thought, smoothing down a dress that needed no smoothing.

A seasoned traveler, able to converse and be amusing in no less than three languages beyond her own native tongue, and part of the international scene since before she could remember, London still felt as if several single-engine planes were taking off in her stomach as the sound of the chimes died away.

This was silly. There was no reason to feel unsettled. It had to be some residual post-traumatic stress because of the accident, London told herself.

But there was no denying that her pulse had kicked up a notch as she opened the door.

Reese was wearing a navy-blue sports jacket over a light-blue shirt. He had on gray slacks and looked very much as if he belonged on the cover of *Heartthrob Monthly*. It was the first time she'd seen him without a white lab coat draped over him.

Her eyes smiled as she greeted him. "You clean up nice."

She was wearing a simple black dress. It looked perfect on her.

Funny, he'd never pictured London wearing something as somber as black. But on her, black wasn't somber. She managed to bring life and color to it.

Reese inclined his head. "I could say the same to you."

She batted her lashes at him in an exaggerated fashion. Teasing or not, he still felt a knot forming in his stomach. The kind that would take hours to undo. "Flatterer."

Slipping his hands into his pockets, Reese waited as she picked up her purse. He glanced around the immediate area. There was no one around. Despite her promise, he'd expected to see the bodyguard right behind her.

"Where's your shadow? Don't tell me that you managed to get rid of him." The man didn't strike him as being easily set aside. The lady had to take after her father when it came to a silver tongue.

Draping a silver-fringed shawl about her shoulders,

she looked up at Reese. "I'd like to tell you that, but I don't believe in lying on first dates."

The word stood out before him in huge neon lights. Until she'd said it, he hadn't really labeled this evening as such. But that's what it was. A date. A bona fide date. He'd absently thought the term and the custom had gone out of fashion, that men and women were now somehow just thrown together by happenstance.

He thought back to London's accident and decided that maybe he wasn't that far from being right.

Reese assumed her answer meant that the man was coming with them. He looked around again. "Then, where is he? Is he going to jump out from behind a door? Or from the elevator when it opens?"

She walked out of her apartment, locking the door behind her. Turning, she threaded her arm through Reese's. "Wallace promised to behave himself and keep a 'discreet distance' away from us at all times so he doesn't spoil the evening."

As long as she was in it, Reese doubted that anything could really spoil the evening.

Pressing for the elevator, Reese thought of telling her that, but then didn't. There was no doubt in his mind that she had enough people flattering her, enough people telling her things she knew they thought she would want to hear, and he didn't want to be lumped in with a crowd like that.

Didn't want to be lumped in with anyone else at all when it came to London. Although he kept telling himself it really shouldn't matter.

It did.

The elevator arrived and they stepped inside. They had it entirely to themselves.

"So, where are we going?" London wanted to know.

He'd debated over that, as well. There were places in and around Bedford that boasted excellent cuisine, fancy decor and fancier prices, places created for the discerning diner. But unless he missed his guess, she'd been to many places like that, taken there by men who wanted to impress her.

Given that her past dinner companions were probably all in a class he didn't belong to, there was no point in trying to compete with them. He might as well take her to a place where he was comfortable.

"There's this restaurant, Malone's, where I used to go to celebrate while I was in medical school."

She smiled. "I'd like that." She wanted to get to know the man he'd been, as well as the man he was. "Who did you celebrate with when you celebrated?"

If he didn't know better, he would have said she was probing for information. Just small talk, he told himself. "Friends."

Friends. London decided to leave it at that for the time being. It was a nice, neutral term that could mean anything, include any gender.

Maybe he just meant hoisting a few with the boys. She wasn't averse to going to a place like that. A quiet little bar would certainly be a change of pace. Wallace might have a canary, but she was determined to enjoy herself.

Without realizing it, she wrapped her arm a little tighter through Reese's.

She might not have realized it, but Reese did.

The moment they stepped out of the elevator and walked through the lobby, the red-liveried doorman snapped to attention. Tipping his cap, he hurried ahead of London to get to the door and open it. Barely a couple of inches taller than she, the man beamed at her with approval.

"You're looking exceptionally lovely tonight, Ms. Merriweather."

London took the compliment in stride, neither preening nor looking down at the man. Instead she smiled graciously. "Thank you, John."

"Fan club?" Reese whispered against her ear as they walked through the door the man held open for them.

His breath against the shell of her ear created a downdraft that zipped along her spine. The reaction surprised and delighted her. There was no doubt about it, there was something electric going on between them, and she fully intended to enjoy it.

She turned her face toward him and replied in a soft whisper, "I give generous tips during the holidays and on birthdays."

He'd left his Corvette parked near the entrance. "You know the doorman's birthday?"

"Knowing a little something about the people you come in daily contact with takes away that depersonalizing edge that always exists." A quirky smile curved her lips. "I learned that at my father's knee. Not that he bothered to teach me anything, I just learned by observing."

Reese didn't know if she was covering up something she viewed as making her vulnerable, or if she was espousing a philosophy she believed in. London Merriweather was a puzzle all right. Warm and open one moment, flippant and distant the next.

He couldn't help wondering which London was the real one.

The doorman followed them to where the car was

parked and insisted on opening the passenger door for her. He'd used his considerable bulk to block Reese's access to that side.

Reese smiled to himself as he rounded the hood and got in on his side. The lady had admirers in all shapes and sizes.

"Those must be some tips," he murmured.

London settled in, buckling up. She nodded at the doorman as he stepped away. "Actually, I haven't given him one yet. He was hired on after Christmas and his birthday isn't for another month." She waved to the man as Reese pulled away from the curb. "I think he's just new and a little zealous in doing his job."

Reese thought it was a little more than that. He guided his red vehicle into the main flow of traffic. "You seem to make people come alive around you, London. You bring out a zest in them."

"Do I?" She turned the comment around in her head and found it appealing. Twisting in her seat, she looked at him. "How about you, Reese? Do I make you come alive?"

"Me? I'm always this way," he told her, keeping his eyes on the road.

But he was lying.

It hurt him to watch her with another man.

To see the smile on her lips, the laughter in her eyes, and know that it was there for someone else.

He never felt more alive than when she turned that magic toward him.

Nor more bereft than when he saw it directed toward someone else.

But that would change soon. He promised himself that. Promised her that.

Soon.

When that day came, she'd smile only for him, laugh only for him. Dress only for him.

Undress only for him.

His palms grew sweaty and his breath grew short. He willed his control back. His breathing became steadier again.

He thought about that sometimes. Late at night in his room, staring at his mural, he thought of that. Of having her.

Sometimes it made a pain twist in his belly, wanting her.

It didn't matter to him that there'd been others. That she'd loved other men. He didn't care about her past. He cared only about her future. And that it would be with him.

He followed her with his eyes, thinking of the day that he wouldn't have to follow her at all anymore. The day that they would be standing side by side. Together.

Forever.

Soon.

Reese held the door open for her as she walked into the dimly lit restaurant. Malone's was owned by a transplanted Texan who'd brought a little of his former home into the decor of the restaurant he loved so well.

Reese tried to gauge London's reaction and decided that the woman would make a fair poker player. Still, he could make an educated guess at what was crossing her mind. "Not what you expected, is it?"

"No," she admitted, "it isn't." The floor was wooden, with a high polish to it. There was a bar running along one wall that looked as if it came straight out of a John Wayne Western. The thought made her smile. She'd always loved Westerns. "A lot of men try to impress me because of what they think I'm used to."

He still couldn't tell if she was insulted that he'd brought her here, or amused. "What are you used to?"

"Facades." The rich were very attached to their traditions and to what they felt elevated them above the rest of the world. Her eyes shone as she looked around the small restaurant. There was a charm here, an intimacy that reached out to her and made her feel at home. "I like this." She turned toward him. "I like this a lot."

He felt a sense of relief wash over him. He'd taken a chance bringing her here. "Good."

A hostess came and led them to their table. It was a cozy booth nestled off to the side. "Do you still come here to celebrate?"

Taking a menu from the hostess, he set it in front of him. Reese shook his head in response to London's question. "I don't have as much time to do that as I used to."

She looked at him in amazement. "Not as much time as when you were in medical school? Just how busy do they keep you at that hospital?"

Things were hectic in emergency, but there were lulls, as well. And he was only one of several doctors on rotation. "I keep myself busy. Between the hospital, my own practice and the reservation—"

Reese couldn't mean what she thought he meant. "Reservation, as in restaurant?"

He liked the way the light from the candle caressed her face. Making him want to do the same. He kept his hands in his lap.

"As in Native American. Navaho," he added before she could ask.

London's eyes narrowed as she studied his face. His

hair was dark, but his eyes were blue. That didn't quite fit the image. "You're not—"

He smiled. Graywolf would get a kick out of this. "No, I'm not."

"Didn't think so. You don't have the cheekbones for it." Although his hair was certainly the right shade, she thought. Blue black, straight and thick. It made her fingers itch.

The food server, a tall, slender college student in his third year as a drama major, came to take their order for drinks. She asked for red wine to go with the steak she already knew she would be ordering, then waited until the waiter was gone.

Leaning her chin on her hand, she looked up at Reese, finding him more and more intriguing as the minutes passed. "So what are you doing on a reservation if you don't mind my asking?"

That she thought he'd mind her probing told him that she had a healthy respect for privacy. He liked that. Reese couldn't help wondering how much she minded having hers invaded periodically because of the nature of her father's work.

"It's in Arizona. One of the other doctors on staff grew up there. Once or twice a year he goes back to offer free medical care to the members of his tribe. Sort of a payback, you might say. A few of the other doctors began going with him. It's a pretty healthy-size group now." It was almost his favorite time, he thought. That was what doctoring was all about to him, helping those who were in real need.

The waiter returned with their drinks and placed them on the table. London continued looking at Reese. "Very noble of you."

He shifted, uncomfortable at the focus her words brought. He looked down at the menu. "Pretty much everything here is good."

Compliments embarrassed him, she noted. She liked that. So many men she knew loved bragging about their accomplishments and beating their chests like the Neanderthals they claimed to look down on.

But then, she'd already sensed that Reese Bendenetti was different.

She decided to follow his lead. "How are the portions?"

"Large."

The information pleased her. "Good, I have a big appetite."

Reese finally raised his eyes from the menu. If he remembered his facts, she only weighed one-hundred and ten pounds. "Oh, really?"

His tone catching her attention, she looked up and saw the skeptical, amused look in his eyes. "Yes, really. If you don't believe me, just watch."

He could think of far worse assignments. "I intend to." Whether she ate anything or not.

She laughed softly as she took a sip of her wine. Glancing around, she tried to see where Wallace had stationed himself. But true to his word, he was invisible.

Taking another sip of her wine, London began to relax—as much as she could with all her nerve endings standing at attention in reaction to the man sitting opposite her.

Chapter 10

As the tables began to fill up, the noise in the cozy restaurant increased. London found herself leaning further toward Reese in order to be heard.

"You know, it's funny that you'd pick a place like this."

The glow of the single candle nestled in clear glass found her face and made love to it. He could see her eyes sparkling with humor even in the dim light. Humor that was at no one's expense. There was no need to brace himself against a put-down.

"Why?"

A fond smile curved her lips as her thoughts took her back across the years to a time when things were so much simpler, to a time when she felt safe and protected. And loved.

"Because I love Westerns."

Her answer surprised him, and he looked at her. "You don't seem the type."

What type do I seem to you, Reese? Cold, calculating, spoiled rotten? I'm not any of those things, not really.

But all she said was, "Looks can be deceiving." And then, because being here made her smile from within, she elaborated. "When I was a little girl, I hated the kind of life my parents led, moving from one country to another. Half the time, outside of the embassy, I didn't hear a word of English being spoken. Sometimes in the embassy, as well. I was very, very homesick and desperately hungry for something that would remind me of the sights and sounds of home."

He seemed genuinely interested, she thought, not because she was the ambassador's daughter—he'd already proven that meant nothing to him—but because she was a woman he was sharing the evening with. She liked that. A lot.

"I thought of television as the last bastion of Americana, but of course there were only domestic programs on." She laughed at her own naiveté. "Except for the occasional Western that was thrown in. Half the time it was dubbed, too, but there's no mistaking John Wayne and his pals for bullfighters, no mistaking Monument Valley—" she named the popular site in Utah where so many Westerns were filmed "—for the Alps. And whenever I did chance upon one in English, I was in seventh heaven. Westerns were my touchstone, my home base." Her eyes swept over the restaurant. From her vantage point she could see a great deal. "In a way, I feel as if I've come home."

He could almost feel her pleasure. A sense of satisfaction that he rarely experienced away from the operating table filled him. If she hated her parents' lifestyle, he was guessing she probably made her feelings known.

"So you rebelled right from the start?"

Nothing could have been further from the truth. In the beginning. And even after her mother died.

"Oh no, I was a good little daughter. Went to classes, learned the necessary languages, did everything I could to make my father proud of me." Because she felt as if he could see right into her, London lowered her gaze to look at the candlelight trapped in her wineglass. "Until I realized that was one of those impossible feats the wicked witch hands out to the heroine in a Grimms' fairy tale. Rather like being told to move the ocean into a pond using a teaspoon." She saw the odd look on his face and guessed correctly. "You never read that one?"

He laughed softly and shook his head. "Must have been one of the stories I missed."

She liked the sound of his laugh. Even soft, it was deep and rich, like black coffee on a cold winter morning. Bracing. "I didn't. I read everything I could get my hands on. It cut into the loneliness."

She'd said too much, London realized abruptly. She was going to have to watch that. There was something about this semistoic man that made him easy to talk to, but she'd never believed in talking too much. If you weren't careful, you gave pieces of yourself away.

Westerns and loneliness. They didn't jibe with the woman he was looking at. He took a sip of his wine and shook his head.

"I can't see you as being lonely."

There was a reason for that. She'd gone into reconstruction mode and carefully rebuilt herself a piece at a time, taking as models people she admired. People she wanted to be like.

Opening the menu again, she perused it in earnest

this time. "That's because I realized one day that no one was going to notice me if I didn't notice myself." She raised her chin ever so slightly as she continued talking. "That's when I decided to grab life with both hands and make the most of it before it was gone for me the way it was for my mother."

So the very independent London Merriweather was actually a product of both of her parents, he thought. Each had influenced her in his or her own way. She was living for both her mother and herself as she thwarted the father she felt had turned his back on her.

Reese found himself wanting to know things about her. About what she'd been like as a child. About what made her laugh, what made her cry. Things that went far beyond the usual kind of relationship he allowed himself to have, that of a doctor looking out for the well-being of his patient.

She wasn't his patient anymore.

He wanted to know.

Making his selection, he closed the menu and looked at her. "Tell me more about the dutiful daughter."

She picked up on the word he'd chosen: *dutiful*. "Why, do you like obedient women?" She hadn't pegged him for a martinet, but you never knew. She'd been wrong before, although not often.

The woman who had heretofore made the largest impression on his life—his mother—was as independent as they came. If he were ever to seek a wife, that would be the first quality he'd look for. A woman who could stand on her own. Who was soft but not weak.

He caught himself thinking that his mother might like London, and vice versa. "No, I'm just having a hard time envisioning you as someone who ever played by the rules."

She wasn't that much of a rebel, she thought, although she liked the way he was looking at her when he said it. What she didn't like was being boxed in. "Well, I did, for the most part. I let myself be sent away to boarding school—"

He vaguely remembered she'd mentioned that to him before. "How old were you?"

"Eight." It was the last time she allowed herself to be vulnerable, to need someone. Because she had and she'd been ignored. When she had needed comfort the most, her father had turned away from her, leaving her in the care of strangers. It was a slap in the face that had taught her to be self-reliant and never to need anyone.

"Eight," he repeated. "There wasn't much you could do about it."

That was where he was wrong. Even at eight she'd been her mother's daughter. Headstrong even though she was vulnerable. Headstrong *because* she was vulnerable. "I thought about running away. And then, briefly, I thought that if I did what he wanted, if I went away to that Swiss boarding school, my father would miss me and come after me."

The smile on her lips was meant to be flippant, but there was a touch of ruefulness to it. And hurt. Reese could see it, even in the dim light.

"He didn't, of course." She curved her fingers around the glass. "He was relieved not to have to deal with me."

Reese thought her description was probably a little harsh. "I don't think—"

London cut him off. "You don't have to. I was there. I know." Her voice throbbed with emotion. London forced herself to get it under control. "My mother was the only person who truly meant anything to him. With

her gone, my father threw himself into the only love he
had left, the diplomatic service." Why was she talking
about this? The conversation had gotten so deep so
quickly. She scrambled for neutral ground. "To his
credit, he is very good at it. My father bought his way
into his first ambassadorship with hefty campaign donations—it's one of those open secrets no one speaks
about in Washington—and turned out to have a natural
flare for it. My father gets along with everyone in the
world—but me."

She flashed a smile at him that went straight to
Reese's gut and threatened the tranquil state of the food
he was consuming.

He had to remind himself to breathe. "Did you stay
at the boarding school year-round?"

She was as honest with him as she had been with herself of late. "He would have liked that, but the school
closed for the summer and during the holidays, so I was
brought home, and when I was old enough and present-
able enough, he had me playing hostess whenever he
threw an embassy ball—they were never parties, always balls, always stately."

She'd tried hard during that time, trying to cull her
father's favor by being the perfect little hostess. She'd
always been ahead of her years that way. But all she ever
received was silence, not approval, and eventually she
played the part for herself, not for him.

She shrugged casually. "I didn't mind, I liked dressing up. And my father was generous with his money—
why not? He has truckloads of it, parting with some to
make his daughter appear attractive so that he could look
better to the people he was dealing with presented no
hardship."

Looking at her, Reese hardly thought that she would have needed anything beyond the light in her eyes to make her attractive, but he kept the speculation to himself.

"It's where I learned to network," she continued. "So it wasn't a total loss. I discovered that people didn't mind parting with money when they were well fed, entertained and feeling just this side of tipsy." She smiled, looking at her own glass of wine. "Fund-raising for charities seemed a natural jumping-off place for me." Taking the bottle he topped off her glass. She twirled the stem in her fingers. "So, now you have my life story, what's yours?"

He didn't like talking about himself. "It's not very interesting."

Oh no, turnabout was fair play. "I'll be the judge of that. Interest is in the ear of the listener." The din around them was getting overwhelming. London leaned farther forward. "What made you want to become a doctor? It wasn't the money."

She said it as if she knew it for a fact. Her statement stirred his curiosity. "What makes you say that?"

She'd ordered prime rib and took a moment now to savor a bite. It all but melted on her tongue. "If it was the money, you wouldn't be going off to the reservation to help people who can only pay you back with thanks, or in trade. With your skill, if making money was your prime concern, you'd be set up somewhere in Beverly Hills, tending the rich."

"Bedford isn't exactly a pocket of poverty," he pointed out.

"No, but Blair Memorial is a strictly nonprofit hospital. That means they do take on patients who can't pay, and perforce, when you're the doctor called in, so do you. That doesn't exactly smack of a man who's out to enrich his retirement portfolio."

He liked the way her mind worked and the fact that she wasn't afraid to display her intelligence. "You're pretty sharp."

She took the comment in stride. "It's my job to be able to size up people." London winked at him. "See how much they can be coaxed to part with. By the way, you're not sidetracking me. I still want to know why you became a doctor."

Like her smile, the wink went straight to his gut, teasing him. He redirected his thoughts. "Didn't that detective your father hired to investigate me cover that in his report?"

His expression was friendly enough, but she could tell that Reese resented having someone probe into his life without his permission. She didn't blame him.

"He covered facts, not motives." She leaned her chin on her fisted hand. "I'm interested in what makes you tick."

That made two of them, he thought. "Not being particularly brilliant when it came to laboratory science, and having no knack for inventing things that people might want in their future, I figured being a doctor was the best way for me to make a meaningful contribution to society."

Was he really that altruistic, or was he just saying something he thought she wanted to hear? "And that matters to you?"

"Yes," he said honestly, then looked at her, watching the candlelight bathe her features. "Doesn't it matter to you?"

As a matter of fact, it mattered a great deal to her. That was why she conducted fund-raisers for charities rather than for politicians who gave lip service to causes they cared about. It was also why she carefully researched and monitored the charities she was associated with.

But she already knew about herself. What she wanted to know about was the man sitting across from her. "Don't try to wiggle out of this. We've already done me, now it's your turn." Her eyes sparkled as she looked at him. "Did you like to play doctor as a boy?"

He grinned at her. "Yes."

And she bet the girls lined up around the block to play with him. "I see."

It wasn't what she thought. "With birds and animals." That was how Jake had come into his life. Jake was a stray, a black Lab that some boys in the neighborhood had tortured. He'd tended to the dog's injured leg and had a friend for life.

She didn't quite get the connection. "Then why didn't you become a vet?"

"Beyond being able to mend the obvious, like a broken limb, dealing with animals can be very frustrating. Animals can't tell you where it hurts." And that, he thought, was enough about him. He looked around, changing the subject. "I think your shadow decided to give you the night off after all. I don't see him anywhere around here."

After eighteen months London knew better. She took another bite of her dinner. It only succeeded in getting better with each taste. Too bad men weren't like that, she mused. "Don't let that fool you."

"What?"

She made a circular motion with her fork to include the general vicinity. "Not seeing him. Just because you can't see him doesn't mean he's not there."

She would have a point if the man they were talking

about was slight instead of six-six and as solid as a brick wall. "Seems kind of hard to hide someone that big."

A trace of affection came into her voice. Wallace did his best to make this as painless as possible for her. It was just that her frustration got in the way at times. "That's what makes him good at his job."

If Grant could manage to hide himself, that made him *excellent* at his job. "How long has he been your bodyguard?"

"Eighteen months." Her plate empty, she retired her knife and fork.

She was right, he thought, she really could pack it away. Looking at her, his first guess would have been that she ate nothing but fruits and vegetables and sparingly at that.

"Is this a permanent arrangement?"

London rolled her eyes and groaned. "Oh, God, I hope not. Not that I don't like the man," she qualified quickly, "but I was almost rid of him and the others a few months ago—"

"And then what happened?"

She shrugged indifferently, looking down at her plate and the single parsley sprig that was left behind. "A white rose was delivered to my apartment."

Did that have some kind of significance he was unaware of? "I'm afraid I don't follow you."

She was getting ahead of herself. Pausing, she debated just letting the whole thing slide. And then something prompted her to share this piece of her life with this man. This piece no one else knew about except for her bodyguards and her father.

"It was from a secret admirer. Wallace instantly took it to mean something else."

It wasn't a stretch for him. He thought of Monica, a

beautiful dark-haired girl he knew in his freshman year at college. "Stalker?"

The speed with which he came to the correct conclusion startled her. "Why would you think that?"

"Was it?" he pressed.

Despite everything, she'd still rather not think that way. "That's what Wallace and my father think, but why would you?"

Then he was right, Reese thought. He felt instantly protective of her. The way he should have been of Monica. She'd been his study partner in bio lab and had poured out her heart to him one evening. She was afraid her ex-boyfriend was stalking her, refusing to accept their breakup. He'd counseled her to go to the campus police. It was the last conversation they ever had.

"I knew someone in college who was stalked."

There was something in his tone that chilled her. She blocked it, the way she did every thought she didn't like, every emotion that came too close.

"And?"

But he shook his head. Monica had a right to rest in peace. "You don't want to know." But *he* wanted to know something. "Was there a note?"

"Yes." More than one. There was even a poem. A bad one, but she found it almost touching in its attempt. "I think it's all pretty innocent, really. If we weren't all so paranoid these days, it would have been just a sweet note, nothing else."

He'd done some reading on the subject since then, educating himself. With stalkers, there were never just one event. "Were there more notes, more flowers?"

She debated saying no, then shrugged. Reese was sharp enough to see through a lie. "Yes."

He appreciated freedom as much as the next person, maybe more, but he found himself shifting sides. Because he'd been the one to find Monica's body behind the library. "Then maybe your father and Wallace have the right idea. It's better to be safe than sorry. Did you tell the police?"

Her father and Wallace had very little faith in the powers of the local police. "Tell them what? That someone sends me white roses occasionally? That his notes are always respectful, almost sweet in nature?"

The waiter appeared just then, a small, black leather folder in his hands that held the bill for their dinner. "Will there be anything else?"

Reese looked at her questioningly. London had already turned down the idea of dessert. She shook her head. "I'm fine."

Reese turned back to the waiter. "That'll be all." The waiter placed the leather folder on the table. Reese took out his credit card and tucked it into the folder. Picking it up, the waiter slipped off to the cash register artfully hidden behind the hostess's desk.

Reese focused on what London had said before the waiter had interrupted them. "He doesn't threaten you, say he wants you for himself, that you belong to him and no one else?" He repeated the gist of the notes that Monica had received.

London shook her head. "No, nothing like that. Personally, I think it's someone who's very shy, that's all, and this whole thing is being blown out of proportion. I deal with a great many people in my profession, Reese. Who knows? Maybe my 'secret admirer' is one of the caterers I work with, or someone in the shop I use to send out engraved invitations. I just don't see the harm—"

He cut her off, a note of passion entering his voice. "The harm is that this can get out of hand. The harm is that one night this guy might decide that the flowers and the notes have gone on long enough and that it's time for you to make a commitment to him—"

He'd managed to press one of her buttons. She raised her voice to match his. "Well then, he's out of luck because I'm not in the commitment business, and if he knows anything at all about me beyond my address, he's probably figured that out."

London's answer wasn't what he would have expected. "Why?"

She thought he was asking how the person who sent her roses could figure out that she wasn't into commitments. "Because I'm not with anyone."

He waved that away. "No, I mean why aren't you in the commitment business?"

He brought her up short with his question. She raised a brow. "Getting personal, are we?"

"You raised the point," he reminded her. "I'm just following it."

She had already made up her mind about him and the part he was going to play in her life. They might as well get this out of the way so he'd know the ground rules. "I'm not in the commitment business because commitments don't last. Promises don't last. Nothing is permanent." She raised her glass. There was just the slightest bit of wine left in it. "Here's to enjoying the moment while it's here and letting the future take care of itself."

There was still a drop left in his own glass. He raised it. "To the moment," he echoed.

Reese touched his glass to hers and watched her eyes as she sipped the last bit of wine. Had she been in love and been bitterly disappointed? He couldn't imagine someone walking out on her, breaking her heart, but then, he couldn't envision his father walking out on his mother, either. But it had happened.

The waiter returned, murmured a thank-you and went off. Reese wrote in a tip and signed the slip. Tearing off the bottom sheet, he pocketed it and his credit card.

Setting down her empty glass, London raised her eyes to his and asked, "Well, we've toasted this moment. What would you like to do with the next one?"

He knew what she was asking and she knew his answer before it was given.

Taking her hand in his, they left the table.

Chapter 11

Wallace found a parking space directly across the street from the apartment building where London lived and eased his vintage beige Nissan sedan into it. The remainder of his dinner from Malone's almost slid off the seat beside him. He managed to catch the container at the last moment before it fell.

He swallowed an oath as he shut off the ignition and settled in.

London and the man she was with had left without warning, their body language giving nothing away about their imminent departure until they'd stood up. He'd only had time to hastily throw the contents of his plate into a container he'd brought with him—the job had taught him to be prepared. He'd spent too many hungry nights on surveillance.

Rising to his feet as London and the doctor left the

restaurant, Wallace didn't have time to wait for a waiter to bring the bill. Instead Wallace had tossed money that he knew would more than cover the meal and a small tip down on the table. He would have liked to have had a drink to go with the rest of his meal, but there was no time for that.

Didn't matter, he told himself. His comfort took a back seat to his job.

He glanced at his watch and suppressed a sigh as he leaned back in his seat. It looked as if it was going to be a long night.

But that—he tried to be philosophical—was what the ambassador paid him for.

London stepped into the empty elevator car. Reese joined her, and the door slowly eased closed, locking them away from the rest of the world.

Looking up, she watched the floor numbers change. As they approached her floor, an excitement tingled through her body, leaving nothing untouched.

Her eyes met his.

The excitement increased.

Without any vanity, London thought of herself as sophisticated, a woman of the world. Due to the nature of her life, she had been one for a long time. Women of the world didn't feel their nerve endings jumping in anticipation because of what they hoped might happen between them and a man who might not be part of their world tomorrow.

And yet she did.

And gloried in it.

London couldn't remember the last time she had felt this alive.

Reese walked with her to her apartment. Instinctively she glanced down at the floor before the door, unconsciously bracing herself.

There was nothing there.

The sense of relief was immediate.

"Looking for something?"

London felt a little foolish, reminding herself of her own theory. That the man who left the roses and notes was harmless. She'd allowed Wallace and her father to spook her.

"Just checking. My 'admirer' leaves flowers on my doorstep. Or rather, the doorman does. He brings them up whenever a delivery is made." The descriptions of the delivery boys varied and according to Wallace, they were all legitimate when he checked them out.

"Have you had him checked out? The doorman," Reese clarified when she looked at him. There'd been that moonstruck look on the man's face when he'd complimented her earlier this evening. Maybe the doorman had gotten this job at the apartment just to be close to her. It wasn't out of the realm of possibilities.

She smiled, taking out her key. Her bodyguard was way ahead of him. "Wallace already did that. He's very thorough, very good at his job." Her smile deepened. "The man leaves no suspect unturned." Inserting her key into the lock, she turned it, then looked over her shoulder at Reese. "Did you want to come inside?"

The question was a formality. They both knew he did. And would.

Still, he glanced behind him toward the elevator. It had gone down to the first floor again and remained there. No one was coming up.

"Isn't this about where Grant comes bursting in, whisking you behind the door and slamming it in my face?"

"His job is to protect me from kidnappers and stalkers, not people I choose to be with. I still have some say in my own life," she assured him. "And he knows better than that." She walked inside the apartment, flipping on the light switch. Reese followed her in. "I made it very clear to him that he's to perform his 'duties' tonight at a great distance. Besides—" turning around, she watched Reese close the door "—I told him that I would be safe with you around."

He wasn't altogether sure about that.

Reese picked up a strand of her hair. The softness unsettled him. Aroused him. "And what's to keep you safe from me?"

She raised her eyes to his, the invitation clear. "Who says I want to be safe from you."

He didn't need to hear any more than that.

Very slowly he took her purse from her hand and tossed it onto the table by the door with only his peripheral vision to guide him. He realized only a beat later that he'd come close to knocking over a vase that was there.

His eyes were on her face.

He could feel adrenaline pumping through his veins, could feel his heart rate increasing.

Taking her face into his hands, Reese lowered his mouth to hers and kissed her. Very, very slowly.

It was like having some kind of hallucinogenic drug injected into her blood stream. The reaction was immediate. And intense.

She could feel the effect spreading through her, taking possession of all of her. Hunger sprang into her loins, her limbs, aching for release, for fulfillment. For him.

Her arms went around his neck and she clung to him.

There was no doubt, no hesitation, no place for either. This was right. In this place, in this time, it was right.

The refrain echoed in her brain over and over again.

The kiss grew, the fire rose, fanned by both of them until it was larger than either.

Somewhere in the middle of the swirling abyss the kiss created, London felt her feet leave the ground, felt Reese's arms tighten around her as he picked her up and turned away from the foyer.

She drew her head back to look at him, confusion in her eyes.

"Where's your bedroom?" he whispered, his throat so tight the words literally had to be pushed through.

It took her a moment to remember. Everything in her head felt jumbled. London pointed toward the rear of the apartment.

He kissed her again, sealing his mouth to hers, and then began walking.

Each kiss he pressed to her lips melted her a little further. Doing the same to him. Sapping his strength a little more.

Reese had the vague sensation of walking for a time. Finally looking up, he saw that they still hadn't reached the bedroom door. It was at the end of the hall.

Curling her body against him, absorbing the warmth of his chest through the clothing—his and hers—that was still a barrier, London looked up at him and saw the smile on his lips. Could taste it even though there was space between them.

"What?"

There was amusement in his eyes. "Your apartment's bigger than the house where I grew up." Not to mention far more elegant. He had a feeling that each piece in it could equal the price of all the furniture his mother had once owned. Certainly the baby grand could.

She wanted to know about that, about the house where he'd grown up.

About him.

About the boy he'd been and even about the woman who had raised him. Questions filled her head, all manner of questions that surprised her.

Personal questions.

She didn't want this to get personal, wanted only to draw the fun, the pleasure out of it—like eating the sweetest part of an orange—and then toss the rest of it away. It was neater that way. Less complicated. Less involving.

She didn't want to get involved, not at any cost, because it would be too great. She knew that, accepted that.

The questions remained, multiplying. Teasing her. Troubling her.

She blocked them out with a resolve that had been years in the making and sealed her mouth to his with a passion that was calculated to take his breath away. It succeeded in stealing hers, as well.

Kissing her over and over again, Reese lowered her until her feet touched the floor.

Her arms tightened around his neck as she pressed her body to his. The hard contours heightened her excitement. She could feel his desire, feel him want her.

An urgency seized her.

Feeling almost frenzied, she curved her fingers along the lapels of his jacket and pulled it from his shoulders, down his arms. She threw it to the side.

Her fingers flew to the buttons on his shirt.

Catching her hands, he stopped her.

Dazed, London looked up at him in mute confusion. And became lost in the smile on his lips.

"Some of the moves have to be mine," he told her quietly.

She swallowed, afraid to draw in a breath, afraid of the moment ending.

Reaching behind her, Reese took the tongue of her zipper and lightly pulled it down the length of her spine. She could feel pins and needles traveling up and down her flesh, breaking every single California freeway speed limit.

Her eyes never leaving his, she shrugged her shoulders. Her dress fell to the floor, pooling around her feet. Displaying her body.

His heart stopped for a split second, then began to beat wildly. She was wearing only thong underwear and black tinted stockings, the kind that came up to her thigh, ending in a flurry of black lace.

He felt his gut tightening so hard, it threatened to snap him in two.

His gaze washed over her, heated, possessive. A sound that could only be termed as appreciative escaped his lips. Cupping her breasts, he drew her close and kissed her throat.

Her head fell back as pleasure filled her and expanded, leaving no space untouched, unlit. She felt as if she could have guided a thousand ships home on her inner light alone.

Her loins ached and she pressed herself against his hardness, eager for the final moment. Wanting gratification the way she had never wanted it before.

It was a long time in coming.

Lowering her to the bed, Reese made love to every

part of her, to her eyes, her cheeks, her hair. To the slope of her shoulders, the hollow of her throat. The curves and dips along her body, caressing, then kissing them. Causing wondrous things to happen along the terrain of her body, wondrous explosions to rack her when she was least prepared.

It was like a wonderful dream.

She never wanted to wake up.

Moaning, trying to maintain at least a shred of decorum, she arched against him as he coaxed each stocking away from her legs. Teasing it from each leg, he kissed each inch that was exposed.

It took a long time for the stockings to finally join her dress on the floor.

Just as she tried to catch her breath, Reese pressed his lips against the small swatch of nylon that still covered her.

She felt the heat of his breath searing into her inner core, making her moist.

Making her crazy.

She couldn't keep from wiggling against his mouth, couldn't keep from arching into him, silently urging him to go further.

To take her further.

When the material seemed to melt away and his tongue found her, she grabbed hold of his shoulders and cried out. The climax was sudden, hard and shook her to the bottom of her soul.

She was vaguely aware of the smile on his mouth as it curved against her skin. Intensely aware of her own need for more.

He brought her to a second climax that racked her body and drained her energy. It took effort for her to even draw a breath.

And then he was above her, his firm body ready for her. Nude, poised.

She realized that she must have somehow clawed away his clothing, but when and how were details she couldn't remember.

All she knew was that she needed him to be with her, to be in her. To take her to the place he'd silently been promising her with every movement of his body.

And still he waited, prolonging the moment. Heightening the anticipation for both of them.

Reese had no idea where all these feelings that were assaulting him were coming from. He was aware of being surrounded, of having every movement choreographed by some unseen power that seemed to be outside his own consciousness.

He was moving to an inner music, an inner fire he had never encountered before.

He wanted to possess her, to feel that final explosive satisfaction that came from having a woman.

He wanted it to continue eternally.

Each time he thought he'd reached a pinnacle, that what he was feeling inside couldn't get any higher, it did. He was not in control here. It was this feeling that had taken over. It was in control of both of them and he could only hang on for as long as possible, enjoying the ride.

Enjoying her.

London felt as if she'd been taken by a huge wave and carried away beyond the point where she could form coherent thoughts. This was a place where thought and fears could not reach. It was a place that was warm and safe and exciting.

"If you don't take me now," she warned him, her

breath coming in disjointed snatches, "I'm going to self-destruct and incinerate right here."

He smiled into her eyes, feeling things he'd never felt before, telling himself it was the moment, not the woman.

"Can't have that," he said, his voice hoarse from wanting her, from the restraint he had been exercising since the moment they'd walked into the apartment.

Because as soon as the door had closed, as soon as he'd looked into her eyes, held her in his arms, he could have taken her there, on her marble foyer, making wild, mindless love to her like the streetwise kid he'd once been.

But she deserved so much more, and if there was only to be this one time for them, he was determined that it was going to be memorable. This much he'd silently sworn to himself and to her.

But the time for promises, silent and otherwise, was over. There was only so much restraint a body could stand, and his was almost past the brink.

It was time.

Balancing his body above hers, Reese used his knee to part her legs, his eyes never leaving her face.

She pressed her lips together, a passenger in the front seat of a roller coaster about to fling itself down a steep incline.

As Reese sheathed himself in her, the power of his entry all but caused him to spin out of control. He brought his mouth down to hers. And for a moment all he did was kiss her, over and over again.

She couldn't take it any longer, couldn't bear to wait, even though she knew she should. London began to move beneath him.

Urged on by her movement, Reese began to move, slowly at first, setting the pace. He could hear her breathing, feel her chest moving as her shallow breaths became shorter. Hear himself as their sounds matched and converged.

Tightening his arms around her, Reese stepped up the pace. A thousand dancing lights surrounded them as they both climbed to the highest crest.

The explosion claimed them both. He heard her cry out his name, felt it echo along his body.

He held her for a very long time, even as the lights in his head faded into the background.

Even as the sound of his breathing slowly leveled itself out.

He wanted to continue holding her until forever descended on them both.

Reese felt he had a good head start.

He knew which windows were hers, had memorized that section on the face of the apartment building. His eyes were instinctively drawn to it whenever he looked up, whenever he kept vigil.

Several minutes after she had entered the building with that worthless cur she'd allowed to accompany her, he watched the lights go out and felt his soul being extinguished.

He knew what was happening, could see it almost as clearly as if it were happening right in front of him instead of twenty stories above.

A guttural sound clawed at his throat, trapped there by sheer force of will.

She'd betrayed him.

He had forgiven her her previous trespasses because their paths had not crossed then, and she could not be held accountable for what she'd done before she'd met him.

But now, now was different.

Now she knew him. Knew he existed.

He'd wooed her, taken the soft, gentle path to her heart. And she did this to him? Gave herself to another man? Let another man touch her, be with her, when by all rights, it should have been him?

It should have been him.

How could she?

Tears stung his eyes as the red flames of rage consumed his sorrow.

He could not tear his eyes away from the darkened windows of her apartment.

The darkness enshrouded him. He felt himself suffocating.

His rage mounted.

Chapter 12

London stirred, realizing that she was beginning to doze off.

The thought that she was comfortable enough with this man to do that ushered in warring emotions. Contentment clashed with fear. As much as part of her was drawn to and yearned for contentment, London knew she couldn't allow herself to let her guard down, couldn't allow herself to reach for feelings that others took for granted. Because she had learned the hard way that those same feelings could leave wounds in their wake that might never heal, that could destroy you.

Awake now, she pulled away from Reese, tucking the sheet around herself. She banked down the ache that was beginning to form within her. "I just want you to know that there are no strings attached."

Her tone was different. The intimacy was gone, replaced by a distance that belied their proximity. What had changed in the last few minutes, he wondered. He hadn't said anything, hadn't done anything but hold her.

Turning, he looked at her face. There were barriers up. Why?

"I think you covered that in your no-commitment speech earlier this evening."

Edgy, annoyed with herself for going deeper into her soul than she *knew* was safe, London took exception to the word he used. Was he being sarcastic?

"It wasn't a speech," she told him. "I just wanted to make the ground rules clear."

"Ground rules?" His eyes narrowed. Had he misread everything that was going on here? "Was this some kind of sporting event?"

She shrugged. The sheet slipped. London quickly tugged it back into place. "Most men would look at it that way."

Had her other lovers? Was that why she'd suddenly pulled back from him? Without allowing himself to get entrenched any further, Reese tried to make sense out of what was being said here.

"I'm not most men, London. I've never found myself yearning to go along with the mainstream."

She knew that. Sensed that. Despite her struggle to remain behind the lines that had been drawn in the sand, she found herself smiling. London tossed her head, her hair raining over her shoulder. "Maybe that's what I find so attractive."

It was an act, he thought. To what purpose? Self-preservation? Or was she as removed from the scene as her behavior suggested?

"And maybe you should stop playing Rita Hayworth in *Blood and Sand*."

He was trying to rattle her, she thought. Well, she wasn't going to let him. Wasn't going to allow him to shake her foundation any further than he already had. "Sorry, must have missed that one."

Definitely trying to shut him out, he thought. "I'm surprised, you've got the part down to a T."

There was nothing left for him to do but to get dressed and go home. He had no idea why he didn't, what compelled him to remain. Maybe it was the look in her eyes that he was sure she wasn't aware of. The one that made him think of a vulnerable girl hiding inside a woman's body.

He made her feel fidgety, restless. As if her thoughts just didn't fit into one another. Sitting up on her knees, she drew the sheet up with her. "I just don't want you reading anything into this, that's all."

She made their lovemaking sound casual. Had it been? He hadn't thought so, he had felt a real connection, but maybe he was wrong. "So, do you go to bed with every man you have dinner with?"

Lightning flashed in her eyes. "No."

He'd struck a nerve. Good. "All right, we'll narrow the circle. Every doctor?"

"No." She knew she should terminate the conversation, ignore it, and yet…

And yet some part of her didn't want him to think of her as the kind of woman she was trying to portray. Some part of her wanted him to know that however briefly it lasted, this had been special.

Was special.

"Then just the ones who save your life." He saw she was about to say something and had a hunch it would be flippant. He gave her the truth. "You went into cardiac arrest on the table."

Her eyes widened. This was the first she'd heard of that. "You didn't tell me that."

"I was saving it." The truth was he hadn't wanted to alarm her and there seemed no reason for her to know all the gruesome details. But maybe she should. Maybe she should come face-to-face with her own mortality. "It helps to have an ace in the hole to play at moments like this."

That sounded far too calculating. From what she'd learned about him, Reese wasn't like that. "You didn't know there'd be moments like this. You're lying."

He wasn't sure if she was referring to her brush with death or to his supposedly saving the information for an opportune time.

"Not about the cardiac arrest. It happens sometimes," he informed her matter-of-factly. "The body goes into shock. There were no aftereffects in your case and I didn't want to upset you." Right from the start he'd had this instinctive desire to protect her. He had no idea why. London certainly didn't seem fragile.

Maybe that was it, he thought. On some level he could see that she was acting, that the woman behind the facade was fragile.

Silence hung between them. It was time to go. Reese reached for his trousers.

London had no idea why watching such a simple action filled her with such melancholy. Shifting so that she was behind him, she rose up again and pressed a kiss to his neck.

The flow of emotion was immediate, filling his veins, taking possession of him.

Turning, Reese pulled her onto his lap. The sheet she

was trying to hang on to was left behind. His arms enfolded her.

"Changing the ground rules again?"

Her heart was pounding. All she could do was look at him. Waiting. Anticipating.

"Playing it by ear as I go along," she breathed.

He knew this wasn't going anywhere, knew it couldn't go anywhere. Neither one of them really wanted it to.

And yet he couldn't help himself, couldn't resist her. So he pretended to play the same game she was playing, with the same nebulous rules. And one rule was that neither of them could be there in the morning.

But for now they had the night, and for now that was enough.

They made the most of it.

One night wove itself into the promise of a next, and a next.

London wasn't sure just how it happened, only that it did. One moment, Reese Bendenetti wasn't part of her life, and then he was. She still told herself that she could walk away whenever she wanted, just as she had always done before. And since she could walk away, she didn't. She postponed it, confident that when she was tired of the game, the man, the moment, she could just shut down and move on, the way she had whenever a relationship threatened to move beyond the realm of casual fun into something more serious. Until then, she would enjoy herself. Enjoy him.

And as one day slipped into another, she found herself waiting for his call, figuratively holding her breath until she heard Reese's voice over the telephone, caressing her ear. Stirring her.

She found she loved the sound of his voice. Deep, velvety, strong. Everything about Reese Bendenetti fairly shouted "protector." A woman could feel safe with him. Safe, but walking on the edge at the same time. Because the moment his lips met hers, the second his arms closed around her, the illusion of safety disappeared.

The man tasted of danger, of things dark and mysterious. And she loved it.

As long as she knew she could get away when the time came.

Later.

Rachel Bendenetti smiled at the young woman sitting on her living room sofa, the young woman who seemed to brighten the very air that surrounded her.

When Reese had called to say he was coming over and bringing London with him, Rachel had braced herself. Having spent a good deal of her life on the wrong side of the tracks, she knew how the very rich reacted to people who had worked all their lives just to survive.

Prepared to be charitable, Rachel discovered that there was no need to overlook thoughtless remarks and demeaning glances. There were none. London Merriweather, born with a golden spoon in her mouth, was bright, vivacious and honestly charming. Rachel could easily see what it was that appealed to her son.

She was surprised that he had been the one to suggest bringing the young woman who had slipped into his life and his conversation to dinner on Sunday. It was a first.

With all her heart, Rachel hoped it was a sign of things to come.

"It's really lovely to finally meet you, London."

Reese slanted a warning look toward his mother. "There's no finally, Mother."

He had a point, London thought. After all, they'd only been seeing one another for—what was it now?— a little less than a month. She tried to pretend that she didn't know the exact number of days, but she did. Twenty-seven.

Still, she laughed. "Don't tell me that Reese had said so much about me. I won't believe you."

She smiled with her eyes, Rachel thought. That was a good sign.

"He has mentioned you," Rachel allowed. "And it's what he didn't say, more than what he said that caught my attention."

That, London thought, left a great deal of room for speculation. In and of itself it shouldn't have picked up the tempo of her heartbeat. But it did.

She caught the look that passed between mother and son. She could almost visualize what life had been like for them. A struggle, with very little money, but with so much love, it didn't matter. Very little mattered when you had love, London thought.

She'd had opulence in her life, never wanted for any-thing material, but she found herself envying them. There was an easy communication between them, a communication without words. The kind that she had once enjoyed with her own mother.

London suddenly missed her mother a great deal.

"I can see where Reese gets his mysterious way of phrasing things."

"We just pay attention to things more than some peo-ple. And we have our own shorthand." Aware of how that might be taken, Rachel didn't want the young woman feeling shut out and quickly added, "I suppose it comes from having to depend on each other for so long."

Sitting on London's left side, Reese realized that he felt a little tense about this meeting. He wasn't really sure why he had brought London here today. He supposed that part of him felt she needed to meet someone like his mother. That was probably presumptuous of him, but he was a doctor and honor bound to prescribe what he felt his patient needed. London wasn't his patient anymore, but she needed someone in her life like his mother, if only for a few hours. His mother had an uncanny gift for making people around her feel good.

Setting down the tray of refreshments she'd prepared on the coffee table, Rachel went to draw the curtain against the intense afternoon sun. As she took hold of the cord, she looked out and saw a beige car parked across the street from her house. There was a man sitting behind the wheel.

Reese had mentioned that London was being stalked. That was part of the reason for this visit. To put London in touch with a more tranquil way of life.

Rachel turned from the window. "Are you aware that there's a man in a beige sedan across the street?" she asked Reese. "He's watching the house."

London nodded. She picked up the wine cooler Reese's mother had poured for her. "That's my bodyguard, Wallace."

Rachel relaxed, then took a longer look at the man in the vehicle. A man shouldn't have to sit out there all afternoon, roasting in a car.

"Ask him in," Rachel urged. "There's more than enough room at the table and I made plenty."

Wallace did not care to socialize. He'd told London it took the edge off what he did. "Thank you, but no," London declined on Wallace's behalf. "He feels he has a better vantage point if he stays outside, watching the house. Besides," she looked toward Reese—it was impossible not to feel safe when he was around, "I don't think anything'll happen to me here."

Rachel smiled and mouthed "lovely" to her son over London's head. Seeing her reflection in the mirror on the opposite wall, London smiled to herself.

Dinner was almost ready. Rachel paused a moment and perched on the arm of the sofa, looking at her guest. "Reese tells me that you hold fund-raisers for charities."

Instantly alerted by her innocent tone, Reese knew where this was going. "Mother."

Both women heard the warning note in Reese's voice. Rachel waved a dismissive hand in his direction as London raised an inquiring eyebrow, waiting to have the mystery cleared up.

Rachel did the honors. She leaned forward and confided to the other woman, "He's afraid I'm going to ask you to do a fund-raiser for Hayley's House."

"Hayley's House?" London echoed. She looked from mother to son and then back again. "I'm afraid I'm not familiar with that one—"

"There's really no reason why you should be," Rachel said. But she was hoping to change that. The more people aware of the small facility, the better the chance that it would receive donations and funding to keep it going. "It's just a small place," Rachel confided. "An orphanage, although they have euphemisms for that sort of thing now. Bluntly, it's a shelter for abandoned babies and deserted children found in hotel rooms, bus stations, alleys, etcetera, thrown away by parents too addicted to some substance or other to realize what they've done—"

Reese watched London's face, attempting to read her reaction. He hadn't brought her here to hear a pitch. He knew how much of her waking hours his mother donated to the facility, but this wasn't the time to draw London in.

"As you can see, my mother's very passionate on the subject," Reese told her. "Once you get her going, there's no stopping her."

London wondered if he was embarrassed, then decided that he cared too much about the older woman to be embarrassed by her. She rather liked that. He wasn't afraid of what someone else might think.

"That's all right," she told him, "people should be passionate on the subject of charities and helping children."

Rachel prided herself on being able to spot a lie a mile away. There were no lies here. She grinned as she looked at her son.

"I like this girl, Reese."

His mother, he knew, liked everyone. But he had to admit it was nice to hear the approval in her voice, even though he was no longer a child but a grown man who didn't need his mother's approval of the woman he chose to spend time with. Still, it was nice to have. God knew he'd gone through his rebellious period. There was a time when he'd given his mother more than her share of grief, although she never complained. She always said that she'd had faith he would come around, even when he hadn't felt that way himself.

"Maybe you'd like to come with me to Hayley's House sometime and look around the place," Rachel coaxed, firmly believing that if you were going for an inch, you might as well try for a mile, or at least a few more inches. "Once you've had a chance to see it, I promise you you'll carry the image around with you for the rest of your life."

All right, she was laying it on a little thick. Reese didn't want London thinking that he'd brought her here with an ulterior motive. "Mother," he warned again.

This time it was London who waved for him to be silent. "I'd like that."

The funny thing was, Reese had to admit she sounded sincere.

And maybe she was, at that.

Rachel beamed at her, ready to accept London into the fold there and then. "Tell me, how do you feel about pot roast?"

London thought of Malone's, the first restaurant Reese had taken her to. A meat-and-potatoes kind of place. Like son, like mother. She grinned. "I don't get it nearly enough."

"Well then, you're in luck." Nodding her head in approval, Rachel rose from the arm of the sofa and went to put dinner on the table.

Conversation for the next few hours was interrupted only long enough to allow one or the other to chew before answering. Otherwise, it went on nonstop over the meal. After dinner, when they were relaxing in the living room, Rachel almost drove Reese from the room by bringing out her beloved album.

The flowers imprinted on the cover had long since faded with age and endless hours of paging through the book. The album featured highlights of her son's life frozen forever in time thanks to the camera she always kept primed and ready. Rachel Bendenetti reasoned that you never knew when the next good picture was coming. Bought the week before Reese was born, it had always been kept within easy reach just in case an important moment came up.

Reese confided that his mother thought almost all moments were important. Rachel made no attempt to deny it.

After spending time giving an informative narrative with every photograph, Rachel retrieved the camera that had made them all possible.

She stood just far enough from the couple to frame them from the waist up.

"Now if you'll just smile for me," she coaxed, the viewfinder against her eye. Lowering it, she peered at the two young people on the sofa. "And scoot together." She motioned with her hand to emphasize her point. "This isn't a wide-angle lens, you know."

Reese looked at London, expecting to hear her demur. She had spent most of her life in front of the camera's eye. He could only guess how she felt about having yet another lens pointed at her.

But to his surprise he saw London move in closer to him. The next moment she leaned her head against his shoulder.

"How's this?" she asked, smiling brightly.

"Perfect." Rachel snapped two photographs in rapid succession. "The second one's for insurance." She never left anything to chance.

And then it was time to go. London found herself feeling reluctant to leave this safe haven, this small, cozy place where there seemed to be only warmth and joy.

"Now, don't be a stranger," Rachel told her, accompanying them to the front door. Looking at London, she nodded toward her son. "You don't have to wait for Reese to bring you. Just give me a call to make sure I'm home and come on over." She winked. "We can have a little girl talk next time."

The wink reminded her so much of Reese, it momentarily took London's breath away.

"Deal," she promised, a beat before she found herself swallowed up in the other woman's embrace. Rachel was used to being greeted and sent off with hugs that were a matter of custom rather than feeling. Rachel's embrace was so genuine, London was touched.

"You know," she said to Reese as they walked away from the quaint one-story Tudor home, her arm threaded through his, "that's probably the first time anyone's mother sat me down to look at their son's life in pictures."

He'd tried to ascertain whether she was bored or not. He had to admit she had looked as though she was interested. "Sorry about that."

The apology took her by surprise. "No, don't be. I liked it. Liked feeling normal…" She hunted for the right word. "Average."

He laughed as he opened his car door for her. "There's nothing in the world that would make you average, London."

She looked up at him before sliding into her seat. "Why Dr. Bendenetti, are you flirting with me?"

He laughed. "Trying my damnedest."

She waited until he had rounded the hood and gotten in behind the driver's seat. The last thing on her mind was the bodyguard sitting across the street. "Why don't we take this back to my place and see how far you're willing to flirt?"

He looked at her for a long moment. Each time he made love with her, he found himself hungering for the next time, wondering when that feeling was going to end. So far it only grew more intense.

"Be careful what you wish for."

All she was wishing for, she insisted silently, was a passionate evening with a very exciting man. Beyond that she refused to think. There were still no strings, nor would there be any.

Because if there were no strings, there was no risk that they would be broken.

London leaned toward him. "For tonight," she said, her mouth inches from his, "let's not be careful."

Reese had no quarrel with that.

Chapter 13

Control had always been an important part of Reese's life. Control over his body, his thoughts and especially his emotions.

Control had been what had seen him through the days when he'd felt like an outcast because his father had left his mother, because they did without and everyone knew.

But being with London had changed all that. It was as if he'd been freed, unshackled, allowed to finally be himself. An utterly different self he'd never even known existed.

The edginess that had slipped into his vehicle along with them accompanied them all the way to London's apartment building, continuing to grow as each moment went by.

By the time he'd parked the car and they got into the

elevator, he felt the last of his shaky restraint about to snap like a brittle twig.

Reese was vaguely aware that London's bodyguard had made the journey with them in the vehicle that followed in their wake. The man would undoubtedly sense that something was happening the moment he saw them emerge from the car. Reese was sure the tension and electricity that crackled between them was evident to the world at large, but right now, he didn't care what Wallace Grant, or anyone else for that matter, thought.

All he cared about was being with her. In every sense of the word.

She felt it, too, he thought. He could see it in her eyes, in her body language. With each floor that went by, the anticipation heightened.

The moment Reese closed the door to her apartment, shutting out the rest of the world, the explosion rocked them both. Her lips found his. Fingers flew, undoing buttons, unbuckling belts, tugging out shirttails and pulling down zippers.

Doing away with cloth barriers that kept them from one another.

What Reese was most aware of was the intoxicating need he had.

The need that had him.

Not for sex, not for a woman, but for her. For London.

He needed all of her. Her mouth, her eyes, her hair, her thoughts. Every single shred that went into that special magic that was London Merriweather.

Reese was like a man completely consumed with unquenchable desire.

There was always a time, a moment, when in the midst of the tempest that surrounded her, London could suddenly step back, look on like a spectator and revel in being desired, in being needed. She would feel confident in her ability to enjoy and then retreat with no regrets, no scars.

But someone had burned the back stairs and there was no retreat for her, no way out, no out-of-body experience that separated her from the man she was with. She was right there, in the thick of everything, unable to separate her thoughts from her feelings, unable to retreat.

This was all so foreign to her that she felt like a woman possessed.

She felt an overwhelming desire not to be adored, but to give back the pleasure she was receiving, to have and to share. To be completely unlike anything she had ever been before. To feel something unlike anything she had ever felt before.

Each time he brought her up to a higher plateau of sensation, all she wanted to do, even as she reveled in it, was to somehow make sure that Reese would feel that same sensation. That he would be trapped in this fiery inferno of whirling sensations and emotions just as she was.

So she touched, caressed, stimulated, provoked, matching movement for movement. And all the while sinking deeper into the world she was trying to trap him in. Not to exercise her power over him, but so that she would not take this new journey alone.

He took her right there, in the very place he had initially been afraid he couldn't get past the first time they had made love together. Her foyer. Now he was just glad he'd been able to close the door in time. With the cool marble floor beneath her and a chandelier glistening above her, he made London his again, just as she branded him.

It could have been a dirt field for all he cared. All that was important was that she was the one he took with him on the journey to ecstasy.

Eyes intent on her face, trying to memorize every nuance, every expression, he entered her. And was taken by her. It was a partnership, with each silently depending on the other. And glad of it.

He wanted to tell her then, as peaceful contentment slipped over him, over them. Wanted to tell her the word that was throbbing in his throat, begging for release.

Wanted to tell her that he loved her.

But the word remained where it was. Silent. Inside of him.

Loved.

Whether he kept quiet because of instinct, or fear, he didn't know. But the word remained unsaid as he gathered London against him. And prayed for many other nights like this.

"Floor's cold," London murmured, her words rippling along his naked chest as she curled her body even closer to his.

He laughed softly, toying with a lock of her hair, marveling at how very soft it felt. How very soft she felt. "I'm surprised it hasn't melted into a puddle beneath us."

She shifted. He felt her lips curve against his chest in a secret smile a moment before she raised her head to look at him. Something warm and giving stirred within him. "I guess we were pretty hot, weren't we?"

"Pretty hot?" He laughed at the weak terminology. "The temperature in hell resembles a skiing resort in comparison." His arm around her shoulders, he pressed a kiss to her forehead. "Would you like to adjourn to your bedroom?"

A small, panicky voice, buried deep inside her, standing on the shoulders of memories, whispered a frantic "No" in reply. She'd already taken too many steps down this road with him. It was time to retreat, to back away before it was too late.

But she nodded her head, determined not to be frightened, not to be cowed.

The next moment she found herself being scooped up in his arms. She laced her arms around his neck. Delighted in the fact that they were both wearing their ardor and nothing more.

She smiled at him wickedly. "A girl could get used to this."

He spared her a look before beginning to walk down the hallway. "That's the general idea."

The general idea. Was he talking about the future?

Please don't promise me something about the future, don't try to give me what no one can.

Somehow she stilled the panic rising in her stomach.

London placed her finger to his lips and warned, "Shhh."

It took him a moment to realize why she was doing what she did. She was telling him that there were still no strings between them. No links to couple them beyond the moment.

He told himself he understood, but he wasn't sure anymore that he did.

Reese kissed her as he walked into the bedroom, passion flooding through his veins. But as he raised his head, something caught Reese's attention. He looked again.

And stopped dead.

There was a flower on her pillow. A long-stemmed white rose. Tucked beneath it was a card.

She saw the look on his face. "What is it?" Twisting around in his arms, London looked toward her bed.

He saw the color drain out of her face.

Setting her down, he crossed to the bed and picked up the note.

"No."

The single word was a stern command to him. He looked at her in surprise, the note in his hand.

London was determined to have no buffers. She couldn't depend on anyone to be there for her of their own free will. To believe that would make her twice as vulnerable as she was at this moment.

"I'll read it. It's addressed to me." Steeling herself, London extended her hand toward him expectantly.

Against his better judgment, Reese handed the small beige envelope to her.

Holding her breath, London opened it and quickly scanned the message. The print could have come from any one of a million printers.

"He's not worthy. No one'll ever love you the way I can."

It was as if the air in her lungs had turned to ice. London let the note drop to the floor at her feet. She felt violated.

Damn it, how had he gotten in here? He had been here, in her apartment, in her room. By her bed.

How?

Reese quickly picked up the note and read it, then looked up at her. He saw the look in her eyes. Fury mingled with fear within him. This wasn't the simple admirer she insisted it was. This was a stalker. "He knows about us."

She nodded grimly. Her voice devoid of all feeling,

she said, "He's got to be watching the apartment, seeing us together…"

A chill went over her heart, climbed along her spine.

Reese didn't understand. "How did he get inside? This is a secure building with a security system inside the apartment." How much safer could they make her? And yet this scum had managed to get inside.

She dragged her hand through her hair, struggling to get ahold of herself. She felt like pacing, like running, like screaming. She stood perfectly still, torn in all directions.

"I don't know, I don't know." Scrubbing her hands over her face, she looked at the pillow. "Get that out of my sight," she cried, waving a hand at the rose.

He took it and the note, putting both aside on her bureau behind the framed photograph of her mother. "The police are going to want to see them."

Giving in to the pent-up emotion, she began to pace. "I don't want the police, I want Wallace."

"No offense, but the man isn't exactly keeping you safe, now is he? Not if someone can get into your apartment and leave this." He nodded toward the things behind the photograph. "The police have more manpower and resources available."

He was right, but she didn't want him to be. London wanted fewer people in her life, not more. If the police were brought in, there would be nothing short of a media circus going on around her. It was the last thing she wanted.

She laughed shortly. "Just what I want, more manpower and resources thrown at me."

She wasn't taking this seriously. Trying to make her understand how grave the situation actually could be, Reese grabbed London by her shoulders, holding her in place. "This isn't a game, London. Someone wants you—"

It suddenly occurred to her that they were having this discussion without a stitch of clothes on between them. A wanton smile curled along her lips as she desperately blocked out any thought about the man who had invaded her private terrain.

"You mean other than you?"

He knew what she was trying to do, she was trying to divert him. Maybe even divert herself. But for her sake he wasn't going to let it happen.

"Other than me. With possibly very sick intentions. This is serious, London," he insisted. How did he put her on her guard without frightening her? Or was she already frightened and this was the way she was dealing with it? He still didn't know the details that went into making up the whole of London Merriweather. But he intended to, by and by.

Determined to distract both of them, she laced her arms around his neck. "I never argue with a naked man in my bedroom."

Damn it, it was taking everything within him not to succumb to the fact that she was nude and supple against him and that he wanted her with every fiber of his being, potentially serious situation notwithstanding. "It's not a joke, London."

She raised herself up on her toes, brushed a kiss against his lips, needing him at this moment more than she'd needed him all the other moments combined. There was just no getting away from the fact that he made her feel safe. Protected.

"I wasn't laughing."

It was incredibly hard resisting her, harder than anything he'd ever done in his life, but with his hands on her shoulders, Reese moved her away from him. His eyes held hers, the eyes being the only place he could look without feeling his knees grow weak.

"London, we have to call."

London bit her lip and then nodded, a flippant remark dying before she voiced it. She knew he was right. And wished he weren't.

With a sigh she surrendered to logic and the inevitable. "I'll get dressed."

He allowed himself one last sweeping glance. "It's either that or have the detectives fall to their knees in worshipful reverence when they get here."

She smiled then. A real smile that began in her eyes. He instinctively knew how to make her feel better.

"Reverence, huh?"

"Worshipful." He crossed to the doorway. His own clothes were still out in the foyer. He pointed toward her walk-in closet. It was best if they remained separate for a few minutes or neither one of them was going to get dressed. "Now put something on before I forget to be smart about this."

She inclined her head and opened her closet. He'd scored another point in a tally she was keeping almost despite herself. She kept it because she was unconsciously searching for that flaw, that inevitable flaw that all men had.

So far there was nothing on the negative side.

Wallace frowned as he used a handkerchief to pick up the card.

He'd followed the doctor stoically when the latter had come down to summon him. He had to admit he was surprised that it was the man rather than London who had come. It was obvious to Wallace that she was allow-

ing this relationship to go further than the ones he'd read
about in the last bodyguard's report on her.

He'd said very little during the elevator ride up. His
words and theories were all for London's ears, not some
flavor-of-the-month who had attached himself to her
side for a time.

Wallace shook his head as he stared at the note. "How
the hell did he get in here?" he stormed, then flushed as
he slanted a look at London. "Sorry." He didn't like to
curse even mildly in front of her. Laying the note back
on the bureau, he blew out a breath, supplying the answer to his own question. "It was probably when I was
tailing you earlier."

Wallace stood over London, looking every bit the
part of the gentle giant in some outlandish fairy tale. Except that the look in his eyes was not so gentle.

"If you'd let us put up security cameras in the apartment…" he chided her.

Wallace got no further in his reprimand. Her objec-
tions still held, even after this. "No. I won't let you do
that. I'd feel like I was in the middle of a peep show."

"Maybe he's right," Reese finally said. He'd held his
peace until now, letting London do the talking. After all,
it was her life that was in jeopardy, her bodyguard asking the questions. But there was a fine line between
brave and foolhardy, and she was being unduly stubborn. "Better a live peep show than any alternative."

He noted that Wallace didn't look particularly happy,
despite the fact that what he said was actually support-
ing the bodyguard. But he wasn't here to make Wallace
happy, he was here to do what he could for London.

When she said nothing in response, Reese crossed toward the telephone on her nightstand.

Her eyes widened and she quickly darted in front of him, putting her hand on the phone before he could pick up the receiver. "What are you doing?"

He didn't even bother looking at Wallace, convinced the bodyguard was probably snarling. "The police, remember?"

She'd let that discussion die away, hoping he would put it out of his mind once Wallace was up here. Obviously, the man had too long an attention span.

"No," she insisted. "I don't want them called in. I've already got three around-the-clock bodyguards. The police can't do any more for me than that, and if the police do get called in, somehow this is going to wind up in the tabloids. I don't want to be on page two." There was a slight hitch in her voice that she damned herself for. She didn't want to get emotional about this, just get her point across. "That'll just bring more crazies out." She put her hand on his in supplication. "Please, Reese, I know what I'm saying. No police. Let Wallace and his team handle this." She glanced at Wallace with a look of confidence. "They can keep me safe."

With reluctance Reese released the telephone receiver. He still wasn't convinced that the police couldn't do more than Wallace could, but she did have a point about the crazies. The last thing she needed was a copycat stalker.

"All right," he agreed, his voice low, steady, "but then, I'm moving in."

That had come out of nowhere and for a second it took her breath away. Collecting herself, London demanded, "What?"

He couldn't decide whether she looked like a deer caught in headlights or a tiger about to charge. In either case, Reese didn't want her to think he was taking advantage of the situation.

"You have a spare bedroom. I'll stay there for a few days when I'm not at the hospital." He wanted her to agree. Most of all, he wanted her to be safe. "Call it insurance."

"You're not a professional," Wallace pointed out, grinding out the words so that there was no doubt in Reese's mind just what the man thought of amateurs.

"Doesn't take a professional to care."

Care.

The word hit London smack in her chest, causing an upheaval. Causing panic. He'd just admitted to caring about her. Caring for her. She looked at Reese, wanting to cling, wanting to run, hating the abundance of both feelings that were flooding her. She was supposed to be stronger than that.

"I'll be fine," she assured both men firmly. "I appreciate you two butting heads on my account, and I'm flattered, I really am, but I won't have whoever this is making me afraid in my own home." She looked from Wallace to Reese, wanting to make this point absolutely clear. "He's never threatened me, he's never done anything but be a gentleman." To Reese she said, "Wallace and the team can take care of me, and you can date me. Nothing has to change."

The trouble was it already had, and she knew it and was afraid of knowing it.

But because playing a part made her feel better, she did so.

As was becoming his habit, Wallace took the note and flower with him, intending to put it with all the others.

Softening, hating to have to pull rank, she looked at

her bodyguard. "If it makes you feel better, Wallace, you can stand guard outside the door tonight."

The almost boyish face looked unsmilingly at Reese. "How about him?"

Cocking her head, striving very hard for a nonchalant pose, she shrugged.

"He's free to do whatever he wants. If he wants to leave, he can leave. If he wants to stay," she looked at Reese significantly, "he can stay."

The way she looked at him at times turned his mouth to cotton and his knees to water. It took effort to look as if he were unaffected, but he did his best as he shifted his eyes to Wallace. "I'll let you know."

With a swallowed oath about amateurs, Wallace walked out of the room and then out of the apartment. The front door closed a little more loudly than it might have.

Reese had already fixed his attention back to London. "I don't think he approves of me."

She couldn't truthfully argue with that. But then, she doubted if Wallace truly approved of anyone she'd dated. He'd lumped them all under the heading of "security risk." "Don't let that bother you. He's just being my bodyguard. What matters is whether I approve of you."

That sounded like an invitation if he'd ever heard one. "Do you?"

She smiled, winding her arms around his neck. Pressing her body against his. "What do you think?"

As he tightened his arms around her, he realized that she'd put nothing on under the dress she'd hastily thrown on in his absence. The fact that she was naked beneath it made his pulse race. He was beginning to think that wasn't ever going to change. What was more, he was relieved it wasn't.

"I think that you are a lady who is used to getting her own way about everything."

Her smile widened, pulling him into the heart of it. "Handsome and brilliant. I think this time I struck gold."

He would have liked to think, as he brought his mouth down to hers, that this time would also be the last time for her.

But he knew better than to try to predict what London would do. She seemed to be content with only the moment, and that meant so should he.

The problem was, the moment was no longer enough for him.

Chapter 14

London shifted on the sofa. The newspaper that was sitting on her lap began to slide off and she grabbed it, nearly sending the telephone receiver tucked between her neck and shoulder tumbling after it. On hold, she'd been debating hanging up and calling again later.

But just as she settled back into place, she heard a deep, familiar voice on the other end say hello. It was about time.

"Hi, Dad, it's London. Your daughter, not the city."

It was an old joke, very worn around the edges, voiced at times in exasperation, at other times in memory of a jest her mother had once made when she was trying to get her husband's attention about a matter concerning their only child.

"London, what's wrong?"

There he was, cutting to the chase as he always did

with her. No glimmer of the charming chitchat he was known for. Was that concern or impatience she heard in his voice? Probably the latter.

The connection to Madrid was not the clearest, and there was static crackling across the lines, thanks, no doubt to the storm she'd heard was roaming its way across the Atlantic. It had taken her a solid fifteen minutes of transfers once she'd gotten through to the American Embassy in Madrid before she'd been put through to her father's personal line.

It occurred to her that if this had been an emergency, she could have been dead by now. The kidnappers her father claimed to be so worried about would have grown exasperated, given up and dumped her body in the river.

She glanced down at the lead story on the front page of the *L.A. Times*. The story that had prompted her to make this call. Freedom could finally be in her grasp.

"Nothing's wrong, Dad." Absently she traced the outline of the man being led away in handcuffs just below the bold caption. "Everything could be very right. Did you happen to read the front page of your favorite newspaper on the Internet today?"

Except for the subdued crackle, there was silence on the other end of the line. So much so that for a moment London thought she'd lost the connection. "Dad? Are you still there?"

A quiet sigh preceded the ambassador's reply. "I'm here, London. And yes, I read it."

She'd thought that he'd be a little more animated than this. Maybe they weren't talking about the same thing. "They caught the terrorist who kidnapped Susannah Parker. It wasn't any huge network of terrorists, it was just one guy, off his nut, working independently.

He's also the one who sent the notes to the other women," she said in case her father hadn't read that far. It was difficult to contain her excitement. "This means we can finally call off the dogs, right?"

"London…" Her father's voice was as serious as she'd ever heard. It was the voice he employed when there was no budging him. "…Wallace called me the other day."

London tried not to scrap her hope. She knew exactly what her father was referring to, what had both Wallace and Reese concerned. Well, damn it, life wasn't without risks, and she was willing to take them in exchange for freedom.

"No offense, Dad, Wallace is a nice man, and there's no doubt he's good at his job, but you do pay him a lot of money to watch me. Did it ever occur to you that he's basing his argument on the fact that he just might want to hang on to this lucrative job?"

Ambassador Merriweather was tired of going around with his daughter about this. Tired of arguing. He'd just spent the past six hours trying to settle a dispute between a major American corporation in Madrid and the minister of industry. He didn't want to have to waste time chasing around this familiar bush with his daughter.

"And did it ever occur to you that your life could be in real danger? That whoever is sending you those notes and flowers is probably deranged?"

The barely tethered anger in her father's voice had her reaching for a dose of protective sarcasm. "Don't think someone can send me notes and flowers without being deranged, Dad?"

Mason nearly lost his temper, something he very rarely allowed himself to do. "This isn't a time for jokes,

London. I won't have something happen to you just because you can't take this seriously."

So near and yet so far. Her frustration got the better of her. Rising, she began to pace. "Yes, I know, nothing must happen to the ambassador's daughter. Think of the way that would reflect on you."

"What are you talking about, 'reflect'?" he shouted at her. "I was thinking of how it would feel."

Now there was a word that she wasn't accustomed to hear coming out of her father's mouth. "Feel, Dad? Do you feel?"

"What kind of a question is that?" he demanded angrily. "Of course I feel."

She sincerely doubted he knew the meaning of the word, much less what it entailed. He was the perfect ambassador, the perfect unruffled diplomat. She'd seen a news clip of him several days after her mother's funeral. He was attending the wedding of some prince from one of those tiny countries that most of the world was unaware of. There'd been a smile on his face. That had convinced her that her father was completely without feelings.

"What, Dad?" she wanted to know. "What exactly is it that you feel?"

He had no idea what had gotten into her. Normally, he told her what he wanted of her, and she eventually did what was requested. He had no patience with this rebellious nature she displayed—this trait that was so like her mother's.

"London, I can't talk to you when you're this way."

She was through retreating. It was time they had it out. And if they didn't speak again after it was over, well, they hardly spoke now, so what did it matter?

"No, you have to talk to me when I'm this way. Not talking to me has *made* me this way. Sending me away from you when Mother died made me this way. You sent me away when I needed you."

He wasn't accustomed to having to explain himself to anyone who wasn't part of the government. "I sent you away to spare you."

That was a lot of hogwash, something he'd told himself to ease his conscience, London thought. "Spare me what—contact with the only person who could have seen me through that awful time?"

She'd been eight years old. What did she know of going on without someone who was a vital part of his everyday existence? Someone who had been his guiding sun? Children bounced back, their hearts didn't break the way adult hearts did. He'd sheltered her and expected her to be fine.

Each word felt heavy as he dug it out. "I was having a terrible time adjusting to life without your mother. I didn't want you to see me like that."

His admission took London by surprise. He'd actually felt something, felt a loss? Resentment crowded her. Damn it, why hadn't he said so? Why hadn't he told her? It would have meant so much.

"Seeing you like that would have helped me, would have made me feel that we both missed her." She took a deep breath, her voice suddenly shaky with emotions she didn't want to release. If he was telling her the truth, then his so-called restraint had cost them both. "And maybe it would have brought us together the way she'd always wanted us to be."

London was right, he realized. She was right. And there was nothing he could say to change that. "London."

There was another long pause, this time it was hers. "Yes?"

"I'm sorry."

This was her father; she wasn't going to read anything further into his words. "Sorry we're having this conversation, or—"

He broke in. "Sorry that I didn't realize how much you were hurting, too." He took a deep, steadying breath. That out of the way, he still was not going to be moved. "But that's still not going to make me terminate Wallace and his men."

She supposed, if she looked at it from his perspective, she could see his point of view. "No, I don't suppose it will." London could hear someone in the background, calling to her father. She was surprised that there hadn't been an interruption before now. This probably ranked among the longest conversations they'd ever had. "I guess that's the rest of your life calling. You'd better answer it."

He had to go, but since they'd cleared things up this far, he had one more thing to attend to. Something that had gone unsaid for perhaps too long. "One last thing, London. You do know I love you, don't you?"

He'd never said that to her before, although her mother had told her he loved her more than once. She'd just assumed her mother was covering for her father, the way all good mothers did.

London felt a smile creeping up from her toes. "I do now."

The connection was suddenly lost. She figured the storm was having its way with the phone lines. Her smile didn't abate. She hadn't won what she wanted, but she'd gotten something far more precious. The impossible had happened. She and her father had cleared the air.

Mentally she reviewed her calendar for the coming month. Maybe she could manage a trip to Madrid around the third week or so. It was a thought.

On her way to the first-floor tower elevators, Alix DuCane turned the corner and just barely avoided colliding with Reese, who was coming from the opposite direction. Both halted abruptly within inches of contact.

The first thing she noticed was that he was smiling. To her knowledge, he wasn't given to looking like that for no reason.

"Well, you're looking pretty chipper today," she commented. Rooting around for a cause, she thought of the surgical list she'd seen at the nurses' station just beyond the operating rooms. "I take it that bowel resection you performed this morning went well."

He laughed. The surgery had gone far better than anticipated. "Yes, but this has nothing to do with a bowel resection."

No, she thought, surgery didn't put a light into a man's eyes, even an excellent surgeon's, like Reese. She wasn't about to let him get away without telling her what did.

"Tell me." She placed her hand on his arm to add weight to her entreaty. "I could use a little happy news."

Reese made no reply. Instead he dug into his pocket and took out a ring box. When he opened it, there was a blue-white, heart-shaped diamond nestled against a black velvet interior.

It took her breath away. "Wow." Alix looked up at him. "Reese, I don't know what to say. This is so sudden. We're not even dating." She saw the sudden bewildered look on his face and laughed. "Relax, I'm kidding." And then she became serious, wanting to share in his happiness. "Who's the lucky girl? I didn't think you ever got to see anyone except for your patients." And then, as she mentally backed up, it hit her. "It wouldn't be that gorgeous one who was brought in the other month, the one who'd tried to find a way to drive through a telephone pole, would it?"

Reese had always maintained that Alix had one of the sharpest minds at the hospital. The brightest of the bright. "You do take all the fun out of things, Alix."

Overjoyed that he'd found someone to share his life with, Alix gave him a quick hug.

"But if I know you, you'll find a way to put it right back in."

She stepped back to admire the ring again. The overhead lighting threw blue-white sparks everywhere in the corridor. "So when's the big day so I can clear my calendar?"

He flipped the box closed and slipped it back into his pocket. "Haven't asked her yet."

That was so like a man. "Well then, get to it. Not that I expect any woman in her right mind to turn you down," she added. And then a thought hit her. Her grin grew wider. "Oh, God, Reese, your mother is going to be so jazzed about this. Have you brought the lady around to meet your mom yet?"

He thought of the first encounter. After a few minutes he might as well not even have been there. "Not only has my mother met her, she's assimilated her. You know that orphanage my mother volunteers at?"

"Hayley's House?"

Alix had gone and held and fed a few babies there herself when time permitted. She'd also volunteered her professional services on occasion.

Reese nodded. "That's the one. Mom's taken her there several times already. She even corralled London into holding a fund-raiser for the place next month."

Alix laughed. Rachel Bendenetti had never struck her as being a shrinking violet.

"Sounds like this is a good match all around." She had to get going. Alix brushed a kiss against Reese's cheek. "I am really happy for you. Now put that ring on her finger, Romeo, and get on with it, already."

He intended to do just that this evening.

Reese made reservations at the most expensive restaurant in the area.

He wanted to propose there, where the lighting was romantic and the atmosphere even more so. There was even a band playing tonight. He knew London liked to dance.

The plan was to give her the ring just before the dessert arrived.

That was the plan. But he couldn't wait.

Tension was all but taking the very air out of his lungs. He was pretty sure London would say yes, but there was still a small part of him that was afraid the evening, the proposal wouldn't go the way he hoped it would. Afraid that after all this time, he'd found the girl of the dreams he didn't even know he had, and she would turn him down.

So when London opened the door in response to his knock that evening, he decided the hell with timing and plans. It was better to get this over with and then take her out to celebrate.

If there was something to celebrate.

Whenever she went out with Reese, London was prepared for a phone call telling her that he'd be delayed because of an emergency. Seeing him standing there brought an instant smile to her lips. At least the evening was off to a good start, she thought. And with any luck it would end that way, too. In her bedroom.

"Hi, you're early." London turned toward the hall table where she'd left her things. "I'll just go get my wrap—"

His heart thumping against his chest, Reese caught her arm, stopping her. "Wait a second."

She turned around obligingly. Her smile faded slightly when she saw the serious look on his face.

Oh, God, he was going to break up with her.

Well, it wasn't as if she hadn't been preparing for this from the first moment he'd walked into her life. More than half a lifetime of training was hard to shrug off. Still, something within her felt as if it was about to go into mourning.

"Yes?"

Now that he had her attention, he felt his mouth go dry, and he forgot all the words he'd been rehearsing.

"I'm not sure how to say this."

She was surprised at him. Didn't doctors advocate ripping off a Band-Aid in one fast motion? This was just like that. Swift if not painless.

"Just spit it out," she told him. "That's the best way. It doesn't have to be fancy. It just has to be said." Although she wished it didn't. She wanted a little longer, just a little longer. Happiness had made her greedy.

Reese was disappointed in himself. Granted, he had never exactly been eloquent, but he'd never been tongue-tied, either. This was a side of himself he wasn't happy about.

"I really thought I would be better at this. Not that I've had any practice," he added quickly.

The last thing he wanted was for her to think he'd

done this before. He'd never proposed, never wanted anyone in his life on a permanent basis before. Until London had come into his life, he was certain that he would just go through it doing all the good he possibly could and that would be enough.

After having met London, he knew it wasn't enough. Not anymore.

He looked so uncomfortable she suddenly found herself wanting to put him out of his misery. "Do you want me to make it easy for you?"

He looked at her sharply. "No."

Reese had no idea what she could do, other than propose herself. He didn't want her beating him to the punch. He wasn't a traditionalist, but there were some things that a man had to do first.

His fingers curved around the velvet box in his pocket. Now or never. If he kept on babbling this way, she was going to think he was certifiable.

He took a deep breath and plunged in. "London, I'd like you to wear something for me."

Had the breakup made a U-turn? Or was this about something else? The conversation she'd heard earlier today with her bodyguard came back to her. "What, a two-way homing device? Sorry, Wallace already proposed that, and I—"

He had no idea what she was talking about, only that he was about to start perspiring if he didn't get this said soon. "No, this."

Taking her hand, he placed the box in it.

Stunned, London stared for a long moment at the black object nestled in her palm.

He wasn't leaving her. He was staying. Saying he was staying permanently.

She didn't know which was worse.

Because as painful as it would have been to see Reese leave, what he was asking of her made things even more difficult. He was asking her to believe that this was going to continue. That they were going to continue. Asking her to believe, when she knew things didn't continue. They ended. For her they always ended.

He couldn't read her expression. She was just standing there, looking at the box. "Aren't you going to open it?"

She didn't want to open it, didn't want to see it. Didn't want to slide down deeper into the quicksand from which there was no escape.

"No." She pushed the box back into his hand. "Let's just go out to dinner, Reese." Again she turned to retrieve her things on the table. "They're not going to hold the reservation indefinitely, even for the doctor and the ambassador's daughter—"

Confused by her reaction, he took hold of her arm, turning her back around to face him. "Maybe you don't understand—"

That was when the need for self-preservation suddenly leaped in between them. "Yes, yes, I do understand. I understand perfectly. You're giving me a ring, or a skate key, or some kind of binding thing and asking me to be part of your life—"

She sounded as if she were accusing him of something. Why was this going so wrong?

"I'm asking you to marry me so we can be part of each other's lives," he insisted.

"We already are," she told him. Didn't he see that? He was the first thing she thought of every morning, the last thing she thought of every night. And she wasn't happy about it. "Why can't you just leave things the way they are?"

There came a time when commitments were made, when people settled down. They'd reached that junction. He thought, hoped, they'd reached it together. "Because I don't want to take it one day at a time anymore."

She shook her head adamantly. "That's the only way I know how to take it."

"I want forever, London." He didn't know how to say it any better, any plainer than that.

Cornered, trapped, she lashed out, trying to make a break for freedom. "What kind of doctor are you? Didn't they teach you anything in doctoring school? There is no such thing as forever."

All right, she was being incredibly practical, especially for London. "Then I want as long as I can get."

"That's what I'm giving you," she cried. Didn't he see that? Didn't he know what he was asking of her? To strip herself bare and leave herself exposed to a pain that was more than she could endure? "One day at a time. It's all I can give you. All you can give *me*. Anything else would be a lie."

She was shouting now, and he tried to break through the barriers she was throwing up between them. "It doesn't have to be that way."

"But it is." Suddenly she was very, very tired. He was boxing her in and she wanted to escape. "Look, maybe going to the restaurant isn't such a good idea right now." She laced her arms in front of herself protectively. Blocking him out. "I'm suddenly not hungry. I just want to be alone for a while."

There was an edginess in her voice. He was accustomed to her being in complete control of herself, confident, poised. She was none of those now. And her body language was telling him that she was walling herself off from him.

"Will you just go? I need my space."

He tried to take her into his arms, but she backed away. Reese felt frustration welling up inside of him. "I'm not going to crowd you, London."

"Then go. Please." Her hands on his chest, she pushed him to the door. "Please."

There was nothing else he could do. He slipped the ring box back into his pocket. Squaring his shoulders, Reese opened the front door and left.

Chapter 15

He'd never known two days to drag by so slowly. Filled with work, both of the emergency and nonemergency variety, the minutes of each day still moved with the speed of two anesthetized turtles.

Reese put in for an extra shift, not wanting to go home. Nothing worked.

Try as he might to crowd his head with thoughts that had nothing to do with London, all his thoughts had something to do with London.

He'd never placed himself on the line before and so had never suffered rejection before. He couldn't say he cared for it much.

Sitting at the desk at the fifth-floor nurses' station, Reese closed the folder on the patient being released today. His cell phone rang and he welcomed the diversion.

"This is Dr. Bendenetti."

"I still get a thrill hearing you say that."

He recognized his mother's voice and wondered what she was doing calling him here. His mother never called the hospital, never called his cell. He felt an odd premonition.

"Reese, I'm sorry to call you on your cell phone, but do you know where London is? I'm worried about her."

That made two of them, but for entirely different reasons, Reese thought. He had no idea where London was. He hadn't seen her since she'd turned down his proposal. Initially he'd thought of going back, but to what end? To yell at her? To try to coax her into changing her mind? Neither seemed the right way to go. So he remained away, working. It was what he was good at. Relationships obviously weren't.

"No, Mother, I don't know where London is." He told himself to drop it there, that anything concerning London was no longer his affair. For all he knew, she was snubbing his mother. Having turned down the son, she might not want to have anything to do with the mother. It seemed like a fair guess. But something prompted him to ask, "Why?"

"Well, I stopped by on the way to Hayley's House to pick her up the way we'd agreed, but she's not answering the door. It's not like her to stand me up."

How could his mother possibly know what was or wasn't like London? Granted she was pretty good at sizing people up, but she hadn't known the other woman for that long.

How about you? Certainly didn't take you long to propose, did it? an inner voice taunted him. "Are you sure you got the day right?"

"Of course I got the day right," Rachel replied patiently. "I never forget anything, you know that."

Yes, he knew that. His mother had a memory like a steel trap. She always had. "Maybe she just forgot." But even as he said it, he knew it wasn't true.

It was as if his mother could read his thoughts. There'd been a time, when he was young, when he'd been convinced of it. "That isn't like her, either."

No, he thought, his mother was right. That wasn't like London. And it really wasn't like London to take anything out on his mother that might have happened between them. He was just looking for excuses, but in truth, there weren't any.

"Did you see any of her bodyguards around?" Maybe whoever was on duty had just gone shopping with London. Or maybe, the thought suddenly occurred to him, London had been in another accident.

"Not unless they're disguised as potted plants or paintings." Rachel's voice grew serious. "Reese, I'm worried. London didn't seem to be concerned about whoever was sending her those notes, but I am. This is a very strange world…"

So she'd shared that with his mother, had she? That meant that London was more concerned about the notes than she let on. That bothered him.

"All right, go home, Mother." He tried not to allow his own mounting concern to enter his voice. "I'll see if I can find her after my shift's over."

"Call me the moment you do." He wasn't fooling her. She knew him too well. He was as worried as she was. Rachel paused before adding, "I've got a bad feeling about this."

The trouble was, Reese thought as he flipped closed his cell phone, his mother's bad feelings were usually right.

* * *

This was absurd, Reese told himself as he rode up in London's elevator some thirty minutes later. He was getting worked up over nothing. The woman could look after herself and even if she couldn't, she had a tag team of bodyguards who could. Nothing had happened to her, she'd just forgotten an appointment. Lots of people forget appointments.

Still, he had seen the rose on her pillow that evening, had seen how pale London had grown when she'd discovered it.

What if…?

Determined not to let his thoughts go there, Reese got out of the elevator and went to her apartment. He rang the doorbell, but no one answered. Not that time nor the ten times that followed in quick succession.

There was no one home.

But there should have been. He'd asked the doorman before coming up if the man had seen London today. The answer had been a firm no. When he'd pressed, the doorman had informed him that he had been on duty from ten this morning until now, and in that time he had not seen her in the building, much less walking out of the building.

Still, the man had to take a break sometime. Maybe London had left then.

Damn it, he was letting this all get to him. There could be a hundred explanations.

He kept coming back to one.

Since she obviously wasn't answering her regular phone, he took out his cell phone and called hers.

There was a moment's delayed reaction before he realized that the ring inside his cell phone was being echoed from within the apartment. Her cell phone was in there.

The knot in Reese's stomach tightened a little more. London was never without her phone. She'd told him she felt naked without it. Either she was inside and not answering for some reason, or—

Reese struggled to curb his initial instinct and not run down the fifteen flights of stairs to the ground floor. Instead he forced himself to take the elevator down. Bursting out through metal doors that were barely parted, he quickly hurried over to the doorman.

"I want you to let me into London Merriweather's apartment."

The other man drew himself up to his full five foot eight. He figured the several inches he lacked were made up for by the uniform he wore. "Hey, look, mister—"

Reese didn't have time for an argument. He said the first thing that came to his mind. It was either that, or grab the man by his lapels and slam him against the opposite wall.

"I'm her doctor and I think there might be a medical emergency." Reese already had his wallet out and flipped it open to show the doorman his hospital identification. "There's no answer from inside the apartment, but I heard her cell phone ringing. She is *never* without her cell phone," he emphasized as the doorman began to mount a protest.

Faced with the look in Reese's eyes, the doorman had no recourse but to back down.

"Okay, sure." He swallowed nervously as he went to the front desk and unlocked the drawer where all the keys were kept. "But you're taking full responsibility for this."

Reese was already shifting impatiently on his feet, ready to take off. "I'll sign in blood if you want, just get up there."

The apartment was empty.

There was no response when he called her name, nothing but the faint echo of his own voice.

"Looks like she's not here," the doorman volunteered timidly. He made no move to leave his post right outside her doorway.

But Reese wasn't so sure. He raised his hand in silent dismissal as he went to look through the rest of the apartment.

London wasn't in any of the other rooms.

Puzzled, worried and annoyed with himself at the same time, Reese made his way back to the front door. As he reentered the living room, something crunched beneath his shoe.

Looking down, he saw that it was a piece of a vase. He recognized it as the one he'd almost knocked over that first night he'd made love to her in her apartment. Where was the rest of it? Had it fallen? Or was there some kind of a struggle here?

Was Wallace out looking for her? Was that why the bodyguard wasn't here?

"Ready?" the doorman asked nervously. He kept looking over his shoulder, worried that the manager might be coming up, or that someone else on the floor might see him and make a report to the manager. He couldn't afford to be let go. "You know, this could mean my job if—"

But Reese wasn't ready to leave just yet. He really didn't even know why, but he suddenly felt an urgent need to find the rest of the vase.

"Wait."

Leaving the doorman, Reese hurried into the kitchen and looked inside the lower cabinet where London stored her wastebasket. The pieces of the vase were inside, neatly thrown away. He took the wastebasket out. Something red caught his eye, and he lifted out a piece.

There was blood on the long jagged edge.

Hers? Had she cut herself picking up the pieces? Or was something else going on?

Had the vase been thrown at someone coming at her? His heart froze.

"Hey, Doc, you coming?" the doorman called out to him.

He put the basket away beneath the cabinet and crossed to the front door again. The doorman quickly locked up and was at the elevator bank in record time, pressing for the down button.

"Are you sure you didn't see London leave?" Reese asked just as the car arrived.

The doorman was the first in. He pressed for the first floor, relieved the ordeal was over. "I already told you, I was at the front entrance all day."

Front entrance. "Is there a back entrance?" Reese asked quickly.

The question clearly threw the other man. "Well, yeah, but that's for the delivery people. Ms. London wouldn't take that." He made it sound tantamount to her slumming.

"Not of her own free will," Reese said, more to himself than to the man with him. He dug into his pocket and gave the doorman a twenty. They'd reached the ground floor and the lobby. "Do you know where her bodyguard lives?"

The doorman thought for a moment. "Don't know about the other two, but if you mean Wallace, yeah, I know where he lives. He's got an apartment over on Grand Avenue in Santa Ana. One of the older buildings. Told me he was saving up to move down to El Toro."

With the kind of money Reese figured the ambassador was paying Grant, the bodyguard could easily have moved to a more upscale area. "What's the address?"

The doorman waited until another twenty appeared to keep the first bill company before he rattled off Wallace's address.

Wallace wasn't at his apartment.

Feeling desperate, Reese knocked again, then tried the doorknob. Something sticky met his touch. When he examined his hand, there was blood on it. Fresh blood.

He thought of the vase.

The sick feeling in his stomach grew. What was going on here?

Like a man possessed, he ran down the narrow staircase to the first floor, the metal stairs echoing each step he took.

Reese used the same story on the superintendent that he had on the doorman in London's building. And the same bribe.

The superintendent, a small, shapeless man with two days' gray-and-white growth unevenly sprouting on his face used his spare key to let Reese into Wallace's apartment. Unlike the doorman he had no compunction about coming inside with him. He liked to look, to snoop, whenever possible. A man needed to know about the people he rented out to. That was what the building owner paid him for.

This time the superintendent got more than his money's worth.

The old man's jaw dropped as he walked over to a mural, drawn like a moth to a flame.

"Wow, he must really have the hots for that woman," the older man marveled, moving closer to take in as much as he could without putting on his glasses. The wall was crammed with photographs and news clippings about London. Curious, he turned to Reese. "She anybody?" he wanted to know, then pressed, "You know her?"

Reese felt as if he'd just been gut shot.

The photographs all collided into one another, a haphazard collage. There were some pictures that had obviously been taken several years ago, but most were recent.

His eyes honed in on a photograph that had to have been taken within the past few weeks. It was the evening he had taken her to Malone's. He could tell by the dress she was wearing.

His head had been cut out.

"Yes," he said quietly to the superintendent, "I know her."

The man cackled, shaking his head. "Wish I did." He looked around, disappointed that the other walls were not similarly decorated. "Wonder if he's got any more pictures or stuff in that storage room he's always so secretive about."

The half-muttered question sent up a red flag. Reese all but grabbed the other man by the shirt. Adrenaline began to pump madly through his veins. "What storage room?"

The man jerked a thumb down, indicating a spot below his feet. "The one in the basement."

"There's a basement?" As far as he knew, the homes and apartment complexes in Southern California didn't have basements.

"This is an old building," the superintendent reminded him. "Different code then. Lucky thing for some of the tenants. They pay extra to have it. I told Grant I needed a key to the place, but he said no, that there was this sensitive equipment there and he didn't want anyone fooling with it." The man snorted indignantly. "Like I'd fool with—"

Reese didn't have time to listen to the other man rave. "Take me to it."

But he remained where he was, shaking his head. "Won't do any good. I told you, I ain't got a key, and he keeps it padlocked. Doesn't trust nobody."

There's a good reason for that, Reese thought. The man was a monster of a magnitude that far transcended any physical flaws. "Do you have bull cutters?"

The superintendent knew where he was heading with this. He led the way back into his apartment and went into his tool chest, a massive red affair with multiple drawers and crannies mounted on wheels.

The bull cutters were inside the cabinet. He took the set out gingerly. "But that's against the law," he protested.

As if the man cared. "We want the law," Reese told him. "Once we're down there, I want you to point out which storage room is Grant's and then go call the police—911," he emphasized.

"Why?" The man's deep-set, mud-colored eyes opened up wide. "What'll I tell them?"

That was a no-brainer. Opening the door to the stairwell, Reese led the way down to the basement. "Tell them to get down here as fast as they can. Tell them a woman's life is in danger."

The superintendent was right behind him. They stopped as they came to the landing. "What woman?"

He didn't have time to write out a cue card for the man. Every second he was here talking to him might be a second that was crucial in saving London's life. He grabbed the bull cutters the superintendent was still holding.

"Which one is it?" Unnerved, the unshaven man pointed to the third door from the wall. The largest one. Reese took off. "Just get them here," he tossed over his shoulder as he ran. "Fast."

Reese approached the storage room door. His heart was in his throat.

Logically, he should wait for the police. But logic didn't have anything to do with the situation right now.

Why hadn't he seen it?

London was being stalked by her own bodyguard, by the very man who'd been paid to look after her. That was why he'd managed to get into the apartment without setting off any of the alarms. He'd been the one to install the security system in the first place.

All the while he'd been entrusted with keeping her safe, he'd been a breath away from abducting her. How sick was that?

As he brought down the bull cutters on the padlock, Reese prayed that he'd find London here. Alive. If she wasn't here, he hadn't a clue where to start looking for her.

The padlock fell to the floor.

Reese threw open the door. The enclosure looked

like a tiny model home, all stuffed into an eight-by-ten area. There was a bed, table and chairs and a sofa arranged before a small television set.

All the comforts of home, Reese thought sarcastically.

A musty smell assaulted his nose. There was a single bulb hanging overhead, illuminating the tiny, pseudo-living space. It was just dim enough for him to need a moment to get his bearings.

Just long enough to hear the desperate, almost inhuman sound.

And then he saw her.

London.

She was bound hand and foot and tied to a chair over in one corner. Her mouth had been sealed shut with duct tape.

She was wearing a wedding dress. A veil drooped over her left eye.

"Oh, my God." His heart pounding, Reese dropped the bull cutters, raced over to London and pulled off the tape.

Pain shot through her, going from her face to the top of her head. It was worth it just to be free of the damned tape. London gulped in air as Reese worked to free her of the ropes.

"It's him. It's Wallace," she cried, fighting back hysteria and the dizzying realization that she'd been rescued. "He's the one who's been sending the poems, the flowers, everything. He said he had to do something before someone like you took me away from him."

Reese untied the rope from around her ankles. Freeing her, he pulled London to her feet. He wanted to hold her, to comfort her, but they had to get away before Grant returned. "Where is he now?"

She almost cried at that. The whole thing had been too horrible to describe coherently.

The words almost refused to emerge. "He went out to get us our wedding supper."

She'd always considered herself strong, but London struggled to keep from shuddering. She'd trusted this man, allowed him into her home, into her life, for the past eighteen months. And all the while he'd been fantasizing about her, planning this. Bit by bit.

How could she ever trust anyone again?

"He said we could marry each other, that all we needed to do was say the words and then he'd be my husband and would always take care of me."

Reese saw the tears in her eyes. For now, he made no mention of them. "When did he leave?"

She shook her head. "I don't know." Time had become a blur. "Ten, fifteen minutes, maybe longer. I didn't have any way of telling."

"That's all right," he assured her, needing her to remain as calm as she could. He didn't want her to fall apart now. "The police are on their way." Reese saw her wobble. "Can you walk?"

Her legs felt numb, the ropes had all but cut off her circulation. But she needed to get out of here before she suffocated. Determination entered her eyes. "I'll crawl if I have to."

"Then let's get out of here."

Reese took her hand. London winced involuntarily. He looked down and saw that there were red, raw lines around her wrists where the ropes had bitten into her flesh. It wasn't difficult to guess why. London had tried to work the ropes off her wrists.

A rage bubbled up inside him.

The next moment London was yanking on his arm, pulling him back from the entrance.

Her eyes were huge as she stared past his shoulder.

There, in the doorway, was Wallace.

Chapter 16

His plans were being thrown all awry.

Bendenetti, always Bendenetti. Why couldn't the bastard just stay away?

The expression on Wallace's face was one of sheer malevolence. "Where the hell do you think you're going?" he demanded, his bulk blocking the only way out.

Reese's hand tightened on London's in silent reassurance. "Get out of the way, Grant. The police will be here any minute."

A look Reese couldn't even begin to describe entered the bodyguard's eyes. The man looked enraged, deranged. Reese moved his body in front of London.

"The hell they are." As his own words echoed back to him, Wallace's eyes shifted toward London. For one slim second a contrite look passed over his face. "Sorry. I shouldn't curse in front of you."

"You shouldn't stalk her, either," Reese told him angrily.

The hatred returned in flaming sheets of rage. He'd always hated pretty boys. The ones who were better at things than he was. The ones who had all the advantages he never had. Wallace curled his fingers into his palms, trying to contain the rage.

"It wasn't stalking, it was courting," he spat out. "I had to do something. She was going to talk her father into dismantling security, into sending me away." Forgetting Reese, Wallace looked at the only person who mattered in this. London. "Don't you understand? I have to be near you. You're all I think about, London, all I want." His eyes pleaded with her to understand. "I'll be good to you, I swear. You'll never want for anything, never feel afraid again. I'll protect you." The emotion in his voice swelled with each word he uttered. "And I won't ever, ever leave you."

He knew her fears, her thoughts. London felt violated, as if he'd found a way to crawl into her mind.

It was hard to keep the revulsion from her face.

"I know all about the way you feel, about being abandoned. I was, too." Wallace was sure that if he just kept talking, she'd see that they were soul mates. He had to make her understand that they belonged together. "I grew up in an orphanage. Don't you see, we were meant to be together." His eyes, soft only a second before, hardened as they shifted toward Reese. "And no one else is ever going to have you."

Numb, incredulous, London stared at Wallace, saying nothing.

His patience at an end, Wallace suddenly reached

past Reese, shoving him aside. He grabbed London's arm. "Let's go."

London literally dug in her heels, but even so, she could offer little physical resistance to the big man's strength. All she had was her own strength of will. He wasn't going to do this, wasn't going to take her again. She couldn't let him. "No!"

Reese grabbed his other arm, trying to pull him away. "Let her go, Grant."

In response, Wallace swung around and hit Reese's jaw, hard. The force sent Reese flying head first against the wall. The blow to his head jarred his teeth and very nearly rendered him unconscious as he crashed to the floor. For a moment his body was too stunned for him to collect himself.

"I haven't got time for this now, London," Wallace told her, scooping her up into his arms. "This is for the best, you'll see. I promise."

Doubling up her fists, London beat on his chest. Though she was no weakling, it was like a fly assaulting a rhino.

"Wallace, put me down!" she ordered. "You can't do this. It's not right."

"You're wrong. Nothing's ever been more right," he said.

His arm tightening around her, he turned toward the entrance. His car was parked just outside the building, and they could still get away. He could marry her later, but he had to save her for himself now.

Behind him he heard Bendenetti moan. The only fly in the ointment. As long as the other man was alive, he would never completely possess London. Bendenetti had to be eliminated.

Holding London against him like a doll, Wallace pulled out the gun he had tucked into the back of his pants with his free hand. "Cover your ears, London."

London's heart stopped when she saw the weapon. He was going to kill Reese. "Wallace, please," London begged. "Don't do this. I'll do anything you want, just don't kill him."

Anything he wanted. Which meant she loved the other man. "I have to. He'll come after you and he won't stop." Cocking the revolver, he took aim.

"No!" London screamed, grabbing his arm. She jerked it upward, and the shot went wild, going through the ceiling. Wallace cursed loudly. The next second London dug her nails into his eyes, and he screamed in pain.

Still dazed, his own vision double, Reese scrambled to his feet. He nearly tripped over the bull cutters. Picking them up, he held them with both hands and swung the heavy tool with all his might at the back of Wallace's head.

The big man crumpled to his knees, then fell on top of London. She screamed.

His head still spinning from his contact with the wall, Reese managed to roll Wallace off London and pull her up to her feet.

She threw herself into his arms.

"Are you all right?"

They asked the question in unison, then laughed with the giddy relief that came from having survived something deadly together.

In the background they heard the comforting sounds of police sirens approaching. It was over.

"I guess the superintendent got through," Reese told her. He continued holding her and didn't want to let her go. Ever.

A sigh racked her entire body. It was over. Finally over. She was free, really free. Free because of Reese. She owed him everything.

London drew back her head and saw the gash on the side of his forehead where he'd hit the wall. He *was* hurt. "Oh God, you're bleeding."

He touched the area gingerly. It was throbbing and felt to him as if it was three times the size of a normal head. He looked down at the blood on his fingers. "I guess I must have hit my head harder than I thought."

"Here, lean on me," she instructed, placing her shoulder beneath his arm.

He looked at her. She looked frazzled and beyond worn-out. This had been some ordeal for her. He should be the one holding her up.

"Maybe we can lean on each other," he suggested with a half smile.

She could have cried she was so relieved, so happy. "Sounds good to me."

"Feels like just yesterday that I was here," London murmured to Reese.

She was sitting up on a hospital bed in the far corner of the emergency room while Alix finished examining her. Refusing to go the usual route and change into a hospital gown, or even be separated from London, Reese was sitting on the chair beside her. The gash on his forehead had long since been attended to and was now covered with a bandage.

Reese laughed shortly. "Feels more like an eternity to me."

"The truth, as always, is somewhere in the middle," Alix commented diplomatically, putting down the in-

strument she'd used to check London's pupils one last
time. "After scads of tests, the good news is that there's
nothing wrong with you that a soak in a hot tub and a
good night's sleep won't fix."

London continued to watch the other woman, waiting for the other shoe to drop. "And the bad news?"

Alix laughed for the first time since she'd heard that
an ambulance had brought Reese and London in. She'd
raced into the E.R. from the fourth floor the moment she
knew, determined to be the one to attend them. Reese
couldn't bully her into backing off.

She was nothing if not thorough, despite his pro-
tests. It was a relief to discover that neither was seriously
hurt. Even Reese's head wound would heal nicely. There
was no evidence of internal bleeding, no concussion.
The prognosis couldn't have been better.

Alix looked at Reese. "It's obvious she's been hanging around you too long." She decided to oblige London and give her a downside. "The bad news is that I
think the wedding dress is ruined."

London looked at the torn, dirty dress draped over the
back of the chair. Her mouth turned grim. "Burn it."

Alix looked from London to Reese. She hadn't been
privy to what had happened just before the ambulance
had brought them here, hadn't really been able to talk
to Reese since he'd shown her the ring he was going to
give London two days ago.

She glanced at the woman's hand and saw that there
was no ring on the proper finger. Had he asked her and
she'd turned him down? Or was he still waiting for the
"right" moment? Then why had she been brought in
wearing a wedding dress?

Tactfully Alix said nothing. "I'll leave you two to get

ready." She picked up both charts and made one last notation on London's. "You're both free to go."

London looked down at the hospital gown they'd had her put on. She couldn't leave in this and she refused to put the wedding dress on again. She turned her eyes toward Reese, a mute supplication in her eyes.

He picked up on it immediately. Even if she had been willing to don the dress again, he wouldn't have let her. The sooner that was out of her sight, the sooner she would really start to heal.

"Alix, you still keep an extra set of scrubs in your locker?"

Alix thought that an odd question at this time. "Yes, why?" And then she looked at London's face and understood. Sometime soon, Alix thought, she was going to corner Reese and get some answers. But not this afternoon. "Oh. Okay, sure. I'll bring them around in a few minutes," she promised.

Charts in hand, Alix slipped out, pulling the curtain closed around them, giving them a small measure of privacy in a nonprivate environment.

Restless, London laced her fingers together, then unlaced them. "She's nice."

"The best." Because his legs still felt a little wobbly, he remained seated. But he reached for her hand and wound his fingers protectively around it.

She smiled, the simple action warming her. "You two been friends long?"

He was feeling his way around. This was the first real conversation they'd had since he'd walked out of her apartment. "Long enough for me to show her the engagement ring."

She nodded. That explained the way Alix had looked

at the wedding dress. A flood of guilt came over her. Again. Just as it had this morning and the night before. And the afternoon before that.

"Reese—"

"London—"

Their voices overlapped, blending together. London welcomed the reprieve. "You first," she said.

"Ladies first," he insisted, stalling for time, not knowing how to form the words that went with the emotions ricocheting around his heart.

He could have lost her today. Forever.

The realization echoed through him, stunning him with its power. It made him determined to put his ego aside and be in London's life, at least on the perimeter, at all costs.

In a way he supposed he could almost understand how Grant felt. He felt sorry for the man the police had arrested. But not sorry enough to regret that, from all indications, Wallace Grant was going to be put away for a long, long time. He wasn't going to be a threat to London anymore.

She took a deep breath. Her ribs ached from when Wallace had grabbed her this morning to keep her from fleeing the apartment. She found herself stumbling to get the right words into place.

"I was going to call you this morning and apologize about the other night—at least explain why I said what I did." She bit her lip. "I happened to mention to Wallace that you had proposed to me, and he must have panicked." She would never forget the look in his eyes. Like a child who had had his only toy taken away at Christmas. "He's been trying to work up the nerve to propose to me all this time."

How could she have been so blind? London berated herself. How could she not have seen any of this coming?

"He did," she told Reese in a small voice. "And he confessed about the roses and the notes. He sent them to make it look as if I was being stalked so that my father would keep him on, but he tried to do it so that I wouldn't be frightened." Her mouth curved in a sad smile. "He succeeded, you know. I wasn't afraid." She couldn't help it. Now that everything was settling down, she felt sorry for the man. "Wallace was really trying to look out for me."

There were tears in her eyes. She had an incredibly soft heart, Reese thought. Any other woman would have been full of anger for what she had been put through, not felt sorry for her stalker.

"London, he's a sick man."

"I know." She took another deep breath and let it out slowly. "Funny, isn't it? The only man who ever promised to stay in my life turns out to be a deranged stalker."

Reese stood up and came to her. "He's not the only one who wants to be in your life permanently, London."

She looked at Reese, searching his face. Trying to find answers to half-formed questions. "You mean you still do, even after all this?"

How could she possibly think his heart was so fickle? "Why would any of this change my desire to marry you? If anything, it just shows me that you need someone in your life to take care of you."

No, she wasn't going to be smothered. She didn't need a keeper. "I don't—"

"Yes," he told her firmly, cutting her off, "you do." This wasn't a point to be argued. "We all do." He took her hands into his. "We all need someone to take care of us and to take care of," he emphasized. "That's what marriage is supposed to be. A fifty-fifty deal. Sometimes it tips a little one way, sometimes the other, but in the end it levels out. You need someone, London. Let it be me." He threaded his fingers through her hair, cupping her cheek. "Because I need you.

"I didn't realize it, didn't know I was missing anything, until you came into my life and showed me how drab it had been up until then. Until you showed me how good it could be. I want you to keep on showing me, London. Until we're both very, very old."

He made her smile. He always did. "Making love into our nineties?" She laughed softly. "They'll want to study us in a lab."

He shrugged. Loving her. Wanting her. "Let them. As long as we're there together, it doesn't matter where we are or who else is around." And then he grew serious. "I love you, London. And I want to be there for you. When you wake up in the morning. When you go to sleep at night. I want to be next to you."

The smile came into her eyes. "Tall order for a physician."

There were always ways around things. "I'll get people to cover."

But she shook her head. "I don't want you to be any different from the way you are right now." And then she smiled again. Broadly. "Maybe a little cleaner, but just as dedicated, just as good, just as sincere as you are this moment. Because that's the man I fell in love with." She stopped, surprised at herself. "Wow, I said it. I really said it." She looked at him to see if the significance had penetrated. "I said I love you."

It was going to be all right, he thought. From now on

it was going to be all right. "No, technically you said 'fell in love with.' But there's no penalty. You get a do-over if you want to say it right this time."

Oh, God, why had she waited so long? This feeling of loving someone, of loving him, was so overwhelming, so wonderful as it rushed through her, freeing her.

"I want to say it right every time." She framed his face with her hands. "I love you, Dr. Bendenetti. Very, very much." She brushed a kiss against his lips. "So much that it scares me. That's why I said no."

Amusement entered his eyes. "So if you loved me less, you would have said yes?"

She laughed, knowing she had to sound like a crazy person. But that was okay. Love could make you crazy sometimes and she was ready for that. "No. But if that offer of yours is still on the table, I'd like to take it this time. I'd like to say yes now."

Definitely all right, he thought, relieved. "It's still on the table."

"Yes now," she echoed, and then laughed. He put his arms around her, and she winced slightly, then shifted. Away from the pain and into him. "New bruises on top of the old ones. I guess the bride's going to be wearing black and blue."

He was looking forward to caring for those bruises. "That's okay. Haven't you heard? I'm a very good doctor."

If her heart was any more full, it was going to explode. "Yes, I have heard that."

He drew her a little closer. "And as long as the bride is mine, I don't care if she shows up at the wedding in Technicolor."

"Oh, the bride is yours, all right." London wrapped

her arms around his neck and brought her lips up to his. "The bride is very yours."

Alix parted the curtain on the side, the scrubs she'd gone to fetch for London in her hand. She stopped short and then quietly placed the scrubs on the bed, fairly certain that her presence had not been detected by either of her two patients. They were very busy wrapped up in each other and the kiss they were sharing.

She smiled to herself as she slipped out. Looked like Reese had finally gotten around to proposing.

Everything you love about romance...
and more!

Please turn the page for Signature Select™
Bonus Features.

Bonus Features:

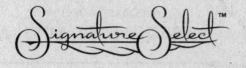

BONUS FEATURES

THE BEST MEDICINE

EXCLUSIVE BONUS FEATURES INSIDE

A conversation with
MARIE FERRARELLA

USA TODAY bestselling author Marie Ferrarella has written more than 150 books for Silhouette! Recently we chatted with Marie about her writing career, family and her favorite things.

How did you begin your writing career?
I began my actual writing career with plagiarism. I was eleven years old and wrote a knockoff of *The Little Match Girl*. Mine was about a little boy named Dickie. *Children's Digest* gave me my first rejection slip. But I had read my story to my best friend and made her cry. The power of the written word was awesome and I was hooked.

Was there a particular person, place or thing that inspired these stories or inspired THE BACHELORS OF BLAIR MEMORIAL miniseries?
Over the years, I have taken care of my mother, my father and, for the last nineteen years, my mother-in-law, as well. All were (or are) in need of a

battery of doctors. I spent a lot of my time in waiting rooms and also talking to a variety of specialists, building up an arsenal of caretakers as well as a rapport with the different physicians. My overactive imagination did the rest.

What or who inspires you?
Professionally, I have always been inspired by Nora Roberts, who I think is without equal in this field. I've also been inspired by bill collectors. It takes a lot of money to raise a family these days.

When you're not writing, what are your favorite activities?
When I'm not writing, I'm usually slumped, facedown, over my computer. However, on those rare occasions when I do have some free time (and have decided that it's okay if everyone sticks to the kitchen floor for a couple of more days), I love to watch movies or read (mysteries, romances, biographies—everything but horrors). I do take the month of December off whenever possible to do Christmassy things, reconnect with my family (and unstick people from the kitchen floor).

Could you tell us a bit about your family?
Ah, my family. Everyone has met my family. My husband, Charlie, is the brooding hero of half my books. My kids contributed to every child I've ever written about—like the overenergized kids in *Mother for Hire*. Even my dog, Rocky (who is a female German shepherd—I am not responsible for

her name, my kids are), showed up in a couple of romances, specifically her training period when I actually slept next to her puppy cage so she wouldn't be lonely. If you want actual details, my husband has a master's in physics and has worked on the space shuttle and space station, my daughter, Jessica, has a degree in digital arts and is now involved in game quality assurance for a major game company and my son, Nik, is in his last year of college and is going to be a doctor—more inside information on medicine. And they all live at home with me (I have had a Ben Cartwright/Ponderosa complex since I was nine).

What are your favorite kinds of vacations? Where do you like to travel?

Okay, I have never been on vacation. Even my honeymoon was spent in Disneyland, showing my brand-new in-laws around. My husband doesn't like to fly; he knows too much about what can go wrong with a plane. Summers for me meant taking the kids to the beach, to amusement parks and to movies. Consequently, to me a vacation is being with the people you love without having to do work in between.

Do you have a favorite book or film?

I love lots of movies, but I have to say that it is probably *Seven Brides for Seven Brothers*, which I saw a total of fourteen times as a kid. It's romantic, adventurous and they sing. Everything I love. As to favorite book, it would have to be *Gone With the*

Wind, followed by *The Once and Future King* by
T. H. White. I adore the Arthurian legends, but if it
were up to me, there would have been a happy
ending.

Any last words to your readers?
Any last words for my readers? Yes, please read.
Seriously, I want to thank each and every one of my
readers for choosing to read my stories. I hope I've
entertained you a little because that is all I have ever
wanted to do.

Marie Ferrarella's next book, *Searching for Cate*, will
be on sale in August 2005 from Signature Select.

TOP TEN
Dreamy Doctor Movies
by Hilda Rasula

There's just something about a doctor with a
good bedside manner...
Sexy, smart and caring, these docs have it all.

1 The Wedding Planner (2001)

Starring Jennifer Lopez, Matthew McConaughey

Mary Fiore is San Francisco's best wedding planner.
With exquisite taste and, ever since her fiancé left
her at the altar five years ago, an unsentimental
heart, Mary is the woman for the job. When she's
saved from an accident by heartthrob pediatrician,
Dr. Steve Edison, sparks fly, and neither one can
deny the incredible connection they share. But when
Mary realizes that Steve is the groom in her latest
project, she knows she's doomed, for she's already
broken the golden rule in her line of work: Never fall
in love with the groom....

2 Spellbound (1945)
Starring Ingrid Bergman, Gregory Peck

The attractive leads are both doctors in this wonderful film from Alfred Hitchcock. The dashing Dr. Edwards is appointed to take over as head psychiatrist at a mental asylum. When he arrives, he immediately falls in love with a fellow doctor, the coolly reserved Dr. Constance Peterson. It soon becomes clear, however, that Dr. Edwards is in fact an amnesiac, and that the real Dr. Edwards is missing—presumed dead. Convinced of the impostor's innocence, Constance goes on the lam with him, and risks her career and her heart as she psychoanalyzes a new patient to try to save the man she loves.

3 Mumford (1999)
Starring Loren Dean, Hope Davis, Jason Lee, Alfre Woodard

In the small town of Mumford, a psychiatrist of the same name moves in and immediately starts attracting business with his unorthodox methods of therapy. By giving brutally honest advice, the doctor helps change the quirky townspeople's lives as no one has been able to do. His identity is called into question, however, when a jealous rival shrink digs up some dirt on Dr. Mumford. Even more alarming, however, is the fact that he's fallen hopelessly in love with one of his patients!

4 Doc Hollywood (1991)

Starring Michael J. Fox, Julie Warner, Woody Harrelson, Bridget Fonda

Fresh out of med school, Dr. Benjamin Stone is driving fast and furious on his way to Beverly Hills, where he has been offered a position at a prestigious plastic surgery clinic. To avoid a traffic jam, he takes a detour, and crashes his car in Grady, the smallest of small towns. Sentenced to do community work in the local hospital, "Doc Hollywood" is forced to stay for a while, to his unending frustration. When he starts to fall for a cute local, though, his superficial ambition might just take a detour of its own....

5 City of Angels (1998)

Starring Meg Ryan, Nicolas Cage

Based on the German cult movie *Wings of Desire*, *City of Angels* centers around Seth, an angel watching over Los Angeles. He is seen by a beautiful heart surgeon, and as they fall in love, Seth must decide if he wants to join the living. This heart-wrenching, ethereal tale is for die-hard romantics.

6 Dr. T & the Women (2000)

Starring Richard Gere, Helen Hunt, Laura Dern, Kate Hudson, Liv Tyler, Farrah Fawcett

In this kooky comedy from director Robert Altman, Richard Gere plays Dr. T, a wealthy Dallas gynecologist plagued by what other men only dream of: too many women. Between his excitable daughters, his airy sister-in-law and her three daughters, his secretary who's in love with him and his ever-demanding patients, Dr. T can't get a moment's peace.... Until a cool new golf pro moves into town who's unlike any other woman he knows.

7 A Woman's Face (1941)
Starring Joan Crawford, Melvyn Douglas

In one of her best performances, the legendary Joan Crawford plays Anna Holm, a woman embittered by a facial scar she received as a child, and the life of crime it has led her into. When she is caught by a talented plastic surgeon, he decides to help her, fearing that if he succeeds, he will have created a monster: all beauty with no heart. The operation is a success...but can love redeem a monster?

8 Baby Boom (1987)
Starring Diane Keaton, Sam Shepard

Known around Wall Street as "the tiger lady," J. C. Wiatt is a corporate power player. She's great at business, but bad at parenting, as she soon finds out when she inherits a baby girl from a distant relative. Complications ensue, and J.C. finds herself living in the country, exiled from the corporate world. When she meets a dreamy veterinarian, though, J.C. realizes that maybe domestic bliss isn't such a bad idea after all....

9 Gross Anatomy (1989)

Starring Matthew Modine, Daphne Zuniga, Christine Lahti

Joe is a medical student who doesn't buy into the fierce competition around him. He's so laid-back that he would rather analyze the body of his cute lab partner, Laurie, than take his studies seriously. When his most demanding teacher falls ill, however, she and Laurie know that they must convince Joe to live up to the highest standards in order to fulfill his potential as a great doctor.

10 Raiders of the Lost Ark (1981)

Starring Harrison Ford, Karen Allen

12 During World War II, roguish archeologist, Dr. Indiana Jones, is hired by the U.S. government to recover the Ark of the Covenant. However, this ancient artifact is also being sought by Nazi agents who will do anything to put a stop to Indy's expedition. Indy solicits the help of his ex-flame, Marion, and the two share a thrilling escapade through exotic lands. Billed as "The return of the great adventure," *Raiders of the Lost Ark* lives up to its claim and its nine Oscar nominations.

THE OFFICE GRAPEVINE
BLAIR MEMORIAL HOSPITAL'S
LOCAL CHATTER...

The gossip mill is buzzing about heart surgeon Dr. Lukas Graywolf. You might remember his rather turmoil-filled meeting with Special Agent Lydia Wakefield. They're married now and there's definite talk about beginning a family. It's a matter, we're told, of getting the two together in the same room at the same time. Both are enormously busy, but very much in love, so we all know it's just a matter of time.

Should a little one be on the way, we have more than a fine selection of pediatricians to offer them now that Dr. Terrance McCall has left law enforcement to join our staff in order to be close to his wife, Dr. Alix DuCane, our newly appointed Head of Pediatrics. Courting favor with the boss will certainly take on new meaning in their family.

You might have heard that two more members of our little family decided to combine their resources and tie the knot. Our very own nurse Jolene DeLuca has taken the charming and immensely eligible Dr. Harrison (Mac) MacKenzie off the market. Not only that, but they've just recently added to our little community, giving Jolene's Amanda and Mac's Tommy a brand-new baby sister. Erika, named after Jolene's mother, is affectionately referred to by one and all as "Little E."

Not to be left out of the baby parade, internist Dr. Reese Bendenetti and his wife, the former London Merriweather (who some of you might recall he so nobly saved from a stalker) recently became the proud parents of twins, Nathan and Belle. Mother and babies are doing fine, Daddy is getting very little sleep, but then, being a doctor, he's used to it.

And last, but by no means least, Dr. Peter Sullivan, will be marrying Raven Songbird (yes, that Songbird, of the fashion design fame) in a ceremony next month at the Songbird estate. According to the bride, whose brother Blue will be the ring bearer, the immediate world is more than welcome to come. The groom has asked that a few less attend.

The Office Grapevine will continue to keep close tabs on what's happening at Blair Memorial Hospital and keep you updated with further details....

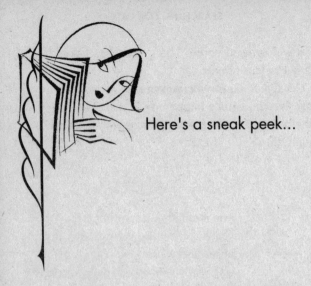

Here's a sneak peek...

16

Searching for Cate
By
Marie Ferrarella
Coming in August 2005 from
Signature Select

*FBI Special Agent Cate Kowalski needs to find the truth
about her life, and that means finding her birth
mother. But her quest brings her up against Dr.
Christian Graywolf and a past he has yet to confront.
The attaction is intense, immediate—and the truth is
something neither is ready for: that all his life Christian
has been searching for Cate.*

CHAPTER 1

"What do you mean it's not compatible?"

Special Agent Catherine Kowalski stared at the short, husky lab technician before her. A basket filled with vials, syringes and other bloodletting paraphernalia was looped over his arm, and he looked at her as if she were a deranged troll having wandered out of a fairy tale.

The drone of voices in the hospital corridor outside her mother's single care unit faded into the background as she tried to make some kind of sense of what the man had just told her.

It's a mistake, a voice whispered in her head. But still, there was this terrible tightening in the pit of her stomach, as if she was about to hear something she didn't want to hear.

This was absurd, she thought. Just a small foul-up, nothing more.

"She's my mother. How could my blood type be incompatible with hers? There has to be some mistake," Cate insisted.

There was no sympathy on the technician's rounded, pockmarked face, just a weariness that came from doing the same laboratory procedures day after endless day. There was more than just a touch of indignation in his eyes at being questioned.

His voice was flat, nasal. "No mistake. I tested it twice."

Her stomach twisted a little harder. Somewhere in the distance, an alarm went off, followed by the sound of running feet. She blocked it out, her mind focused on what this new information ultimately meant.

No more surprises. I can't handle any more surprises. Cate had graduated near the top of her class at Quantico. In the field, there were few better. But on the personal front, she felt as if her life had been falling apart for the last few years.

And this might be the final tumble.

Cate's eyes narrowed. Her voice was low, steely. "Test it again."

Submitting to the blood-typing test had been nothing more than an annoying formality in Cate's eyes. She'd thought it a waste of time even as she agreed.

Time had always been very precious to her.

Ever since she could remember, for reasons she could never pin down, she'd always wanted to cram as much as she could into a day, into an hour. It was as if soon, very soon, her time would run out. Over the years, every so often, she'd tried to talk herself out of the feeling.

Instead, she'd proven to be right. Because there hadn't been enough time, not with the father whom she adored. Officer Thaddeus Kowalski, Big Ted to his friends, had died in the line of duty, protecting one of his fellow officers during the foiling of an unsuccessful liquor store robbery. She was fifteen at the time. It seemed like the entire San Francisco police force turned out for his funeral. She would have willingly done without the tribute, if it meant having her father back, even for a few hours.

When she was a little girl, they used to watch all the old classic Westerns together and her father always told her that he wanted to die with his boots on. She'd cling to him and tell him that he could never die. He'd laughed and told her not to worry. That he wasn't prepared to go for a very long time.

He'd lied to her and died much too soon.

As had Gabe Summer.

Special Agent Gabriel Summer, the only man she had ever allowed herself to open her heart to. Gabe, who had stubbornly assaulted the walls she'd put up around herself until they'd finally cracked and then come down. Gabe, who somehow managed to keep an upbeat attitude about everything in general and humanity in particular.

Gabe, who had nothing more than his arm found in the rubble that represented a nation's final departure from innocence on that horrific September 11 morning in 2001.

Like her father, Gabe had left her much, much too

soon. They never had the chance to get married the way they'd planned, or have the children he wanted so much to have with her. The lifetime she'd hoped for, allowed herself to plan for, hadn't happened. Because there wasn't enough time.

And now, with her mother diagnosed with leukemia and her bone marrow discovered not to be a match, Cate had thought at the very least she could donate blood to be stored for her mother so that when a match would be found—as she knew in her heart just *had* to be found—at least the blood supply would be ample.

But now here was the stoop-shouldered man myopically blinking at her behind rimless eyeglasses, telling her something that just couldn't be true.

"I can't test it again," he informed her flatly. "I've got work to do."

Lowering his head, he gave the impression that he was prepared to ram his way past her if she didn't let him by.

Cate planted herself in front of him. At five foot four, she wasn't exactly a raging bull. To the undiscerning eye, she might have even looked fragile. But every ounce she possessed was toned and trained. She was far stronger than she appeared and knew how to use an opponent's weight against him.

She temporarily halted the technician's departure with a warning look. "Look, a lot goes on in the lab. You people are overworked and underpaid and mistakes *are* made. I need you to test my blood again.

And then, if you get the same results, test hers. Just don't come back and tell me they're incompatible, because they're not. They can't be."

The small man stepped back, his eyes never leaving her face. "Look, lady, you're AB positive. Your mother's O. I don't care how many tests you want me to run, that's not going to change. You give her your blood, she dies, end of story." He drew himself up to the five-foot-three inches he came to in his elevator shoes. The vials in the basket clinked against one another. Annoyance creased his wide brow, traveling up to his receding hairline. "Now I've got other patients to see to."

"Problem?"

Cate recognized the raspy voice behind her immediately, even before she turned around. It belonged to Dr. Edgar Moore.

Doc Ed.

Tall, with a full head of thick silver hair that added to the impression of a lion patrolling his terrain, Doc Ed had been her family's primary physician long before the term had taken on its present meaning. It was Doc Ed who had held her and comforted her when she'd found out about her father's death. And it was Doc Ed who had called her at the field office to tell her to come home, that her mother needed her even if Julia Kowalski was too stubborn to get on the phone and place the call herself.

Cate had gotten herself reassigned to the San Francisco field office where she'd initially started her career. That allowed her to see to her mother's care. It didn't help. Her mother's condition was worsening by the week. By the day. Time was slipping away from her and there wasn't anything she could do about it.

On the verge of feeling overwhelmed, Cate sighed with relief. Reinforcements had arrived. Doc Ed would put this irritating person in his place.

She refrained from hugging the doctor, even though she felt the urge. Instead, fighting for control over her frayed emotions, banking down the scared feeling growing like an overwatered weed, Cate brushed aside a strand of straight blond hair that had fallen into her face.

"Doc Ed, could you please tell this man that his infallible lab *has* made a mistake."

The doctor's warm gray eyes looked from the annoyed technician to the young woman he'd known since her first bout of colic. "How's that?"

Cate took a breath and collected herself. She hadn't realized that her temper was so close to snapping. The restraint she'd always valued so highly was in short supply.

She gestured toward the technician and stopped to read his name tag. "Bob here is telling me that I can't donate blood to my mother. That our blood types are incompatible." The laugh that punctuated her statement was short and mirthless. And nervous. "We both know that can't be true."

The moment the words were out of her mouth,

they tasted bitter. Like bile. Instincts honed on the job pushed their way into her private life. Once again whispering that something was wrong. Very, very wrong. That the twisting feeling in her gut was there for a reason. There were no planes flying into buildings, no bullets fired, no cells mutating and turning cancerous, but something was still wrong. She could feel it vibrating throughout her whole body.

Because Doc Ed's affable face had taken on a look of concern.

Cate suddenly felt like throwing up. Like running down the hall with her hands over her ears so she couldn't hear anything, anything that would further shake up her already shaken world.

She did neither. But it was all she could do to hang on. She'd spent a good part of her life trying to be tough, trying to live up to Big Ted's reputation. He'd had no sons and she felt she owed it to him because in her eyes, he'd been the greatest father to ever walk the earth.

But she wasn't sure just how much more of life's sucker punches she could take and still remain standing, remain functioning.

"Can't be true, right?" Cate heard herself asking quietly. Holding her breath.

Doc Ed sighed. "Cate, maybe it's time that you and your mother talked."

Every bone in her body stiffened, braced for an assault. She could feel the hairs on the back of her neck standing up.

"We talk all the time, Doc." Her voice was hollow to her ear.

Behind her, Bob, the lab technician, took his opportunity to hurry away. She heard the rattle of the vials as he escaped down the hall. But her mind wasn't on the other man. It was centered on the expression on Doc Ed's face, which did nothing to give her hope.

She wasn't going to like whatever it was that she was going to hear. She was willing to bet a year's salary on it and she had never been a betting person.

"At least," she added, "I thought we talked. But I guess I thought wrong."

Doc Ed made no answer. Instead, he lightly cupped her elbow and guided her back into the room she'd vacated several minutes ago when she'd seen the technician making his rounds. Her mother had been dozing off.

Cate had waylaid the lab tech in the hallway, once again stating her impatience. She wanted to begin donating blood, the first of what she intended to be several pints. Frustration had assaulted her even before he'd opened his mouth to tell her the bad news.

Ever since she'd learned that her mother had leukemia, Cate had felt completely frustrated. There was nothing she could do to change the course of events. When her bone marrow turned out not to be a match, it had just fed her impatience, making her that much more determined to be able to help somehow. She'd immediately taken it upon herself to spearhead a search amid the San Francisco Bureau personnel and their families for a donor. So far, there had been none who matched.

More frustration.

And now, this, whatever "this" was.

"Julia." Doc Ed's gravelly voice was as soft as Cate had ever heard it as he addressed her mother.

The pale woman in the bed stirred and then turned her head in their direction. The look on Julia Kowalski's face told Cate that her mother was braced for more bad news. Resigned to it.

Don't be resigned, Mama. Fight it. Fight it!

Cate found herself blinking back tears as she approached her mother's bed and took the small, weak hand into hers.

She could almost *feel* time slipping through her fingers. Her soul ached.

Julia tried to force her lips into a smile as she looked at her daughter. "Yes?" The single word came out in a whisper.

"Cate just found out that her blood doesn't match yours." Moving over to the bed, Doc Ed took his patient's other hand and held it for a long moment. "Julia, it's time."

"Time?" Cate echoed. A shaft of panic descended, spearing her. She fought to push it away without success. Her heart hammering, she looked at the man who, over the years, she'd made into her surrogate grandfather. "Time for what?"

"Something that you should have been told a long

time ago." His words were addressed to her, but Doc Ed was looking at the woman in the bed as he said them. "I'll leave the two of you alone now." Releasing Julia's hand and placing it gently on top of the blanket, Doc Ed made his way to the door. Pausing to look at them for a moment longer, he added, "I'll be by later to look in on you, Julia. And Dr. Conner will be by shortly."

Cate was vaguely aware of the reference to her mother's oncologist as she watched the door close behind him.

Sealing her in with her mother and whatever secret the woman had kept from her all this time.

...NOT THE END...

Look for the continuation of this story in Searching for Cate *by Marie Ferrarella, available in August 2005 from Signature Select..*

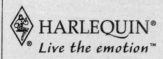

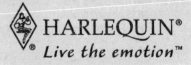

COMING NEXT MONTH

Signature Select Collection
VELVET, LEATHER & LACE by Suzanne Forster,
Donna Kauffman and Jill Shalvis
Hot new catalog company Velvet, Leather & Lace is launching a
revolution in lingerie—and partners Jamie, Samantha and Mia
are coming apart as fast as their wispy new underwear! At this
rate, they might get caught with their panties down. And the
whole world will be watching!

Signature Select Saga
NOT WITHOUT PROOF by Kay David
When hired assassin Stratton O'Neil is framed by a dangerous
drug cartel, he is forced to protect Jennifer Rodas, who is also
a target—which means drawing her into his dark world of high-
stakes murder and intrigue.

Signature Select Miniseries
THE BEST MEDICINE by Marie Ferrarella
Two heartwarming novels from her miniseries, *The Bachelors
of Blair Memorial.* For two E.R. doctors at California's Blair
Memorial, saving lives is about to get personal...and dangerous!

Signature Select Spotlight
MAKING WAVES by Julie Elizabeth Leto
Celebrated erotica author Tessa Dalton has a reputation for her
insatiable appetite for men—*any* man. But in truth, her erotic
stories are inspired by personal fantasies...fantasies that are
suddenly fulfilled when she meets journalist Colt Granger.

Code Red #12
JUSTICE FOR ALL by Joanna Wayne
Police chief Max Zirinsky's hunt for a serial killer leads him to
Courage Bay's social elite. He needs a way to infiltrate their ranks,
and turns to hospital chief of staff Callie Baker. Her solution:
pretend they're dating. But the attraction is all too real, and
neither of them can "pretend" for long. But the killer sees
through their relationship. And for that, Callie will have to die....